RAPTORIVA

VICTORIA
RIVERA

First published in the United States by Prosey Books, an imprint of Pocketful of Prosey LLC.

Cover art by TrifBookDesign
Maps and interior art by Daniel Brown
Layout, typography, and formatting by Victoria Rivera

www.toririv.com

First published May 15, 2024
Second Edition

For Rocco and Bellamy,
my very own little dinos.

Note From Author

This story is inspired by real-world places and the things, people, and languages in them. However, it is neither historical fiction nor an alternate history of Earth. It takes place in a unique setting that also includes dinosaurs and other prehistoric creatures from various geological time periods (as well as special breeds, hybrids, and a few fictional species). I have obviously taken creative license with the overall concept and many details, and simplified a few items for better readability, but I hope readers will feel as excited about this fantasy world as I do. I wanted to write a story that incorporates my passion for dinosaurs and my love of Latin America; this is my ode to both.

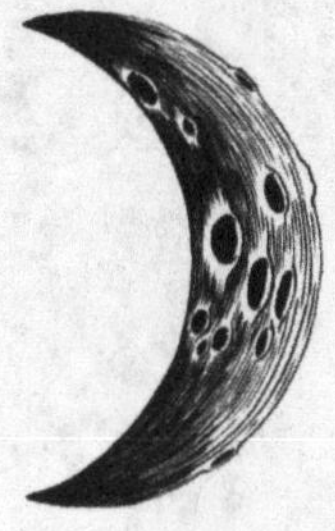

Some parts of this novel may deal briefly
with sensitive subject matter.

....

For a detailed list of content warnings, please visit:
www.toririv.com/cw

RUNAQA
Masi
TISQU
ALETA
GULF OF WAYAQA
Lake Weqe
Silver City
Port Sach'ara
Port Anqas
RUHPARIY
QHUSI
Willkaparqui Mountains
Urubamba Mountains
SUMAQ
Volcanic Region
QOLQE
Lake Wayllu
Nansa
KANTUTA BAY
Lake Umiña
YUPA
UNU
Huandoy
Lake Sillu
ALLPA
AMACHAKUNA
Tukukuq
Pirqa Mountains
GULF OF ALLPA
Mt. Wiru
ANQAS OCEAN
Murkroot
THE TAIL

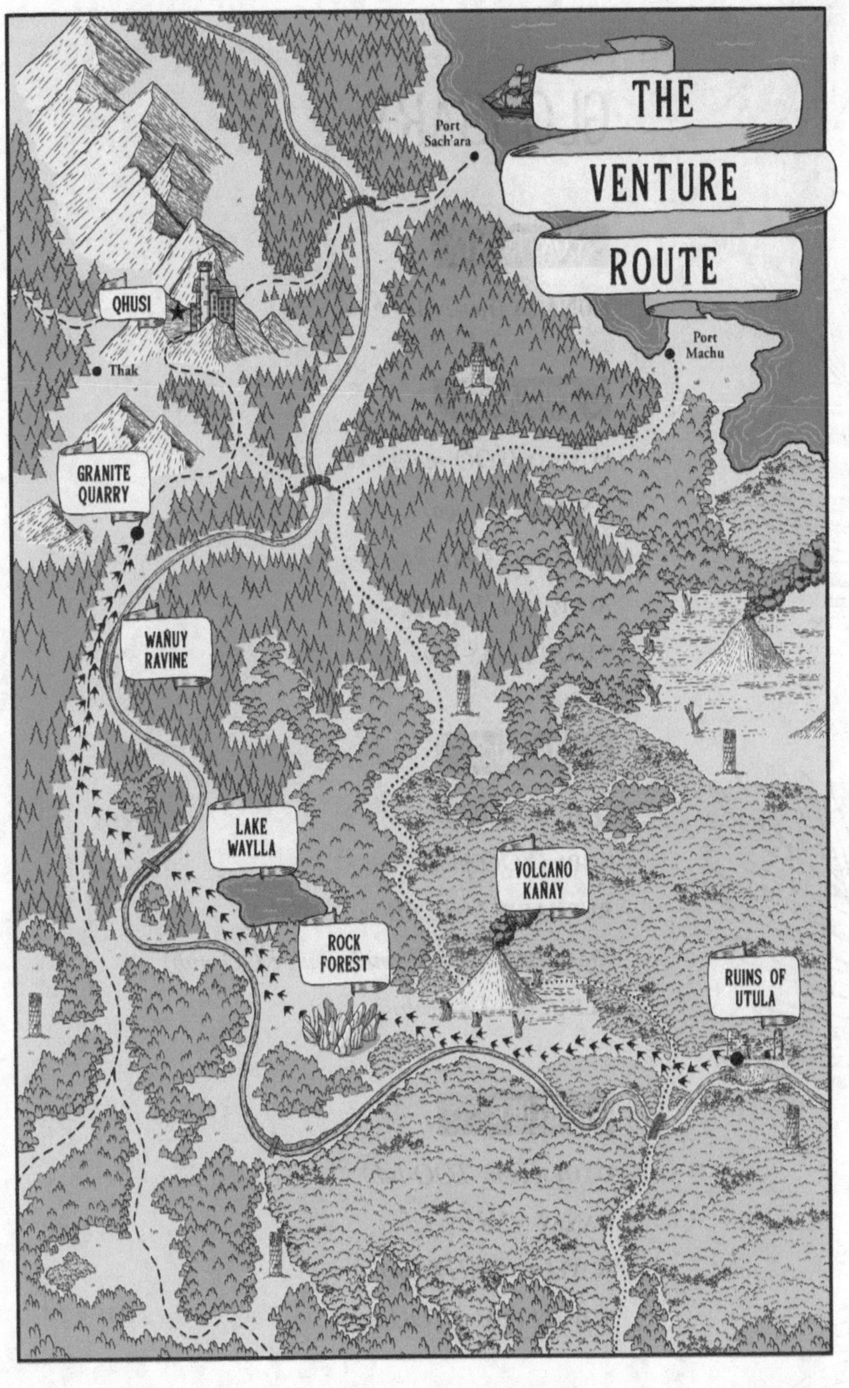
THE VENTURE ROUTE
Port Sach'ara
Port Machu
QHUSI
Thak
GRANITE QUARRY
WAÑUY RAVINE
LAKE WAYLLA
ROCK FOREST
VOLCANO KAÑAY
RUINS OF UTULA
VENTURE ROUTE
AMARU RIVER
MAIN ROADWAY & TRADE ROUTE
ABANDONED TRADE ROUTE

GLOSSARY

CONTINENT

RUNAQA *(roo-NAH-kuh)*

TERRAINS

SUMAQ *(SOO-mahk)*

UNU *(OOH-noo)*

QOLQE *(KOHL-kay)*

ALLPA *(AHL-puh)*

TISQU *(TISS-koo)*

CAPITALS

QHUSI *(KOO-see)*

YUPA *(YOO-puh)*

RUPHARIY *(roo-PAR-ee)*

AMACHAKUNA *(ah-mah-chuh-KOO-nuh)*

ALETA *(ah-LAY-tuh)*

OTHER

UTULA *(ooh-TOO-luh)*

KAÑAY *(KAHN-yahy)*

WAYLLA *(WAHY-luh)*

WAÑUY *(wahn-YOO-ee)*

QORA *(KOR-uh)*

NINAN *(NIH-non)* / **APO-KIMSA** *(AH-poh KIM-suh)*

SAKAY *(SAH-kahy)*

OLLAN *(OH-lun)*

QHAPAQ APO *(KAH-pahk AH-poh)*

PIDRU *(PIH-droo)*

TAMYA *(TAHM-yuh)*

MULLU *(MUH-loo)*

HAKAN *(HAH-kahn)*

RIMAQ *(RIH-mahk)*

APO-HUK *(AH-poh HOOHK)*

APO-ISKAY *(AH-poh ISS-kahy)*

RUYAN *(ROO-yun)*

KILLAY *(KIH-lahy)*

TAKAN *(TAH-kahn)*

JAYLLI *(HAHY-lee)*

MICHIQ *(MIH-cheek)*

PAQARI *(pah-KAR-ee)*

QHAPAQ IZHI *(KAH-pahk EE-see)*

QHAPAQ ACHIK *(KAH-pahk AH-cheek)*

QUYA URPI *(KOO-yuh OORP-ee)*

GORGO *(GOR-goh)*

RAPTORIVA *(rap-toh-REE-vah)*

Clade: Microraptoria **Wingspan:** 13-16 in **Weight:** 1-2 lbs

Small, four-winged, paravian dinosaur. Capable of short-range powered flight and long-range gliding through the use of pennaceous feathers on both front and rear limbs. Scales and plumage are medium to dark iridescent green, with occasional markings of red.

The Runaqan Compendium of Reptiles

ONE

A **SMALL, TOOTHY SNOUT** slipped through the opening of Qora's knapsack. Qora nudged it back inside and tightened the drawstring.

"Shhh," she said, although there was no one in the woods to bear witness. And had there been anyone, they would have been more likely to notice the eoraptor carcass she was carrying. She shifted under the weight of the twenty-five-pound dinosaur slung over her shoulder and strained her ears to pick apart the sounds around her.

First, a low growl in the distance, which most certainly belonged to one of the armored struthiosaurs that made their homes in burrowed holes. The clicky back-and-forth of dromaeosaurs, a pack of four—Qora scrunched one eye and tilted her head—no, six—less than a quarter mile off. Wind whistling through mountain conifers. The burble of water. The punctuating cries of a rhamphorhynchus exactly seven seconds apart. Finally, the gentle vibrations of a herd of protoceratops migrating across the meadow on the other side of the stream, number indeterminate. But even though it had been four years, no sound could ever completely drown out Ollan's voice in her mind, screaming her name.

Qora—run!

A familiar ache swelled in her chest. She rubbed her thumb along her crossbow foregrip three times, touched the trigger with the pad of her index finger, and checked that the bowstring was taut against the bolt in the flight groove—always loaded, always ready. She wouldn't make the same mistake twice.

Her knapsack wriggled, which prompted her to pick up speed. She hurried onward, avoiding the large piles of ruck that dotted the forest floor. Her black dinoleather boots were already covered in mud, the soles and laces caked with it; she didn't need reptile waste on them too.

Fifth Bell tolled from the campanario, audible even though the city of Qhusi could barely be seen from here, particularly through the mists that surrounded its mountaintop locale.

Qora counted the bell's chimes silently as they went off. *One, two, three, four, five.*

Out of breath and breaking a sweat, she adjusted the eoraptor, with its dead eyes and copper-toned scales. It had taken her most of the day, crouching in the underbrush, before she'd finally hit it, which on its own had been a stroke of luck to find—but it had been several minutes after that when she'd spotted a godsend. Something more valuable than months' worth of other trades combined, scales green and iridescent and shimmering like a gem, with four wings and a coarsely feathered tail. It had only taken a bit of dried meat, laced with the sleep-inducing nectar of puñuy blossoms, to lure it to her. Now she just had to wait for the puñuy to take effect. She hushed the knapsack again, but it had already begun to settle down, internal movements slower, more lethargic.

This was a dangerous game to play; Qora knew that. But she thought of what awaited her at home, and she had to believe it would be worth the risk.

Soon, the capital city broke through the mists that clung to its perimeter. Qhusi was the closest place in Sumaq to the High World, people always said, because its citizens practically lived among the clouds, although Qora often thought the clouds were good at hiding things nobody wanted known.

She moved out of the trees to see a sprawl of stones climbing up the domed earth. Retaining walls created tiered levels where shops, homes, and gardens had been built. Stairways snaked between buildings. Other mountains, with their sacred spirits, jutted up in a protective panorama.

Only then did Qora let her crossbow hang against her hip by its woven strap that she wore across her chest. She hurried through the side streets, panting up the incline, bypassing teams of stegosaurians yoked together packing down new gravel on the roads.

She reached the main roadway, which cut the city in half. All along its cobblestone sidewalks, vendors had stands set up with every imaginable product on display. Dyed and woven fabrics. Dinoleathers made into belts, bags, shoes, and riding gloves. Jewelry made from wooden beads, forged metal, colored stones, or reptile teeth and feathers. Barrels full of quinoa, amaranth, maize, and maca. Meats hanging with their swirled pink flesh.

Qora maneuvered through until the central buildings were visible, along with the traffic that flowed between them. Ankylosaurs transporting sacks of grain, city officials with their copper helmets patrolling the streets on megaraptors, common single riders on rhabdodons, and the occasional triceratops with feathered bony frill carrying the wealthy in canopied seat boxes.

Even in her haste, though, Qora couldn't help but pause to glance up at the castle carved into the side of the adjacent mountain. Kallpa House—accessible only by flight—loomed over the city, serving as a reminder that the qhapaq, the supreme leader who lived there, was both physically and spiritually high above everyone else. The bulk of the castle had been chiseled and shaped from the mountain rock itself, while additional walls and embellishments were layered and fit together from external rocks. Enormous black pterobeasts with eighty-foot wingspans flew back and forth across the divide, carrying important members of the household in gondolas that hung from ropes harnessed to the reptiles' bodies. What must it be like, Qora thought, to travel that way, peering down as the world shrank?

"Two days!" Cried a sharp voice, calling her attention back to her lowly place. A man stood in the city square, shouting into a horn that amplified his voice. "Two days left to enter the Venture!"

Good, Qora thought. Two days and she wouldn't have to hear these stupid announcements anymore. She was glad the Venture only happened every five years. She'd been twelve when the last one was held in the neighboring land of Unu, and too young to care much the time before that. Unfortunately, this year's event would be hosted on her home Terrain, making its promotion more difficult to escape—for two more days at least.

By the time she reached her destination, Qora's dark braids were frayed, hair stuck to the back of her neck and edge of her forehead. Her skin felt flushed and humid, which she suspected had more to do with what was in her knapsack than it did with her physical exertion. For now, the creature it held remained motionless, but she couldn't be sure for how long.

The building before her was that of the old marketplace, more than a hundred years ago when the city hadn't been so vast. Now its upper levels were home to fabricators of rough-spun clothing and shoddy tools, while the subterranean level was its own sort of market known as the Underground.

Inside, Qora let down the hood of her green bayeta hunting jacket. A wave of fermentation filtered into her nose, and the din of haggling traders overwhelmed her ears.

She gazed at the row of taxidermied dinosaur heads that lined the far wall, mostly medium-sized bipeds, each frozen mid-bite and mounted on polished wood. Mismatched tables were littered with beverage cups and gambling tokens, along with items of value (gold rings, rare reptile feathers, and bottles of foreign liquors). Thirty or so people sat throughout the dim space with money and goods between them. On the other side, a few dozen more were cheering and howling around a large enclosure, watching two shirtless men go at each other with their fists.

Gorgo—"The Gorgosaur"—had bags under his eyes today, although his muscles bulged as they always did and he bared his teeth as menacingly as ever. His opponent, Qora didn't recognize. Young, maybe eighteen, disheveled with dark, shaggy hair. He wasn't short, but Gorgo's large form dwarfed him nonetheless.

When the boy moved, Qora's pulse rushed. His rhythm, the way he reacted to each strike like he knew in advance when it would be coming. It was more of a dance than a brawl. Qora sucked in a breath when he nearly took a blow to the jaw, but he was slippery as smoke. Gorgo's fist was nothing but a kiss on the boy's cheek.

Sakay, whose uncle ran the Underground, stood near the back counter with his tattooed arms crossed, watching the fight with a wry smile. He scratched the side of his head where his black hair was cut close to the scalp, geometric designs shaved into it. Longer hair was tied in a knot near the crown of his head. His ears were pierced with obsidian studs and he wore a necklace whose charm was a dinosaur tooth the size of Qora's thumb. Twenty years old and he helped run this place like a middle-aged chieftain, as shrewd as most of the better traders when it came to negotiations.

Qora wove between the tables to get to him, graceless with the carcass she carried but careful not to bump the knapsack. Somebody muttered, "I guess that little toy crossbow actually works," but Qora pretended not to hear, resisting the urge to tell the man that it was actually a compact military weapon and if he ever had doubts about its functionality, she'd have been more than happy to demonstrate on his chest.

Sakay looked up from the fight. "Qora." His gaze trailed to the eoraptor and a grin broke across his face. Before he could say anything else, the young fighter in the enclosure landed a punch so hard something cracked. Gorgo cried out and lunged forward.

The audience chanted what Qora assumed was the younger fighter's name. *Ninan! Ninan! Ninan!*

Ninan shifted from the center line and threw a power punch, utilizing the force of Gorgo's own attack against him. Qora cringed.

Meanwhile, Sakay was bobbing and weaving like he could steer the fight from all the way over here, fueled by vicarious energy.

"Sakay." Qora snapped her fingers twice, but Sakay's eyes were fastened to the fight. "I don't have all the time in the world."

He swatted the air in her general direction. "Give me a minute."

Her shoulder ached under the eoraptor carcass, which she heaved onto the counter. Blood finally flowed freely into her right arm, making it tingle.

The fighters circled each other, shuffling their feet, upper bodies jerky with feints. Gorgo's muscles bulged, threatening in their size, but the weight of them added a lag to his movements. He was always an instant behind, always just shy of landing a hit. Ninan slipped most of Gorgo's punches and rolled seamlessly with the rest. In between, he attacked from a low angle, exploiting weak spots. Within seconds, he wrestled Gorgo to the floor and pinned him there, cranking the man's arm at an angle that sent a crawling feeling down Qora's spine as she watched through a fence of her fingers. The referee counted to ten and the crowd chanted the numbers with him in unison, erupting at the end.

Ninan released Gorgo and stood tall. Then he snatched a cup of pisco from someone in the audience, chugged whatever was left inside, and slammed it to the ground. The ceramic shattered, shards spewing everywhere. He raised both fists high and everyone cheered again.

Sakay applauded. He stroked his chin and sighed before he finally took a good look at the heap of animal flesh Qora had set before him. He reached out to examine the reptile. Even in this dull light, the scales were a lustrous, rosy gold. The reptile also had a long, elegant skull and fine purple quills down the back of its head. He ran his hands over the scales, slick and gleaming.

Any other day, Qora would have been eager for him to praise the kill, eager to argue with him over what he would owe her for it. But today, her mind was elsewhere. Today, her kill was only an excuse to talk to him. Her heart hummed. She looked around to see that everyone was still engrossed in their games and their trades, then leaned forward and lowered her voice. "There's something else," she told him. "Something I need to—"

The sound of a screeching chair cut her off. One of the seated men stood, slipping both hands under the table in front of him, upturning the whole thing. Everything on the surface went flying. Pink and red stones plinked as they spilled and spread out over the wooden floor.

"You think you can pass off that second-rate rumipuka as rosinqa mineral?" The man picked up the other trader by his shirt collar and balled a fist.

Sakay groaned. "I have to take care of this. Wait here."

"But—"

"Just hold on, alright?"

Qora turned away and set her elbows on the counter in front of the eoraptor, burying her face in her hands and resisting the urge to scream into them. Sakay would be angry—of course—when he saw what she'd caught, but he was the only one who could help her, the only one she could trust. Instead, he was worried about two idiots squabbling over rocks.

It wasn't *those* rocks that were causing the real conflict anyway, she thought. At that very moment, a man in the corner was discreetly trying to sell a sack of skyrock pebbles. Now *that* was a rock to squabble over.

Qora craned her neck to observe the exchange, the way the trader leaned forward and kept his voice low, his right hand forming the sign with all four fingers touching the thumb—the rough shape of a dinosaur's head. Who could resist the ability to subdue most reptiles with one substance? These celestial rocks, controlled and processed by the qhapaqs for centuries, would never come cheap, though—not when most people believed that Sky Mother herself had dropped them from the High World so humankind could survive among monsters.

Qora had seen these deals often enough by now that she could recognize them at a glance, and was wondering if she should warn Sakay this was going on under his uncle's roof when a whistle—a descending pitch—cut through the background noise.

"Nice kill," said a voice.

Qora glanced over to see Ninan, the boy fighter. Glistening with sweat and marked with emerging bruises, he pulled on a gray, striped poncho. One corner of his mouth rose as the dark skin of his chest disappeared beneath knitted wool.

Warmth flooded Qora's face. She stepped back, unsure whether the boy was sincere.

"Incredible reptiles," he continued. "And a nightmare to catch, from what I've heard."

There was something almost regal about him, Qora thought, and she couldn't decide whether it was his posture or his demeanor. It was subtle, but noteworthy. Otherwise, he was as rough and ragged as most of the others here. Dirt under his fingernails, a few scrapes and scratches, the odor of sweat floating off of him. Not that any of that necessarily bothered her.

What did bother her was that he didn't seem to be looking directly at her when he spoke. His gaze seemed to fall somewhere past her shoulder. She subtly turned her head, at which point she caught sight of an older man just on the other side of where she stood.

Qora clenched her jaw. It was enough to momentarily put off her frustration with Sakay, who had become distracted—yet again—talking to some red-lipped woman selling potions made of dinosaur blood.

Ninan's thick brows pulled together and his eyes flicked from the eoraptor to Qora, then to her crossbow. "Oh. I'm—I'm sorry," he said quickly, wiping sweat from his forehead. "I just assumed it was your father's." He indicated the man behind her.

"My father's dead," Qora said.

One of the traders at the nearby tables chuckled and said,

"Best not to upset the kid. She can be moody sometimes."

Qora's crossbow, fully loaded, burned against her hip. She maneuvered the weapon into position and aimed at the trader. One click and the bolt zoomed out and pierced the loose fabric of his sleeve, nailing it to the table. The man jerked back so abruptly he tipped over in his chair, his sleeve ripping clean through as he fell, leaving only a scrap of material attached to the landed bolt. He scrambled to get back up. "You little—"

"Enough," Sakay interjected, coming toward them. He stopped in front of Qora and turned to face the man, blocking him from her view.

"You have a problem with me talking to this little *kantuta*, huh? We all know you only let her come around for what she trades you in *private*." He clicked his tongue and winked.

Qora spanned her weapon again but Sakay grabbed her wrist and held her in place. "She doesn't miss unless it's on purpose, so consider yourself the beneficiary of her kindness. I'm sure you won't see that twice."

The trader spat on the floor and wiped his mouth with his torn sleeve.

Sakay stood a little straighter. "Get out, or I'll let her shoot you for real."

The man narrowed his eyes, challenging Sakay, who, in response, shrugged and released Qora. Qora loaded a new bolt and the man put up both hands.

"Okay, okay." He muttered several curses under his breath, then gathered his things and stalked out.

Sakay whirled around and crossed his arms, glaring down at Qora. "Do you think you can manage to keep your bolts in your quiver for once, please? My uncle's trying to run a business here, and I'm sure he'd prefer that it didn't all go to ruck on my watch."

Ninan twisted his lips.

"Is this funny to you?" Qora demanded.

"No," Ninan replied. "I didn't mean to offend you. If anything, I'm even more impressed now that I've seen your skill in action—"

Qora scoffed. "Oh, now you're *more* impressed?"

Sakay took her by the elbow and pulled her away from Ninan. "Would you relax? You can't be in here five minutes without riling up at least one of my patrons, and I don't have the patience for it today."

Qora jerked her arm out of Sakay's grasp and pinned her gaze on Ninan like she would a target in the woods. "Of course. How inconsiderate of me. I wouldn't want to disturb the *great* company you keep."

"Don't rag on them too much," Sakay warned. "I'll probably be paying you out of the golds I just made off this one." He patted Ninan on the back.

"What did you put money on *him* for anyway?" Qora asked. "I thought Gorgo was your favorite bet."

Sakay shrugged. "Decided to mix things up a little—bet on the underdog for once. Except it turns out he wasn't much of an underdog after all. Quite the stylist, no need for brawn. It's like he trained with professionals." He looked at Ninan. "Twenty golds on you for the next fight?"

"Can't make the next one," Ninan replied. "Previous engagements."

"Tomorrow, then." Sakay gave a terse nod.

Ninan reciprocated, then left to collect his winnings, and Qora bored imaginary holes into his back with her eyes.

Sakay smirked. "I thought you didn't have all the time in the world …"

Qora scowled back at him. "I don't. You're the one who's been off flirting with swindlers."

"She wasn't a swindler. Aquilops blood is a legitimate painkiller and anti-inflammatory. And jealousy isn't a good look on you, *kantuta*." He emphasized the word satirically, but it was still a cutting remark. The men in here liked to belittle Qora this way, hunters and traders who thought she was too young and fragile to handle a weapon—soft as the kantuta blossoms that grew between the highlands and the eastern forests.

"Don't call me that."

"Come on, I'm kidding. If you're any kind of flower, you've got more thorns than petals. You're the kind with toxic pollen, or one of those carnivorous sundews that gobbles up insects."

Qora's knapsack bumped once against her ribs, reminding her what she was here for. "Are you going to pay me, or what?"

"See? That's exactly the attitude I'm talking about." He returned to the eoraptor and pried open its mouth. "You know, I've heard these smaller teeth make for some fine little necklace beads. Apparently the women in Qolqe are crazy for them. But they have to be just the right size ..." He tested the sharpness with a fingertip and hissed.

"Sakay. I'm not here for the eoraptor."

He paused to look at her squarely. "What?"

Qora darted her eyes at the knapsack, which, as if on cue, began to stir. "There's something else. Something I found after I hit the eoraptor."

Sakay glanced around. "Come with me."

In the storeroom, he closed the door behind them and steered her away from it.

"Don't be mad." Qora held the knapsack, its captive creature quickly turning restless. Her fingers trembled as they worked at the drawstring, making the knot worse with each tug.

Sakay put both hands on top of hers. "Calm down. You're never going to open it like that." He took it from her and loosened it, careful to keep the creature from bursting out all at once.

The small opening was enough for that tiny, toothy snout to reappear, snapping and snarling, before the creature shoved up and revealed more of its iridescent-green head. It flapped its wings inside the knapsack.

"A *raptoriva*?" Sakay all but shouted the word, startling himself. He glanced at the door. "Are you crazy?"

"You already know the answer to that."

He growled through his teeth. "Seriously—Were you even *thinking*? Spirits, Qora. I swear. The only time you aim first and shoot after is when you have your weapon. When it comes to anything else, you do the exact opposite."

"I need the money, Sakay. And if you can connect me with the right traders, this'll get me a rexload. I don't have much time. Weeks, if I'm lucky."

Sakay jerked back as the raptoriva reared its tiny green head, revealing a splotch of red on the underside of its lower jaw. He held it by the neck, the rest of its body swaddled in the knapsack.

Qora didn't want to reckon with her conscience. Of course the raptoriva deserved to fly free. But it would certainly be well cared for—idolized, even—in some highborn's aviary, well fed, groomed daily.

"I can't lose another brother," Qora said. "Please. Will you help me?"

TWO

A TUNNEL OF CURVED BONES marked the entry point to the quinoa farming community of Thak, and although the tunnel had been made from the rib cage of an enormous sauropod—such that walking through it gave the sensation of being swallowed up and digested—it seemed a small embellishment when compared to the vast fields of red-tipped stalks that lay beyond. The surrounding mountains were not as tall and looming as those closest to the capital, but they stood proudly, faded and green against the horizon.

Ninan swayed on the back of a rhabdodon as he rode through, holding reins in one hand and rubbing his sore jaw with the other. The reptile beneath him had scales as red as the quinoa, with black markings and a shawl of black-and-white feathers over its shoulder blades and forelimbs—a smaller cousin breed to the iguanodons that had helped plow the fields this past spring. She was no megaraptor, though, Ninan thought. Sure, she didn't require meat to survive, and she could shift between bipedal and quadrupedal posture ... but she was slow. The memory of swift cliff rides on raptorback induced a painful sense of longing.

Here in Thak, the air was thicker and warmer, and the work was endless. The people lived a good fifteen miles from the city, but they seemed content in this remote place, harvesting grain and weaving cloth and spinning wool.

Twenty-five adobe homes faced a central gathering place. Women hung laundry while children collected dried llama dung for the evening fires and hefted grain to the storehouse. Ninan gazed up at a rising pillar of smoke, which signaled the workers to come in. It was a method he'd only seen in remote areas like these, where people often spread out far and wide. The "smokers" were made of saltpeter and sugar—heated until the two created a thick substance—rolled up inside a thick papyr tube that burned quickly.

The men, young and old, who had been deep within the crops, sickles rustling, began to settle their motion, throw the last few bundles onto the drying heaps, and merge homeward.

Ninan slid from the rhabdodon and walked her to the dinoshelter, inadvertently drawing several children toward him as he went.

One of the boys, who wore a colorful woven cap with earflaps, shoved his way to the front. "You're back!"

"What'd you bring us?" said a little girl as she huffed to keep up.

"Bring you?" Ninan said. "Why do you think I'd bring you anything?"

"Come on," said a second boy.

Reaching the dinoshelter, Ninan removed the rhabdodon's saddle, along with his own belongings, and nudged her into a stall. "I don't know what you're talking about. I don't have anything you'd want."

"Please?" said the girl. She looked to the rest of the group, a collection of ragamuffins of various heights in various states of disarray—from dirt-smudged faces to worn, rough-spun clothing with patched knees—as if for confirmation that they all deserved whatever hidden goods Ninan might possess. One of them held three squirming compsognathus hatchlings as casually as if they were an armful of potatoes. The children all nodded with pleading enthusiasm.

"You won't be interested in what's in my bag." Ninan pulled the strap onto one shoulder and patted the main compartment, which was stretched over a lumpy mass. "It's just sweet anise bread and fried squash cakes."

The children all chattered at once, swarming him with their tiny fingers.

"Alright, alright!" Ninan held the bag above his head. "Everybody line up."

With impressive speed, they arranged themselves along the shelter wall, several of them bouncing on their toes as they waited.

"Now don't go getting everything all sticky, alright?" Ninan said, doling out the breads and cakes. "Your mamáys will never let me hear the end of it."

They all nodded and immediately bit in.

"Off you go, then." Ninan shooed them out of the shelter like wild sciurumimus and watched them skitter back to whatever they'd been doing before.

As he removed the rhabdodon's reins and hung them, Pidru appeared in the doorway. The boy was close to Ninan's age, but more slimly built, with a weariness that seemed to add to his years. His dark hands were rough from labor, his clothes worn thin because his father had used them for years before he had. He carried a small sickle and wiped his forehead with the back of his wrist.

"Nice of you to finally join us," said Pidru. "Now that it's quitting time."

Ninan frowned. "Don't be scaly. I came bearing gifts." His bag was empty now, but he was sure Pidru had seen the children on their way out.

"I've been here all afternoon busting my hindquarters while you've been wasting money at the market?"

Ninan withdrew a handful of silver coins from his pocket. "I think I can spare it."

Pidru scowled but took one of the coins and turned it over a couple of times. "You don't have to be such a showoff, you know."

Ninan clicked his tongue and grinned. "Come on. You're not really mad, are you?" He offered the rest of the coins. "Your mamáy can finish paying her taxes now. At least for the season. I pull my weight, even if it's not cutting stalks."

"You think you're too good for cutting," Pidru said.

"I'm not good *at* it. Everyone here can out-cut me in their sleep. They look at me like I'm a complete ruckhead. Anyway, who needs a sickle when I've got these?" He held up his fists, all bruised and swollen.

"You *are* a ruckhead," Pidru replied. "Or at least you will be if you keep taking punches like that."

"But I'll be a well-to-do ruckhead, won't I?"

Not that the money Ninan could make on his own would ever compare to what he used to have, but it certainly seemed to stretch further, the farther one lived from Qhusi.

Before Pidru could argue, a girl poked her head in, black hair in a top knot. Her nose, in silhouette, was the same shape as Pidru's, although smaller. "Pidi, aren't you coming to eat? Mamáy wants to know if—" She spotted Ninan an instant later and gasped. "Ninan! Where have you been?"

Ninan winced when she wrapped her arms around his waist

too abruptly. "Hi, Tamya. I went to Qhusi for a bit of work."

"'Work'?" Pidru repeated.

Tamya deflated and released Ninan. "You mean you were fighting again."

"You don't have to make it sound like a crime," Ninan told her. "It's perfectly legal—and lucrative. Anyway, how did you know? When did you get so smart?"

She shrugged. "I'm not a kid. I notice things."

Pidru shook his head. "Twelve is still very much a kid, Tamya. Although, so is eighteen—for some people."

Ninan blinked at him, unamused.

New smoke—this time from the cooking fires—carried the scent of roasting maize and vegetables all the way to the dinoshelter, reminding Ninan it had been a while since he'd last eaten. He'd hurried to get home from Qhusi, and his entire supply of breads and cakes had been depleted upon arrival. *Little velociraptors*, he thought. His stomach leapt.

He followed Pidru and Tamya to the central gathering zone, where families produced a variety of foods to share among the community.

Oviraptor meat sizzled on spits over flames. Sweet potatoes roasted in clay ovens. Pidru and Tamya's mamáy diced small peppers with some of the neighboring women.

Another woman worked at a griddle made from a sheet of flat stone laid over river rocks, with a blazing fire underneath. She motioned for one of the older girls to bring a basket of dinosaur eggs—large ones that could barely fit in one hand—and began cracking them onto the hot surface.

Within a few minutes, everyone had a ceramic bowl of something to eat, a bit of this and that, with corn beer or well water to drink. Ninan tried to go slow with his hash of sweet potatoes and corn, knowing the other boys his age had much more of a right to scarf down their food like starved reptiles, having cut hundreds of pounds of crop without a rest. He sat next to Pidru on a short retaining wall, eating quietly. Tamya was perched on a different wall among her friends, nibbling on a piece of corn bread. For all the work everyone had put in to harvest the quinoa, none of them ate a bite of it; it all went to Qhusi, mostly for interterrenal trade. The grain was a profitable commodity, much more valuable for business than as everyday sustenance for the locals.

Pidru flexed his fingers, all callused and cracked.

"Oh," said Ninan, setting down his bowl. "I almost forgot." He fished around in his bag until he found a small container and gave it to Pidru. "For quick healing." *Quick as silvers can afford*, he thought. It wasn't the near-magical cure of tyrannosaur or spinosaur marrow he himself had once had access to—a godsend for some of the deeper lesions he'd suffered in the past. But of course that kind of medicine could only be obtained in far-off places and on dangerous missions. To these people, even simple ointments from psittacosaurus oil were a luxury.

Pidru examined the container. "You're the worst, you know that?" He opened the ointment and dabbed a bit of it onto his palms, then rubbed them together and sighed. "You make it a chore to hate you—and sometimes, I really want to hate you."

Ninan nodded. "That's fair." He knew he hadn't been the most agreeable guest. Ninan had been quiet about where he'd come from, desperate enough to accept the kindness of strangers who were willing to feed him and give him a place to sleep. If he'd told them the truth, they never would have let him stay. And since then, he'd tried to keep up and learn, but even after almost a year he hadn't been able to fully adapt to this lifestyle. He longed for the air at high altitude, for the megaraptor paddock at dawn, for thick dino steaks and fine pisco, for a bedmat set off the ground and stuffed with ornithomimid feathers. He missed his old friends, regardless of how quickly they'd renounced him the second he'd fallen from grace.

Glancing at Tamya, Pidru added, "I always used to wish I had a brother."

"Is that right?" Ninan said.

Pidru pinched his lips together like he was suppressing a smile, and returned his attention to his meal. "I guess you'll have to do."

Ninan gave Pidru a shove, and Pidru reciprocated with double the force.

𝕯𝕯𝕯

A short while later, two children raced by in a frenzy. Ninan and Pidru looked up to see Tamya joining them, followed by several others.

"The courier's back!" Tamya said over her shoulder.

Heads lifted from their food. People turned toward the source of excitement. Children were practically skipping through the community, informing each household in turn. Anyone inside their homes emerged, peering out with a curious and hopeful gaze.

A man emerged from the far end of the road, meandering toward the people on the back of a green avaceratops—a smaller ceratopsian with two front horns, a mottle of brown down her back, and a splay of colorful feathers across her frill.

The community members bustled, and while Ninan would never fully understand the excitement over such a small event, he supposed he couldn't really blame them for looking forward to it. Otherwise, there wasn't much to do but work, and worry about paying what seemed to be exponentially rising taxes. Those who couldn't pay were often forced to donate time to state crops, or to other industries that served the qhapaq, like the skyrock quarries. Some even died there.

Ninan looked at Pidru, who cast a wistful glance at the setting sun. He'd told Ninan that he'd always used to watch it with his father—returning after the day's work was done to admire the trimmed field—the evidence of their labor awash in the glow of dusk. But Pidru never returned to the fields after work anymore.

The courier passed through the sauropod-rib gateway and slid down from his reptile's saddle, its back lumpy with packages. The community members went to him and gathered around, each giving him their names and a description of what they'd been expecting.

It was an interesting ritual, Ninan thought, the way the people showed off what they'd received, read letters together, shared news from the city.

The news this evening, however, was dominated by the upcoming Venture. The event everyone had been talking about for months was finally about to begin.

Ninan recalled the previous Venture, whose prize had been a chest of rosinqa gems nested in a den of smilodons. A weeks-long journey through Allpa's tropical savanna, facing dire wolves and several species of deadly spiders in addition to some of the more prominent dinosaurs—particularly dracovenators, who liked to bite off the heads of their prey before digging into the rest of the body. As if the journey hadn't been enough on its own, the competitors had then been required to successfully evade or kill the dozens of vicious saber-toothed cats that guarded the prize.

Competitors never had a clue what they'd signed up for until the announcement that took place three days prior to their sendoff. And even then, they were only told the prize they'd be chasing and given a map to guide them to it. The true danger wouldn't be revealed until someone arrived at the end. But if they could make it, they'd earn the item *and* an enormous sum of money.

Two Ventures ago, the prize had been an ancient artifact—the golden shield of one of the qhapaqs who had ruled the Old Empire—to be found upon the snowy peaks of Huandoy. When the final three competitors had reached the appropriate summit, they discovered that the shield had been installed among a colony of pterodaustro, whose long bills were lined with hundreds of thin spike-teeth. Before emerging victorious with the shield, the champion had had his right arm torn from its socket and shredded before Venture watchguards had finally come to retrieve him.

Every endpoint was a long journey from the start, to test the endurance of the competitors—and give them time to interact along the way. These interactions were made public as the Venture coordinators sent out heralds, who flew over the competition route daily and returned to the city with updates. Artists depicted scenes, and fictionists spun stories, and everyone sat on the edges of their seats biting their nails.

Plenty of the people who entered weren't even expecting to win; they only wanted the potential fame that would come with the spectacle of it all. They might have to give up and turn back halfway through, but they'd return to a nation that knew their names—at least for a while.

For others, it was financial desperation that drove them to

enter, the prize itself and the large sum of money that came after obtaining it. Only fifty competitors from each Terrain would be selected—after a series of entrance trials—and each competitor's family was guaranteed a smaller sum of money if they died along the way. In fact, landmarks at each leg of the journey functioned as checkpoints, guaranteeing payments for reaching them.

Ninan suspected it was easier to construct narratives for the competitors when they had compelling motivations for competing. The man whose property would be lost if he couldn't pay his past-due taxes. The orphan who must prove himself worthy to marry a highborn's daughter. The greedy gambler who never met a challenge he didn't like, so long as there was a monetary prize involved.

Unfortunately, a good number of them would die within the first twenty-four hours.

Although Ninan missed the city—only having recently mustered the courage to sneak into its lowlier venues to fight—he was grateful, at least, to be away from the tiresome reminders of the Venture (with the exception of these bits of chatter from the locals about it). The public's growing terrenal pride only reminded him of the emblem that had been permanently inked on him in infancy, the one he could not erase but which no longer granted him any status.

And then, as though these thoughts of his former life had magically summoned a demonic, physical manifestation of it, a shrill sound halted the conversations around him.

Ninan looked up. His breath lodged in his throat.

A man in a dark uniform soared over the distant treetops on a single-rider flying reptile—a giant albino pteranodon with faintly dappled wings. He tore through the sky, the pteranodon's wingflaps stirring the air as he crossed into the quinoa field.

"Mullu," Ninan whispered. He looked around, pulse beating like a ritual drum. The people had turned raucous, scattering in in all directions in a panic.

Mullu descended, coming straight to Ninan, arrow to prey. Whether Ninan were to run, hide, fight, it didn't matter; his whereabouts were clearly known. The qhapaq could raid the whole of the farming region if Ninan tried to disappear.

Pidru was positioned to flee but hesitated, seeming to sense that Ninan knew something.

Tamya took Ninan's hand and tugged at him. "Come on!"

The pteranodon tipped back its point-crested head, opened its mouth, and screeched.

Ninan gently pried himself from Tamya's grasp. "This is about me. I'm the one he wants. You both need to go."

Tamya and Pidru exchanged glances, but Ninan shouted "Go!" and they both headed back toward the houses, although not without casting concerned looks over their shoulders.

Mullu landed the flyer like they shared one mind, fluid and sure. Perfectly graceful except that the half-ton pteranodon was so large, it crushed quinoa stalks fifty feet across before it came to a full stop and tucked away its wings.

Ninan forced a confident stance.

There was a time when his confidence wouldn't have been forced in front of Mullu, though, he thought. Back when the man had known him under a different name. Respected him. Would have had to kneel before him.

Chief attendant to the qhapaq himself and Mullu still had had to obey Ninan's command. But those days were over.

In another fluid movement, Mullu dismounted and turned to face Ninan, no more than two yards from where the boy stood. He was dressed in black, wearing a helmet with skyrock embedded on the rim. On his chest, he bore the symbol of the Three Crescents in red. He brandished a skyrock-tipped staff, then nodded at the saddle strapped around the base of the pteranodon's neck.

"Get on. Your father wants to see you."

THREE

IN NEAR DARKNESS, the abandoned dye bath outside the stone house looked like a pool of blood, color-sapped petals and mashed berry skins floating on the surface. That careful balance of ingredients to produce the perfect hue had been for nothing, Qora thought.

A rainbow of loose yarn skeins hung from the drying rack, flecked with wind-blown debris and beginning to tangle. It had been weeks since Qora's mamáy had taken anything to market.

Qora's knapsack was empty now and her pockets were full, thanks to Sakay's help, but she wouldn't be able to get to an apothecary until morning—and she would have to go all the way across the city to the Kichka District to find the right one.

It had been an eerie meeting with the smuggler—the man Sakay had determined would be the most discreet and generous. Qora had been instructed to arrive at a specific location on the outskirts of Qhusi, and to come alone, no exceptions.

"This is a bad idea," Sakay had said. "I can't just let you go alone."

"He explicitly said he won't meet me any other way. It makes sense to have as few people involved as possible. The fewer witnesses, the better."

"Or he wants to take advantage of you."

Qora had given him a sharp look.

"Financially," Sakay had clarified. "I didn't say who my 'client' was, or any details about you—for that reason."

"Thank you for the forethought, but I'm used to people trying to push me around. And I'll have a weapon."

That hadn't quite satisfied him, but eventually, he had let Qora leave.

The location had been a narrow, deserted passageway between city buildings, where the smuggler had already been waiting. He'd been broad shouldered and fierce, in a wide dinoleather belt and alpaca-fiber cloak dyed black. One look at him and Qora had felt she would have just as soon turned back, forgotten the whole thing—but it would have been worse to have given up so quickly.

"Well, you're practically an infant." His comment had made Qora wish she'd thought to take out her braids, but even though they aged her down, they kept her hair off her face in the windy woods stalking prey. Still, the smuggler had been impressed with Qora's prize and had been surprisingly easy to deal with.

Tomorrow couldn't come soon enough.

Now Qora huffed and dodged the brood of little, feathered compsognathus that squeaked and scuttled across her family property, taking care not to step on any tails. Qora had bred them from wild hatchlings to keep mice out of the grain, and to lay eggs for cooking, but the compies reproduced so quickly it seemed like they were everywhere all the time—and their bright-green coloring made them hard to miss.

The property was cramped compared to the land Qora's family had once owned. It certainly wasn't the meadow near the foothills, whose lush grasses Qora's mamáy had named her for, but the plot was livable.

Qora's family even kept a dozen alpacas within a palisade, covered in a rope net to keep out reptilian predators. Mammals were precious commodities—for wool or fiber to make textile yarns, and also for milk—and most people were lucky to have any at all. For that reason, it was best to only make meat out of reptiles.

Inside, the house was cluttered with different pigment sources. An open sack of red hibiscus blossoms dried out from neglect, bowls of tara pods and collpa once meant to produce a slate-like shade of blue, and ch'illca leaves—the same kind Qora had used to dye her bayeta jacket green.

Regardless of so many aromatic items, however, the whole place smelled of holy wood, its sweet scent catching Qora off guard. Her eyes fell first to the bowl on the floor, where a tiny bundle of the blunt-cut wood pieces smoldered, and then to the kneeling shaman, who wore woven skirts over her narrow hips, a necklace made of some small dinosaur's vertebrae, and an embroidered cap with little beads around the rim. The shaman knelt over a bedmat, where a young boy lay half asleep, and spoke rapidly in a soft tone to invite Sky Mother's blessings.

Qora's oldest living brother, Hakan, stood off to the side with their mamáy, head bowed. At just thirteen, he was taller than everyone else in the house. Tight-lipped and wide-eyed, he seemed to warn her to stay back and keep quiet, although Qora already knew she was in trouble for her late arrival.

As the shaman shook a bundle of chakapa leaves over the small boy's body to cleanse the energy that surrounded him, Qora's mamáy clasped her hands, grayish and stained from all her years working with dye.

Her mamáy was a petite woman, but her energy—when it was at full force—could dominate a room. Lately, though, she was like a rag that had been wrung too many times, lank and drab with her energy sapped out. Even her onyx-black hair, which she wore long but tied back, seemed to have lost its luster.

Qora remembered the time "before." She remembered her mamáy's vibrant hope, her round belly that seemed to have grown from nothing overnight. She remembered spending summer days scampering in the grass with Hakan, the two of them pestering Ollan, whose deepening, adolescent voice occasionally sounded like the screech of a newborn rhamphorhynchus. She remembered the day that her mamáy had suddenly turned quiet, how the shaman had then pulled Qora aside to explain that the child her mamáy had been carrying had turned quiet, too—permanently.

It hadn't been the first of her mamáy's children to turn quiet. Thanks to Qora, it hadn't been the last.

Ollan's voice had been so loud just before turning quiet, Qora thought. So loud, she didn't think she'd ever not hear it again.

Qora—run!

Baby Rimaq had come shortly after the loss of the previous pregnancy, a bright ray in the darkness, but his light was dimming now.

He looks so small, Qora thought of the boy on the bedmat. Littlest brother, beacon of hope, consolation. His doll-perfect face was sallow, specked with blisters, some crusted over while others remained red and tender. Bits of dried mucus had accumulated on his thick lashes. His eight and a half years seemed like nothing in the wake of this illness.

The shaman continued to rattle chakapa leaves, employing different rhythms and motions. She followed this ritual by wafting tobacco smoke over Rimaq, and finished with a song of healing.

After a series of parting pleasantries, the shaman saw herself out, leaving the family to themselves.

Qora's mamáy picked up a clump of alpaca fiber and carded it with her fingers—an idle task to keep her mind busy, Qora figured, as she likely wouldn't be spinning the fiber to yarn any time soon. Then her mamáy cast a sharp look at Qora's boots.

Qora squinched her toes inside the dinoleather. In all the chaos with the raptoriva and the golds, and then having to wait for the shaman, she'd forgotten to take them off. Sometimes she liked to think that it was only their dirty nature that bothered her mamáy—the fact that they had mud and probably a little ruck dried onto them—rather than the boots themselves. Under different circumstances, maybe. As it was, Qora and her mamáy had very different ways of grieving.

Hakan, seeming to sense the tension in the air, cleared his throat. "I'm going to go put the compies in their coop for the night."

Once he'd gone, Qora said, "Sorry I'm late," then slipped her feet out of the boots without untying the laces and set them outside the door.

"Sky Mother's envoy spirits require devotion from everyone in the household," her mamáy said.

Qora frowned. "Does Sky Mother really just want us to stand around pleading for miracles? Wouldn't she rather we actively went out and looked for them?"

"You mean by wasting all your working hours stalking reptiles in the woods?"

"That's not—"

"It means nothing that I've asked you repeatedly not to do it? There's plenty of work in the city, but you'd rather risk your life—and my sanity—tromping through ruck?"

Qora huffed and went to her brother. She knelt beside the bedmat, resisting the urge to stroke the boy's cheek, knowing it would only cause him more pain. Instead, she settled on slipping her hand under his palm—one of the few places where the theropox had not affected him.

"City work is a con," Qora said. "People drudge away till their fingers bleed and get almost nothing at the end of it. I can spend the same daily hours hunting dinosaurs and trade them for the same or even three times the wage."

"You never know when to quit, Qora. As if it's not enough that you nearly lost your life once, you have to tempt the keepers of the Grave World again and *again* …"

It was true, Qora thought. She didn't know when to quit. Or maybe it was that she simply *couldn't* quit. Not since she'd first realized she could kill a reptile for more than its meat. The market, always flush with dinoleathers and bone jewelry, had been proof of that. The shimmer of a dromaeosaur-leather belt hanging on display, the clack of sharp tooth-bead necklaces dangling against each other. People wanted those skins; they wanted those teeth. They were willing to pay and Qora was eager to receive. It was a power she wanted to wield, no matter the risks. More than that, it was a way to spit into the face of her demons, to tell them she would not be driven out in fear.

"I can get the sparkshade," Qora said.

Her mamáy's fingers, tangled in alpaca fiber, paused. She looked at Qora. "What?"

Qora stood and took out a small, velvet sack. She turned it upside down, spilling several gold coins into her palm.

Her mamáy covered her mouth and stared at the coins for several seconds, inhaled slowly and said, "What have you done?"

"I got what we needed."

"You know what I mean. That's *gold*, Qora."

"It was a trade." She offered the coins to her mother, who flinched like they were cursed. "You won't even touch them?" Qora asked. "Rimaq is so fragile, Mamáy. I'd trade my *soul* to give him more time. Maybe I just have—but if I did, it was worth it."

It was the only way they ever would have been able to afford sparkshade, a silver honey produced from the nectar of inqa-lillies grown in soil laced with skyrock dust—and the singular product known to be able to obliterate deadly viruses.

"I appreciate your dedication to your brother, Qora, but you must not fall victim to a false dilemma. It doesn't have to be your soul or his life. There must be a way to keep both. There are other ways to solve this."

Qora sighed. "What—more prayer? More rituals?" She slipped the coins back into the sack and offered them again.

Shakily, her mamáy accepted, brows furrowed. "Promise me you haven't brought a curse on our home with these golds."

"I can't promise that. But I can promise I'll get the sparkshade, and that the sparkshade will help Rimi to recover. He'll have the strength he needs to fight the theropox."

Her mamáy held the sack to her chest and eyed Rimaq, who had fallen asleep. He was half covered, because it hadn't seemed right not to have a blanket on him at all, but a mist of sweat glistened on his face.

"Qora, you can't keep doing things like this. I swear, sometimes it's like you're trying to … *prove* something."

Qora sat back down beside Rimaq, trying to imagine how they'd ever cope without him. Sometimes it felt as though everyone she'd ever loved was leaving her behind in the world, one by one. First Ollan, then her papáy. Now Rimaq.

"I know you wish it had been me instead of Ollan."

Her mamáy sighed. "Again with the false dilemmas …"

Paying closer attention to the sweat on her brother's hairline, Qora pressed a hand to his forehead. He winced at the contact.

"He's too warm," Qora said. "I'm going to get him some water."

She hurried to the well behind the house.

When she reached the well bucket, she dipped her head back and growled. The handle had fallen off again, its rusted metal and splitting wood prone to malfunction.

She fumbled with the parts, trying to make them fit back together, but each attempt seemed to cause everything to fall apart all over again. Suddenly she felt a hand on her shoulder—a delicate touch. Qora stopped.

She wasn't sure how she'd let her mamáy sneak up on her. She supposed it was because she'd spent more time attuning her senses to dinosaurs—hours sitting up in high branches listening to their sounds and observing different species, their packs, their patterns, their habits—rather than to people.

"'Be precise or do it twice,'" her mamáy said.

She was always spouting similar phrases, and this one more often with Qora than with Hakan or Rimaq, which made Qora angry. Qora, of all people, knew the importance of precision— the precise way to hold her weapon, the precise spot on a reptile to shoot for a perfect kill—but there were times when she couldn't fathom how anyone could worry about small details when a situation demanded fast action. That was the irony of being hasty or impatient, her mamáy would have said: Haste often led to mistakes, and mistakes would often cost double the time to repair.

Even in her anger, though, the motherly touch calmed Qora

a little. She slowed down, concentrated, worked the pieces again, and within a minute she had everything set up to draw the water. She felt her mamáy's hand slide gently away. While she longed for that touch, she also felt a certain sense of relief without it. Qora had done too much harm to deserve it.

It was unnatural, Qora thought, to feel so distant from the woman who had borne her, from the woman in whose body her fragile life had formed. Now it seemed they couldn't be farther apart, even standing right next to each other. The most familiar strangers.

"Thank you for getting the golds," her mamáy said quietly. "But … please … no more of these kinds of risks."

Trembling, Qora nodded once. "I'll go to the apothecary at dawn. And that'll be it, I swear."

As Qora's mamáy took her hand, a pair of copper-helmeted men emerged on megaraptors, treading onto the property.

Qora withdrew, feeling instinctively for her crossbow even though she'd left it inside.

Her mamáy's eyes widened with concern. "City officials?"

The officials dismounted and approached Qora directly.

Relax, Qora told herself. *There are plenty of reasons for—*

"What is this?" her mamáy demanded. "What's going on?"

Qora backed away but the officials flanked her. One of them took her by the arm. "You're under arrest."

The Terrain of Sumaq shall be represented, additionally, by the symbol of the Three Crescents.

Let the first be the sickle that cuts the quinoa. Let the second be a claw for the reptiles that inhabit our land. Let the third be the light of the quarter moon, and the protection of our beloved moon spirit.

Each of these three shall also represent the Three Worlds: the Grave World below (from which the quinoa seeds sprout), the Earth Itself (upon which the reptiles walk), and the High World above (in which the moon spirit dwells).

All who live and work under the qhapaq shall have the honor and obligation to wear this symbol in perpetuity, as it shall be branded upon the back of the right hand, so that such service to gods and Terrain may never be forgotten.

Statutes of Sumaq, Book VII, Article IV

FOUR

NINAN PEERED OVER THE SIDE of the pteranodon at the wafting mists that spanned the gorge below. It was only as the mists parted that he had a full view of the steep drop that separated Sumaq's capital city of Qhusi from its ruling Kallpa House. The thinner mists, which hung like sheer curtains in front of the castle itself, blurred its details, much the way Ninan's memory of his old home had been blurred in his mind all these months. No matter how many times he'd arrived from the sky just like this, no matter how many years he'd spent at the castle as a child, the whole place seemed to have lost its sharpness whenever he'd tried to picture it lately. Now, as the pteranodon dipped for its final descent, Ninan felt his stomach dip too.

This was real. He was returning home.

But *why*?

His exile from this high place—from his titled place among his family—was supposed to have been permanent. He wondered if his recent prizefighting had somehow drawn the attention of the qhapaq's staff, if his presence in the city—even incognito and in an obscure place like the Underground—had displeased the supreme leader. Would Ninan be punished for it now? He swallowed hard.

The pteranodon landed on one of several stone-paved

landing pads that made up a large, open area leading up to the castle's entrance. Nearby, a pterobeast gondola full of Kallpa House staff was simultaneously set down, while another carrying a couple of ambassadors lifted away. Other pteranodons, which were only a third of the size of the pterobeasts, arrived and departed around them. The flyers screeched at one another, but otherwise did as they'd been trained to do. Ninan had always found their posture disturbing, the way they propped themselves up on their forelimbs, which looked like inverted elbows—made worse by the little claws that protruded from the bend. At least these ones had some feathers, he thought, thanks to the cooler mountain climate; on past travels he'd seen desert flyers with nothing but skin and scales that drew attention to their jagged, bony figures. He flinched as the nearest pterobeast swung its massive head around and twisted its long neck; its equally long and pointed beak could knock out a passenger with one swipe.

For that reason, the handlers wore skyrock-studded breastplates and helmets, and carried skyrock-tipped staves and plenty of skyrock dust to keep the flyers in line.

The bigger the breed, the more you need.

Mullu slid down and motioned for Ninan to do the same, removing his riding gloves and revealing the Three Crescents—branded onto the right back of his hand—that all employees of Kallpa House bore.

The mists thinned again, an inevitable break in their constant ebb and flow, revealing the magnificent carved-out walls and pillars of Kallpa House. Other walls, constructed high and wide, set the castle apart from the initial slab, while the mountainsides that had not been carved up—at least not to such an extent— were cut into flat tiers, each landscaped for a different purpose.

Ninan immediately picked out the reptile paddocks on the

lower levels and the combat training grounds above them, with several levels of specialized microcrops in between, and garden viewing areas on top.

As Mullu escorted Ninan into the courtyard, workers looked up from their activities, many of them stunned with recognition. Mullu, however, gave them his typical, granite-faced warning glare and they all averted their eyes.

Ninan and Mullu then passed a grand fountain, with its spinosaur statue at the center spewing water from its mouth. Multiple stairways came into view, some leading up to balcony terraces and higher levels of the qhapaq's home, others leading downward to cellars and subterranean storehouses.

A reptile handler headed off toward the menagerie carrying an archaeopteryx whose wing feathers were a gradient of magenta and yellow. An impressive addition, Ninan thought, although he didn't like to think about the underhanded ways Qhapaq Apo got his hands on exotic animals—mostly reptiles—for his collection.

Finally, Mullu led Ninan to the summit hall, so called for both its high-point location within Kallpa House *and* its use as a gathering place for important meetings. It had been the location of many negotiations between Qhapaq Apo and leaders of other Terrains. It had also been the last room of Kallpa House that Ninan had set foot in before he'd been forced to leave, the place where his fate had been determined.

Inside, four high-backed seats were set against the wall. The largest seat was made of mahogany and carved with a collage of carnivorous reptiles.

Fitting, Ninan thought, although he remained silent as Mullu directed him to stand before the empty seats.

Tapestries lined the hall, bearing embroidered scenes

of historical battles or epic encounters from folklore, most involving fierce reptiles and shiny blades; one depicted a scene from Sumaq's legendary air battle with the Kastillans, fought on the backs of pteranodons over the Urubamba Mountain Range. Racks of spears spanned the east wall, relics of the ruling family's ancestors, fletched with expensive dino feathers.

Various birds and reptilian flyers were on display throughout the space, many of which Ninan could not name. They were all rare, of course, and so Ninan wasn't sure why he bothered to try and recognize any of them anyway. Epidexipteryx, he was fairly certain, was the name of the one by the door. Another, on the far wall, was likely a nyctosaur, as he'd heard such reptiles had similarly long, branching head crests. The only one he knew for sure, though, was the little green one that held the place of honor in the gilded cage at the north corner: raptoriva, a shimmering flyer with four wings. There had been a few sightings of these recently, owing to the volcanic smoke covering so much of the eastern coast and driving them westward.

Mullu stood off to the side with his hands clasped behind his back. Moments later, Qhapaq Apo entered, dressed in sleeveless red and black robes that bared his tan, muscular arms. He wore the gold-plated likeness of the top half of a spinosaur skull as a headpiece, a special sort of crown that flaunted the terrenal symbol—because although the Terrain of Sumaq no longer incorporated the lands where such large predators dwelled, it had once been the hub of the Old Empire that had. The spinosaurs were endangered now, and what was left of them remained only beyond the Pirqas.

The qhapaq set his square jaw firm and looked at Ninan. The man was silent, however, and took his seat right of center.

The quyas entered behind him, three wives dressed in robes

similar to that of their husband. Their dark arms were more delicate, and decorated with gold bands. The first wore a crown of gilded dinosaur teeth, while the second and third wore simple circlets. The first took her place to the left of the qhapaq, and the other two sat on either side of the central pair. It was a visual representation of the arrangement that all Sumaqi leaders upheld: a primary wife whose child was assumed to continue the family line, and two additional wives whose children would act as reserves—should the first prove inadequate. Three wives, in similitude of the symbol of the Three Crescents. Once each had produced a male child, the qhapaq was to lie with her no longer. For this reason, the qhapaq kept an entire wing of the castle dedicated to his mistresses. Additional children would be illegitimate, of course, although many would go on to serve the qhapaq closely in some way.

Ninan found himself reaching toward his mother, the third wife, but quickly retracted his hand and made a fist at his side. He mouthed the word *mamáy* and the woman heaved a breath that seemed to be relief—as she had, after all, been unaware whether Ninan had lived or died—her dark eyes watering as they met Ninan's. He pressed his lips together and gave a subtle head bow, wishing he could speak to her, but he wouldn't know whether that was possible until the qhapaq provided the reason for calling him here.

"Apo-Kimsa," said the qhapaq.

Ninan flinched at the sound of his name—his *real* name.

His Majesty Qhapaq Apo Kallpa, because he was so grand and formidable (having taken power at the ripe age of seventeen) had named each of his sons after himself: Apo-Huk, Apo-Iskay, and Apo-Kimsa. But no one had called Ninan by his birth name in so long, it hardly seemed to belong to him anymore.

"I'm called Ninan now."

The qhapaq stroked his chin, taking in Ninan's appearance. "Hmm. Well, I suppose it suits you. A common name for a common boy."

Of course it did, with his unkempt hair and his muddy boots and a face tinged with bruises. Nothing about him was princely anymore. He couldn't even fully remember what that felt like.

"One of the few things I've chosen for myself," Ninan replied

He thought again of the emblem tattooed on the back of his neck just below the hairline, a small shield with a roaring spinosaur inside of it—the emblem of both the Terrain of Sumaq and the Kallpa family alike. His hair was just long enough to cover it, but it lurked there, a reminder of his now-lost heritage. It was a tradition of royal families to mark their children this way, the very beginning of the things that would be forced upon them.

"Oh, you chose many things for yourself," the qhapaq argued. "You *chose* to gamble away your monthly allocations at raptor races and high-stakes token exchanges. You *chose* to disgrace the House of Kallpa in public on numerous occasions. And you certainly *chose* to find yourself among renegades during a time when our nation's image has grown fragile. I'm not sure what you expected from me, but it certainly could not have been lenience or mercy."

Ninan couldn't argue with that. He had indeed spent his money on games and bets and drinks. He'd gotten into drunken brawls and stumbled into the wrong places, one of which has been some sort of gathering of renegades. It had been unintentional, but his presence there had been enough to brand him a traitor and get him banished from Kallpa House forever.

Ninan shook his head. "I didn't expect anything. I stopped

expecting anything from you *long* before you stripped me of my title and flew me out to the wilderness to fend for myself. If there was one thing I *might* have expected, it was that you wouldn't care enough about me to notice I wasn't around—much less what I was doing while I was out. But … I guess you only notice those beneath you when they harm your ego."

If Ninan hadn't been expecting it, he would have missed the hand gesture the qhapaq directed at Mullu, who promptly stepped forward and struck Ninan across the back with a skyrock staff.

Ninan bit his tongue to keep from crying out, and crumpled to his knees. On the way down he caught a glimpse of his mother's face, her eyes glossy with emerging tears—but she kept her trembling hands folded in her lap against the fabric of her dress, her fingers ringed with rosinqa stones.

Once he had steadied himself, and the initial onslaught of pain had subsided, Ninan asked, "Is this what you dragged me back here for? Another beating?"

"While I'd relish the chance," said the qhapaq, "to discipline you further … no, it is not. I've brought you here to present you with an opportunity."

Opportunity? Ninan kept from laughing only to avoid another strike against him. He'd heard that word too many times from his father, and it was always intended to make the listener believe they were the recipient of some grand prize when, in fact, it was a proposition. Qhapaq Apo didn't "extend opportunities"; he made business deals.

"An opportunity for *me?*" Ninan said in a noticeably inauthentic tone. "I'm honored. Here I was wondering how you found me—why you would have even bothered to look for me at all, especially considering I'm not one of your heirs anymore."

"Yes, well," the qhapaq said, "There wasn't much looking to

be done. Prizefighting isn't the most inconspicuous of activities. Especially not for those with skills like yours."

Ninan huffed. "That almost sounds like a compliment."

"A compliment, perhaps, to the instructors that *I* appointed to train you—many of whom you disrespected and whose lessons you missed. It's no wonder you lack achievement in other areas. I'm surprised *anything* stuck." The qhapaq stood and approached him, emphasizing that he had to look down to meet Ninan's eyes.

"Then I guess I don't understand why you think I'd be interested in this … 'opportunity,'" Ninan replied.

"An opportunity that you do not deserve, but which I am willing to extend in order to restore the broken image of the Kallpa household. The Terrain is in need of a more united mentality."

"You must be awfully desperate if you need *my* help to do that." Ninan caught sight of his father's commanding gesture once again, but this time he reflexed fast enough to catch Mullu's staff in a tight fist. In the same motion, he sprang to his feet and twisted the weapon away, flipping it back on the assistant.

As Mullu prepared to unsheathe a blade, the qhapaq simply said, "Leave him be."

Mullu let up, reluctantly, and kept his eyes trained on Ninan.

"A point for my son," the qhapaq told him. "In whatever game he thinks we're playing." He began to walk in an observational circle around Ninan, looking over his appearance, his posture. He took the staff and returned it calmly to Mullu, then turned back to his son. "You've always been adept at defending yourself with your hands, *Ninan*—setting the bar high for your brothers, despite their age and size over you—I won't deny it. I allowed them to test you. Encouraged it, in fact. Somehow, you always managed to hold your own."

Sure, Ninan thought, if holding his own meant taking dozens of punches to the gut before he'd finally figured out how to block properly. If it meant narrowly escaping the full force of Apo-Iskay's favorite knife—which had left a deep scar on Ninan's upper ear—until he'd learned that his brothers were incredibly fallible without their weapons and thus had developed underhanded ways to manipulate them physically.

The qhapaq stopped to face him. "The question is … Can you employ your skills for a greater purpose?"

Ninan had to fight to slow his breath, to tamp down the anger that simmered just under the surface of his composure. "What purpose would that be, exactly?"

"The purpose of redemption," said Qhapaq Apo. "I'd like to offer you the opportunity to earn back your title—to return to the life into which you were born, and regain all the privileges that come with it."

Ninan shook his head in disbelief. Earn back his title? His inheritance? His "honor"—whatever that meant?

"How?" he asked.

The qhapaq rested his palm on one of the trapezoidal plates of his necklace. "Our longstanding laws state that one who has been disinherited, even in cases where treasonous behavior is concerned, may be both redeemed and restored, should he perform an act of valor, particularly when such an act is done within the context of nationalism.

Ninan narrowed his eyes. "I'm listening …"

"Enter the Venture" said the qhapaq. "And win."

Ninan scoffed. "Are you insane?" He should have known it hadn't been the end when he'd been disinherited. The qhapaq had always been particular about his image, about the image of his household—and his first attempt to cleanse it hadn't been enough. Especially not when the other Terrains were watching. "You want me to participate in that stupid game? *Those* are your terms? If you want me dead, why don't you just execute me yourself? It would look much better publicly—really show off how ruthless you are."

"The Venture is a display of skill and endurance," Qhapaq Apo said sharply. "A tribute to the warriors and hunters and crusaders that built the Old Empire, with its vast trade networks and its mines and quarries. The whole of Runaqa will be watching. I, even in my eminent position, can't redeem you simply by saying so—no one would truly recognize your place or respect you—but if you can endure the Venture—at least make it to the end alive—you'll have earned back your place in the eyes of not only Sumaq but all Five Terrains. If you can manage to win, even better."

Ninan inhaled slowly, stiffly, taking it all in. Lips pursed, heart pounding. His father couldn't be serious. He was likely asking Ninan to traverse hundreds of miles of some kind of wilderness, and face countless wild and vicious reptiles—and that was to say nothing of the desperate and greedy competitors who would fall all over each other with blades. Stepping on the others. Murdering anyone who got in their way. The Venture was a call to some of the most brutal people on the continent. Everyone else would be quick casualties.

"For your own safety, you would not share your true identity until the games are over. You would compete in disguise, acting as a common Venturer," the qhapaq explained. "How convenient that you already embody the part."

"I'll embody the part of a dead man. There's no way I can do this. I'd be lucky just to make it past the first few days alive—and you want me to try to *win*?"

"Kallpa House will provide you with resources, so far as we're allowed to do," Mullu explained. "You'll be given state-of-the-art weaponry, advanced armor, an ample food supply, skyrock and skyrock dust to protect you against the reptiles. All discreetly, of course. Hidden under common clothes and within a common carrying pack."

"I've appointed Mullu as a herald," the qhapaq added. "He'll keep an eye on you—although, this being an international event, the other Terrains will be watching as well, and we can't allow anyone to believe we've assisted you or shown you favoritism. This would defy the entire purpose of the assignment."

"So this isn't really about me proving myself. It's the *illusion* of proving myself—to preserve the image of Kallpa House."

"The House to which you will once again belong, so long as you manage to survive. Then we'll tell everyone you've returned, all heritage restored. I think it will be a wonderful conclusion to the Venture, for the Five Terrains to witness your redemption at the champion's homecoming ceremony."

Ninan's mother gave him a pleading glance from her seat, even though she knew he couldn't easily say no to this. Kallpa House beckoned him. The view of Qhusi from above, the clear mountain air, the comforting mists. His old room, his old clothes, and clean, abundant water. He'd never be hungry and he would once again have the Terrain at his fingertips. The dark shadows of the household seemed minimal when he really thought about it—like the silly nightmares of a child, which he could dispel with logic. And, after all, Mullu had said he would be given every possible resource at his disposal during the Venture—food, weapons, protections. Many other competitors could only afford to leave with the clothes on their backs and a bit of hunting gear. Some were good in combat but lousy at feeding themselves, while others were decent hunters but couldn't hold up against better fighters. If Ninan was careful and could avoid making enemies, all he would really need to worry about would be the challenge at the end, whatever monster guarded the prize. Even then, with the state-of-the-art weapons he'd been promised, he might be able to do it. Who cared if his father only wanted to repair his own reputation? Ninan wouldn't have to hide anymore, or worry that someone might discover his past.

Although it did also occur to him that he might never see Pidru or Tamya again. He didn't imagine it would be permitted that he spent time in such places, but he was no stranger to sneaking out when it suited his whims. Would his friends forgive him, though, once they knew the truth?

He'd been considering the details for too long, hesitating. The qhapaq stepped forward and said, "Or maybe all that bravado that first lost you your princehood is the extent of your courage. So courageous in your rebellious acts against your household, but no bravery in sight for something that actually poses a true danger."

Ninan's jaw clenched in response. He lifted his chin and met the qhapaq's eyes. "Fine," he said. Maybe it was time to show his father what he was really made of. "Let's get started."

FIVE

THE CREAK OF RUSTED HINGES spurred Qora to consciousness and she squinted at the morning light. She wasn't sure when she'd actually managed to doze off, between the drunken moaning that had come from the cell beside her and the sheer devastation of being there in the first place. She rubbed her eyes and rolled her neck, her whole body tight from having slept curled up on the floor. It was as though she'd taken a physical beating, even though it had been more of an assault to her entire sense of self.

The guard held the barred door open and Sakay appeared behind him.

"Spirits, Qora—are you alright?" Sakay rushed toward her. He grabbed her by the shoulders and looked her over, then examined the cell as though it had been some kind of torture chamber, but there was nothing except a bench, an empty water cup, and Qora.

"How did you know I was here?" Qora asked.

"I got word that some of the reptile trades had been compromised, so I went to your house to check on you, and your mamáy told me what happened."

With an impatient gesture toward the outside of the cell, the guard said, "Any day now, kid. I'm not going to stand here forever."

"You're really just letting me go?" said Qora.

"Temporarily," the guard clarified. "Thanks to your benefactor."

Sakay didn't meet Qora's eyes.

"No …" Qora said. "You don't have money for that."

"I made a little extra on an 'underdog' yesterday," he reminded her. "Besides, this is my fault. I never should have let you make that trade. I should have talked you out of it."

"Like you *could* have?"

"Fine, then. I should have tied you up and gagged you while I set the little flyer free."

Qora stepped out of the cell and the guard escorted her and Sakay to another officer, who explained what would come next.

"Your case has been evaluated and your course of discipline has been determined," he said. "You have four weeks to pay in full." He returned her belongings and then issued her a document, rattling off the legal details in a dull tone, informing her that because of her age and because she was not yet married, her parents were responsible for whatever sum she was unable to pay on her own, and that the fine could only be forgiven in the event of her death, in which case the city would not pursue her family financially—only because she had not inflicted permanent damage to property or persons, and because she would be unable to offend a second time, on account of not being alive to do so.

Qora looked at the number and her stomach twisted itself into a hard knot. A strangled voice came out of her. "This is more than everything I own. More than my family's land. My arresting officers have already seized my profit from the raptoriva—isn't that enough?"

"This is a first offense," Sakay told the officer. "She's a kid."

"Doesn't matter," said the officer. "Fifteen is the legal age of criminal accountability and she's seventeen. Plenty of girls her age are responsible for entire households."

"Is there really no other option?" Sakay asked.

"If she'd rather sign a labor contract, we can arrange it here."

"An indenture," Qora concluded. "Work for free until the fine is paid?" And of course that would leave her unable to hunt, or even work for a regular wage that she could contribute to household expenses. Without her help, her mamáy would never be able to keep up. Not to mention Rimaq wouldn't likely survive the next few months if he didn't get that sparkshade, which may have been stardust for how financially out of reach it was from Qora now.

"With a sum like this, though," said the officer, "You'd be looking at ten to fifteen years. You'd be required to live in the labor dormitories and would only be allowed to leave upon full payment."

Sakay's mouth hung open. "Ten to fifteen *years*?"

"Due to the fact that criminal wages are less than half the terrenal minimum. Although, at her age, and with a bit of cleaning up, she *might* be able to pay off a few years sooner if she'd be willing to perform"—he lowered his voice—"special favors."

Qora recoiled. Sakay lunged at the officer but Qora held him back; as much as she would have liked to give the man a bloody nose, she didn't need another crime on her record.

"Didn't think so," the officer said, straightening his uniform. "I suggest you come up with a payment plan, and fast. Or tell your family to start packing."

)))

Qora followed Sakay to where he'd stationed his rhabdodon.

"You go first," Sakay said. "I'll get on behind you."

Qora stared at the empty saddle, her eyes burning with the tears that screamed behind them. Heat swelled in her chest, in her limbs, putting a fire in her cheeks. She couldn't breathe, couldn't think. She put her hand on the saddle horn and slipped her foot into the stirrup, but she lacked the strength to pull herself up. Part of her wanted to go back into that cell, to curl up in the corner and stay locked away from the world, from the stupid things she'd done.

"Qora." Sakay put a gentle hand on her back. "I'm sure there's something we can do. Get on the rhabdo; I'll take you home and we'll talk about it."

But Qora didn't want to talk about it. She couldn't face her mamáy after this. Her family would have been better off if Qora had done nothing at all. All their incomes combined couldn't cover the fine. They'd have to forfeit the house, the alpacas, their land … and Qora would still be indentured for a decade or more. In fact, it would be better for her family if she were *dead*; like the guard had said, that was the only thing that could absolve her family now. She squeezed her eyes shut like she could block all this out for a second, but it was waiting for her like blinding sunlight on the other side, leaking through her meager defense. How could she have let her family down so horribly—*again*?

As she inhaled slowly to calm herself, a familiar-looking young woman cocked her head from across the street. "Sakay?"

Sakay turned to see the woman with her red lips and her dinoleather case of potions.

Aquilops blood is a legitimate painkiller and anti-inflammatory.

Qora hadn't noticed at the Underground just how long the woman's hair had been, a black silk curtain that fell seductively over her shoulders and down her back.

Sakay seemed to give a little shake of his head, as if to say this wasn't a good time, but the woman didn't notice—or if she did, she didn't care. She waited for a triceratops-pulled cart to pass and then raised the hem of her skirt a bit as she stepped into the street and crossed to greet him.

"Nice to see you again," Sakay said, although he darted an apologetic look at Qora. "Qora, this is Sonqo. She's a vendor—"

"I remember," Qora said flatly. "I mean, I can see that." She nodded at the potions case. If only mystical cures like those were as effective as advertised. Maybe children wouldn't be dying of theropox.

"It's been an incredible morning so far," Sonqo told them, "what with all the excitement downtown."

"What do you mean?" Sakay asked.

"I've sold almost everything I brought out today; in fact, *all* the vendors are making a killing because of the Venture. The city square's packed with people signing up last minute."

Suddenly Sonqo's unnaturally red lips became more interesting for the information they conveyed.

Of course, Qora thought. She'd heard it on her way to the Underground yesterday afternoon. Today was the final day.

"That's great," Sakay said, with what sounded to Qora like forced enthusiasm. She hoped he wasn't holding back on her account, but it didn't matter anyway because she was about to leave them to their conversation.

"Yes," Sonqo replied, "Although now that word's getting around, vendors from all over town are starting to—"

"Excuse me," Qora muttered as she gave the street a quick traffic assessment and stepped off the curb.

Sakay reached out but Qora was already halfway to the other side. "Qora! Wait! Where are you going?"

Numbly but quickly, Qora made her way up the street as though some other force was controlling her body. She pushed past other pedestrians and kept her eyes forward while Sakay's voice faded behind her.

Within a couple of minutes, she reached the city square, where several long lines of people waited. At one end of the square were four booths, each with a registrar seated behind it taking names. And, as Sonqo had said, the place was crawling with vendors.

They sold baskets of empanadas and netted bags of fruit, tonics for hair loss, beaded bracelets, newly cobbled shoes, quipus. Plenty of everyday goods, along with the occasional "potion" or other crackpot commodity.

One older woman sold dimetrodon eyeballs from a jar. "Breach the cracks of a broken mind!" she said in advertisement, "Heal an injured brain! Achieve mental clarity! Open the mind to innovation and creativity! Receive revelation from the gods! Used by history's greatest artists and inventors!"

Sakay had mentioned trying one of these before, known colloquially among traders as "brain berries," but he'd said it had tasted like a meaty grape and had had no effect on him whatsoever—other than upsetting his stomach.

Regardless, Qora couldn't help thinking that a little mental clarity wouldn't hurt her right now, were it truly possible to obtain it from a jar for a silver or two.

A lot of dinosaurs and pelycosaurs *did* have truly mystical qualities, though. Powdered pachyrhinosaur horns could give a miraculous (but short-lived) burst of physical energy; pegomastax urine could fight infections; ground-up struthiosaur scutes could combat anxiety; bone marrow from a tyrannosaur or other oversized theropod could supposedly rapid-heal deep flesh wounds. That was all thanks to evolving alongside the skyrock—which was ironic, since skyrock caused the reptiles so much discomfort. But these things were not as easy to come by as some vendors and traders would have people believe. Almost anyone who purchased such mystical items was usually paying for llama eyeballs, or human urine, or genuine desert sand.

Most people ignored the woman and her jar. Hopeful entrants waiting in line partook mainly of the food, while surrounding spectators or encouraging friends and family made up the bulk of other customers.

Qora stopped to watch from the fringes and looked over the people in line. Burly older men and eager teenage boys and hunters ready to test their skills. A woman got in line, too; she was tall and muscular and walked with an erect-shoulder kind of confidence.

Soon Sakay caught up, out of breath, and came to her side. He took one glance at her and said, "No. Absolutely not. Don't even think about it."

Without looking at him, Qora said, "Why not?"

A journey of a couple of weeks—or potentially less, depending on effort and setbacks—didn't seem like so much time compared to spending the rest of her youth and then her young adulthood working for the qhapaq while her family was left to rot without her. And the prize and the money would be all she needed and more. There was no way she'd find a way to make that much money in the same timeframe by any other means. And Rimaq didn't have much time. Meanwhile, each checkpoint would allow her to earn something toward her debt, so the longer she could manage to survive, the better.

"Because it's suicide!" Sakay said.

The Venture didn't intimidate Qora, in *theory*. She wasn't

unfamiliar with standing alone in a habitat full of dinosaurs and having to defend herself. She knew every groove of her crossbow and she could pick apart sounds in the underbrush like they were musical notes. She struck fast with accuracy. More than that, Ollan had taught her that the speed and size of an animal didn't matter so much as understanding its limitations and exploiting them, outsmarting the animal in ways only a human could do. That was where human power lay, after all—in wit. Although it was her brother's ghost that made the whole idea so terrifying. The stuff of her ongoing nightmares.

Blood rushed to her head. Memories cut across her mind like lightning veining over a dark sky. A reptile's vicious roar, sharp teeth shredding flesh. Her screams. Ollan's screams—and worse, Ollan's silence that had followed.

She felt like she might vomit. Still, what terrified her most about it was also the very reason she *had* to do this. She couldn't be responsible for the loss of another one of her mother's sons. And there was money even if she didn't make it to the end, too, which was something. Qora would be able to provide nothing during an indenture.

"At this point," Qora said, "I'm worth more dead than I am alive."

"Don't say that."

"It's true. You were right when you said I'm a plant with more thorns than petals—that I'm toxic."

"That is *not* what I said."

"I'm like a poisonous vine that's grown beyond control, and can't help but cause destruction. If I get pruned back in this competition—or even fully uprooted—maybe that's not the worst thing."

Sakay scrubbed a hand over the buzzed side of his head

and groaned. "Gods, you're melodramatic. You can't think like that. Take a minute to breathe before you jump on the first opportunity to be someone else's target practice. Trading the raptoriva was that 'shoot first aim after' kind of situation I was talking about just yesterday, and this is too."

"There's no time," she said. "Sometimes you have to shoot your shot, whether you've aimed well or not." That should have been its own expression, she thought, like all her mamáy's little sayings. It was truer than most of them, too. In any case, this was the only way to combat that "false dilemma" her mamáy kept warning her about; she wouldn't choose between her family losing everything quickly or losing everything slowly—she'd take a chance for them to keep it all, even if she lost herself in the process.

"It's not that simple. You can't just sign up and immediately get in. There are entrance trials—tests you have to pass before you even have a chance at being selected—otherwise there'd be hundreds of participants from every Terrain. You might be an excellent shot, but what about speed? What about endurance? I heard you have to stay on the back of a raging carnotaurus for a full twelve seconds without falling off. Can you do that?"

Qora stepped into the registrar's line. "I guess we'll find out."

It was at the onset of the eighth year of the fourth era that Sky Mother rained fiery rocks from the High World, destroying the wicked that dwelt upon the land, while also providing that blessed skyrock.

And those who survived were deemed worthy to remain, and from thenceforth would wield the power to subdue the reptiles.

And the large rocks cooled and dotted the continent, clustered heavily in five regions, whereby the Terrains of the Old Empire would establish their core cities.

Thus, the highborn leaders of these cities began to gather and process the skyrock, guarding it and governing its use.

Cord Record 452, Segments 8-11

SIX

"WHY EXACTLY AM I HERE?" NINAN ASKED. He'd arrived at the trial grounds—what appeared to be seized farmlands divided into various courses and ranges, with a sprawl of equipment tents, domesticated reptiles, animal handlers, attendants, guards, and judges—and met Mullu through a side gate to avoid the long line of entrants checking in at the front. "If my father's going to let me bypass the entrance trials, there's nothing for me to do but watch. Seems like a waste of time."

"Plenty of would-be competitors watch the others complete trials while they wait their turns," said Mullu. "Along with spectators from the general population." He nodded at the crowds gathering along the outside of the barriers near the entrance, looking in. "It's important for you to make an appearance. This is the only portion of the competition that we have sole control over, which thankfully allows us to manipulate these results in your favor, but it still must look legitimate when Sumaq sends forth its chosen fifty competitors. Those selected need to have at least seen your face before, spotted you at the shooting and throwing range, in the combat ring, and so forth."

"And you don't think anyone will recognize me as … ?" Ninan pointed to the back of his neck.

Mullu gave him a dreary look. "You flatter yourself. Most

people think you're dead, and others have entirely forgotten you. The majority have never seen you up close to begin with. Anyone born high or connected enough to have known you and remembered your *former* appearance won't be desperate enough to compete in this barbaric display. Not to mention as the third son, and the son of a third quya, your existence is of much less consequence than your brothers'. Your bedraggled veneer should keep you well out of suspicion. So long as you maintain the length of your hair to cover the emblem, there should be nothing to worry about."

As if this assessment of his personhood weren't insulting enough, Ninan had had to spend the night in one of the lowliest rooms at Kallpa House—like some stranger in what used to be his own home—with guards posted outside the door. He'd been too coddled during his childhood to be fit to live among regular people—as he'd learned quickly in Thak—and now he was too disgraceful to be part of the "polite" society in which he'd been raised. There didn't seem to be any good place for him.

"Well," said Ninan, "If I'm that unimportant, why even have me compete? If, by some miracle, I manage to win, who would even care?"

"That's the point. Your job here is to *make people care*. Make yourself worth something."

Ninan stared at Mullu, the man who so dutifully carried out every one of the qhapaq's orders—even something as piddling as escorting a disgraced former-prince to these trials and providing instruction. Ninan couldn't understand such fierce loyalty to his father, and had often suspected that Mullu might share a bit of Kallpa blood. After all, many highborns believed that the gods had chosen the illegitimate offspring to be loyal servants to those of pure lineage. Thus, Mullu surely must have felt himself to be some divine servant, doing noble work.

Mullu led him around the backside of a row of tents, to a point from which Ninan could observe better while remaining mostly out of sight. Entrants had slowly begun to spill onto the grounds through the front gate, which was marked off by red pennants bearing the Three Crescents on each one.

Ninan brushed his thumb over the ink-stamp on his forearm—another Three Crescents, along with his entrant number that he would show to the recorder at each trial event, for keeping track of scores. The ink, he'd been told, would take several days to fade.

"The other competitors," Mullu informed him, "will get the usual earful of warnings, instructions, and disclaimers once they've been officially selected. You, however, will hear it from me now."

"How fortunate," Ninan mumbled.

"Each of the Five Terrains is holding its own trials as we speak, on their own land. Other Terrains may have different rules, but traditionally, each Terrain's fifty competitors will be chosen based on their ability to pass at least three of five trials."

Looking around, Ninan could easily determine what the trials were.

Barriers separated lanes of a partitioned racetrack, with caged—and apparently very hungry—dromaeosaurs waiting on one end—a test of speed; those who weren't fast enough wouldn't necessarily be killed, but wounds would be brutal. An elaborate ropes obstacle course implied a test of agility, operating under the time constraints of a sand timer that looked to provide about ten minutes. A fenced-off area was divided into two sections, one in which tiny parvicursors darted back and forth, the other with a platform divided into stations—a test of accuracy and precision with ranged and throwing weapons against moving targets. More fencing sectioned off a small arena, where reptile handlers wearing skyrock-studded vests fed juvenile carnotaurs, preparing for the same event that was common during reptestrian exhibitions and would require a rider to remain mounted while one of the reptiles flailed violently, a test of endurance. And finally, something Ninan was most familiar with, a fighting ring, a place for testing resilience.

"Won't more than fifty of these people," Ninan said, gesturing around, "be able to pass three of these five trials? There must be several hundred entrants here."

"Of course more than fifty will pass. But passing is only half the battle. Each performance warrants a numerical score, with points awarded not only for skill but also for effort and presentation. All the better so that Qhapaq Apo can select whom he believes will be the most interesting."

"Why not narrow the selection to whomever can pass all five?"

"This is not just a competition, Apo-Kimsa, it's a show. Part of what unites the audience is the ability to mutually admire or mutually despise the characters involved."

"Characters," Ninan repeated bitterly.

"Yes. The best characters must have weaknesses, must fall short and be given the opportunity to rise. Thus, the fifty chosen will not necessarily be the most agile or intimidating; some will be chosen on their ability to draw a crowd, to gain admirers, or to add tension to the narrative that will follow the competitors from start to finish."

Ninan recalled the last Venture again, how everyone had been eager to receive the daily reports, the way it had been all they talked about for weeks—and yes, the way everyone had had their favorites, retelling the events and glorifying or vilifying different competitors as though they were heroes or villains in folktales. The competitor who had gained the most attention hadn't even won; he'd been a skyrock quarryman from Qolqe, who had successfully wrestled three smilodons with his bare hands, but ultimately lost the prize to a more skilled Tisquvian hunter in the final hour. Still, he'd been revered as a hero, and many people had considered him the true champion. He'd received accolades, money from patrons, titles of honor, even managed to find himself a highborn wife who would never have looked at him twice before the Venture. It was no wonder Ninan's father wanted him to be a part of this competition; even if Ninan didn't win, as long as he came out alive, and maybe managed to do something brave or noteworthy, he'd have the nation's attention. But could he really win them over? Make them love him?

"The sendoff," Mullu continued, "will take place on the flats of the old granite quarry at the capital's southern boundary. Each competitor will be given a map of the route and required to leave on foot. However, should you possess the ability to tame some wild animal to use as transportation *after* the sendoff, or manage to procure another means of transportation—engineering a pull-cart or the like—such endeavors are acceptable. Past competitors have been known to take down a transporter or a courier and commandeer their animal, and there is no rule against this; however, most travelers know better than to be near the designated route during a Venture. Even nearby villagers tend to evacuate, to avoid being targeted for resources."

Ninan felt a thickness in his throat, although he wasn't sure why. It wasn't as though spending his energy caring about the fates of bystanders had ever done any good. Everything his father directed was a hazard to ordinary citizens.

"Each Terrain's leader appoints two heralds, for a total of ten heralds," Mullu said, changing the subject. "The heralds will travel by pteranodon, make camp each night a ways behind the competitors who are farthest behind, and during the day fly out every hour—or more frequently if conflict is evident—to gather information as to how the competition is progressing and how the competitors are interacting. Heralds are permitted to land, observe from afar or at close range, anything short of speaking to competitors directly. It won't be *impossible* for you and I to be in contact, in the event of an emergency, but it will be very difficult."

"Got it." Ninan combed a bit of hair from his face with his fingers. "I'm on my own, and people will be watching my every move."

"Correct. However, there will be opportunities to obtain new resources, should you lose any along the way. You may recall from previous Ventures that once a day, at midday, heralds will airdrop a round of supplies—often similar items but of different quality, to encourage competition for the best item. Pouches filled with low-grade skyrock dust, for example, as well as purer forms. Thus, should one competitor locate an airdropped pouch of inferior skyrock dust, it will be clear that someone else has located a better one, incentivizing interactions."

Ninan remembered many vivid recountings of disputes over airdrops that had resulted in irreparable bodily harm and even death. "As long as everyone back home is entertained, right?"

Mullu ignored his flippancy. "Every evening, one herald from each Terrain will fly back to Qhusi to deliver updates to the competition coordinators, replenish herald supplies and airdrops, and then return to camp. With representatives of all Terrains present at camp and during flybacks, all heralds will be held accountable by the others—particularly to avoid exactly what you and I are doing right now."

If that wasn't a perfect representation of how the Terrains interacted with one another on just about every matter, Ninan didn't know what was. Always watching each other like condors, lying in wait to take advantage of failures or weaknesses. The Five Terrains had once been a single, flourishing empire, and Sumaq had been the empire's most powerful region, believed to be blessed by the gods. While the ancient showers of oversized meteorites had fallen over the whole of the continent of Runaqa and over much of the sea, it had been Sumaq that had seen the majority of these celestial gifts. That had left the other regions jealous and greedy, Ninan's father had told him, once leaders had determined the full extent of skyrock power, and that was when the fighting had begun. But despite the rivalries from which the Venture had been born, Qhapaq Apo always insisted that the empire would be whole again, that he would be the one to reign over it, and that all "lost lands" would be fully recovered "in due time." Not including, of course, the independent land to the far south, simply known as The Tail.

"Without fail," Mullu said, "nearly half the competitors will be dead or will have surrendered within the first five miles, and the remainder will likely be halved again within the next few days, due to lack of survival skills, and death by wild reptile. That has been the trend."

"'Surrendered'?" Ninan asked. "Is that when they wave the white pennant?"

"Yes, competitors will be provided a white pennant flag. Should one choose to leave the competition early, they must wave the pennant in the presence of a herald and they will receive flight transportation back to the capital—along with an onslaught of shame upon their return."

Ninan didn't need to hear anything else to know that those last words came with a warning directed at him. This wouldn't be a prizefight in which he could tap out if his opponent was too brutal. He was only allowed to leave this competition two ways: as a champion, or through the Grave World.

"I believe that's everything we needed to discuss," Mullu said. "Now, I have herald business to attend to, so I urge you to go forth and be seen. Don't make too much of a ruckus, but feel free to participate in a trial or two—only those you're certain you can pass. Pass/fail scores will be posted at the end and I've already arranged for your name to appear on the boards with full points. Don't delegitimize it by being foolish. Understand?"

Ninan nodded and waited for Mullu to leave, giving him a few seconds to put some distance between them before he emerged onto the trial grounds. Entrants were lining up for trials, probably beginning with the easiest—based on their skills—before moving on to those that might expose their weaknesses or injure them before further testing. That was what Ninan was planning to do, at least. He joined the group gathering outside the fighting ring, settling among them and cracking his knuckles.

Soon, the trials began.

The fight mediators looked over the group and selected two entrants whom they deemed well matched in size and strength.

"First to end up on his back is out," one said.

After a starting bell, the fights proceeded. It wasn't a realistic fight, Ninan thought, putting matched fighters together. They always did this when it came to the better organized sport fights hosted by higher class officials, but in the real world, there was no such parity. The strong preyed on the weak. The weak were born into environments in which they were never meant to thrive, sometimes never even had a chance. Only a scrappy few ever fought their way out, and usually at a high cost.

Ninan knew that all too well. He would never forget the first time he'd tasted his own blood in his mouth. Flat on his back, grass rustling in his ears like insects as he'd struggled against Apo-Huk's weight pinning him down. Then another punch that had made his skull creak. Bleary-eyed, he'd only been able to come up with one solution: spit in his brother's face. It hadn't been that clever, but it had deterred Apo-Huk long enough for Ninan to wriggle out—and at least he'd been fast. That was only the beginning. A few months later, Apo-Iskay had fractured a couple of Ninan's ribs, and for that, Ninan had stolen a jar of meat drippings from the cookhouse, doused Apo-Iskay's clothes, and shoved him into the cellar with a swoop of microraptors, bolting the door behind him. More beatings had followed, along with years of unscrupulous stunts and retaliation and brawling, but Ninan had learned one thing about himself: He was a survivor. Maybe it wasn't completely insane to believe he could survive this too. Then again, as vicious as his brothers could be, they were a far cry from dracovenators and pterodaustro.

"You really think you've got a chance in there, sweetheart?" said one of the entrants.

The voice belonged to a young man with distinctive features—a lighter, Kastillan blend that many people considered exotic and beautiful, but which Ninan found to be highly overrated. The man's face looked like it had been carved out of sandstone, and he had one of those perpetual brow quirks that gave him a smug demeanor. He also wore a dinoleather belt with multiple compartments for throwing-stars—four- to six-point blades manufactured overseas that had become popular weapons during the past several Ventures. He spoke to a woman waiting among the other fighters.

"That depends," the woman replied. She was taller than the average woman, with trim but well-defined arms, and she wore her hair in a tight crown braid. She pinned the man with a death glare. "Will I be fighting *you*?"

The man looked her up and down, and shrugged. "I guess I wouldn't mind laying hands on some of that."

She lunged at him and would have decked him in the face, if it hadn't been for mediators holding her back.

"Save it for the ring," one of them said.

"Or better yet," Ninan chimed in, "the Venture." He caught the man's eye. "*If* this guy even makes it in, that is."

The man regarded him with a scoff.

"Names?" the mediator said, ignoring the verbal exchange.

It took Ninan a second to realize the mediator was speaking to him, too.

"Ruyan," said the other man.

"Ninan."

The official assessed them in turn, then barked, "Into the ring."

Ruyan grinned and removed his throwing-star belt, which he handed to an attendant, then ducked under the rope. Ninan followed.

The recorder came in and wrote down their stamped entrance numbers, then slipped out. They stood facing one another for an instant before the bell rang.

At a glance, Ninan might have agreed that he and his opponent were well matched—Ninan was shorter, but they weren't *too* different in build—except that under Ninan's loose, rough-spun cotton shirt, his body lacked the bulk and definition he'd once had. After a year eating a diet heavy on root vegetables and grain, with meat only as an occasional luxury, he'd turned downright lanky in comparison to his old self.

As they circled one another, Ruyan feinted to one side, but Ninan didn't take the bait. He kept his form, moved confidently. He shook his hair out of his eyes and pushed his loose sleeves up past the elbows.

"What lovely arms you have," Ruyan taunted at the sight of Ninan's bared skin. "The ladies must envy you."

"If you're comparing me to the entrant you just insulted a minute ago, I'll take that as a compliment." Ninan threw a glance at the woman, who crossed her arms and responded with a look that said, *"Finish him."*

"It was a joke," Ruyan said. "Lighten up." He raised that quirking brow even higher. "Not that you need to lighten up *physically*, that is. I wouldn't want you to completely disappear. I'd have no one to obliterate."

Ninan threw a fast punch.

Ruyan grunted and clutched his jaw, stepping back. "Son of a reptilian *cow*," he growled.

"Best not to speak about my mother that way," Ninan said. He feinted, prompting Ruyan to raise his arms in a block, at which point Ninan pummeled his torso. Ruyan stumbled before taking three aggressive but useless, hook-like swings at him. Then he managed to land a fourth to Ninan's already sore jaw.

Pain spidered through Ninan's teeth. He hissed inward, grimacing. It took him a moment to right himself, and he quickly became subject to a new onslaught of attacks. Soon he was barely keeping Ruyan at bay, and quickly found his back against the rope perimeter.

"Come on!" one of the entrants shouted from behind. "Take him down!"

Then the woman's voice: "Lay those 'delicate' hands on him!"

His lips twisted and he turned his body to dodge the next swing. He grappled with Ruyan, holding him in a clinch before striking him twice.

Ruyan backed up and wiped blood from the corner of his mouth. He spat red at Ninan's feet. "Well, I will say … You're almost as *handsy* as your mother." The words had only just passed his lips when Ninan tackled him to the dirt.

Ninan got three additional punches in before the mediators sounded the bell. Ninan stopped, panting, as the referee raised his arm for him, and the onlookers erupted in whooping and hollering.

Ruyan sat up and spat again, scowling.

"Next pair," said the referee.

〉〉〉

Many entrants were already on the sidelines treating wounds. On-site medics tended to bloody gashes and broken limbs and assessed whether the wounded were fit to continue the trials.

Ninan was grateful he wouldn't have to take part in every trial required of everyone else. Although, he reckoned he might be able to stay mounted on a raging carnotaur; he'd helped break megaraptors before, and even avoided being thrown from a particularly violent one. The obstacle course didn't seem too intimidating either, except for some of the steeper climbing walls and their small handholds; Ninan had never been much of a climber. And he may have been fast as a child, but he doubted he could outrun dromaeosaurs, especially when the only escape route was straight ahead with no possible deviations, or obstacles to hide behind. That left the range, and Ninan grimaced at the thought. Aim and precision had never been a priority over improving self-defense, and he hated to admit it but he'd neglected most weaponry skills development in favor of bare-knuckle fist-fighting—the idea being that the enemy could rob him of a weapon, but not so easily if his weapon was his own body.

He stopped at the range for a moment to observe. Apparently entrants were allowed to shoot using their weapon of choice. Those waiting their turn held longbows, crossbows, slings, throwing knives. One entrant even had a spear.

As he looked around, some anonymous attendant approached him, handing him a longbow, a quiver, and a pair of archery gloves. "From Mullu," the woman said. Then she lowered her voice. "He asked me to tell you to keep off the range, but to let people see you with the gear out here." After she left, Ninan fiddled with the gloves, which only had three finger partitions—for the index, middle, and ring fingers—so that the wearer's thumb and smallest finger would be bare.

Which way do they go? The thumb of a glove was usually the indicating factor, but neither of these had one. He would have tried them both ways, but he didn't want to look like an idiot, so he slipped them on quickly and chose not to think about it any longer. He set the quiver strap across his chest, the way he'd seen another bowhunter do, then figured out how to use a small clip on the bow shaft to attach the bow to a hook on his quiver strap so that the bow rested against his back. *This is why I hate this stuff,* he thought.

Now that he was all set, he craned his neck to see the range more clearly and caught sight of the little, darting parvicursors—the targets—just before he heard the click of a weapon. One of the parvies suddenly sprung back, taking a bolt to the head.

The people watching clapped and whistled. A few seconds later, another click. Another parvy down. The shooter completed a total of ten shots in a row, all clean as polished coppers. Ninan pushed through the other entrants to see whom the fatal bolts belonged to.

Then he blinked hard to make sure he hadn't lost his mind.

What in the Five Terrains …

In that same green jacket and black dinoleather boots she'd been wearing the day he'd met her at the Underground, the girl—Qora—stepped forward and accepted the applause with a stoic nod.

SEVEN

QORA WAS GRATEFUL that the ranged weapon trial had been an easy success. Even though she wasn't used to shooting with so many people watching (or with *anyone* watching, for that matter, not counting her little stunt at the Underground the other day when she'd nailed that trader's sleeve), she'd blocked out her audience and focused straight ahead, just like she'd learned to do on her morning sprints.

And sprinting was the only thing that allowed her to pass the *following* trial: the speed trial. The fact that she'd practiced the very skill of making sure she could outrun the quick-footed carnivores in the woods—at least for a long enough stretch to get somewhere safer—had given her a leg up. Two legs up, in fact.

In this case, her safe place was the exit gate at the end of the racing lane. The exit was lined with skyrock and halted the dinosaurs within two feet of it, such that they would not follow an entrant through. She'd never had to use her speed quite like this before, trapped in a partitioned route with teeth gnashing at her back. If it had lasted any longer, her panic might have gotten the better of her; as it was, she took the last yard at a leap and tumbled through the protective gate. She hoped to all gods and spirits she'd never have to do anything like that again.

Afterward, she had to take a few minutes to gather herself.

While she may have been able to outrun the dromaeosaurs, she couldn't outrun the guilt that still followed her, or the memory of spending that night in a cell.

Once she'd signed up for the Venture, she'd gone home to let her mamáy and brothers know she was alright, but hadn't had the nerve to confess what she was planning.

"Did anyone hurt you?" her mamáy had asked. *No.* "How did you get out?" *A friend.* "What's going to happen now?" *I don't know.*

It had all been too much, and Qora had brushed off further questions. "Don't worry. I'll fix this."

Her mamáy had not appreciated her brusque reply. "The same way you fixed everything *last* time?"

With that, Qora had felt a crushing weight on her chest. She'd packed a few supplies, kissed Rimaq's limp hand, and gone off to practice for the trials. It had been very late when she'd returned, and by then her family had already been asleep, so Qora had stayed by Rimaq's bedmat for a few minutes, fallen asleep there, and left before dawn to check in at the trial grounds.

Now she was partway through—although, even should she succeed, she wasn't sure she'd feel *successful.* Being selected for the Venture was the obvious goal, but she dreaded it as much as she needed it.

"A scavenger must not complain about the state of his meal," her mamáy would have said. The Venture was a gift, in its own grotesque way, and Qora was going to accept it, despite the dangers involved.

When Qora moved on to the obstacle course, she spent several minutes watching other entrants to identify the trickier parts of the course so she could avoid their mistakes—the mistakes that would cost them too much of that limited ten minutes allotted.

On her own turn, she found it challenging, but nothing she couldn't handle; she'd spent plenty of time wending her way through twisting, woodland undergrowth on hunts, climbing trees, and scaling rocky mountainside vantage points to spot the small flyers with the better meat on them.

Then, having passed enough trials to qualify, she weighed the risks of participating in the remaining two. She'd never ridden a carnotaurus before, much less an angry one, and the thought of going up against a grown man in a fistfight made her stomach turn. Still, a higher score might win her favor with the judges, and there seemed to be a lot of entrants who were doing well on more than one trial. She couldn't risk not being selected to progress to the Venture.

The only question was, who would she rather try her luck with—an aggressive, human brawler, or an unruly reptile spurred by skyrock dust?

She thought of the prizefighters at the Underground and all that those fights entailed. Bloody teeth clattering to the ground, punches so forceful they broke the skin on impact, eyes swollen shut so tightly that the only fix was to slice the surrounding skin— usually with whatever rusty razor someone had on hand—and let them bleed themselves back down to size. It was worth noting that Gorgo was deaf in his right ear, and that one of his fingers didn't bend properly anymore. Qora looked at her own fingers and shuddered.

And that's how she found herself on the back of a juvenile carnotaurus.

The reptile was calm while its handler got Qora situated. Despite being in a saddle, Qora could feel the carnotaur's movements beneath her, the large bones and thick muscles shifting under its skin. Her heart thrummed. She tried to distract herself by focusing on pointless details—the carnotaur's two short tapered horns, its comically small arms in comparison to the rest of its body, the scales that merged into dark pebble-spikes.

"Now," said the handler, "hold tight to the braces." He indicated a set of bars attached to an upward extension of the saddle that encircled the carnotaur's neck, one bar on each side. "When you hear the whistle, that's when your twelve seconds start."

For some reason, Qora thought she'd have a moment to process what the handler had just said, but the whistle came almost instantly after. The handler flicked a fistful of skyrock dust at the carnotaur and it let out an ear-splitting roar. It flung Qora forward, her hands nearly slipping from the braces. She hugged her body close to the carnotaur and tightened her grip, squeezing her eyes shut and praying to every spirit she could think of. *Don't let me die here.*

The seconds passed in an agonizingly slow manner while the carnotaur bucked and flailed. The force of its flinging tail traveled up to its head in a powerful wave, which crested under Qora's legs and threatened to launch her across the arena.

Any second now. Any second now.

She was so close—she had to be. Her head throbbed and she was clenching her teeth so hard she thought they might shatter, but she was sure it was almost over.

And then came a buck that tore her fingers from the bracing bars. She flew off the saddle, briefly airborne, and struck the dirt. There hadn't been time to think, but she tried to throw herself into a roll. Instead, she landed at an odd angle. Her diaphragm spasmed, refusing to let her pull air into her lungs. She pushed herself up onto all fours and tried to breathe, feeling like she might suffocate right here in front of everyone.

A medic rushed to examine her, instructing her to sit and relax so she could inhale properly again. She was informed that she'd lasted eight seconds, and that she'd made a solid—but unfortunately failed—effort. Qora wasn't sure it had been worth the try.

As she moved weakly beyond the arena, raucous noises drew her to the fighting ring, where two men had apparently been occupying the space for far too long. Qora convinced herself she would just have a look, get an idea what to expect. She was surprised to see a woman among them, tall with lean muscle, hair twisted out of her face in a crown. Beautiful and menacing. Qora had seen a few women at the other trials, but most of them, like her, seemed to be avoiding this trial, saving the worst for last. Why men derived so much pleasure from physical violence was a mystery to her.

"Come on!" an onlooker shouted. "Put him on his back and get this over with! Other people still need to compete!"

Neither entrant was backing down. Both continued to circle one another, panting, darting with quick steps. Both were bloody, dirty, and swollen.

The referee raised his voice. "Sudden death! First to land a strike above the neck wins."

The circling turned more dramatic, the bobs and weaves more exaggerated. Qora felt like she was watching two roosters trying to peck each other. Finally, one of them struck and the other's nose spewed red.

"Winner!" the referee called.

Another mediator was already looking over the crowd to select the next pair.

"You've passed me over *eighteen times* now," said the menacing woman. "I'll fight any one of these ruckheads and have them down in less than two minutes."

The other entrants groaned and booed as she shoved against them toward the mediator.

"It wouldn't be a good trial of skill," an entrant told her. "They're trying to set up an actual challenge here."

"Yeah," said another.

"Yeah!"

Everyone jostled one another, all sweat and stale breath. Before Qora realized what was happening, she was sucked into the mass. She tried to remain stable but lost her footing and tumbled onto one of the other entrants, a young man with a split lip and several bruises, but whose light, exotic features easily outshone the flaws.

He braced her and settled her back upright.

"Thanks," she told him. "Sorry."

He chuckled. "Usually I like to buy a girl a drink first, but … I don't mind."

Her face heated. Not knowing how to respond, she said nothing. Due to the way everyone was crowding, she still had to stand uncomfortably close to him, and she debated whether it would be worth falling on anyone else to try to get out.

"Aren't you a little young to be a Venture entrant?" The man hooked a thumb onto his belt, which held several throwing-stars. Many of the blade points were already bloody.

He clearly passed the range trial, she thought, observing the stars. She tried to inch over and give herself some space.

Another entrant pointed at Qora. "Hey, what about *her*?"

"Me?" Qora shook her head. "I only came to watch. I haven't decided whether I'm even going to—"

"Put her in! That's a fair match. Then we can move on."

The mediator nodded and waved her forward.

"No, really—" Qora insisted, but the group acted like some kind of collective intelligence, urging her to the front. She locked eyes with the woman, whose stare was hard and bitter. This was insulting to her, a capable twenty-something woman forced to fight a teenage girl who had none of the required skills for this trial.

"Names?" said the official.

"I'll give you my name when you give me a fair fight," said the woman. The recorder was already taking her by the forearm to read her stamped entrant number for the score book.

"Her name's Killay," said another entrant. "She works down at the forge. I've seen her throw a knife but I doubt she can throw a good punch."

Killay swatted the recorder away and narrowed her eyes.

Qora hesitated, like not saying her own name might keep her from this savagery, but a thwack on the shoulder from some angry brute in the group made her blurt it reflexively. "Qora—but I'm *still* not—"

"In you go," the mediator barked.

With a heavy sigh, Killay trudged into the ring. Her fists were already clenched, but Qora was sure it was less in preparation to hit her than it was due to the circumstances of this fight.

Qora offered the woman an apologetic half smile while she lifted her own arm to show the recorder her stamp.

The bell rang.

Killay stretched her neck once to each side. "Don't take this personally." Her fist slammed into Qora's gut, folding her in half. The carnotaur arena had already thrown her a similar punch, and a second one now was almost enough to make her vomit.

She managed to hold it in, slipping Killay's next strike in the nick of time.

The sounds surrounding the ring were a muddle of entertainment and annoyance.

"This is the kind of fight I'd pay to see."

"Hurry up. Let some real fighters get in there."

"My money's on the tall one."

"At this pace, we'll be here through the night."

Qora kept her distance for a moment, taking a deep breath to gather herself. It took some effort to block out the commentary, but she tried to focus, thinking of all the fights she'd glimpsed on the days she'd gone to the Underground. Most of her memories involved a blur of men chanting and hollering around the fighters, rather than the fighters themselves or the techniques. The only fighter who stood out to her right now was that boy—that obnoxious boy—with his slippery-as-smoke maneuvers and his copper skin and his stupid compliments to the wrong people. She groaned internally.

No. This was not the time to be proud; There was much to learn from him.

Think, Qora told herself. *What would* he *do?*

She recalled the way he'd faked a punch—not just a flimsy arm motion, but a full-body commitment to the ruse—before slipping to the opposite side. She herself was fast enough, and deft; she'd proven that much on the racetrack and the obstacle course.

With impatient steps, Killay bounded toward Qora. Qora ducked clumsily to avoid a jab that she was sure would have blackened her eye. With a hopeful grimace, Qora feinted a left hook, then slipped to the right to deliver the punch. It was a weak and reckless punch, but it seemed to startle Killay. Qora went for the abdomen and jabbed weakly again before Killay struck her across the nose.

Flashes of light filled Qora's vision and she staggered backward, catching herself on the rope.

"Hey," someone said.

Squinting, and biting back a scream, Qora wiped a stream of bloody mucus from her nose. She turned toward the voice, which sounded vaguely familiar.

Oh gods. It was him.

Right there on the other side of the rope, watching this whole embarrassing display unfold, was Ninan. He had a longbow clipped to his back, and—wait, why was he wearing his archery gloves like that?

"Not a good time," she mumbled.

"Word of advice?" He leaned toward her. "Turn your hips into your punches."

Qora's mind was foggy. Her entire head throbbed. "What?"

"You're not hitting with any power. Just like you put your whole body into that feint, put your whole body into the punch. Your fist is the messenger—everything behind it is the message."

"No coaching!" said one of the mediators.

Ninan put up both hands innocently and stepped away from the rope. He raised his eyebrows at Qora, who turned back in time to see Killay coming for her. One sweep of the woman's long leg was enough to land Qora flat on her back—once again with the wind knocked out of her.

In another muddle of events, Qora heard a bell and then a bout of cheering—probably not in favor of Killay, but because this fight was over and now the "real" fights could resume.

"You alright?" The man with the throwing-stars materialized and offered his hand.

She regarded the gesture but stood on her own, brushing off her clothes. "Bruised ego for sure, but otherwise, fine."

Together, they ducked under the rope and out of the ring.

"Can't pass 'em all," he said. "I only passed four of the five."

One of her nostrils dripped onto her upper lip and she quickly wiped it with her sleeve. "Did you pass the fights?"

Before he could answer, someone else answered for him: "With flying colors."

It was Ninan again, leaning casually against one of the posts to which the ropes were tied.

Qora sighed and pinched her nose to stifle it.

"And, by flying colors," Ninan added, "I mean *blood* red, *flying* off his face.'"

"Let's try again, then," the man growled. "Outside the ring."

Ninan chuckled. "Ruyan here likes to talk a big game," he told Qora. "Throws a half-decent punch with his words, but … not so much with his knuckles."

Ruyan bristled. "Choose a time and place—"

"You know what?" Qora interjected. "I think I'm finished here. Nice to meet you, Ruyan. Ninan, it was … unexceptional … seeing you again."

She shoved her way back to the central gathering area between trial zones, which should have led back to the entrance—which would now be her exit—but her mind and her body were both weary and she could hardly think straight.

"Qora." Ninan caught up to her. "It is 'Qora,' isn't it?"

"Sure," she deadpanned.

"I just wanted to say, nice work at the range earlier. I saw you shooting. It was … impressive, to say the least."

"More impressive now that you know it was me?"

He huffed. "No. Just … plain impressive. That's all. Are you going to hold my idiocy over me forever?"

"Probably." Qora spotted her way out and nodded at it. "Anyway…"

"Word of advice, though?" he added, glancing at Ruyan, who was visible talking to a medic. "Avoid that guy."

Qora laughed. "Word of advice?" she repeated. "Your archery gloves are on backwards." And then she walked away.

EIGHT

NINAN HELD ON TIGHTLY as the megaraptor raced along the cliffs. He had to squint as the cool air tore over him, mist condensing and clinging to his hair and lashes like dew.

He'd forgotten what it felt like to ride such a lithe animal who, despite her thunderous legs, seemed to glide over the earth, with her head bent forward and her tail oscillating. This megaraptor was midnight blue, with feathers sprouting backward against the crown of her head and down her neck in layers—not as elaborately as some of the males of her species, but still a beauty in her own right.

Kallpa House came back into view, a sight that made Ninan's shoulders sag. An hour on the cliffs hadn't been enough to fill his emptiness.

He was grateful, at least, that his brothers had not been present since his return. Apo-Iskay had married last summer and was currently living in Qolqe, the home of his bride (the ambassador's daughter), while Apo-Huk (with two wives already, both of whom were kept and pampered somewhere within Kallpa House) was away supervising the installment of a new Sky Temple at the western border. Both, of course, would eventually return to Sumaq for the Venture's sendoff ceremony, but otherwise, Ninan hoped he wouldn't have to face either of them for a good while.

When Ninan approached the paddock, Mullu was there waiting on foot.

"The competitor list is now available for viewing." Mullu fell into step beside the trotting raptor. "Just a formality for *you*, of course. But it comes with the coordinators' announcement of the Venture prize and its location as well."

Ninan tugged the raptor's reins until she stopped. "Let's see it, then."

Once inside, the staff escorted Ninan to the dining hall, where he received a platter of poached microceratus eggs, finely seasoned dinohyus sausage, a bowl of sweet quinoa with lucuma compote, and a glass of purple-corn chicha garnished with cinnamon sticks. Another staff member provided a sheet of papyr, with words inked below the Roaring Spinosaur shield and Three Crescents.

The following entrants have been selected to compete in the fifteenth quinquennial Runaqan Venture.

Ninan scanned the list until he found his own name planted near the middle.

Well, it was *almost* his name.

Ninan Chakuq

The qhapaq certainly couldn't list him as a Kallpa, and had thus provided a surname that wouldn't hint at his lineage. And "Ninan" was a guise too. Nevertheless, it was daunting to see his name in writing next to all those others—others who had actually *earned* their place on the list, he reminded himself. Others who would be bustling to get to papyrs just like this one, which were surely already posted throughout the city, to find out who had been chosen.

Below the fifty competitor names came the prize they would

seek and the specific location they'd be traveling to.

These brave competitors will seek a Golden Spinosaur Tooth hidden at the ruins of Utula

"Of course," Ninan said aloud, although he was alone at the table now.

If it wasn't finding some way to incorporate the national symbol of the spinosaur into every mural or tapestry, it was stringing the smaller teeth into necklaces or fusing them to form crowns. It was monuments built to the spinosaur as though it were an additional god to be worshiped. The qhapaq had even begun an experimental hybrid breeding program a few years ago to produce miniature spinosaurs—nicknamed "sailbeasts"—a sort of raptor-sized terrenal mascot, a few of which had escaped their confines and terrorized the locals before the Guard had captured them and put them down. Now that the qhapaq had managed to get the Venture to take place on Sumaqi land, he would be sure to make a point every chance he got—starting with his selection of the competition's prize.

Some prize, too. It may have been a novelty to other competitors, the thought of such a large reptile's tooth, not to mention the amount of gold used to coat its surface, but Kallpa House kept gilded spinosaur teeth in practically every room. They were gaudy decorations, each mounted vertically on polished granite platforms and encrusted with jewels at the base. Ninan could just picture one of those on some pedestal in the middle of the crumbling ruins of Utula, surrounded by concealed traps whose triggers would draw atrociraptors to the scene. Or maybe it would be positioned at the top of one of the towers, surrounded by an overwhelming swarm of eudimorphodons.

He stared at his fine breakfast, the kind of meal he'd craved for months, and suddenly felt nauseated. The Venture was upon him, and instead of watching from a distance—happily oblivious to all the gory details but for what would be told in the streets and spread through narrative papyrs—he would be in the middle of it all. A gamepiece for the qhapaq to set in motion.

Ninan had been given so many instructions he could hardly keep them all straight. And that was nothing compared to the supplies his father's staff was working to provide him with.

He would wear an inconspicuous traveler-style poncho of woven cloth, but it would be double layered and lined with copperskin—a sort of chain mail made up of thin, overlapping plates of copper shaped into protective scales. Underneath a cotton shirt and basic trousers, he would also wear a dinoleather vest, treated to be hard and nearly impenetrable, as an armor. He would wear a belt with subtle skyrock studs, and common-looking boots with steel reinforcements in the toes.

As for weapons, he would carry a lightweight, sports-grade longbow with its metal painted like wood, two longblades, and a leather rollup full of utility knives and other tools.

Supplies included firepowder (for quick-start fires), an oilskin tarp to cover the ground when he made camp, a camouflaged tent system, high-energy dehydrated food that would bloat to three times its size, water cleansing drops, a bandaging kit, a tincture made from the cells of desert allosaurs that would keep his body from losing water too quickly, a rapid-heal tyrannosaur marrow balm, and a lamp filled with purified sauropod oil that would burn as little as a quarter ounce per hour without producing smoke, soot, or odor. And, of course, a pouch of pure skyrock dust. "This is as much a danger," the qhapaq had said of the skyrock dust, "as it is a protection, if you don't conceal it properly. Many competitors will kill for it without the slightest hesitation."

This Ninan already knew, one of the few things he remembered vividly from past competitions. Many competitors had spent all their money to start with a strong skyrock supply in hopes of using it on whatever reptilian monsters waited at the end—but no one had ever had any left by the time they reached the prize. There were too many times along the route when encounters with dinosaurs had required them to use it up, and too many more times when other competitors had stolen it. He could see the appeal, though; the good kind could ward off just about any reptile with its scent alone—undetectable to humans but potent to dinosaur scent receptors—and keep them several yards away. The fact that he would have some with him gave him infinitely more confidence in his ability to win.

His weapons supply, however, was less reassuring. Despite working with the qhapaq's best trainers, there wasn't time to significantly improve. His aim with the longbow was acceptable, but only so long as his targets were steady. His blade technique wasn't terrible, but there would be much better blade-swingers in the competition. Thankfully, these more refined weapons were easier to use than some of the rough blades and bows he'd used on sporting hunts in Thak (until the others in the group had stopped inviting him along). He could only hope that what his father provided would be enough.

On a whim, though, he enlisted the kitchen staff to help him produce an additional weapon of his own, recreating Thak's saltpeter and sugar blend used for the smokers. Mullu mocked the idea of wasting time with a farming community's signaling system, but Ninan had other uses in mind for it. He simply said, "An enemy who can't see well or breathe well is half as difficult to overcome."

In all this chaos, Ninan hadn't had the chance to speak

with his mother. They had only exchanged sorrowful glances whenever they happened to be near one another, but the qhapaq or Mullu had always been present too. Finally, after nightfall, when Ninan had a moment alone in his room—the temporary room assigned to him—she came to his door.

"Mamáy," he said wistfully when he opened up to find her standing there, backlit by the sconces in the hallway. He pulled her against him and soaked her in like medicine. A tremble moved through his bones as he tried to quell the storm brewing in his chest.

She cupped his face. "There's something I wanted you to have." Her Qolqese accent was familiar and reassuring.

She'd always tried to speak like a Sumaqi, but many of the sounds went against her linguistic instincts. Ninan thought for the first time how difficult it must have been for her, leaving everything she'd ever known to become a quya in a foreign land. Now that he knew what it was like to have a life torn away, to live among strangers and try to muddle through unfamiliar routines, he had gained a new respect for her.

She released him and handed over an object wrapped in red velvet.

Carefully, Ninan pulled back the edges to reveal a dagger sheathed in white dinoleather—albino dilophosaur, from the look of it. The sheath had been cut to follow the shape of the dagger's edge. He slid it out so the serrated, dinosaur-tooth blade was showing. It had been filed thin and flat to produce a sharper edge, and etched with Qolqese religious symbols. "This comes from your ancestors," Ninan deduced.

His mother nodded. "I can't offer you much in the way of protection—your father has taken care of the physical things, at least. But I will pray to my gods for you each day and night, and those symbols will bring you good fortune."

He took her hand and held it for a long time. "This has all happened so fast. One minute I was trying to find my place in the quinoa fields, now I'm back here cheating my way into the Venture, for spirits' sakes ..."

"Your father's ways are mysterious," she said. "You must be careful—not only in the Venture but in whatever future interactions you have with him. I do not trust what he does."

"What do you mean?"

She shook her head and traced the stone pattern of the doorframe with her fingertip. "There are many things. He has always been secretive, always determined to rise among the other Terrains. Of late, he has been focused on sending large shipments to the island nation."

"What does he want with Tisqu?" Ninan asked. "With its size, it's of little benefit to us as an ally. At least, I shouldn't think so—not to him. Shipments of what?"

"Skyrock."

"He's been sending skyrock *out* of Sumaq?" That didn't make any sense. Qhapaq Apo was notorious for the way he hoarded the stuff. To distribute it elsewhere ... Ninan couldn't fathom why.

"I've only caught glimpses of records," the quya admitted, "but it looks that way. He seems intent on winning favor with the Tisquvians. For what, I can't say. And he's also had guards posted at the old military stronghold on the eastern front."

"But that hasn't been used in ... decades."

"As I've said—beware. When you return, there will be much to discuss."

Ninan felt his throat thicken. "What if I don't come back?"

She cupped his face again and stared into his eyes sorrowfully. "You will."

"How can you be sure?"

"Because the qhapaq desires it," she told him. "And the qhapaq gets what he wants."

NINE

QORA SNATCHED THE PAPYR from Sakay. "How did you get this?"

It was early enough that the Underground was empty. The usual patrons were either sleeping off hangovers or out procuring new things to trade.

Sakay turned his back to the counter and pulled himself onto it with the heels of his hands so that he was sitting on its edge. "Stole it from the tax collector's bulletins."

She was going to argue with him over the ethics of this—to scold him about all the hopeful entrants who would have to look elsewhere to get such vital information about their fates—but all she really cared about right now was the list of names, and whether hers was on it.

Her index finger trembled as she dragged it over the list, a weary effort to ground her to the task of finding the right combination of letters that would make or break her family's future.

Sakay pinched her finger between his own forefinger and thumb and moved it near the bottom of the papyr.

Beneath her fingertip it read: **Qora Kanchaya**

"No ..." she said through a breath. She looked up at Sakay. "Really?"

He scoffed. "Sweet serrated teeth, Qora—I should hope so. Do you think I would have bothered to set a gaggle of pamparaptors loose to cause a diversion so I could steal an announcement that *didn't* have your name on it?"

Qora stared at the list, blinking hard to make sure she wasn't imagining things. She'd only passed three of the five tests. Without a doubt there would be competitors on the route who had passed all five, and she shuddered at the thought of going up against any of them.

What had the judges seen in her? Was there a good opportunity for entertainment at her expense? She pushed out a heavy breath and shook her head. It didn't matter how or why; all that mattered was that she had a chance now. A chance to make up for what she'd lost—and what she'd lost for her mamáy and the boys.

She scanned the rest of the document to learn that she would be seeking a golden spinosaur tooth at the ruins of Utula. She'd never been that far before, never even been beyond the foothills. She'd only heard stories, mostly at the Underground, between men who traveled all over the Terrain to trade exotic goods. She knew the great river led there, for the most part, and that it was an old fortress built by Kastillans during the invasion. It would be crumbling now.

"This is two hundred and fifty miles from here," Qora said.

"Yep. Two hundred and fifty competitors, two hundred and fifty miles. That's what you signed up for. You sure do know how to get your sickle-claw stuck in the timber." Sakay hopped down from the counter and snatched the announcement from her. "Now," he said, "We've got work to do."

Sakay took Qora into the storehouse and fished around until he found a few supplies for her. Char cloth and sparking stones; a canvas hammock that could roll up tight into a little bag; a compass; a multiknife; a machete; a container of dinofire ointment.

He taught her to make a low-smoke fire, keeping fuel tight to the flame. "Smoke is incomplete combustion," he said. "You'll still need to watch out for pterodactyls when making camp near the river, though," he added. "They cluster their big nests on the ground, usually on riverbanks. The closer you get to the jungle, the more of them there'll be, and they're drawn to bright lights and loud noises."

"Why?" Qora hadn't seen many pterodactyls here in the mountains. Aside from the oversized flyers employed by the highborns, most local flyers were relatively small, like the rhamphorhynchus that barely made a meal for two, or troodons cooked for special occasions.

"Because they like to pick off weakened animals that have already survived an attack," he explained. "Loud noises imply conflict—a thunderfooted chase, screeching and roaring, that sort of thing. Plus they've got eyes trained to pick out arapaima in the water; those fish scales are pretty flashy when they get going in the current. Anyway, you'll have enough to worry about already; you don't need a five-hundred-pound flyer on your tail too. So do your best to keep quiet, and no fires after dark near the water."

Qora went home and later returned with a traveling pack, one she'd used before on longer hunts, and Sakay gave her specific instructions on how to arrange its contents. "I was lucky enough to see the Venture sendoff in person when I was fifteen—but it wasn't pretty," he told her. "You're going to have arrows and bolts at your back. So all the tough stuff goes at the back of your pack, to fortify you like the armored body plates of an ankylosaur.

At worst, you'll get a pack full of holes. Still, other competitors might try to pick you off by the legs, so that's where these come in." He held up a pair of long, narrow, metal plates with a slight curve to them, and pointed at her boots.

"Won't that make it hard to run?"

"You can ditch them after the sendoff. But also, we're going to practice."

They went to the fields outside the city and Sakay sent Qora to run lines through the grass. Line after line until her calves were practically numb, until her knees were sore, until she dripped with sweat. Then she did it backwards, shooting bolts on the move while Sakay chased her with a sack of straw as her target.

"What about my head?" Qora asked between gulps of water when they'd finished.

"Keep it down."

𝕯𝕯𝕯

As a "respite," Qora and Sakay spent another couple of hours on machete work. Sakay said, "I haven't been to the jungle myself, but my uncle has, and he says it's dense as a pachyceph's head. You'll be hacking for hours at a time, and if you don't hold the machete correctly, you're going to get godsawful blisters. You have to use the blade's weight to your advantage; let the hilt work like a hinge in your hand, no need to wear out your elbow or your wrist."

Sakay demonstrated a pinch grip, looser at the bottom than at the top and had Qora replicate it. She worked on it over and over, hacking at bushes and underbrush. Soon, the afternoon was fading.

"I think we'd better call it a day," Sakay said.

Wearily, Qora nodded. Her heart ached to continue, to train until her fingers bled, but her body was ready to collapse, and it wouldn't do her any good to wear herself too thin before the competition even started.

"Take it with you." Sakay pointed his lips at the machete. When Qora frowned, he clarified, "To borrow. I expect to get it back."

She squeezed the hilt. "Thank you. For all of this. You really didn't have to help me."

"Believe it or not, Qora, I like you. You're stubborn, and you don't take ruck from anyone. Which can be frustrating as a businessperson, but, as a friend … Well, let's just say I'd want you on my side in a fight."

She scoffed. "Sure you would."

"I'm serious."

"Except I'm not worth much without my crossbow." She raised the machete close to her face and stared at her haggard reflection in the metal. She could take on most reasonably sized dinosaurs with a bolt, but there would be different kinds of monsters in this competition—people so hungry for money and glory they'd scheme and scrounge and kill each other. And of course the jungle itself was a monster, too. Unrelenting heat and humidity, impassable growth, insects that hungered for human blood.

"That's a load of guano." Sakay snatched the machete back and pointed it at a rotted tree stump. "See that?"

Qora nodded.

He pulled the weapon back behind his head and flung it forward like an oversized throwing knife, its hilt wobbling as the blade lodged in the wood. Then he wrenched it out and handed it to Qora. "You try."

She gave him a look like he'd lost his mind, but obeyed. At first she didn't hold her wrist firmly enough, the machete veered to the side, and she missed the mark by an embarrassing distance. The second time, she hit it, but not with enough force, and the machete clunked to the ground. It took her eight tries before she got the blade to pierce the stump.

"Beautiful!" Sakay exclaimed. He handed the weapon back to her. "Practice that and you'll have a backup skill—even at a distance. No one'll see it coming."

Before they parted, he gave her a package, with several smaller packages inside, each containing different kinds of dried food—meat, root vegetables, fruits.

"This is too much," Qora said. "You've already given me other supplies. Besides, if you haven't noticed, I'm not half bad at providing food for myself." She pulled an imaginary trigger.

Sakay rolled his eyes. "Yes, I've noticed. But just because you're good at hunting doesn't mean you don't hate it." He glanced at her boots. "I know what you're thinking about whenever you have to take a shot."

The boots were stiff from the metal inside, despite being otherwise well-worn and flexible. Qora remembered, though, how stiff they'd felt in the beginning, and to this day she still wasn't sure if it had been the newly worked dinoleather or the looming shadow of what she'd killed to have them made. She wiped a drop of sweat from her temple. "If you know, then why do you antagonize me so much?"

"Because you have to deal with your demons one way or another. Might as well toughen up." Sakay shrugged. "You don't develop reptile-thick skin by people going easy on you. Plus my uncle would have my head if he thought I was going easy on *anyone*—especially some kid who tends to cause a ruckus every time she comes in."

Qora's eyes shifted to the pile of food between them and she raised an eyebrow.

"This doesn't count. Special occasion. One-time deal. Don't come to me later expecting more favors, alright?"

Despite the heaviness of the situation, a smile clawed its way out of her. "Alright."

"Now," he said, waving her off, "Go take down some monsters—*kantuta*."

⁑⁑⁑

On her way home, Qora deliberately went by way of the stream that trickled through the woods. *Thuqa*, the locals called it. A trail of saliva compared to the great river she would be following to get to the ruins of Utula. And with all the Venture entailed, she knew she couldn't go without taking as many extra precautions as possible.

When she reached the stream bank, she inhaled the pungent, earthy scent of a mushroom patch. The tuffets of yellow fungus bloomed over a log like flowers, with gill-striped undersides.

"These ones are special," Ollan had told her. He'd been seventeen at the time and Qora eleven, just months before he'd joined the Guard. "When night falls, they glow." He'd gathered up a cluster and they'd taken them home and stayed up till dark. When night fell, the mushrooms glowed green, phosphorescent and magical. For days, Qora had kept them in a jar next to her bedmat, mesmerized by their beauty. Until, of course, she'd forgotten to keep them wet and they'd shriveled up.

Now, she uncorked that same jar, which she'd brought in her pack. She arranged a bed of moss and leaves, and moistened it with stream water, then used a knife to carefully pry up the bark where the mushrooms grew, setting a cluster inside the jar.

It wouldn't be practical to build fires all the time during the competition, but this way she wouldn't have to operate in complete darkness, especially as the moon spirit's light would be minimal while the moon waxed slowly over the next two weeks. She hoped she would survive long enough to see it again.

Then, a trail of black-tipped feathers led her to a hollow in the earth where the ground sloped against rock. As expected, she soon caught sight of a sinornithosaur and made a clean shot through its heart.

Normally, she wouldn't pursue a sinorn. They were venomous, their meat was bitter, and their skin and feathers weren't particularly valuable. But a venom-tipped bolt could be the difference between a mild wound and a major one, and she wanted to be sure she had that option.

The head was just small enough that Qora could grip it in one hand. She pried open the sinorn's mouth, poised the fang over the opening of a second jar, and pressed on the gland at the back of the jaw—something she'd once seen a physician do to make anti-venom—until a greenish liquid came out, drop by drop. Highly corrosive on bare skin, paralytic in the bloodstream. She did this for both sides until the container was full, careful not to get any venom on her hands, then capped off the jar with its cork lid. As she rearranged her pack and looked at her jars side by side, she paused. The mushroom jar was glass, transparent to make use of the glow—but the other two, one for the dinofire ointment Sakay had provided, and another for the sinorn venom, were nearly identical. With the sky darkening over her, she made a mental note to mark the jars later, then headed home.

When Qora arrived at the house, she found Hakan sitting on the front steps surrounded by compies. He held one in his lap, letting it nip at a small reservoir of grain in his cupped hand. Something about this gentle act made him seem younger, childish, even though he was well on his way to young manhood.

Slowly, she approached and sat beside him. "You know they can feed *themselves* ..."

She'd seen these compies capture smaller reptiles with their tiny, three-fingered claws and bite them in half. More often than not, they had their snouts in the grass snatching up crickets or worms. Then again, they probably appreciated a meal they didn't have to work for, as much as anyone else would.

"The company's nice," he said. "*Compy-ny.*"

Qora laughed.

More grain specked the ground, where other compies fed, although a few of them nudged each other trying to get at Hakan.

"Did the shaman come again today?" Qora asked.

Hakan nodded. "Not that it did any good."

Qora was glad to hear her own sentiments echoed by someone else. Sometimes she'd thought the gods and spirits didn't interfere as often as people believed they did; she wondered if maybe they were similar to the rest of nature, simply existing, giving of themselves in ebbs and flows the way the rain might nourish crops after a dry spell or the way the sun could warm the chill in one's bones or the way medicinal plants grew along the riverbanks. All blessings were available, and some would befall those who were in the right place at the right time while other blessings required harvesting. Determining what was a blessing, or a miracle, or a godsend, was the hard part. She'd thought she'd "harvested" the means for a cure when she'd traded the raptoriva; now she wasn't sure the reptile was the gift it had appeared to be.

She likewise wasn't sure that the Venture was the next best step; all she knew was that she had to do *something*.

"It's Mamáy's way of fighting, I guess."

"Right," Hakan agreed. "'Even grass has a blade,' she keeps saying."

"Of course she does."

It was another phrase their mamáy used often. Small efforts weren't useless; one should fight with whatever weapon he or she happened to have, whether it was something as fragile as hope or as thin as desperation.

"What happens now?" Hakan tickled the compy in his lap, who chattered softly in response.

Qora sighed and dipped her hand into the grain sack beside her. She sprinkled a bit more grain onto the ground, and the compies squawked as they raced to pick at it. "I don't know. I've obviously made a mess of things. But I'm going to do everything I can to fix it, okay?"

Even if I die trying.

⟫⟫

That night, Qora's nerves kept her wide awake for a long time, a buzzing in her head as loud as the combined noises of the forest, only she couldn't pick apart the conflicting thoughts the way she could pick apart reptile calls. Everything was a jumble she couldn't quiet down. At some point she slept—she must have, because she couldn't remember being awake the whole night—and fully woke at dawn. She'd agonized over how she was going to tell her mamáy and the boys what she'd decided to do, that she'd be leaving that morning, but it was clear to her now that there was no way to do it. She couldn't stomach the look on their faces, couldn't listen to Hakan's pleas not to go or her mamáy's disapproval.

And so, in the milky light, with a small lantern burning, Qora unrolled her mamáy's quipu on the table. The bundle of camelid-fiber cords was frayed and worn from use. Her mamáy had tied knots into it, untied and retied them so many times. A hundred cords, each in alternating colors of red, black, and beige. The knots were supposed to form patterns that would correspond to numbers and letters, a way to keep track of sales and household finances. Only a few knots were tied onto the cords now, the last of mamáy's profits from before Rimaq had fallen sick. Qora pinched them with her fingernails one by one and tugged them loose, then set to work on her own knots.

When she'd finished, she kissed her still-sleeping mamáy, then Hakan, who snored softly like a pot of simmering water, and then went to Rimaq's bedmat and kissed his palm.

Finally, she adjusted the quipu so that the cords were laid out in a clear, neat row:

All my love, always. Please forgive me.

They would find out soon enough what she meant.

Flyers perched high will drop
guano on those below.

Sumaqi proverb

TEN

THE OLD GRANITE QUARRY looked almost like a stadium, with tiers cut into the mountain six hundred feet high—marbled gray and white, with horizontal lines marking each row and vertical scores where slabs had been removed and carted away for construction.

Citizens cluttered the rows and looked out over the two hundred and fifty competitors who stood on the flats below, most of whom had been loaded onto the back of a long-necked sauropod and transported from Qhusi in a group. The sauropod—a supersaurus—chewed on the branches of surrounding trees, seemingly oblivious to the now-empty seats installed down the length of its neck and spine.

Ninan waited with his hood up. His poncho was heavy, what with the copperskin mail lining the material. Other competitors wore copperskins too—chest-length collars made of larger scale-plates strung together. These would only protect the heart, however, while Ninan's extended to the hem of his poncho.

He lifted a foot and tested the weight of the metal concealed in the toes of his boots. He'd already done this a dozen times, and adjusted his pack, which was much heavier than it appeared. He patted his right pocket, where he kept a compact smoker that he hoped would get him through the bloodbath that was about to occur; he'd practiced his plan several times beforehand, and was already mentally mapping where he would run after the departure signal.

The flats spread wide and eventually met the roadway, covered in cut stones of the same granite. Only a small portion of the roadway was paved this nicely, leading up to the capital in one direction and for a few miles toward the next city in the other. Then it would fade to cobblestone, or even packed earth on the smaller branches, narrowing as it went.

It was only in his boredom, as the competitors waited for the sendoff ceremony to begin, that Ninan became keenly aware of someone staring at him.

A young man—Unuvian, Ninan guessed, since he wore a blue poncho embroidered with the symbol of a triceratops. Athletic build, long legs, muscled arms. He must have been Ninan's age, give or take a year—but more likely give—and carried a bundle of rope, along with a pickaxe and a pack that was bulky with additional tools and weapons. He wore dinoleather gloves and a firm scowl.

When Ninan caught his eye, the young man didn't look away. In fact, Ninan was sure he was doubling down on the intensity of his gaze. Then the qhapaq appeared at the forefront of the horde, allowing his guards to escort him up to a platform—a particularly large slab of granite that had been positioned here for this purpose—and raised his voice.

"Thank you all for attending this magnificent event!"

Behind him stood the qhapaq's three quyas and his first two sons. He wore a more elaborate headpiece today, preening like he'd sprouted the feathers directly from his own head—a self-assured reptile in the presence of inferior species. Apo-Huk and Apo-Iskay each wore headpieces as well, although not as grand.

Apo-Iskay had begun to grow a bit of a belly, Ninan thought wryly; not so tough now that he'd spent a few months eating that infamous cheese-and-potato stew in Qolqe.

Ninan's brothers had refused to acknowledge him, even within the privacy of Kallpa House, which had been fine by him. He doubted earning his way back would change anything, either.

"Today we are gathered for the commencement of the Venture," said the qhapaq, "where fifty competitors from each Terrain will embark on a journey down our hallowed mountains and into the jungle where the ruins of Utula await them. Brave Venturers from Sumaq, Unu, Qolqe, Allpa, and Tisqu will seek the gilded spinosaur tooth that honors our great land."

Applause followed, and coordinators doled out canvas maps, white pennant flags, and mysterious wooden tubes.

"Watchguards stationed at one of Sumaq's southern watchtowers will be on standby," Qhapaq Apo explained. "You will use your firestick"—he held up a wooden tube like those the competitors were receiving, and pinched a thin cord that came out of one end—"to send up a pyrotechnic signal once you have completed your quest and obtained your prize …"

Ninan received his own firestick, lightweight, about twelve inches long. It smelled of sulfur and charcoal.

"… at which point the closest watchguards will fly to meet you, and return you to the capital via pterobeast."

What a relief that would be, Ninan thought, after dozens upon dozens of miles on foot. The pterobeasts could cover more than eighty miles in an hour, where humans walking might be lucky to cover somewhere between ten and twenty in a day depending on the terrain. A journey that would take competitors up to two weeks would take a large flyer less than three hours, passing over all the trees and the creatures that lived among them.

It would be an interesting bookend to his past year, Ninan thought, should he win. The last time he'd flown in a gondola had been after his trial at the summit hall. Attendants had flown him out to the wilderness, lowered him down, and shoved him out. It should have been only the wilderness he'd had to face, but enemies—angry at the rumors surrounding his alleged treason— had discovered the location and prepared themselves to attack. Ninan couldn't remember how long he'd been running, seeking refuge in outbuildings on farms and within thick crops. He'd had to scavenge for scraps, and been close to starving when he'd reached Thak and discovered a small potato garden, where he'd stuffed his face with the raw root vegetables, not caring that they tasted like literal dirt, and fallen asleep with a sour but full stomach in an empty stall of the dinoshelter. He would never forget waking up in a pile of straw—or the look on Pidru's face when he'd found him there.

Pidru's mamáy had taken Ninan inside, given him fresh corn bread, and wiped his face clean like he was a small child who'd been out playing and lost track of time. Ninan had been far enough from Qhusi that nobody recognized him—and he was already a lesser Kallpa brother at that. The community was kind, and it had felt safe. As good a place as any for Ninan to live out a simpler life where his reputation wouldn't follow him.

He didn't have that safety now. If the other competitors were to discover his true identity, a good number of them would probably want him dead, target him—either for being such a poor excuse for a Kallpa, or because of the oft-despised qhapaq who had spawned him. He'd draw both sides like a prized kill.

While the qhapaq continued with instructions, Ninan

paused to look at the map, scanning the route and the landmarks. Prior to his arrival, Mullu had provided him with an *additional* map, whose roads and paths would line up with this one, but which also revealed a few lesser-known passages—shortcuts, in some cases, or alternatives to the more dangerous or crowded segments. He would have to stop and compare them when he got the chance.

"Red pennants will mark the route every five miles as a guide. Remember that you may use your own *white* pennant to surrender at any point," said the qhapaq, "and a herald will remove you from the competition peacefully.

"At dusk, the heralds will blare horns once for each remaining competitor—subtracting those who have died or surrendered—to alert remaining competitors as to how many are left to beat. However, once the number of remaining competitors reaches five or fewer, the horns will no longer blast. You must then use your keenest senses to stay ahead."

Sporting, Ninan thought. Who didn't love a potential ambush at the last minute? He rolled his eyes.

"At the midpoint of the route, you will come across a smaller prize, in similitude of the main event. Your clue: Lift your gaze to the gods in gratitude."

Ninan had to remind himself that, although this had all the trappings of a game, it would have grave consequences too. The usual laws of the land didn't apply now; theft and murder would be commonplace, and everything was designed to incite conflict or to drive competitors into greater danger. To those back home, it would be epic and dramatic through the lens of the herald reports, an ongoing tale to inspire and engage listeners; it would be a list of numbers—how many days were left and how many competitors had been savagely ripped apart by velociraptors and who had slashed whose throats—while its true horrors would never have to be experienced up close by anyone but those directly involved.

Ninan broke a sweat under his arms and his breath quickened. He looked around at the other competitors to see if any of them betrayed similar feelings. Most were raptly staring at the qhapaq as he repeated more of the instructions and information Mullu had already relayed to Ninan before the entrance trials. Some were double-checking their packs and supplies. Others eyed each other like they'd eye a gang of venomous sinornithosaurs. A few fidgeted with weapons or cracked knuckles or bounced on the balls of their feet.

There was a bald man dressed in black who looked like he belonged to a band of marauders; a highborn who wore a necklace made of bronzed theropod teeth; a few young men wielding slingshots; a feral-looking man with his face painted up to look like a dromaeosaurus, silvery white with black markings and an artistic representation of jaws that spanned the distance between his ears. There were bits of dinoleather armor everywhere, vests or headgear or simple arm and leg guards, although one man openly wore a full suit of it. Each competitor appeared hardier than the last.

Then Ninan identified a familiar green bayeta jacket. A familiar crossbow. A familiar steely gaze. If he hadn't been so preoccupied with preparations the past few days, he might have thought to scan the list for her name. He supposed it should come as no surprise that she'd made her way into the Venture. From what he'd seen, that girl was as obstinate as a pachycephalosaur; she certainly deserved her place here. His anxious fingers found the smoker in his pocket again and he thought, *But she doesn't deserve what's about to happen.*

ELEVEN

QORA GRIPPED HER CROSSBOW and rubbed her thumb along the foregrip—one, two, three times. At least three. Always. Index finger on the trigger. Bowstring taut on the bolt. Strap fixed to the handle, comfortable across her chest. She flexed her toes inside her boots, muscle cords tensing all the way up her legs against the metal in the back.

She left up the hood on her jacket. The lightweight wool barely kept off the autumn chill, even with the long-sleeved shirt she wore underneath. She wiped a sweaty palm on the dark fabric of her pants and tried to steady her breaths. The straps of her worn, brown bag full of supplies were tight on her shoulders, a tightness made worse by the emotional weight she carried there.

Her blood felt like it was sputtering through her veins. She could hardly focus on the qhapaq's words; she could only focus on his face, his demeanor, the pride with which he spoke to the crowd—and how he didn't know or care that he was responsible for Ollan's death. As if his excessive taxes weren't enough, he seemed to bear no shame in endangering his own citizens on a regular basis, and here he was, glad to do it again with the Venture for the sake of nationalism. Sure, the entrants had *chosen* to participate—even vied for the opportunity to do so— but she knew she couldn't be the only one who was here for reasons beyond their control, out of desperate hope to change their circumstances.

There were so many people around her, so many watching from the granite tiers and so many more on the flats loaded up with weapons. Some of the competitors were younger, closer to Qora's age, while others were older and even beginning to gray, with all ages in between.

"As you can see on your maps," Qora finally heard the qhapaq say, "the first quarter of the journey follows the trade route that extends from the capital. The latter portion intersects the river and runs nearly parallel to some of its banks."

Qora studied the illustrations that detailed the topography, the roadway, waterways, and the landmarks the competitors would pass. Several miles after the departure from Qhusi, they would skirt the length of Wañuy Ravine. In a few days, they'd reach the banks of Lake Waylla. Next would come a rope bridge that crossed the twisting pattern of the river Amaru. They would travel through the Rock Forest and eventually to the Volcano Kañay. From then on, it would be a mass of thick rainforest all the way to Wiqi Falls, which spilled into a pool that flowed right up to the ruins.

Among the competitors, Qora spotted the woman who had nearly broken her nose in the fighting ring—Killay—who wore a chest bandolier full of throwing knives, and a shorter bandolier around each thigh, her brown hair in the same tight crown braid, looking like she could level any beast with her facial expression alone.

Trying to see if she might recognize anyone else, Qora looked past the man who stood next to her—a thirty-something in a full suit of dinoleather armor, arms crossed. She was sure she was nearly young enough to be his daughter, although he was so foreboding she couldn't really imagine him having children. She must have looked ridiculous to him, she thought, and even more ridiculous when compared to him side by side.

There were more foreigners than not—two hundred, to be exact, with the combined groups of fifty from each of the other four Terrains—some of whom indicated this clearly by the colors they wore. Unuvian blue, Qolqese silver, Tisquvian purple, Allpan gold. Qora, however, would not have dared to wear red for Sumaq; red would have been asking for trouble. The vibrant color of fresh blood against the green woods that surrounded them and the verdant jungle ahead? She'd chosen her color for a reason, long ago, and she wasn't about to change it now. After several minutes scouring the enormous group, Qora's eyes landed on Ruyan, who seemed to have seen her too. His lips turned up as if in amusement, and he had an easy confidence in his sparkling, gray-brown eyes. Qora only nodded her acknowledgement before refocusing her attention on the instructions.

"As always, the heralds," said the qhapaq, "will fly by pteranodon to assess the damage, count bodies, witness conflict, and to make the daily airdrop—small resources that might be helpful as the days wear on, in similitude of the mystical rocks that Sky Mother rained down millennia ago."

A row of ten heralds waited on the sidelines, lined up like a small troop of soldiers. Each wore a black uniform with three stripes on the left sleeve in his or her Terrain's colors.

The qhapaq went on to explain that the particular pteranodons the heralds would be riding were also trained to smell death and locate corpses, and he suspected they would be very busy in the coming weeks.

Meanwhile, everyone else would eagerly await the reports.

Then professional fictionists would recount and embellish the tales on street corners while artists depicted the scenes in pigment or on wood carvings. What a grand show it would be.

Qhapaq Apo then launched into a long-winded ode to Sumaq and its magnificent heritage, along with dramatic promises of how these valiant citizens of Sumaq would compete to exhibit their skill and bravery among the Five Terrains. The words muddled together and Qora found herself gripping her crossbow stock so tightly she felt like the skin of her knuckles might split. She nearly jumped out of her skin when another competitor moved into her periphery.

A faintly smoky scent hit her nose, with an undertone of burnt sugar. Ninan kept his face forward but glimpsed her sideways. He rested a hand on his hip, where a dagger hung from his belt, part of its sheath peeking out from under his poncho. Albino dinoleather, Qora noted, which was rare, and was usually used to sheath antique blades made from the serrated teeth of large theropods, because its lack of color matched the enamel. Sakay traded and sold blades like that sometimes, and not for cheap.

Strange, she thought, *that Ninan would have such an ornamental weapon.* It was too nice for a boy as rough as he was. He must have won it in a fight—or maybe stolen it.

The qhapaq concluded his praise for the nation and circled back to final instruction. "On this date, the moon spirit hides her face. You have until the sun sets, prior to the *full* moon, to reach your prize."

Fourteen days, Qora thought. *Fourteen days and this will all be over.* Could she *last* fourteen days with these brutish treasure hunters? Not to mention a jungle full of dinosaurs she wasn't familiar with?

A parade of red Sumaqi flags fell in line behind the platform, the image of a Roaring Spinosaur emblazoned on each one.

Qhapaq Apo raised his firestick. It was larger than those the competitors had, but was otherwise the same. A filled tube, a cord on one end. "On my signal …"

Ninan leaned close to Qora. "Word of advice?"

Qora tensed and ran her thumb over her crossbow foregrip again. *One, two, three.* "No thanks," she told him.

"Make sure you know where you're headed before the starting blast goes off," he said anyway, as the qhapaq curled a fist around the firestick's cord. "Don't get spooked by the smoke—just run straight through, alright?"

A muscle in the qhapaq's forearm hardened visibly before he wrenched the cord from the tube.

Qora half-turned to look at Ninan. "Smoke?"

His eyes locked on Qora's for an instant—and then a squealing, fiery light shot into the air.

From the crown of the summit
To the valley below
Where the mists bring sweet spirits
And the mountain ferns grow

May we always revere these
Soil growths and sky rock,
In Sky Mother's chosen
Resplendent Sumaq

Final verse of the Sumaqi national anthem

TWELVE

NINAN LIT THE SMOKER before the *boom* echoed off the granite. He shot forward, eyes on the trees, trailing thick plumes of smoke.

The red lights of the qhapaq's firestick spidered across the sky, startling nearby flyers perched on branches.

Other competitors coughed and stumbled, disappearing into the smokescreen.

Ninan couldn't leave everyone behind at once, though. The grind of metal on metal overlapped as competitors fought around him. Arrows hissed past his head—shots in the dark, thanks to the visual obstruction he'd created. Several slingstones thwacked his pack and another struck his thigh. A machete came up against his copperskin from behind—then a small axe blade—but neither cut through. A club to the ribs nearly had him doubled over, but he managed to keep moving.

Competitors flailed blindly at whomever was closest, trying to take out as many others as they could on the way to the road. Ninan pushed onward, drawing out his longblade and yanking his copper-lined hood tighter around the sides of his face for protection.

The flats turned to pavingstones beneath his feet. The roadway was wide and pale, running southward. Pine forest sprawled on both sides of it. The pavement would eventually lead all the way to the capital of Unu, but only matched the Venture route for about sixty miles, and would not serve as a guide for long.

Ninan tried to block out the sounds of battle. He scanned the scattering competitors that had gone before him, looking for a flicker of green, but he didn't see Qora. Not that it mattered; *he* was supposed to win, which meant he shouldn't care what happened to her. Still, he hoped he hadn't trapped her back there in the thick of the chaos. As scaly as she seemed, he didn't quite wish her dead—especially not like that.

Even having made it this far, the uppers of his boots were flecked with blood, soles slippery and red, and he didn't dare stop to find out specifically why, but he imagined there were bodies broken open all across the stone, insides spilling out.

It was hard to maneuver nimbly with so many supplies strapped to his back—all his gear and the longbow he still hadn't efficiently learned to use. At least most of the other competitors were at the same disadvantage as far as extra weight and bulk.

Panting, Ninan prepared a second smoker while he ran. With his focus on lighting it, however, he neglected to watch where he was going and barreled directly into a pair of competitors engaged in a knife fight. The smaller of the two took the opportunity to slip away, thanks to Ninan's interference, but the other, a burly Qolqese man with arms like war cannons, picked up Ninan by the scruff of his poncho.

"What's this?" The man jabbed a thick finger into one of several new holes on the fabric, touching through to the copperskin lining. He tore open the top layer of the poncho with his knife and revealed the thousands of tiny, tightly linked metal scales underneath.

That was all it took to publicize Ninan's wealth.

Before Ninan could position himself for defense, half a dozen other competitors converged on him.

He tried to fight them off—an uppercut, a leg sweep, a throat punch—but no matter his skill, there were too many, and they'd caught him off guard. They ripped off his pack and wrestled over its contents. They tore weapons from his belt. His supplies diminished one by one—longbow, food, medicines, skyrock products. In the span of what must have been less than a minute, three men dropped dead from yet another competitor's throwing knives, while two others ran off in separate directions with stolen goods. A remaining few came to pick off what was left, but Ninan spewed smoke before they could pounce. He quickly picked up his ravaged pack and sprinted away.

He kept a quick pace for at least a mile, panting as sweat tracked down the sides of his face.

This thing had barely begun and already he was in horrible condition to keep going.

He tried to take a mental inventory of what he'd lost. Most of it could be replaced, if he was clever—or if his father could send more resources—but someone had yanked his mother's serrated-tooth dagger from his belt, and he had no idea which competitor it was.

Wearily, he went on, seeing fewer and fewer competitors. They'd either fallen behind or spread out, if they weren't dead by now. Heralds followed those who had managed to progress to this point or beyond, circling areas where sounds of conflict were most evident. He strained his eyes looking through the treetops until he located Mullu—three Sumaqi-red stripes on the left arm of his uniform. Ninan waved and ran alongside the pteranodon's shadow until Mullu began to lower. Other heralds had descended too, in response to competitors who had already had enough and waved their white banners to request a flight home, so Ninan hoped there would be no suspicions over Mullu's landing, at least this once. From what Ninan could see, there were no competitors in his immediate vicinity.

Mullu touched down where the trees stood a bit wider apart. There was room for the pteranodon to settle itself without snapping any branches, but only just.

"Your father's not going to be happy about this," Mullu said, guiding the reptile forward while he remained mounted. "Look at you. Torn to shreds, baring your copperskin wealth for all the world to see; it's meant as a last resort, not to take every hit someone throws at you. And your pack is practically empty."

"There were too many competitors." Ninan pinched his waist, where a cramp had begun to build, and winced. "I'm lucky I got away with my life."

Mullu glanced around as if to assess privacy, then detached a sheathed longblade from his own belt and tossed it to Ninan. "That's the best I can do for now. I'll make sure you get my airdrop first thing tomorrow; look for me at the back of the formation when we fly out. Everyone else tends to cluster on the first few heralds' drops to see if it's something worthwhile— although it will be. We're mindful of what competitors will be most desperate for."

"Pisco?" Ninan said.

Mullu met the joke with a cold stare. "Medical attention. The first drop is always an assortment of salves and bandages." After a survey of the other heralds overhead, he added, "I'll see what I can gather from the dead—assuming other competitors haven't robbed them bare—and try to smuggle something useful into the package. Don't miss it."

With that, he commanded the pteranodon into an upward sweep and left Ninan alone again, his shredded poncho fabric fluttering in the wind of the flyer's wingflaps.

Ninan sighed and hooked the new blade onto his belt. His pack was far too light; he could tell by the way it sat—or rather, sagged—against his spine. Did he dare assess the damage?

He knelt for a moment and opened the pack. Inside, he found an oilskin tarp rolled up at the bottom, the allosaurian hydration tincture, a few bandages, a handful of smokers, a waterskin, and two dehydrated meals. In the outer pockets, he still had his firestick, white pennant, and map (along with the additional, secret map he'd received before the sendoff). But he no longer had a tent, firepowder, or any ointments. His only weapon now was the longblade Mullu had just given him.

He suddenly felt a crushing weight against his chest. How was he going to survive this?

I can still do it, he told himself. Everything would be fine. That's why Mullu had been appointed a herald; Kallpa House would take care of him. *The qhapaq gets what he wants.*

Ninan tried to take comfort in that thought, but the words felt meager when he considered the many miles—and monsters—ahead. With shaky hands, he took the waterskin and removed the cap, bringing water to his lips. As he took a sip, a sudden *thunk* against the ground made him spill it.

He dropped the waterskin and spun around, assuming a fighting stance.

A young man appeared to have dropped from the trees and landed in a crouch. Slowly, he tipped his face up and locked eyes with Ninan. "Thought you looked familiar."

Familiar? Everyone at Kallpa House who knew of Ninan's return had assured him he would be unrecognizable. His chances at success during the Venture seemed to be growing worse by the minute.

"You …" Ninan observed the young man's Unuvian blue clothing, the athletic way he'd apparently descended from the branches above, the pickaxe on his belt, the worn dinoleather gloves. "You were watching me earlier. At the flats, before the sendoff." Recognition aside, it took him a moment to process what it meant that another competitor had apparently been here, lurking in the trees, for some period of time.

Ruck.

His eyes wandered to the place where Mullu had landed with the pteranodon; there was no way their exchange could have gone unseen.

"Who are you?" Ninan asked.

"The princeling doesn't remember me …"

Ninan's stomach twisted. *Princeling.*

If there had been any doubt as to his identity, his interaction with the qhapaq's chief attendant would have cleared that up instantly. "*Should* I?"

The young man stood up straight and shrugged. "I'll give you my name but I'm sure it won't make a difference. It's Takan." When Ninan couldn't produce any response, Takan scoffed. "Like I said …"

"Look, if I ever offended you in some way—"

"'Offended' me?" Takan chuckled bitterly. "That's an interesting way to put it. But I guess I shouldn't be surprised that you'd belittle the memory when you're *such* an important person." He touched his chin. "Except … *are* you?"

Ninan followed Takan's gaze, which roved the length of him pointedly. Ninan knew he was filthy and battered. A drop of blood hung at the edge of one of his nostrils, his clothes were torn, and he had the resources of a lowborn. Whoever Takan was, he'd apparently seen him in a much different state before, but for the life of him Ninan could not recall when that might have been.

"What do you want?" Ninan wiped his nose. "If you're hoping to get something valuable off of me, others have already beat you to the punch."

"I have what I need." Takan pointed his head at his own pack, which was practically bursting at the seams. And he didn't have a scratch on him. He must have gotten ahead of everyone, sped off before the chaos could overwhelm him. He looked up at the branches, where he'd been hiding. "Anyway. You really ought to watch your head, princeling. You never know what might be going on above you."

A grunt in the distance prompted Ninan to turn and look for the source of the sound. Another competitor, mid-sprint, arched his back and collapsed with an arrow in his spine. When Ninan turned his attention back, Takan was gone.

THIRTEEN

QORA'S LUNGS BURNED, but she kept running. One, two, three strokes on her crossbow before she curled her fingers back around the foregrip and spared a glance over her shoulder.

She'd only had an instant to determine which direction she would go. Then she'd had to sprint with all her might to stay ahead of the smoke that had quickly blanketed the flats. The metal in her boots had been too stiff to warrant comfortable sprinting, just as she'd expected, although Sakay had been right to insist she reinforce them; several competitors had fired in her general direction and not one had succeeded in taking her out of the competition. In her periphery, she could see part of an arrow lodged in the side of her pack, which she didn't yet dare stop to remove.

She continued to put mileage between herself and the other competitors, fleeing from all human sounds. Her body begged her to slow down.

Just a little longer, she told it.

It must have been half an hour before the echoes of the sendoff stayed put behind her, before they no longer wafted after her like the smoke whose scent still clung to her clothes. Smoke and burnt sugar. *Just run straight through, alright?*

Ninan had given them both a head start. But why? Why

should he bother to warn her?

Maybe he had thought himself noble for doing poor little Qora a favor. Him and his "words of advice."

The sounds of the initial battle still played in Qora's mind—arrows and slingstones sinking into flesh, skulls cracking on paved road, spectators booing and cheering and shouting.

At this point, Qora finally slowed to a brisk walk, assessing her surroundings, making a mental catalog of her supplies. She didn't love being in the woods, but she was familiar enough with them to feel confident in her ability to navigate them. For a moment it was almost as though she were out hunting on a regular day: not pleasant, but nothing she couldn't grit her teeth and bear.

Except this was no regular day—and Qora realized she might never see a regular day again.

Would she live to rise at dawn with her brothers and eat amaranth cereal before feeding the alpacas whose fiber her mamáy used for yarn? Would she live to see the racks of colorful yarn drip-drying outside her house, to watch her mamáy dangling her drop spindle while she waited for vegetables to roast in the clay oven? Such mundane things that it hadn't occurred to her she might miss. Now she ached for mundane. She'd kill for it. In fact, she just might have to.

Qora took a swig of water then quickly depleted her entire supply. She went to the stream to refill.

After a couple more miles of walking, though, the land began to look different. The slope of it, the pattern of the trees. Regions she'd only seen once or twice on longer, more adventurous hunts. She kept moving, stopping for short breaks to drink water, avoiding the map in her pack. But soon, there was no denying it anymore. She was officially in unfamiliar territory. Now her only clue to what lay ahead was the ink drawing on the canvas map—and somehow, she didn't think it could do justice to the scope of it.

Throughout the remaining hours of the afternoon, she kept her ears tuned to sounds of activity, although she wasn't used to listening for people and dinosaurs at the same time. She avoided indications of other competitors, veering laterally whenever she got close enough to spot someone else. From afar, she saw another competitor, with what appeared to be a dislocated arm that dangled awkwardly at his side, waving his pennant; she shuddered as one of the heralds landed to retrieve him.

As the sky grew orange and dim, Qora grew weary. Even though the air had cooled, sweat condensed under her arms and around her neck. Her body heat released another wave of the smoky scent she thought would have faded from her jacket by now, and she couldn't help wondering whether Ninan had survived the sendoff, or whether he was lying cut open on the roadway somewhere. And if he *had* survived, she wondered how soon he would give up all that benevolence and try to kill her, when conditions turned dire and inhibitions faded in favor of the inevitable desperation to survive and win. She pictured his sepia complexion, his boyish smirk, his dark eyes. Could there be a killer behind them?

Along the route, wild compies darted in and out of thickets. They were skinnier and more skittish than the compies at home, and lighter in color. Brown sciurumimus scurried up trees, blending into the bark. There were several reptiles that were far too large to consider hunting but which were peaceful and kept to themselves: a herd of speedy gallimimus stopped at the stream to drink, a parasaur chewing on plants and guarding a nest full of dappled eggs, and a couple of mid-sized ceratopsians with tiny horns along the top edges of their bony frills.

In accordance with the map, Qora came to one side of Wañuy Ravine—which meant she'd forced herself to travel an impressive twenty-five miles, verified by the number of red pennants she'd spotted along the way. The ravine's dropoff was blunt and covered in moss. She peered down at the rocks that cluttered the bottom, and shivered.

She wanted to keep moving, but she also knew she couldn't overdo it on the first day. She had to save her strength. While gaining distance was important, so was her ability to stay alert on the route. There were eleven and a half hours of daylight each day, and she wanted to utilize every one of them.

As darkness fell, it would be more dangerous to keep traveling anyway, so she looked for the best place to set up camp, somewhere ensconced but not near the thicker bushes where predators would like to hide.

She found a couple of sturdy tree trunks that would suspend her hammock, then set down her pack. She slipped the metal out of her boots and massaged her calves. She chugged water and gorged herself on troodon jerky.

Even though it was chilly, she wouldn't make a fire tonight, she'd decided; no sense advertising her location—although she suspected there weren't many competitors who felt threatened by her. She hated to admit it, but she knew that was likely the only reason she'd made it off the flats alive.

"That little toy crossbow ... "

"If anything, I'm even more impressed now ... "

"Let some real fighters get in there ... "

Everyone had been too busy bludgeoning the more menacing adversaries to worry about her. Of course she also knew she had to be grateful for that. Sakay would have said to use that to her advantage any chance she got—and as pathetic as it felt, she planned to. This wasn't a time for pride; she had to get through this if there was any chance to help Rimaq.

Thinking of the sendoff, and of the savagery she'd left behind, Qora took a few minutes to dip some of her bolt tips in the sinorn venom before she got too comfortable. Not that the growing tension in her chest and shoulders was *comfortable* …

She set out the glowing mushrooms as dusk still clung to one last sunlit glow, and unrolled her hammock. But as she went to tie up the first end, the underbrush rustled.

Qora stopped dead, holding her breath.

Someone spoke—two voices—arguing. Darkness was coming on so quickly, she could just make out two men, no packs on their shoulders, smears of dirt or blood (or both) on their clothes and faces. They dodged each other, one with some kind of utility knife, the other with a dagger.

"Hand over the skyrock," said the one with the dagger. He seemed to have a slingshot as well, tucked into his pants, but perhaps hadn't had the chance to load it.

"Come on. You'd really rob one of your own? We could work *together* …"

Surely they were far too engaged in their own conflict to notice her, Qora told herself. All she had to do was keep quiet, stay hidden.

If only she hadn't set out a glowing light right next to her.

The first competitor tackled the second just before Qora tossed her jacket over the mushrooms to cover them—but it was too late.

"Wait—did you see that?" the second demanded, apparently unimpressed by the knife against his throat.

The first shoved him down harder and said, "Nice try." But he did glance in Qora's direction, squinting.

"I'm serious. There's someone there."

The two men paused, both staring at Qora's camp. Qora, who had ducked behind a tree, held her crossbow to her chest and performed her usual self-soothing routine.

Bowstring taut. Bolt snug. Trigger ready.

She listened for their footsteps the same way she would have listened for signs of game. She parted her lips and inhaled slowly, heart drumming against her ribs.

No one had raided her yet, and now—as one of the few competitors who still had ample supplies—she would pay the price.

"There's a full pack," said the second man. "We could split it."

"I don't need trouble with other competitors. I just need your skyrock."

"No … It might be no trouble at all. I could've sworn it was a girl …"

"The one with the knives?"

Silence. A head shake, maybe. "Looked smaller. Just a kid."

Quiet steps now, but Qora could hear them. She peered carefully around the tree as they approached, signaling to each other.

You go that way, I'll go this way, Qora imagined.

Blades raised.

As soon as one of them was close enough, Qora took her first shot. Her target moved and the bolt soared past him.

"Ruck!" He ducked and scoured the ground until he found a stone the perfect size for ammunition. He brought out the slingshot and loaded it. The sling croaked as he stretched it back.

A second later, tree bark splintered next to Qora's head.

She trembled, gripping the crossbow to steady herself while she figured out what to do next.

The ravine was still a few yards away. It was dark enough now that the men might not be able to tell where it dropped off. Qora peered around again. The shooter was crouched behind a boulder, but Qora could make out the light-colored wood tone of his slingshot, which peeked up, waiting for Qora to reveal herself. She got on her knees and patted the ground until she found a large rock, which she pried up, dirt shoving under her fingernails so tightly it hurt. She hurled it away, toward the ravine. Both men shot, racing past her to get closer to the decoy.

Qora followed, spanning her crossbow in advance, watching them get within a few feet of the ravine. They looked around trying to find her.

Her loaded bolt still had a sheen that told her the venom on it was potent. She sank it into one of the men's thighs and he bellowed, grabbing the bolt like he was fighting the urge to rip it out. The other went for cover while Qora spanned, loaded, and sank a bolt into his shoulder blade; he crumpled to the ground screaming. Qora loaded one more venomous bolt in case she needed it, but both men squirmed and writhed for several minutes until they finally seemed to lose consciousness.

In the dusklight, Qora crept toward them. The first lay on his back. He was larger than the second, so Qora was surprised the venom had taken effect so soon; it could take longer on a bigger body.

Qora knew she was supposed to run now, but all she could think was that both men looked as dead as if she'd shot with intent to kill. As she took a shuddering breath, the man on his back twitched. Qora retreated, but the man's eyes sprung open and his fingers cuffed Qora's arm.

He was weaker and slower than he would have been without venom gradually taking over his body, but he dragged Qora down anyway. She clambered on hands and knees. He lunged at her, grabbing the collar of her shirt and jerking her backwards. Still holding her crossbow, Qora swung the weapon around and clipped him in the face, cutting a deep mark onto his cheek and across the bridge of his nose where the loaded bolt scraped him. The bolt's venom began to dissolve into his open wounds and he doubled over.

Qora made a run for it—but then she suddenly remembered where she was and stopped short, gasping for air.

The man stumbled toward her. He pulled out his knife and wagged it like he was drunk. Qora kept her eye on the blade, letting him approach.

He charged forward.

Qora waited.

Waited.

Waited.

A little longer.

At the last possible second, she slipped out of the way.

He careened over the edge of the ravine and plummeted into its depths. Branches cracked and snapped on his way down. His body crashed at the bottom. Qora cringed at the sound— bones shattering on boulders.

A chill spread through her limbs, one that had nothing to do with the drop in temperature now that the sun had gone down. One of Qora's braids has fallen out and wind blew loose hairs over her forehead. She wrapped her arms around herself.

Cautiously, she looked over the man on the ground closest to her, to see if he had anything worth taking. A couple of knives and a slingshot were all he had on him; the rest must have been wherever his camp was, but Qora wasn't going to go looking for that in the dark.

Above her, heralds flew over carrying lanterns that almost appeared to be floating on their own. The horns blared over and over. Qora counted them.

One hundred and four.

That meant that one hundred and forty-six competitors were either dead or had surrendered. More than half were out of the Venture now, but almost as many still remained. Qora took a steadying breath, packed up her things by mushroom light, and went off in search of a different place to sleep.

As if she would be able to sleep.

FOURTEEN

NINAN WOKE SHIVERING. The oilskin tarp underneath him was poor insulation against the cold ground. The metal scales lining his poncho did him no favors either, but he wasn't about to remove any armor when there were still so many competitors raging around.

If it hadn't been for the skyrock-studded belt that thankfully hadn't drawn enough attention to end up stolen, he might have been mauled by velociraptors in the night—he'd heard them scritching all around and making their warbling cries to one another, and they'd even sniffed around his camp before the skyrock had warded them off.

He used the last of his water to hydrate one of his two remaining meals and had to force himself not to inhale the food all at once. Even after he'd eaten, his stomach groaned and gurgled, not even half satisfied after the day he'd had yesterday or the energy spent on a near-sleepless night. And there was only a single meal left unless Mullu could manage to get him something else. Ninan certainly couldn't hunt with Mullu's longblade; he would have been ruck at hunting even with the bow he'd had at the start.

The morning remained milky and brisk even a couple of hours after dawn. Those two hours felt like ages to Ninan while he walked on and on, watching the skies and hoping for some relief. He was only able to take advantage of one of the shortcuts on his secret map thus far, which might have saved him *half* an hour, although it didn't help him advance so much as it allowed him to simply keep up. It would prove itself more useful later on, in the jungle, when he could use the abandoned trade routes to avoid having to cut through the vines and the underbrush, but for now, he only hoped to maintain a good pace.

Later, a few other competitors moved along within view, but remained distant, probably too worn and ravaged to start fights with anyone. Some traveled in groups of two or three, always of the same nationality as far as Ninan could tell, wearing the same Tisquvian purple or bearing similar Allpan smilodon patches or murmuring to one another in a language only they among themselves understood. Competitors would team up this way sometimes, Mullu had told him, temporarily allying themselves to increase the likelihood of one of their own winning rather than a foreigner. But of course alliances would have to end eventually.

Ninan passed through a few raided camps—dead fire pits surrounded by less useful items cast aside, packs slit and emptied, a splatter of dried blood here and there, a far-flung boot—and several dead bodies that the heralds' pteranodons would sniff out later. A couple of the bodies were bare naked; it made sense that they might have been stripped of whatever dinoleather or copperskin collars or durable shoes they'd been wearing, but what is really so bad that some other competitor would need to steal trousers and undershirts? Nothing was off limits, it seemed, or too petty to kill for. After he'd lost nearly everything at the sendoff, Ninan had comforted himself with the thought that, while he'd had little to survive on, he also had little to covet, but now he wasn't so sure. He could be targeted for something as simple as a waterskin—and worse, there was someone out there who knew who he really was.

After another mile or so, the clouds began to burn off and the soil released the damp scents that only came out when heat willed them to. Far behind, the high mountains of Qhusi rose above the landscape shawled in white vapors, already faded and emitting an almost artificial quality, like a mural drawn with chalk pastels. And from the trees that stood between Ninan and his homeland emerged a group of dark flyers, one by one, shooting up into formation.

Ninan's stomach tensed. His limbs surged with energy summoned from a dwindling reserve. He couldn't linger; he had to get Mullu's airdrop. Immediately he broke into a run; the flyers would pass him soon enough, and then it would require a painful effort to keep Mullu within view.

The heralds blared their horns again, but this time it was a single, long note rather than several shorter ones, to alert competitors that soon there would be resources to compete for. Competitors would know to look to the skies—if they hadn't already heard the pteranodons' warning cries or seen the fluttering shadows cast by those massive wings—and position themselves to receive whatever might fall upon them. Ninan didn't see any competitors in his immediate surroundings, but he was sure anyone within a mile would be moving toward the drop-off points.

Mullu was at the tail, as he'd said he would be, pulling back slowly as the formation spread out. The heralds were waiting now, turning their pteranodons in spirals to keep them flying over the same general spot, to give competitors more time to gather.

Ninan pushed his throbbing muscles. His copperskin jangled

against his abdomen. His toes slammed into the reinforcements in his boots. Mullu was now stationed ahead of him, but Ninan kept the herald in view, racing toward him. He caught Mullu's eye; Mullu nodded once, looked to the other members of the group—who were now dropping burlap sacks stamped with Sumaq's spinosaur-and-shield emblem in red ink—and let the bounty fall to the ground. Ninan memorized its location and dug deep within himself to find more speed.

Then, at the edge of his vision, he caught sight of another figure moving alongside him. He turned his head.

"Nice to see you again, princeling." Takan ran with ease—barely out of breath, even though he had a full and heavy pack—as he swung a rope-cord with stones attached to both ends. Before Ninan could process what Takan was about to do, the primitive bola soared toward him. Ninan couldn't outrun it in time; the cord cut him off at the shins, its stone-weighted ends flinging around until it wrapped both his legs and he lurched forward, his whole body slamming down. He couldn't catch his breath for several agonizing seconds, and meanwhile, Takan had surpassed him and disappeared.

As soon as he was able, Ninan untangled himself and got to his feet and hurried to catch up, taking the bola with him. But by the time he arrived at the drop spot, Takan was already several yards onward, bag in possession.

You really ought to watch your head, princeling.

Takan had planned this. Trailed him. Sought out Mullu's airdrop. And why wouldn't he? He'd heard Mullu tell him he'd fall back.

The *whumpf* of bodies hitting the ground was audible from somewhere in the woods. The scrape of metal on metal. Shouts, grunts, wails of agony. Ninan stood numbly as the pteranodons clustered in multiple areas to see which competitors had taken the bait—and who had stolen the bait, and who had won it back, and who was about to bleed out for it before others snatched it away and carried it off in different directions.

Ninan thought it would only take a few minutes for the desperate and furious sounds to fade, but they continued long after the drops. He stumbled on empty-handed, a sting forming behind his eyes. Mullu was somewhere else taking notes, falling in line with the other heralds, and may not have even realized Ninan had missed his salvation.

Who was he kidding? He wasn't a winner; he couldn't even catch a falling bag. It had barely been twenty-four hours and already he was primed for starvation. Some prince he was.

No—he corrected himself—he wasn't a prince. Not anymore. All this pampering and catering to him in preparation for the Venture had made him forget. And he wasn't exactly on his way to earning his title *back*, either.

Not a prince. Not a crop cutter. Not a hunter or a warrior or even an athlete. No resources or equipment to hide behind anymore. All he really had were his fists and a bit of smoke, neither of which gave him much of an upper hand when others carried spiked clubs and hunting bows and—apparently—bolas. He clutched the bola now, raising it to observe the intricate way Takan had wrapped the end-stones. He wasn't sure he'd be able to utilize this weapon himself, but he stuffed it into his pack anyway, sighing.

If he wanted a chance to finish this competition, he was going to have to get clever. He was going to have to fight dirty. And as he considered the way the airdrops had lured so many competitors to one place—like traps for unsuspecting animals— he suddenly became very clear on how to do it.

FIFTEEN

WITHOUT SKYROCK, QORA HAD TO BE on full alert throughout the night, every night. And the nights were long. Hours upon hours of light sleep, interspersed with noises that pulled her awake in a panic. Usually it was only smaller theropods whose species she wasn't familiar with—but that was enough to keep her on edge. She felt like she'd almost kill for skyrock dust right now, and she had no doubt plenty of other competitors already had. She cradled her crossbow as she slept, finger on the trigger. She didn't make fires. She shot reptiles that were too big to eat—so that they didn't tear her to shreds in her sleep—and had to leave them to their decay, which pained her; she was grateful whenever vulturous dinosaurs found their way to the carrion she'd left behind, and more grateful that it kept their bellies full so they didn't come after her too. She also fended off more wild compies than she could count. Unlike the healthier compies at home, the ones out here weren't content with insects and rodents; they nipped at Qora's legs and tried to burrow into her pack for her dried foods.

After the first few days, the fighting seemed to be less frequent. With fewer and fewer competitors, it was easier to avoid encounters with anyone, as long as Qora was tuned into her surroundings.

Some idiot kept making fires during the day—for midday meals after a hunt, maybe—sending up smoke for all to see. She'd watched other competitors racing off toward them, blades held aloft and prepared to raid. Then there had been grunts and shouting, and shuffling of forest debris, and rustling of thickets and ferns, and finally silence. Qora figured these encounters would have resulted in the death of whomever had built the fires, or at least left him with too few resources and forced him to surrender, but the next day, she saw the smoke again. Some people never learned.

For the most part, though, other competitors seemed to be focused mainly on survival now, on covering more ground. Petty fights meant the loss of what little resources most people had left, which meant a lower chance at getting to the ruins. Although that didn't stop a few of them from resorting to other sorts of dangerous measures. Qora came across multiple competitors trying to use skyrock (likely stolen) to capture wild reptiles for transportation—a woman with her hands coated in skyrock dust coaxing a parasaur, a man with skyrock bracelets attempting to mount a wild rhabdodon. One competitor had some luck with a large protoceratops, but the reptile's stride wasn't much faster than a person on foot, especially as it stopped repeatedly to nibble on ginkgo shrubs and made a fuss every time the tree growth was too thick for its wide berth to pass comfortably.

By the fourth day, Qora trudged along parallel to the narrowing route, determined to keep at least a few hundreds yards of distance from it, but her map showed an upcoming water body—a segment of the snaking river that she soon would intersect—with a solitary bridge that was, essentially, a continuation of the roadway she'd been working so hard to avoid (in hopes of avoiding other competitors). Looking at the map more closely, however, she determined that to go around it would force her to follow the river's curves for the remainder of the journey—adding dozens of additional miles—and she'd still have to cross it at the end to get to the ruins. Thinking of Rimaq, and how time was of the essence, she knew there was only one option.

Stroking her crossbow, Qora took a deep breath and headed toward the road.

Eventually, she came upon the rope bridge. It was stretched from one end of a gorge to the other, twisted cables suspending the walkway, about a hundred feet across.

Her stomach churned. She didn't like the idea of crossing a path she knew the other competitors could be crossing at any moment. They could all spread out when there was foliage, weaving in front of and behind each other over dozens of miles of forest and for several days without ever knowing it, but they had to come back to the main route when it was time to go over water—at least when that water was at the bottom of a gorge. Either that or they'd have to climb down and cross the water directly, but that would take extra time, and the water was swift and full of aquatic reptiles and carnivorous fish, not to mention no one wanted to risk getting their firestick wet. Any shallow, easily passable segments would be far out of the way.

The bridge itself hung in solitude, with no evidence of human activity—although a few of the surrounding trees had had their smaller, lower branches cut, internal wood visible beneath the bark. Not the way a reptile might break or bite them, Qora thought; maybe someone had been improvising weapons from pointed sticks.

Qora kept her hand on her own weapon as she crossed. The whole structure swayed with her movements. The ropes groaned and creaked. She had to remind herself it was only perceived weakness in the bridge; these had been constructed to support riders on dinosaurs, after all.

By the time she made it to the other side, she was so distracted gripping the cables and watching her surroundings that she almost didn't notice what was under her feet. Before she stepped off the bridge, she gasped, supporting most of her weight on the last section of the cable and drawing backward.

The exit path, covered with leaves like the rest of the forest floor, had a break in it—a hole in the ground three feet wide. But it wasn't the kind of hole that a diictodon would burrow, leaving a ring of piled dirt around the edge, and it was too deep to be a footprint. Qora couldn't quite put her finger on what was wrong about it; it just seemed unnatural—misplaced.

She crouched to get a closer look. The cover of leaves extended over flattened clods of soil held together with fine roots. Long, lightweight branches—the other ends of the cut-off branches she'd seen a minute ago—crossed the opening, forming a type of grate. As she moved the leaves and dirt, she revealed an even larger opening with a steep slope below, which angled down onto wooden spikes that jutted at varying lengths like saber-teeth.

A dinofelis trap. Named after saber-toothed dinofelis cats, an open mouth in the ground that could swallow and kill.

Qora gagged and covered her mouth.

At the bottom lay a limp body, impaled in several places, limbs drooping as flies buzzed over the sallow skin.

It was a courier. He wore the typical blue shirt, with the white band tied around his right arm. He wasn't even a competitor, nothing to gain from this game, but apparently everything to lose.

Who would do something like this?

A stupid question, Qora knew. Of course there were plenty of competitors who would. The trap clearly hadn't been set for an animal; It had been deliberately set where human traffic would be concentrated. Except anyone setting it would know there would be plenty of non-competitors passing through, innocent employees of the state. It was a brutal last-ditch effort to possibly kill a competitor, but with low odds. A coward's method.

Shaking her head, she stepped back, and something hard came up against the underside of her boot.

She knelt to see what it was.

A white weapon—a tooth dagger.

Qora picked it up and turned it over. Its sheath was missing, but there was no mistaking it. The same size, the same serrations. Too rare for there to be two floating around the same competition. Another wave of nausea pulsed in her belly, the place where she had once felt a flutter when she'd thought—like an idiot—that Ninan had complimented her.

Nice kill.

She had actually blushed when she'd seen him coming toward her, all sweaty and battle worn and radiating confidence. And at the entrance trials, some small part of her had been glad for his advice outside the ropes, however useless it had been to her untrained fists. Even at the sendoff, when he'd warned her about the smoke, she'd questioned herself, wondered whether it was necessary to cling to her grudge like she did her crossbow. Now she felt pathetic. That boy wasn't just cocky; he was cruel.

With her face burning at the very thought of him, Qora kicked away the rest of the trap's cover, trying not to look at the rotting corpse inside. She staked some of the sticks in the ground to mark the trap, should anyone else come through in a hurry. As she shifted some of the debris, she also happened to find the dagger's sheath, which she slipped onto the blade before she stuck it in her pack.

As midday rolled around, Qora hungered for meat. Her dried food supply was dwindling and her body weak. Still in isolation, for what she could see, she found a good place to set her belongings, marked by a fallen tree, while she hunted for something that could build her strength. She only ventured about fifty yards from the site as she crept toward a rhamphorhynchus—dark gray, with white spots—as it perched in the low branches.

Qora aimed carefully, bracing the crossbow against her inner shoulder. She took a breath.

Click.

Her bolt pierced the rhampho's head. The rhampho flopped down and rustled when it hit. Qora was about to retrieve it when the faintest movement on the ground behind her made her tense. She spanned and turned simultaneously toward the potential threat, already loading another bolt when she found herself facing a man with one hand raised in surrender and the other tucked against his chest, a bloody bandage covering most of his right arm.

"Sorry," the man said breathlessly.

Ruyan.

Blood pounded in Qora's head as she assessed him.

Injured. No throwing-stars or other weapons. A withered look about him. White pennant hanging from his pocket.

Even with his chestnut hair mussed from exertion, he maintained a certain charm.

"I swear I wasn't trying to sneak up on you," he continued. "I was coming through this way when I saw you hunting, and I stopped. Didn't want to scare away your game."

"Oh." Qora still held her weapon at the ready, but lowered it slightly. "That was … considerate of you."

It was strange holding a conversation with someone, after four days on her own. Only four days, but they'd been long ones, stretched out into seemingly endless hours on seemingly endless terrain, lost in her own paranoid thoughts while anyone within view had been a threat to her safety. She wasn't sure what to make of this now, how to navigate such a calm and casual situation.

"Incredible shot, by the way." He nodded at the rhampho. "On such a small target. I can't imagine how much practice it must have taken you to develop a skill like that."

No kidding, she thought. Hours with Ollan while he'd corrected her form over and over, guiding her in the same pattern as his trainers had taught him and probably with as little mercy in his critiques. "Thank you," Qora said, relaxing. "What happened to your weapons? And your pack?"

"Got raided the first night," he told her. "And again two nights ago."

"And your arm?"

"Tried to snare a pamparaptor but it sank its teeth into me a couple of times before it ran off. That's when I decided I'd had about enough of this whole thing." He gestured to the pennant. "Just waiting to spot the heralds on their next patrol."

As much as Qora was glad to have one less competitor in her way, it was still so early to have to bow out. "That's unfortunate for you."

"It is," he admitted. "Better to quit while I've still got my life, though. Especially with someone out there setting pit traps."

Qora thought of the tooth dagger in her pack. Ninan would have probably been pleased to see Ruyan skewered on spikes.

She could just imagine his reaction: *"A test of his intelligence, which he passed with flying colors—and by flying colors, I mean 'blood red' and 'corpse blue.'"*

"So cruel." Qora shook her head. "I saw the one at the last bridge. So much for a contest of skill; as far as I can tell, the Venture's more like a showcase of underhanded brutality."

"Yes, well … you seem to have done well in staying out of it. That's good."

"I've escaped it narrowly. So far."

Ruyan smiled flatly and fidgeted as he cradled his arm. "I don't suppose you'd have any medicine, would you? I can't figure why such a small bite should hurt so much, but it's as bad as if the teeth were still cutting into me."

Qora nodded. "Right. Pamparaptors have something in their saliva that amplifies the pain of their bites. Most of the smaller dinos do, actually. Or other irritants that cause itching."

"That explains a lot. I got a troodon bite once and I swear it hurt less than this."

She glanced in the direction of her things. "I have a salve. It's not strong, but it might help." She started walking and Ruyan followed. Even though he didn't make a move in her direction laterally, Qora squeezed her weapon and kept a few feet between the two of them.

"There's still a good chance you can make it to the ruins unscathed," Ruyan offered. "The conflicts have subsided for now. Of course competitors may be more desperate—and more willing to kill for what they need—but they're also weakened, which is an advantage. A lot of them won't be thinking clearly, won't be at the top of their game. Not everyone has the good sense to know when to quit." He tapped his own chest.

Mentally, Qora went over everything she had on her,

anything someone else might want. She still had some food, her few weapons. She wasn't entirely useless to the other competitors, even if they didn't think she was anyone to worry about as far as beating them to that golden spinosaur tooth.

The two of them reached the fallen tree where Qora had left her belongings. She glanced over her shoulder at Ruyan before she bent to go through her pack. Ruyan pressed his lips flat and sat on the fallen tree, waiting patiently. After opening the flap, Qora dug around for the salve container. "This should take the edge off, at least." She found the container and uncorked it, but the color and consistency made her pause. Syrupy and green. "Definitely not that one." She'd completely forgotten to label the containers, in all her preparations before leaving. She set down the sinorn venom slowly so it wouldn't slosh. Then she located the outwardly similar salve container and sat beside Ruyan as she went to open it.

"You know," he said, brushing her wrist with his fingers, stopping her, "I'm sure it's a terrible time to say this, but … I've found you fascinating since I first saw you."

Qora slipped out from under his touch and set the medicine between them so he could help himself. "'Fascinating'?"

He regarded the medicine but didn't open it. "The judges must have thought so too—since you're here."

"I did my best. That's good enough for some people, and not enough for others. But whatever the reason, I should really get going. If you're not going to use—"

She looked down to find his hand resting gently on her knee. Her muscles tensed. She shifted away. When he touched her again, she pushed his hand off. "What are you doing?"

His expression darkened. "You're going to pretend you're *averse* to me now? After falling all over me at the trials?"

Qora scoffed. "It was crowded. I lost my footing …"

"And afterward? When you kept so close?"

"I don't think you understand what 'crowded' means." She stood and went to put away her things.

In a second, his hands found her waist. "If you say so …"

She spun around and shoved him.

Almost instantly the back of his hand came across her face, rattling her skull. But despite her shock, one thing was very clear to her: He'd used his "injured" arm.

A lump formed in Qora's throat as she pressed a palm to her cheek.

But what about the blood?

Then it occurred to her that there were plenty of dead bodies with bloody bandages he could have stolen to wear.

When she scanned the woods, her gaze fell on a mass in the distance—a pack set up against a tree, and the hint of an oilskin tarp rolled up on the ground. Far enough away that she wouldn't have noticed it, had she not been looking for it. Few supplies maybe, but not the camp of a man who'd been raided twice, or a man who was planning to leave the competition any time soon.

She went for her crossbow, but Ruyan grabbed her by the shoulders and slammed her forward against a thick tree, his arm across her back, pinning her.

"I don't like it when women play games with me," he growled.

Dread crept through Qora's veins like sludge. When she screamed, Ruyan pushed her face into the bark, scraping her cheek until hot pinpricks of blood broke through. She tried to throw her elbows back but the angle was all wrong and she didn't reach him. The more she moved, the harder he pressed and she screamed again, involuntarily, from the sting of it. She stomped on his foot with the heel of her boot and he let up pressure enough for her to slip out. She rushed for her weapons, both of which were somewhere on the ground next to the scattered contents of her pack.

She had her sights set on Sakay's machete. It was just beyond all her containers and wrapped-up supplies. She reached forward, ready for it. Then—

Thunk.

She was horizontal, face-down in the dirt. She struggled under Ruyan's weight as he held her in place.

Twisting her body so she could get at him better, she slashed his face with her jagged, untrimmed fingernails. They wrestled until Qora ended up on her back.

In her periphery, the machete blade gleamed, but it was still too far away. Anything within reach was something useless—a pack of dried meat in the opening of her pack, the container of medicine.

The containers.

Qora strained and struggled until she got a hand free, then stretched to reach the uncapped venom. Her fingers curled around it. Gripped it.

She thrust it at Ruyan.

At first he was startled, squinting to keep the liquid out of his eyes. But it would only take a second for him to feel the effects.

Qora pushed him off and scrambled backward.

He screamed and collapsed and writhed in the dirt. His fingers looked like claws, the way he held them all curved and contorted over his face like he wanted to scrape off all his skin.

She ran and snatched up her crossbow. By the time she reached it, Ruyan was getting to his feet, grunting, his skin red and swollen. Blisters were already beginning to form, marring the face he had once displayed with so much charm.

With her pulse overwhelming her ears, she aimed her crossbow at him. He lunged toward her and she didn't have to think about it.

Shoot first, aim later.

She pulled the trigger.

He fell in a heap, with her bolt coming out of his heart.

With shaky hands still fused to her weapon, Qora picked up her pack, leaving the empty venom container behind, and ran.

ꗥꗥꗥ

That same chill came over Qora again—the one she'd felt at the ravine—even now, amid the rising heat of the lakeside.

One foot in front of the other, Qora told herself. That's all she could focus on right now. Not the ache spreading from the center of her body outward to all her limbs. Not the dead man she'd left behind.

She reloaded on the move. Then she brushed her hands over her machete sheath to find it empty.

Ruck.

She couldn't go back there. Couldn't look at what she'd done. There would be blood pooled up around the body by now. His face would be something out of a nightmare.

She told herself Sakay would understand if she left it— wouldn't he?

His voice in her head said otherwise. *"You have to deal with your demons one way or another, kantuta."*

With wary, hesitant steps, she dragged herself back up the incline to where she'd left Ruyan, her stomach twisting itself into

146

knots the whole way.

She arrived and scanned the woods, everywhere she was sure she'd been. The imprints of her struggle marked the dirt, but Ruyan himself was nowhere. The machete was gone, too.

It hadn't been that far. And how could she miss a grown man's corpse?

It was only when she located a splintered, blood-tipped bolt—and a handful of loose, copper scales—that it made sense.

A copperskin collar. Hidden under his shirt.

Bile rose into her throat.

Her bolt, no matter how accurate or precise, had cut him— but not deeply enough to kill.

"The Spinosaur and the Raptoriva"
from Asiri's Apologues

Once there was a spinosaur, who boasted that no other reptile could defeat him.

The giant herbivores three times his size came, but he bit through their long necks and severed their heads. The stocky, horned reptiles came, but he cut through their armor. The smaller carnivores with sharp teeth and claws came, but he used his size to overpower them. The pterobeasts came from the sky, but he waited for their descent, ripped off their wings, and left them for dead.

The spinosaur slayed hundreds of reptiles, until not a single clade dared to send another forward to face him. "You?" he said to the sinornithosaur. But the venomous sinorn declined. "Or you?" he said to the ankylosaur. But even the armored ankylosaur declined.

Finally, the spinosaur, desperate to show his power, saw the raptoriva settled firmly in a tree, her green wings blending into verdure. "You have been silent," he said. "Might I persuade you to fight me? It's true that I could kill you with the very breath of my roar, but at least you would die honorably for your bravery."

The raptoriva replied, "No, thank you," and turned away.

Refusing to take no for an answer, the spinosaur let out a ferocious roar that shook the trees and rattled the earth and disturbed all that dwelled there.

The raptoriva, angry that the spinosaur had disrespected her, flew swiftly on her four wings into the spinosaur's face and blinded him with the tiny claws of her feet. The spinosaur shrieked in pain, and the raptoriva flew down his throat and shredded his insides.

As the spinosaur toppled to the ground, finished off by the impact of his own weight, the raptoriva crawled up from his belly and out of his mouth.

SIXTEEN

IT HAD BEEN FOUR DAYS NOW, and Ninan's method had been fruitful. With his cunning diversions, he'd been able to steal several packages of dried food, along with a few camping supplies, extra clothing, and a couple of tools. Nothing so major as ranged weapons or skyrock, but it had been enough to keep him going—which was fortunate, since Takan had managed to intercept Mullu's airdrop to Ninan every day but one. The one bag had contained friction matches and sauropod oil, for creating smokeless flames. Ninan had used these items to fry scavenged dinosaur eggs in a stolen pan, which he'd eaten with likewise stolen jerky, dehydrated potato slices, and fruit.

It didn't seem that Takan had told anyone about Ninan's identity, otherwise he imagined there might be people seeking him out. This wasn't much of a consolation, though, because Takan could easily be saving his knowledge for some more sinister plan. But Ninan tried not to dwell on that at the moment; right now, it was all about survival and moving ahead.

At least he still had the advantage of the secret map. He'd used two off-route trails to gain some extra ground more quickly, one of which had led him to a place where the river gorge narrowed, allowing him to utilize a different—albeit more rickety—bridge than what the other competitors would have had to cross, which had put him well on his way to the next landmark.

A few hours into the morning on the fifth day, the glimmer of Lake Waylla appeared through the trees. The surface of the water was so vast and reflective that it almost seemed to be an extension of the sky. For such a large body of water, the lake was surprisingly quiet, so different from the burble of Thuqa or the hasty surge of the river rapids that poured from Qhusi's mountain peaks.

Tall reeds screened off a segment of the lakeshore's near side. Ninan stopped where the reeds were thickest, hiding his clothes and his few supplies among them, and began to wash. The water invited him with its cool depths, pulling him in, urging him to wade further—but he resisted the urge to stray from the waterfront, in favor of keeping his things close. He only waded up to the waist, then wet his face and hair, scrubbed dirt from his arms, and rinsed away the stink of his sweat. The blisters on his feet and the torn skin on his knuckles stung almost pleasantly as the water cleansed them, and his muscles welcomed the smooth fluid.

He tipped his head back in the lake until his ears filled, dampening the sounds of animal cries and wind through leaves. Literally drowning them out.

If only he could stay like this, he thought. Weightless. Buoyed up rather than pressed down. Carried rather than carrying the weight of his father's demands.

After relishing this feeling for a good while, he'd almost forgotten where he was until aggressive shouts pulled him from his trance.

He tensed, gradually lifting his head until he could make out what he was hearing. It was close—but not enough to cause him immediate danger. The reeds hid him, he reminded himself.

He changed position and moved through the water with only his eyes and nose above the surface, approaching the reeds until he could peer between them.

Three men came swiftly across the bank: the first, on the run, carrying a small burlap sack with a red stamp on it—this morning's airdrop; the second, in pursuit with a recurve bow; the third, close behind with a dagger.

Both pursuers dropped their packs, lessening the weight on their backs, which allowed them to catch up quickly, but the first man reached for a low-hanging tree branch and pulled himself up. He grabbed the next branch and the next, finding footholds in the smallest crevices among the bark.

"Shoot him!" said the man with the dagger.

The other, with a loaded bow, hesitated. "I've only got two arrows left."

"Then don't miss. We can retrieve them after—from his chest."

The man in the tree clambered higher, and then maneuvered around so that the trunk shielded him from the other two men. An arrow skimmed the bark and went soaring into the woods.

Ninan scanned the ground and quickly spotted the men's supplies that remained in the grass behind them. The packs weren't stuffed, by any means, but they might contain something useful. If he hurried, he could investigate before the other competitors noticed. He crept out of the water and carefully eased his legs back into his pants, which clung to his wet skin on the way up.

"Give us the airdrop," said the shooter, "and you won't die today!"

When the man in the tree didn't respond to his request, the shooter sent up another arrow.

Then came a grunt. The branches swayed violently as the man dropped, his body hitting the ground with the sound that had become all too familiar to Ninan these past few days.

Whumpf.

The man's limbs splayed around him. The arrow stuck out of his right eye as blood pooled behind his head.

Shirtless, and still dripping with lake water, Ninan eased toward the supplies, ever mindful of the other men, who had snatched up the dead man's airdrop and were now crouched over the body searching for additional loot.

Among the abandoned supplies, Ninan found that one of their packs contained another oilskin tarp, more jerky, and some additional friction matches. As he lifted the flap of the other pack, its buckles jangled loudly.

He went rigid.

The man with the bow—but no more arrows, thankfully— turned to see Ninan by the packs. "Kill him," he told his companion.

The man with the dagger charged, but Ninan didn't run— he readied his fists.

Ninan dipped to miss the blade. He blocked the man's swinging arm, then threw an uppercut. Another uppercut. He went for a third, but the blade sliced his shoulder.

Ninan growled through his teeth and grabbed the man's wrist, twisting until the dagger fell. He flipped the man around and cranked his arm, pressuring the bone. A second later, the other man came to assist. Ninan used a double collar tie— two hands pressed to the back of the neck, shoving down the head—to control and maneuver the first man in front of him as a human shield against the second.

The muscle memory from his training kicked in. *Don't let*

them work together; make their numbers a disadvantage.

Then it was push-kicks, a knee to the gut, more brain-rattling punches, and soon both men were unconscious heaps.

Ninan panted as the pain of his cuts and bruises flared in the wave of calm that replaced the fight. The cut on his shoulder leaked blood in a clean stripe, and would need a bandage.

Looking around, Ninan determined that there was little to steal here, and he wasn't sure it had been worth the trouble. It would all depend on what was in that airdrop. He glanced at the corpse under the tree with an arrow standing plumb in the eye socket.

Before he even opened the sack, he caught a whiff of its contents. Chalky, metallic. Eagerly, he tugged at the drawstring and widened the opening, staring down into the silvery powder. He dipped his fingers into it and pinched.

It was low grade skyrock dust, but skyrock dust nonetheless. If this was what had been in the airdrop, that meant someone had gotten their hands on the good stuff—and that someone else had probably pried those hands off of it, slashed a few throats, broken a few limbs. Surely several of these sacks had changed hands over the course of the morning. Ninan would have to hide it well, otherwise he'd end up like the competitor beside him. He stared at the arrow for a moment, grimacing.

We can retrieve them after, the shooter's friend had said.

Finally, ashamed that it had taken him so long, he registered that there was a bow here somewhere. A ranged weapon. And there was no one left to fight him for it.

He found the weapon lying on the ground a few feet away. Then a bit of searching led him to the first arrow, which had lodged in the dirt. Retrieving the second arrow was much worse, however, and Ninan cringed as he tried to wrench it from its target. Its tip was metal and barbed and held firm in the flesh where it had landed. It took several squelching pulls before it came out, bringing gobs of bloody tissue with it.

Retching, Ninan swirled the tip around in the lake to clean it, then rinsed his shoulder wound, bandaged himself, and pulled on his dinoleather vest and shirt.

Now invigorated from his victory, he summoned from within himself a more hopeful energy, and headed off with his new supplies.

SEVENTEEN

QORA STOOD NUMBLY ON THE LAKESHORE, watching the water lap against the reeds and make them sway.

She ached to step into its depths, to feel the fresh water on her skin. Others had done it; she'd seen from a hidden place as several men had stripped down and sunken themselves to bathe, all parts boldly on display. *Nothing to be proud of,* she thought. She'd gone on to locate an isolated spot with some coverage so that she could have a stretch of water to herself, but now she couldn't seem to gather the courage to use it. If someone were to see her, they might take it as an invitation. *Anything* could be an invitation, it seemed.

The scrapes on her skin reminded her of that. She inhaled slowly through her nose and held her crossbow to her chest, watching her distorted, watery reflection.

Qora wasn't about to assume she had any particular luster in terms of appearance; she was fine to look at, she supposed, but she'd never stained her lips or worn her hair long and flowing like Sakay's vendor friend Sonqo; she didn't parade around in layered skirts or have eyes well suited to dark liners or colored powders. But sometimes men—especially on a long, lonely journey like this—were just after a warm body. *That* she did have, and it suddenly felt exposed on all sides.

Finally, she knelt and splashed a bit of water on her face, pushed her sleeves up as high as they would go and wet her arms. When she'd surveyed her surroundings carefully, certain there was no one else nearby, she forced herself to take off her boots and roll up the hems of her pants and soak her feet for a few minutes, knowing she'd regret it later if she didn't allow herself some relief.

For the next while walking, she saw no one. She thought of the previous day's horn blares, fifty-three in total. But some of those competitors were ahead of her, others lagging behind and hopefully ready to wave their pennants. The width and vastness of the landscape skewed her ability to encounter too many of the rest.

She did come upon a man skinning a sciurumimus, but when Qora panicked and raised her crossbow, he only nodded blandly in acknowledgement. She noted the sprinkle of feathers at his feet, how scant they were for a sciurumimus; the climate was getting warmer by the mile, and the reptiles more bare in its wake. Reassured, she nodded in return, and kept moving.

As the sun worked its way higher, Qora once again found the landscape forcing her back to the main route. There was no longer a paved roadway, but there was still a worn trail that presented the opportunity to run into other competitors again.

Bolt snug in the flight groove, finger on the trigger.

A quarter mile or so down the path, she glanced up into the trees and stopped in her tracks. Again the trees were blunted in a few places, finer branches hacked off. Sure, the forest was thickening, but not so much yet that competitors would need to start cutting their way through—and even should they choose to, it wasn't the trees that sprawled in all directions, it was the undergrowth, the ferns and thickets and vines below.

Qora thought of Sakay's machete and felt sick.

To borrow, he had said.

Ruyan was somewhere out there with it and she had no idea if she'd be able to get it back, or whether she even wanted to try.

Meanwhile, Ninan had likely concealed another dinofelis trap somewhere nearby, and if Qora wasn't careful, she might step right into it.

Terrors at every turn.

She tried to mentally work out the process. It would take at least an hour to dig a pit that size, if not longer, and even more time to cover it and blend it in. Ninan must have risen early and done it before dawn, or maybe even set it up the previous night. With all that effort, he would have had to put it somewhere that would really count.

Except there appeared to be nothing of significance here. No bridge forcing the steps of an unwitting competitor, no spring where someone might stop to refill a waterskin, no clusters of fruit where someone might pause to eat.

Qora then spotted a traveler's satchel lying in the grass.

Her body tensed.

Had someone already fallen in? Or was the satchel empty and simply abandoned?

As she appraised the potential dangers of the situation, the underbrush began to swish and twitch.

She stepped back and raised her weapon.

Flashes of clothing and hair moved among the leaves, and then someone finally pressed through—a teenage boy carrying a blue egg the size of a papaya.

"Whoa, whoa, whoa," said Ninan. He fixated on Qora's crossbow and flinched. Cautiously—questioningly—he held out the egg. "It's all yours. There are five or six more in the nest."

Qora blinked hard. "What?"

Ninan's eyes darted toward her full pack. He raised a single brow, then tucked the egg under his arm. "Never mind. Seems like you're pretty well stocked."

"Where's the trap?" Qora demanded. She couldn't figure why Ninan would hang around so long after setting it, rather than moving on and gaining more ground, unless he got some sick satisfaction out of watching people die. Then again, maybe he hadn't just been hoping to kill someone—maybe he'd wanted to collect whatever goods they had on them once they'd been impaled.

"What trap?"

"I'm not stupid. Where did you hide it?" Still aiming at him, she snatched up a broken branch and poked at the ground with it. "Here?" Another poke. "Here?" She poked several places along the path, all of which held firm under her scrutiny.

Ninan cocked his head. "Have you been eating pamparaptor? You know, not a lot of people know this, but the liver can make you hallucinate. No one usually likes the liver, so it's mostly a non-issue, but since most of us are out here trying not to starve, it's easy to end up accidentally—"

"Here?" Another poke at the dirt.

"Not a lot of meat on them though," he continued, probably trying to distract her. "Most of their length is tail—although I guess that's true for most theropods."

Qora was still furiously testing everything, keeping her weapon trained on Ninan while she looked elsewhere. He stood calmly, like he was waiting for her to finish, which infuriated her even more. She wouldn't finish until she had revealed the trap and marked it.

"It's a cheap tactic," she told him. "Dirty, underhanded,

cowardly. You know there are some regular people traveling out here—people who don't deserve to get caught up in this stupid game, let alone die for it. And if you can't face other competitors and hold your own, maybe you don't belong in this competition."

"I still don't know what you're talking about …"

Qora stood closer to him now. Close enough that it wouldn't take an ounce of skill to shoot him square in the chest. He looked damp—partially wet hair, clothes splotched like he'd dunked himself in the lake and hadn't dried off properly before getting dressed. The thumping in her own chest picked up speed. She hadn't killed anyone directly and on purpose yet—although not for lack of trying. Ninan had probably taken enough lives by now to deserve it.

Slowly, Ninan raised his free hand like he was trying to calm a wild animal. "Why don't you just put that down, okay? I'm not going to hurt you."

Stepping closer to him and reaffirming her aim, Qora said, "Maybe not *yet*." She could still smell smoke on him vibrantly. Not a campfire smoke, but the distinct, sweet smell of the smoke bomb he'd released at the sendoff. Strange that it still hadn't faded after several days.

"Why would I hurt you? I tried to *help* you."

He had a point, but then again, Ruyan had seemed helpful at first too.

Ninan backed away, nearing the satchel in the grass.

It was possible he had a weapon in there too, Qora thought. "Don't touch it."

"Don't touch what?" He followed her gaze and frowned. "*That?*"

"I can shoot you faster than you can grab anything you might want to use against me."

"That's not even mine—" In a swift move, he reached out and got a grip on one of her crossbow's limbs.

Qora tried to pull back. "Then *whose*—"

Ninan took another step backward and instantly sank below ground—pulling Qora down with him.

EIGHTEEN

IN THAT INSTANT, Qora was Ninan's anchor—and it was clear to him that she did not want to be. Still wearing her pack, she'd already had enough dead weight to worry about when he'd inadvertently pulled her down. Qora had remained partially above ground, slowing Ninan's fall and giving him time to secure himself on something else.

Ninan caught a flash of what was below: poles of wood, sharpened to fine points and embedded at the bottom of a pit. He scrambled until he caught hold of a thick bundle of roots that had gnarled their way through the dirt, but it was too late; whatever grip Qora had had, she lost. She slipped, clawing hopelessly at the grass until it was no longer within her reach. She dug her boots into the cruel slope of the pit. The dirt eroded slowly until she skidded to a stop beside Ninan. Her weapon dangled at her hip, strapped around her body, adding more weight.

"Is *this* what you meant?" Ninan grunted, trying to pull himself higher. "You think I had something to do with this?"

Panting, Qora raised one foot and shoved it into a new spot and held herself there. "Well, *now* I'm not so sure."

The symbolism of the pit wasn't lost, Ninan thought. It was warm and humid, like the mouth of a dinofelis would be. The

161

slope was slick like an enormous tongue and seemed to draw them in, urging them toward the sharpened row of wooden teeth below. Ninan's egg was oozing out, its broken shell scattered. The satchel lay between two of the spikes, ripped open, rocks spilling out.

That was the bait, Ninan thought. Draw someone in with the hope of free supplies, then impale them with this trap.

"Clever," Qora muttered, having apparently made the same connection.

Unlike a living predator's mouth, however, the trap was stationary. The only thing actually working against them was gravity, their own weight.

"We need to stop fighting the slope and lower ourselves," Ninan said.

Qora adjusted her position, tightening her grip on a new set of roots—toes threatening to slip—and looked down. "You mean we should go slowly …"

"That's right. Those spikes are only a problem for us if we hit them at speed. On impact. Otherwise, there's enough room to stand between them, and some space around the edge."

Qora nodded.

She slammed the toe of her boot into the dirt to create another foothold, then located another bundle of roots to hold onto. Ninan followed her example and they both eased downward, bodies close to the soil, nose to nose with insects and worms.

"I think you owe me an apology," Ninan said as he dropped another inch.

"Not yet. We'll see."

"'We'll see'? Do you really think I'd be stupid enough to fall into my own trap?" Ninan touched down.

"Maybe."

Stepping from her final foothold, the roots between Qora's fingers tore out with a snap. She slipped again—only this time, the weight of her supplies threw her off balance. Ninan leapt and caught her by the arm before she keeled over and impaled herself, but the damp earth under his boots was too soft to give him support. He stumbled sideways, feet lost on uneven ground. His leg caught on the point of a spike.

He registered Qora's gasp before his own pain.

The point had punctured his skin—centimeters only, it seemed, but it had been enough to set off several alarms in his mind. He strained his face, sucking air through his teeth.

"Spirits," Qora breathed, dropping her pack and weapon and kneeling beside him.

Ninan had collapsed against the dirt wall, and eased himself until he was seated.

"I'm so sorry …" Qora said.

Ninan scoffed. "*Now* you're sorry."

Qora rummaged through her pack and took out multiple containers. She nudged his hands away from the wound and began to apply pressure.

Ninan hissed.

"It helps with the bleeding," she told him.

"Helps me bleed *more*, you mean? It feels like you're trying to squeeze the rest of it out."

She responded with a hollow scowl before she shoved the hem of his pant leg up to the knee, then opened her waterskin and rinsed the wound. Ninan clenched his teeth.

Qora dabbed his leg dry and opened one of her medicines. "Dinofire," she told him.

One mutual look between them confirmed that he understood her meaning. He braced himself for the burning sensation.

The red ointment stained his skin as if with more blood, but dried quickly and formed a seal over the wound. Ninan closed his eyes and counted his breaths to distract himself. The dinofire felt like it was soaking into the entire limb, like boiling water into porous rocks. Finally, it tapered to a numb heat.

Then Qora set to work on bandaging. The small muscle in her right forearm bulged as she worked, something she must have gotten from spanning her crossbow all the time, Ninan thought.

"You're pretty deft at all this," he said as he watched her. "If not a little rough."

She focused on his leg. "With three brothers, someone's always bleeding from somewhere."

He tried to imagine her tending to three boys of various ages. Scolding them too, no doubt. *Were you hoping to lose an eye?* She might say. Or, *Maybe next time you should watch where you're going.* But he imagined that despite her annoyance, she really loved them. He himself had never been tended by a sibling, only struck—by word and by hand—and left alone to dwell on it.

"If you have any other wounds," she added, "Now would be a good time to re-dress them."

"I don't really have any other—" he started.

But she'd already noticed the patch of dried blood on his shoulder. The thin cut underneath was relatively fresh, newly congealed and still sore.

"That one's pretty much healed," he told her.

Regardless, she tugged his shirt collar down to take a look, but then quickly seemed to forget the whole thing, staring with rapt attention at his armored vest.

Even though Ninan could barely feel it through the dinoleather, Qora's touch made the hairs on his arms stand on end. Only then did he realize how close she was as she examined the cut marks in the leather surface, the stitching of the vest. He was sure she would notice the way it was tailored to his body—not something he could have lifted off another competitor.

He tugged his collar back up. "It's not as expensive as it looks."

"Really? Because it looks *very* expensive. Not unlike that tooth dagger of yours I spotted next to the first trap I ran into."

Ninan froze. How did she know about the dagger?

"Tooth dagger?" he repeated.

"Don't play dumb. I saw it on your belt at the sendoff."

He narrowed his eyes, not sure whether it was pointless to keep up the ruse. She'd already seen the vest, after all, and it wasn't as though the dagger gave away his identity. "Fine. It could have been mine. But I lost that before I even made first camp. I don't know who left it there, but it wasn't me."

"Still, it's impressive that you can afford so many fine things."

"Winning fights pays well."

"Not *that* well."

He rolled his eyes, not about to try and defend his money—or, rather, his family's money. "Hang on ... You said 'first trap'?"

"Yes. That's how I knew what to look for. At the bridge. You didn't see it?"

Ninan shook his head. "Must've been set up after I'd already passed." Of course he couldn't tell her that he'd taken another bridge—a smaller one on a more remote path, thanks to yet another one of the benefits of his upbringing. "Anyway ... Thanks for the patch job." He indicated his leg, then pushed himself up. "But we need to get out of here."

Qora touched a tentative finger to one of the spikes, grasped it by the base, and wiggled it. Then, with a grunt, she ripped it from the ground and stood up.

"What are you going to do with that?" Ninan glanced skeptically at the two-foot spike.

In response, Qora raised it over her head and plunged it into the sloped wall as deep as it would go, giving it an extra shove for good measure. Then she kicked herself another foothold and grabbed the blunt end of the spike. It angled in her grip, pulling its own hole slightly wider in the dirt, but otherwise it held her weight. She looked at Ninan. "Think you can climb?"

Ninan was a bit slower than Qora, but in a few minutes, they'd removed all the spikes and embedded them in the wall in a pattern of footholds and handholds. Should she or Ninan fall, the bottom was bare now, with only holes where the spikes had been.

The gash on Ninan's leg felt like it was splitting open each time he put pressure on it, and it was difficult to hold himself upright against the slope, but finally, Qora made it out with her pack and reached down for him, giving him a much-needed boost to push through the pain.

Once he was above ground, he collapsed onto the grass, panting.

Qora glanced guiltily at the open trap, and even more guiltily at Ninan's leg. "Where's your stuff? I'll grab it for you."

Ninan nodded vaguely at where he'd stashed his pack before he'd gone off hunting eggs. "Actually, wait—"

He'd been a second too late to consider the fact that his dinoleather vest should be the least of his worries when it came to exposing more of his high-cost gear. Qora was already gaping as she looked over the copperskin that showed through the cuts of his poncho.

"Is this yours too?"

Technically it belonged to the qhapaq, so Ninan felt justified saying, "Not *exactly*—"

"It is." She looked at him with sudden clarity. "You were wearing this poncho the day we left Qhusi."

"Nothing in the rules against protecting yourself."

"No, there isn't," she agreed. "But this … this is a whole other level. You've got money. Lots of it."

"So what?"

"So then why have you been fighting at the Underground?"

Ninan sighed. "I don't really feel like getting into it, alright?"

How could he even begin to explain? How could he say that he was the son of the qhapaq's third wife, always relegated to the fringes of his own household? That he'd eventually been cast out to scrounge for his own money and food, and that now he was attempting to prove himself worthy of a legacy he could never seem to uphold?

"Let me guess," she said. "Your life of wealth and privilege isn't *exciting* enough for you?"

"If only it were that simple."

"And now you're trying to … to … what? To *prove* something by competing in the Venture? Or are you just in this for the interterrenal attention?"

It stung how far off she wasn't. Interterrenal attention was the ultimate goal, but he hardly wanted eyes on him in this condition—robbed and wounded and slinking through the underbrush stealing eggs.

"Anyone who enters the Venture has very severe, very personal reasons for doing so," he said. "It's not fair for you to belittle someone else's."

"There are people in this competition who are on the verge of starvation, or imprisonment, or losing everything they own. People whose very lives depend on their success. Meanwhile, you"—she held up the copperskin in demonstration—"have been prancing around in the most expensive armor, and worse, pretending to blend in, hunting a prize that can't possibly mean as much to you as it does to someone else."

"You don't know what anything means to me. You don't know me at all. Maybe I don't even want to *be* in this competition—did that ever occur to you?"

He was surprised to hear these words coming out of his own mouth. Obviously the Venture hadn't been his ideal solution to restoring his old life, but he'd chosen this. He'd accepted the assignment. Although, the more he thought about it, the more he began to question whether he'd really had the option to say no. Would the qhapaq have really let him go back to Thak to live out a lowborn's life?

Qora scowled and dropped Ninan's poncho where she'd found it, then set about gathering sticks and other debris, her jaw noticeably tight. Ninan looked on as she marked the trap—apparently to warn others of its presence.

"Word of advice?" Qora said over her shoulder. "Watch where you're walking from now on."

Ninan scoffed. "I wouldn't have gone anywhere near that thing if it hadn't been for you waving your weapon around like a lunatic. It seems more likely that *you're* the real danger here …"

"The real danger that helped you get out."

"Well, I'm not sure it was worth it if it means I have to listen to you lecture me about everything I own *and* my reasons for being here."

"Alright. Next time I'll just let you die."

"Please do."

"Deal."

"Perfect."

Qora looked to the forest, then back at Ninan, then turned to go. He stood as still as he could to keep up the act that he wasn't ready to collapse on the spot. She glanced back and it took everything in him not to tell her to wait, but she was already moving fast. Ten paces into the trees. Twenty. Fifty.

Soon, she was out of sight, with no remnant of her but the markings she'd left around the hole in the ground, and the sting of her criticism.

〉〉〉

A mile or so later, Ninan paused to catch his breath. The wound was wearing on him more than he'd expected. Every step was like thorns in his leg, particularly as the dinofire ointment continued to burn while it healed. Then, for a moment, he thought he heard Qora's footfalls, the scuff of her boots in the dirt.

Wishful thinking, he told himself. *Wait—why would I wish for that?*

As he listened more closely, he realized just how wrong he'd been about the source of the sounds.

He froze.

Through the trees, he saw flashes of orange and black. Multiple figures preening, despite minimal feathers. He'd seen them in illustrations and reptile compendiums, but never so close.

Atrociraptors.

They weren't large. Maybe thirty or forty pounds each. But each one had a mouthful of knife-sharp teeth, and limbs tipped with equally sharp claws. They sniffed the air in turn—hunting. Ninan wasn't adept enough with his looted recurve bow to feel confident defending himself against them. His skyrock-studded belt might not be enough to ward off that many, and he didn't want to waste too much skyrock dust this early if he didn't have to. Cautiously, he dipped into his pack and powdered his hands with a small amount—just in case. However, he planned to stay downwind of them. That would mean moving toward the river. He was all stocked up on water, and freshly washed from the lake, so it wasn't strictly necessary, but if going slightly out of his way kept him from being torn to shreds, it would be worth it. Besides, now he was injured.

Then, the old fisherman, weary from his labors, lay down in the empty pterodactyl nest and fell into a deep sleep.

When the pterodactyls returned, one of them said, "But what is this? Humankind has not been known to associate with the likes of us."

Another replied, "It must be a gift from the gods. They know that we have subsisted only on fish and small mammals, and that our bellies are never truly full."

"Humankind is selfish," said a third. "He will be more useful as meat. From henceforth, let us feast, and be content."

Excerpt from "The Fisherman in the Nest"

NINETEEN

ATROCIRAPTORS. THREE GANGS in the past mile and a half. Someone else might not have noticed, but Qora was familiar with the cadence of their low vibrations, could pick it out amid the swish of leaves and the swell of the river. Almost a purr. Something about it was slightly different from what she'd trained her ears to hear, though; the frequency was higher, more urgent. And she couldn't figure what the gangs were doing within sight of each other. Raptors of any kind had territories, marked them with a strong scent to keep other gangs away, and rarely crossed paths.

Qora kept closer to the route than she would have liked, yet again pressured to go where she was more likely to run into other people, and weighed the risks. Was a pack of atrociraptors really worse than competitors desperate for weapons and food? Men were not only violent, they were also vengeful. Reptiles, at least, had patterns to their behavior, some code of honor by which every one of them would abide—even if it did permit them to be vicious.

She passed another red pennant marker, estimating that she'd traveled just under a hundred and twenty miles thus far, keeping an average pace of nearly twenty-four miles per day. She worried, however, that she might not be able to continue at that pace, as her muscles ached with every step, and as the climate warmed and the landscape turned more treacherous.

Regardless, she moved south toward the river, instinctively keeping away from the reptiles, with an eerie feeling slinking up her spine. Over the next half mile, those ruddy-brown figures seemed to be closing in on the area, a strange and abrupt migration. And worse, competitors began to converge too.

Daytime was rapidly bleeding to dusk, and every visible human gaze swept upward as the heralds flew over. Horns rang out, loud and sharp.

One, two, three, four, five …

The echo of the day's final count—*seventeen, eighteen, nineteen*—seemed to mock the remaining competitors, who had inadvertently reunited to avoid the monsters surrounding them, only to then encounter the monsters among themselves.

Twenty-five, twenty-six.

Silence.

The sudden hiss of an arrow made Qora duck. An instant later, some other competitor slumped into the ferns with that arrow in his chest. Fists flew, blades swung. Qora kept low and hurried toward the riverbank, away from all the fights that had begun to break out.

When she reached the bank, she gazed down its length and spotted six or seven huge nests about a quarter mile off, barely visible, clustered at the water's edge. Pterodactyls of all sizes sat within them, indigo blue with pale markings. They chattered in communication, a distinct sound that Qora was already committing to memory—a gentle croak that quickly turned shrill—something else for her ever-growing, auditory catalog of the creatures she might encounter, because she'd be damned if she ever caught herself unprepared again.

Several of the pterodactyls turned their attention to the clamor in the woods nearby.

Qora suddenly remembered what Sakay had said. *Drawn to bright lights and loud noises.*

Loud noises, particularly those implying conflict. A situation where they might pick off prey wounded by other predators.

And those idiots—Qora caught glimpses of the other competitors—were roughing each other up as comfortably as if they'd been brawling on their own city street.

A few of the pterodactyls squawked and took flight, soaring up over where the competitors had amassed. Grunts and shouts turned to blood-curdling screams. Arrows and bolts went high; a pterodactyl here or there would swerve and crash, while others dragged competitors away. More pterodactyls followed. Qora gasped and tucked herself behind a tree, panting. She hugged her loaded weapon to her chest and performed her silent ritual.

Stay still. Keep quiet.

She was so focused on steadying her breath, on listening to the croaks and squawks and squeals to gauge their distance, that the blade against her throat came as a surprise.

Qora's stomach dropped.

The shabby likeness of a dinosaur stared back at her—the man with his face painted white and black, marked in reptilian patterns. Those features were hard to forget, even though days of sweat and trips to the river had muddled them.

"Give it here." His lips drew back and bared yellowed teeth.

Qora winced. "Give what?"

"All of it. Whatever you've got."

Qora subtly tightened her grip on her crossbow handle. The curving limbs of the weapon were small, but they were made of metal, and they flared out on the ends, forming points where they held the bowstring.

She maneuvered the crossbow sideways, thrusting a point into the man's belly. He made a guttural noise as he folded, dropping his blade. And Qora ran.

But the man was back on her before she could shoot. He'd come from behind, tightened his arms around her shoulders, directed her away from him and jammed her hand on the trigger, forcing her to fire her bolt into the rapids.

Qora wrestled uselessly against him. He tried to tear off her pack, and when he couldn't, he cut the flap and snatched at the items inside. Contents spilled along the bank.

He picked up her firestick.

An arrow soared between them, just shy of nicking the man along its trajectory—although it probably wouldn't have deterred him anyway. Qora spared a glance at its source, only to see Ninan approaching the bank, out of breath and limping as he hurried to nock another arrow in some old bow that didn't seem suited to what Qora now knew of his finances. She was surprised he'd caught up so quickly, considering her own speed after she'd left him behind, and the fact that he was injured.

Qora leapt for the firestick, firming her grip on it, but the man's grip was firm too. He held the end with the sparkcord and, in an effort to keep it, jerked back, taking only the cord with him, stumbling and landing flat. The man rolled to dodge a second arrow from Ninan as the firestick snapped and sizzled in Qora's palm.

Before Qora could process the danger, red sparks spewed from the tip. She thrust the tube at the man's face. He screeched at the fiery sparks and shoved her arm vertical, just as the firestick launched a bright flare that streaked above the treetops and exploded.

All three competitors looked up. Flashes of red strobed over them. Seconds later, the cry of a pterodactyl pierced the air. Then came another cry, and another. There must have been at least five wild flyers coming, Qora thought.

Bright lights and loud noises.

In a matter of seconds, the flyers arrived, bluish and looming with wingspans at least thirty feet wide and pointed beaks that looked sharp enough to bore holes through a log.

Qora and Ninan both turned back for the trees.

The painted man tried to follow, but one of the pterodactyls swooped down and plucked him up by his shoulders. He unsheathed a larger blade from his belt and swung at the pterodactyl until it dropped him—and realized too late that this was not a favorable outcome. His leg bones splintered when they hit the ground. He screeched as the pterodactyl took him up again and carried him away.

The final sparks of the firestick flashed as Qora and Ninan raced deeper into the woods.

Qora found her crossbow and quiver, hastily arming herself as another pterodactyl came in from the side. She slumped to the ground and rolled to a sitting position, then shot at the flyer's underside. It swayed and plummeted, still flapping and screeching even after it hit the dirt. Qora reloaded and shot again, but the pterodactyl crawled toward her, relentless.

Heralds approached at a distance, drawn to the commotion—not so different from the pterodactyls, Qora thought, except that the heralds were preying on the spectacle rather than the meat of human flesh.

Ninan held the grip of his recurve bow but appeared to have no arrows left. Yet another pterodactyl swooped in, dividing Qora's attention as she fought off the first one and struggled to reload in the darkening woods. In a desperate act, Ninan swung his bow like a bludgeon, smashing the airborne pterodactyl square in the snout as it came at him. It slowed, flapping angrily, then chomped off one of the bow limbs.

With his leg wound, Ninan wasn't fast enough to get away. He stopped to remove his belt, then swung it in a wide circle—it must have been studded with skyrock, Qora thought, too horrified to be resentful at the moment—but the flyer hissed and tore it away. With three flaps of those giant blue wings, it lifted Ninan dangerously high.

"Qora!" Ninan shouted.

Qora finally shot the other pterodactyl between the eyes, then fumbled to load another bolt. Within seconds, Ninan was dangling higher in the air than the painted man had been, and Qora hoped he wasn't stupid enough to try to get the flyer to drop him too.

She locked the bolt in place and shot.

A miss.

Come on.

The flyer lifted Ninan higher still, and swooped off down the bank.

Span.

Load.

Shoot.

The next bolt zoomed high but fell short. Qora stomped.

Ninan's figure shrank into the distance.

Why should I even care? Qora asked herself. This was to her advantage. Another competitor dead and gone.

Still, she couldn't shake the guilt that she'd been wrong about him, at least as far as his intention to viciously kill competitors and travelers in underhanded traps, even if he was some spoiled highborn. And not only had he come to her aid just now—or tried to, despite his horrendous aim—he'd used his last two arrows to do it.

She hung her head back and groaned.

Knowing exactly where he was going to end up, she picked up her quiver of bolts and dashed after him.

Hopefully she could get to him while he was still alive.

TWENTY

NINAN SQUEEZED HIS EYES SHUT, breathing through clenched teeth as he tried not to hyperventilate.

The pterodactyl dragged him through the air by his shoulders, its claws pinched tight while his body hung heavily below. It was only thanks to his dinoleather vest and the straps of his pack that the claws didn't pierce his flesh.

Don't think about the height.

No matter what he told himself, his body knew this wasn't normal. His heart slammed against the inside of his chest like it was trying to get out. His veins felt like they were on fire.

He'd given up shouting, more worried about being dropped prematurely than where this creature was taking him and what it planned to do when they got there. Some part of Ninan thought he might be able to come up with a plan in that time, figure out a way to break free when they were close to landing.

But the entire trip took only a few seconds before the pterodactyl descended on a cluster of giant nests on the ground at the edge of the water. He got the chance to observe the scene for an instant: eggs the size of human heads, grayish and spotted; *actual* human heads, and other various human and animal body parts ripped from their trunks, while pterodactyls young and old fed on them; piles of fish bones discarded along the perimeter.

Somewhere, a man screamed like his limbs were being ripped off, and suddenly fear gripped Ninan more tightly than the claws that kept him airborne.

Then he was dropped into the mayhem.

The stench forced bile into his throat. Rotting flesh on a bed of guano.

Ninan crumpled at the bottom of the nest—hard-packed twigs, branches, dry grass and leaves, with a sticky sealant. The reptiles snapped their tooth-ridged beaks. First Ninan felt them on his feet, then his legs. The young pterodactyls were as big as he was. He kicked and swatted with a fury. His pack protected him from behind, although the reptiles snapped at it, tearing some of the smaller, outer compartments—including the one that held his secret map, whose routes he'd used to catch up to everyone after the pit trap.

"No!" he cried as one of the pterodactyls ripped the map away and shredded the canvas. The reptiles also scattered the majority of his friction matches. But of course he had more important things to worry about right now.

His dinoleather vest buffered the attacks on his chest and ribs but the reptiles came for his face too. He thrust his hands forward, thinking it would only be a matter of seconds before they bored holes into every part of him, cutting through his fingers to chisel out his eyes.

A hiss stung his ears. The closest pterodactyl flared its nostrils and recoiled.

Ninan's hands were still coated in skyrock dust. It wasn't much, but he'd been sure to lodge some of it under his fingernails when he'd seen the atrociraptors.

Atrociraptors that had never actually emerged, he realized. Everyone had fled from the looming threat, apparently for nothing. He'd have to consider the implications of that later.

He reached out to the other pterodactyls, letting them smell the dusty residue. They hissed and backed away. This bought him a couple of minutes as he tried to climb up over the rim of the nest, but larger pterodactyls from other nests advanced on him, snapping their beaks at his traveling pack. He wondered briefly if he might be able to reach inside and grab the entire pouch of skyrock dust, but there wasn't time.

He made it partway over the edge, only to find two more nests butted up against it, and all the while the pterodactyls yanked on his clothes and limbs, fighting over him, pulling him back. Still, he managed to launch himself into an empty nest.

With an instant of mobility, he grabbed hold of his blade and hacked at the reptiles on his heels. A youngling clamped onto his ankle and he sliced its neck. It screeched and swiped a wing-claw across his cheek. A grown pterodactyl came to its aid. Two more followed. They overwhelmed Ninan, the largest of them undeterred by the skyrock dust on his hands.

The bigger the breed, the more you need.

His forearms took the brunt of the attack.

Little by little his energy faded. His strength dissolved and his resistance crumbled. He was buried in a mess of blue, stretched-membrane wings and what was left of other men and animals who had lost the will to fight. The stench of decay and waste choked him. There was nothing left to do.

Then, out of nowhere, the reptiles began to spring back.

Ninan peered through shaking fingers to see crossbow bolts stuck between scales—two, three, four—every few seconds there was another, until the pterodactyls fell dead. Weary, Ninan glanced down the bank. Outside the cluster of nests, Qora spanned, loaded, and shot as fast as she could. If Ninan hadn't been fighting for his life—or at the very least, his limbs—he would have allowed himself to watch her slinging bolts, mesmerized by the vision of her slaying monsters like a warrior queen from folklore. Instead, he stumbled as he climbed over the other nests. Reptiles squealed and fell around him. Thanks to Qora, he escaped the cluster and leapt to the ground, which was thick with mud and sludge. He pushed off against the pain in his leg and limped until Qora met him. The rest of the reptiles scattered into the air and across the nests in a frenzy.

"We have to go," Qora said, ducking under Ninan's arm and bracing his middle.

Out of breath, he replied, "No kidding."

"No," she said, "I mean we *really* have to go. I'm out of bolts."

⟫⟫⟫

Once they were far enough from the bank and with plenty of foliage to cover them, Ninan allowed Qora to deposit him in a seated position, propped up against a thick log.

They couldn't be sure how many competitors had died by pterodactyl or by one another's hands in recent conflicts, but the woods felt almost quiet now. They'd have to wait until tomorrow's horns for more information—after the pteranodons had had time to sniff out the corpses for the heralds to identify and count.

Qora listened intently to the night for several minutes, shushing Ninan whenever he tried to ask what she was doing, and finally determined that the threat of atrociraptors had subsided.

Ninan, who still heard the ongoing chorus of chirping night flyers and growling land reptiles—which he hoped were nestled in caves and dens—wasn't convinced. "You can tell which is which?"

"I can tell your voice from mine, can't I? It's the same thing. They all have patterns, rhythms. Some are smooth, others are rough; some sing, others croak."

"They all sound pretty much the same to me."

"What doesn't make sense is the atrociraptors' behavior," she continued as though she hadn't heard him. "Why did they cluster like that? And then they just suddenly … dispersed?"

It could have been some strange, natural phenomenon, Ninan thought, but he remembered what Mullu had said before the entrance trials. *This is not just a competition, Apo-Kimsa, it's a show.* All that talk about the way things had been set up, manipulated to incentivize "interactions."

"Probably intentional," he said. "Maybe they were being … herded."

"How?"

He shook his head. "Skyrock, I'd guess. The Venture coordinators should have access to plenty of it. I wouldn't put it past them to try and set up a battleground by forcing everyone together in fear of carnivorous reptiles … and then simply letting the reptiles go back to their usual activities."

For a split second, he imagined himself as one of those atrociraptors, moved about by forces he couldn't see, driven onward by his own sense of discomfort and his instinct to avoid it.

"Hmm." Qora pursed her lips bitterly, then pulled out a glass container that immediately glowed green, underlighting her face.

Ninan frowned. "What's that?"

"Mushrooms."

"Mushrooms?"

"Bioluminescent. The darkness causes a chemical reaction that makes them emit light. I have to keep them moist so they stay alive, but they're useful."

She handed Ninan the container. It held five mushrooms with round caps that glowed green, thick stems nestled on bark and moss layered underneath, a buildup of moisture on one side of the glass.

"Sky Mother looks after us," Qora said.

Ninan returned the mushrooms. "It seems she does."

The gods had always been more of a formality in Ninan's household. Figures featured in fine art or mentioned in passing as part of the cultural rhetoric, but little more. Sometimes he thought he felt a spiritual presence in his life, guiding him or giving him hope; other times, his existence felt bleak and pointless. Particularly now.

Sitting still made him more aware of every wound and injury in a way that fighting for his life had not. Without the bloodrush of a will to survive in the clutches of angry monsters, he focused on the lesions, the places where the reptiles had snapped at his skin or bit into him, the muscles between his neck and shoulders that throbbed deeply from the prolonged pinch of pterodactyl foot-claws. Who had been watching over him? No gods he knew of. Only Qora.

"Here." Qora offered him a full waterskin. She knelt in front of him, pouring water into his mouth. He was too weary to insist that he could hold it on his own—which would be close to a lie anyway—and he choked down the water, so thirsty he could hardly bother to swallow correctly, dribbling all over his chin and the front of his clothes. Qora dabbed his skin and vest with a cloth and said nothing, continuing to offer him more as the night darkened.

When he stopped for a breath, Qora sniffed the air around him. "You still smell like that manufactured smoke from the sendoff."

Ninan bent his head to his chest and inhaled. "Yeah, I guess I do. I've been burning it often enough."

She narrowed her eyes. "What do you mean?"

"I set off smokers every day. Other competitors come running because they think someone's got a fire going, hoping to raid, but then I ... well, let's just say I'm always ready and waiting for them."

Qora's expression soured. "You lure them to you and then you *kill* them?"

"What? No. I just give them a beating. They've come with the intent to rob me, after all; I think that's fair. Don't you? Equally fair if I grab a few supplies off them."

"Sure." She stared at him.

"Anyway. I thought I told you to let me die ..."

She set down the water and unwrapped a few items from her pack, one of which appeared to be a portion of leftover meat. "You heard the guys at the Underground—I'm not exactly known for being cooperative." She set the meat on a cloth in his lap. "Eat. You must be starving."

The smell of the meat—a gamey aroma—gripped him, but he held back. "What makes you say that?"

"This morning I found you foraging for eggs ..."

"Maybe I like eggs."

She gave him a sideways look and began to gather up sticks. "You have a weapon, but you obviously don't know how to use it. I saw you shoot, remember? A little while ago at the river? You probably couldn't hit the broad side of a triceratops."

Ninan picked at the food but said nothing.

"Sorry." Qora softened. "That was rude. I know you were trying to help." She rolled one of the sticks between her fingers. "I mean, you *did* help."

She was selective with her sticks, tossing a couple of them back and searching for others, amassing a collection where each piece was similar in thickness and relative straightness. Once she seemed satisfied with the lot, she tightened a fist around the bundle and sighed. "Thank you, by the way."

Ninan swatted the air, but even such a small movement was painful. Finally, he ate. He tried to pace himself, but he was so hungry he ended up eating most of the meat in a matter of minutes. When he looked up, Qora was watching with raised eyebrows.

Mouth still half full, he looked down at his lap guiltily.

Qora sat with her sticks and stripped the bark with a small knife. "I already ate. Once I'm done with these bolts, I can hunt again tomorrow. It's not any trouble."

Ninan grumbled at her breezy reply.

Not any trouble.

She stopped to look at him again, this time with a roving gaze that made it seem like she was tallying up the scrapes on his face and arms. "That was really dumb, you know. Coming down to the bank with your leg like that."

"I know."

After she'd stripped all the sticks bare, she began to shave off knots and bumps. "Why'd you do it?"

He lifted a shoulder. "Seemed like the right thing to do. Thought you deserved a fair chance at this whole thing, I guess."

"I appreciate the effort, but none of this is fair and you know it. Not in the Venture, not in life."

"If I can tip the scales now and then, I try to. Anyway, why did *you* come after *me*? Taking on more than a dozen flyers by yourself? That was pretty dumb too."

"It was on the way."

"On the way?"

Qora nodded. "The nests were banked downriver. It gained me a quarter mile toward the ruins. Plus, I can't travel safely at night anyway; it wasn't like I had anything better to do."

"Probably could've gotten some extra sleep."

"Sometimes I'd rather not bother to try."

Ninan huffed. "Can't argue with that."

He would sleep better now that he had some skyrock dust, though, if that weak stuff even worked.

Suddenly he wondered about Qora, whether she had any protections besides her weapons, but he wasn't sure whether he should ask. "Well, I'm glad I didn't inconvenience you too much."

"You inconvenienced me the perfect amount."

"Oh, good."

He watched her for a few minutes while she perfected the sticks, deftly turning them to bolt shafts. The way her fingers worked, the smooth lines she made. "For what's it worth," he told her, "I'm sorry about that day at the Underground."

Qora shook her head. "It's fine."

"No, it isn't. You deserve credit for what you can do."

"I don't need credit."

"Still, I'm sorry."

She'd moved on now to whittling tips. "You're not the only one who's made that assumption."

"Can't say I'm surprised." He'd seen how the other traders treated her. He imagined they felt territorial over the Underground and simply didn't like her making money in their domain. And while plenty of women held military positions, it wasn't uncommon for more brutish men to cling to ideals of the past. Ninan hadn't meant to underestimate Qora so easily; it was only because she was so young, and so apparently out of place among the other traders and hunters, that he'd made a foolish assumption.

"That's why I always used to lie," she said. "The first time I brought in a kill, I told Sakay it was my papáy's. He believed it, even though it didn't make sense that a hunter would send his young daughter to negotiate a trade—because it made more sense than if I'd killed it myself. But eventually he figured it out. I couldn't help arguing that my shot was from a 'perfect broadside angle,' or demanding more money when I knew how hard it was to get some of those reptiles and how valuable they were. And of course he never *saw* my papáy ... since I no longer have one."

"What happened to him? If I can ask."

"Died in a wall collapse when I was nine. He was a drystone worker. Caught in a bad spot on the wrong day."

"I'm sorry."

She shrugged.

"Where'd you learn to shoot like that anyway?" he asked. "Not that you had to be *taught*, necessarily—"

"My brother."

Ninan nodded at the crossbow. "That his weapon? It looks military, and you're not old enough ..."

"He was in the Guard," she confirmed.

"'Was.'"

"Right."

Ninan leaned back against the log. "Sorry again."

Qora's expression spoke of loss, but there was other pain

there Ninan couldn't quite decipher—something that went deeper than the death of a loved one—a *compilation* of sorrows, he thought. Ninan himself hadn't lost much, but he also didn't love much, and the family relations he had were tainted by rivalries and discord. Still, all of that had shaped him, and he wondered what it was, exactly, that had shaped Qora.

After finishing the last of the tips, Qora loaded one of her new bolts into her crossbow and stood. "I should get going." Beyond her assistance to Ninan, it seemed she had only stopped to re-arm herself.

"Going where?"

"I don't know. Somewhere else. You'll be fine, won't you? I'm sure you've got something useful in that bag—other fine protective gear to keep you safe from monsters and men alike."

Ninan glanced at his traveling pack, little more than a limp pile of canvas. If he'd had half the things he'd set out with, Qora would have been right to assume he was relatively safe and protected. Now having lost most of his supplies, and having spent multiple days scraping by, he had a sense of what she and some of the other competitors might be dealing with.

He swallowed. "Why don't you … stay?"

Qora tensed noticeably.

"You're already here," he reasoned. "That waxing crescent is hardly enough to see by, and those mushrooms won't light more than a foot or two ahead of you. Besides, there's that whole 'strength in numbers' thing …"

His visit to the pterodactyl nests had given him a new perspective, suddenly making the threat of reptilian predators all the more real. But aside from not wanting to withstand the usual nighttime horrors alone—at least not tonight—he found within himself a growing aversion to the idea of Qora out on her own in the darkness, too.

"Nothing I can't handle." She shouldered her pack, tucked the mushroom jar under her arm, and turned to go.

"I have skyrock dust," he blurted.

Mid-step, she stopped. She didn't look at him just yet, frozen like she was actually considering. Ninan wasn't sure how much she'd had to defend herself during these brutal nights, but he figured she might not want to deplete her fresh supply of ammo if she didn't have to.

She threw him a sharp look over her shoulder. "Really?"

"I mean, I stole it off a dead guy—who I didn't kill, by the way. It's low potency, probably diluted with chalk or talc. Just looted it today."

In the mushroom glow, Ninan could almost swear that Qora's eyes were watering.

"I also have an oilskin tarp," he added. "Figured I'd lay it flat, pour the dust into a barrier along the edge on top of it and collect it in the morning so it can be used again. Have to be careful of wind, though."

"Resourceful," Qora said.

"I dusted my hands with it earlier. That's actually what saved me, I think, from the pterodactyls—until you came after me, that is."

Qora slowly returned to where Ninan sat and put her pack down, but didn't drop her weapon. She looked at him squarely. "Alright, I'll stay. But you better not make me regret this."

TWENTY-ONE

QORA'S HAMMOCK HUNG ABOVE where Ninan slept on his tarp, utilizing the vertical space above the ring of skyrock dust and keeping them both within its bounds. Qora had scoured Ninan's supplies and taken all his weapons—something he seemed to think a bit extreme, but he hadn't protested. He sleep-breathed roughly two feet below her, creating a hush that helped wash out the sounds that usually kept her wide awake and alert.

She still clutched her crossbow in her sleep, but for the first time in almost two weeks, she didn't startle awake at every rustle of leaves or shift in forest debris. She fell asleep to Ninan's rhythm and, for the most part, stayed that way all night.

In the morning, she woke at the first sign of dawn, gently stepping over Ninan and packing her things in silence. Before she left, she took one last look at him—his thick eyelashes and bruised jaw and mussed hair—then set his serrated-tooth dagger beside him. An apology of sorts. She had to admit she was relieved to learn he was innocent, and amused to learn that all these idiotically obvious campfires had been a smoke trick, intentionally set up by him.

She wasn't sure whether she should have saved him, though; he may not have deserved to *die*—and he'd helped her, for whatever reason—but he could still become an obstacle for her later. It might have been best to let the nature of the competition take care of him; after all, he'd entered knowing the risks and accepted them. But it didn't matter now, she supposed. What was done was done.

TWENTY-TWO

NINAN UNSHEATHED THE TOOTH DAGGER and ran his fingertips over the surface. Tree sap clogged the crevices between serrations and dirt stained the enamel; he'd have to clean it when he had the time, but for now, he was just relieved to have it back. Qora, however, was gone, like some ghost of the night, a spirit whose form could not be seen in daylight but whose essence lingered, haunting him.

This dagger had been the incriminating factor, the thing that had led Qora to believe he was a heartless architect of deadly snares. He wondered who had had it before her, and how many times it had changed hands since the initial theft. But at least now Qora knew he wasn't malicious.

Not that he cared what she thought of him.

Carefully, he lifted the edges of his oilskin tarp and let all the skyrock dust fall to the center, then scooped it back into its pouch. Despite Qora having fed him the night before, his stomach groaned, and he had nothing to hunt with now that one of those pterodactyls had halved his recurve bow. He tried to use Takan's bola to trip up a small oviraptor, but the cords landed wrong—due to Ninan's complete lack of skill with them—and the oviraptor dragged the weapon off into the woods. He ended up slicing some bristled-sawgill mushrooms from a rotting log, and wondered whether it would have been both more flavorful *and* more filling to have eaten a handful of dirt instead. Maybe he'd try scavenging for eggs again later.

After that, it was a long morning of walking, as always. The terrain was changing gradually, and seemed to provide new challenges every time Ninan had just adapted to the previous ones. And today, his body was sore and stiff in a way he hadn't experienced before, thanks to those wild flyers and his narrow escape from them.

Later, the Rock Forest was visible in the distance, and Ninan braced himself for the wearisome journey across rocky terrain with little to no shade, while his leg continued to throb.

Before he got terribly close, though, a shadow danced over the ground in front of him, prompting him to look up. Mullu soared on pteranodonback, urging the flyer into a descending turn. Ninan checked his surroundings instinctively, but it occurred to him now that Mullu had probably already done that—and from a better vantage point—otherwise he wouldn't be landing in the first place.

Ninan approached the man as the pteranodon touched down.

"We only have a minute." Mullu removed a weapon from the flyer's saddlebags and handed it down.

A crossbow.

"How did you—"

"The body count's high after last night," he explained. "More than two dozen. The 'dons have had their work cut out for them, but it's given me plenty of opportunities to land without suspicion—and a good number of spoils to choose from."

Ninan examined the crossbow. It had a polished wooden stock and foregrip, a curved handle, and a metal flight groove, limbs, and trigger. It was bulkier than Qora's compact, straight-handled weapon with its sheen long worn off, and frankly, he couldn't imagine himself operating it with any amount of grace.

You probably couldn't hit the broad side of a triceratops.

"Thanks," Ninan told him anyway.

Mullu tossed him a bag full of smaller, mystery items. "You might find some of that helpful as well. The most coveted goods were already picked over by other competitors, but there's a bit of food, tools ..."

Looking into the bag, Ninan found a package of dry-cured organ meats, a mosquito net, medicine, bandages, knives, and a quiver of bolts for the new crossbow. He sifted through it all, then wrinkled his nose at the organ meats—hearts and kidneys and livers that appeared to belong to smaller reptiles—wondering what sort of competitor had been the one to lose them. Had it been one who didn't *want* to waste? Or one who *couldn't afford* to? It was like he was right back in Thak, living off the scraps of nature. He tried to console himself with the idea that at least he wouldn't have to cook these shriveled things, since they were already cured and flavored.

"Best pick up the pace," Mullu added. "Your father's not pleased with your progress."

"Shame he hasn't gotten his wish yet—neither a valiant son, nor a dead one."

"If you don't get a leg up, you're much more likely to be the latter." Mullu clicked his tongue and shouted "Rise!" at the pteranodon, and in a billow of whitish wings, he was up and gone.

Those who expect treasure from
All the things that shine,
May find a gleaming dagger
Embedded in the spine.

From "The Gem of Utupya"

TWENTY-THREE

QORA NEARED THE ROCK FOREST, marked by crude drawings on her map. She'd heard of it before, a place that was said to be a mass of tall rock formations, many of them narrow like pillars. No one knew for sure what had created them, but some believed they were formed by lava, flowing under the earth and breaking through, spewing up and hardening, then wearing thin. The Volcano Kañay wasn't much farther, and so all of the surrounding land was likely rampant with liquid fire bubbling under the surface.

Like death, Qora thought. A fiery threat, always lurking and ready to bust through. She thought of Rimaq, delicate and small, while the Grave World beckoned him daily. The idea scraped her nerves raw, and she walked on faster, like she might be able to physically outrun it if she put forth enough effort.

With this category of thoughts on her mind, however, it seemed an eerie coincidence that she then came across a corpse—a man lying across her path. Flies buzzed over a gaping gut wound. She covered her nose and mouth and approached slowly.

The man's dark hair had begun to gray at the temples. He had wrinkles on his forehead deep enough that Qora imagined them to be permanent even during times when he hadn't been particularly expressive in life. He was barefoot. He had no weapons on him (those belonged to some other competitor now).

She stopped to look at him, forcing herself to face the reality of it. So many had been killed in the past few days that it had begun to feel commonplace. Qora hadn't known any of them, but she was sure not all of them had deserved it. This man might have had a family; he might have even hoped to change their future by winning the Venture. Any family still would, of course, receive a sum of money for his sacrifice—and she wondered if he, like her, was worth more dead than alive.

The last stretch was a blur, more woods and grass and thinly clouded sky. By mid-morning, Qora came upon the foretold collection of rocky formations that protruded from the ground, jagged and dark gray with whitish minerals and lichens on them. There were hundreds of these formations, all rising up in different shapes, clustered together, ranging in height from three or four feet all the way to fifty or more. The trees were thinned out significantly around their perimeter and cleared completely from their midst, which was about a quarter mile across. Qora imagined the lava—millennia, or maybe hundreds of millennia ago—bursting through the ground and burning whatever had been there before.

The formations of the Rock Forest towered over her. Broken rocks filled the spaces between them. Persistent, leafy plants pushed up through cracks and crevices. When she got up close, she explored the formations' texture. The shape of one of them reminded her of a parasaur's head, the top of the rock forming a long, back-swooping crest shape on one side and the likeness of a snout that split like an open mouth on the other.

She considered going around, skirting the outer edge of

the cluster of formations. It would be a shorter distance to pass through them, but she'd also have to watch her step the whole way to keep from stumbling on uneven terrain.

Then she reasoned that a higher vantage point might be helpful in deciding her route, and she went up, stepping and gripping. When she reached a spot—relatively high up, although nowhere near the tops of the highest formation—she sat.

Other formations spanned out below, dark like trees hacked off and burnt. Sinister as it was, Qora's heart swelled at the sight of it. Everything below seemed small for once, rather than daunting and overwhelming. As long as she was up here, she could pretend she was unreachable, untouchable. She could see what was ahead and what was behind. All this air was hers to breathe. She basked in this feeling for a few minutes, catching her breath, resting her legs, sipping her water.

Her fantasy shattered, however, as Ruyan emerged from the bordering woodland.

Qora's stomach turned sour.

There was a bloody patch on his chest, dried and brown—where her bolt pierced his concealed copperskin collar. His complexion was sallow, and crusted over with blisters. Sakay's machete hung from his belt.

Ruyan hadn't seen her yet, as far as she could tell. He consulted his map, then appeared to scan the tops of the formations. Qora waited, still as the stuff she sat on, barely breathing.

When he entered the Rock Forest, Qora ducked and began to lower herself to the shorter formations closest to her feet. Ruyan progressed gradually until he was near enough to see her—but he seemed to be looking for something else, something beyond her. Qora had just turned to secure her footing when another distantly approaching figure caught her attention. Then another two. First the competitor with the pickaxe and rope. Next, the one with the suit of dinoleather armor, cracked and coated in grime. And finally, Killay with her bandoliers and a dwindling supply of knives.

Everyone was moving deeper into the formations—but why?

Then it hit her like a stampede of ceratopsians.

"Lift your gaze to the gods in gratitude."

She'd assumed the midpoint prize would come as another airdrop, but the qhapaq had also said it was "in similitude of the main event." The Venture's final prize was always located in some dangerous place and often in some precarious position. And what, in this case, could be more precarious than the tops of these narrow, eroded formations?

Qora lowered herself faster.

As her boots hit the rocky ground, she looked up at all the formations, trying to find what was significant among them, whatever she'd missed before. There was nothing on the near side of the Rock Forest, however; it couldn't be that easy. She continued to look among those at the far side, but there were so many variations within the rock—with some formations blocking others—that it was a wonder any of the competitors actually believed they could find the prize here.

What a waste of time, she thought.

Just like the airdrops, which she had avoided at all costs. And that was probably part of the reason she was still in the game. Vying for those airborne supplies had cost many competitors their lives. This was no different.

She shook her head and turned to back out of the Rock Forest, not wanting to get caught up among more competitors coming through—but the crunch of another pair of boots behind her sent her into fight mode.

She aimed her weapon.

Ninan held up both hands, palms out.

Qora sighed and let her shoulders relax. "Seriously? How are you here already?"

He shrugged. "Must've woken up just a few minutes after you left."

Qora frowned.

"What?" he said. "It's not like I'm *following* you. We're going to the same place, remember? And this is a landmark."

He seemed to have picked up a few things along the way, Qora thought, taking note of a new fullness to his pack and a clunky crossbow hooked to the back of it.

Shaking her head, Qora said, "Okay. Fine. Good luck with this." She gestured at the haphazard cluster of formations. "I'm going around."

"You mean you don't want to get into a bloody fight over whatever prizes are up there?"

As he pointed, Qora glanced up and spotted what everyone else seemed to want.

Somewhere in the center of the mass, atop each of the tallest, narrowest juts, was a rope-net bag full of copper balls. Five bags in total.

Qora didn't recognize them as anything in particular, and looked to Ninan for explanation.

All he said was "Ruck."

"What are they?"

"Firebombs. Military weapons," he explained. "Copper casing with two compartments inside, both full of incendiaries. On impact, the compartments break and react. The whole thing explodes."

Qora thought this over, quickly understanding why such a

thing would be valuable. Not only for killing other competitors with little room for error, but also for fighting whatever monsters waited at the end of this whole thing. Provided a competitor could get the firebombs there without accidentally detonating them. It was almost tempting—such a vast amount of firepower in small containers. She'd be crazy not to admit that she needed this more than most.

But a distant screech pulled Qora's attention to the western horizon, where five white, winged figures approached.

The heralds, looking over the route for action. And when Qora looked back at the prize that was up for grabs, something made her think they might get to see some.

"Look," Qora said.

A tattooed, Allpan woman scaled one of the formations for the firebombs. She had a spear strapped across her back, and climbed with the ease of a spider.

Meanwhile, the others advanced. Loose rocks clacked under the shifting weight of their bodies. Some of the competitors were visible between formations. Knowing they were approaching on all sides, Qora felt like all her blood had pooled in her lower legs, weighing her down where she stood.

"Let's go," said Ninan. "It's not worth our lives to have those."

Qora nodded. She did need the firebombs, but she was much more likely to be victim to an explosion while other competitors grappled over them. Ninan was right; it wasn't worth the risk. She followed him and pushed forward through the Rock Forest, hurrying over the uneven terrain, ducking behind formations as needed. The prize formations were at the Rock Forest's far side, and she and Ninan passed them as the Allpan woman reached the top and snatched the netted bag. Ninan cringed when the copper balls *tinked* together, but the minimal impact failed to set them off.

The Allpan woman descended, now with difficulty as she held the firebombs. Strategically, she stopped and slipped the spear through the netted bag's holes, then adjusted it in her straps so her hands were both free. Except that the spear stretched the hole wider, tearing it to double its width. One of the firebombs slipped through the opening.

Terror filled Ninan's eyes. Qora followed his lead a few yards out of the way before he screamed "Get down!"

Another *tink*, only louder this time, and then a blast followed, fast and sharp, with an echo. They crouched beside the boulders covering their heads. Gravel spewed over them, hitting their backs like hail. A second firebomb struck the ground, spewing more rocks, each emitting a flash of heat and a puff of black smoke that rose and dissipated almost instantaneously.

The third firebomb didn't sound, but additional formations cracked and crumbled from their bases, having cracked during the explosions. Ninan and Qora glanced over their shoulders at the formations. Together, they stumbled backward, then veered sharply out of the destruction path in time to avoid the crash. They took refuge behind the safety of another pillar, hefty and wide, from the final onslaught of tumbling rubble. Qora closed her eyes and waited.

It must have been at least two minutes before everything settled, before the rocks stopped shifting, before the dust hanging in the air thinned enough to see through.

The heralds circled overhead.

A fight broke out as two competitors raced to climb one of the formations that still stood bearing firebombs.

Killay scrambled up another pillar while Ninan and Qora

climbed over and between the rubble to get out.

Ruyan ran past in pursuit.

Pressure built in Qora's body like another firebomb, aching to bust her open. *I could shoot him right now—and make it count this time.*

Ninan urged her along, but she hesitated, weighing her options. She couldn't waste this opportunity.

The only thing worse than a raging animal was one that had survived a shot. Ruyan had a bolt puncture, and a marred face that would never be the same; he wouldn't forget who had caused that. And if Qora could take him out now, she'd never have to worry about him again. She wouldn't have to fear his shadow in her dreams.

Another teetering pillar, however, spurred her to keep moving. She and Ninan had to clamber over new piles of rubble, some of which were jagged as blades. In her panic, her ankle twisted in the mess. Her knees buckled. She caught herself, but a sharp pain cut into her dominant hand. Crimson seeped down her palm. The sting set in, hot and severe. She bit back a scream.

Killay and Ruyan went head to head now, both eager to get to the remaining firebombs. Ruyan got hold of the back of Killay's shirt collar and dragged her down from her climb. She twisted and pitched a fist. He lunged—she ran. She turned back and flung a blade that sank into his hip. Ruyan made a guttural sound before he yanked out the knife, lunged at her again, and directed the blade into an uppercut, twisting it into her abdomen until she collapsed. The woman didn't even scream, just choked on her own reaction, mouth agape as her eyes rolled upward. Ruyan removed the knife, panting, and looked over.

That's when Qora knew he'd seen her.

She stopped and positioned her crossbow, the gash in her

skin tearing wider. Blood wet the handle and her fingers slipped. She clenched her jaw against a new surge of pain as she worked the trigger.

Ruyan bled from the hip but stood tall and faced her, his teeth bared in a raging glare, daring her to shoot.

"It didn't work last time." He put a fist to his chest to jangle the damaged copperskin collar under his shirt. Then he pulled back his arm and flung his knife. Qora ducked. The blade lodged in a cluster of rocks.

Ruyan came forward, but two strides in, his legs faltered and he hunkered down, clutching his wound. Still, he seethed. "We're not finished!"

"I think we are," Qora said.

He crawled through broken rocks, wincing at what must have been sharp edges biting into his knees.

She pointed her crossbow and aimed for his head.

Ruyan reached into the rubble, then raised his hand, fingers curled around a dusty—but fully intact—copper ball.

Qora stopped dead.

Ruyan lifted his chin. "Agree to disagree?"

TWENTY-FOUR

Qora stood with her crossbow braced against her chest, peering down the barrel as she aimed. Her form was all angles and lines, everything precise and calculated.

Her finger twitched against the trigger.

"Qora, don't."

She didn't acknowledge him, but didn't proceed either. She seemed to be warring with herself, weighing the risk, with a hatred in her eyes Ninan hadn't seen even in the face of the mockery she'd openly detested at the Underground.

"You'll kill him, sure," said Ninan, "but if that firebomb hits just right, those pillars will come down on *all* of us."

"Run, then," she told him. "I'll give you a five-second head start."

He rested his fingers in the crook of her elbow, the gentlest touch. She was solid for a moment, but slowly he felt her form soften. She released a breath and lowered her weapon.

Ruyan sneered. "That's a good girl. Do what you're told."

And just like that, Qora was sharp again.

Click.

Ninan yanked her off course before the bolt shot out. Ruyan ducked. The bolt clattered against the rocks.

Qora hissed out her pain, curling up her bleeding hand. "What is *wrong* with you? I almost—"

"It's not worth it!" he told her. "Come on ..."

Pteranodon wingflaps kicked up dust as the heralds swarmed, soaring over the wreckage.

"Why are you still here?" Qora shook off Ninan's grip.

Ruyan stood feebly but pulled back his arm, firebomb positioned for launch.

Qora hurried to span and load another bolt, but her eager, bloody fingers fumbled. Ninan grabbed her by the crossbow strap and pulled her away as the firebomb went airborne. She resisted him only for an instant, and then it was clear she had seen the shining copper orb overhead. Together they rushed to outpace it. They reached the edge of the Rock Forest as the firebomb struck a smaller formation, smashing apart, blasting the rock to pieces, and spewing fire. With hazy vision, they stumbled toward the woods.

Ninan hissed as a jolt of energy punched his spine. He lurched into his next steps, struggling to keep his balance as rubble and streams of smoke shot up behind him and Qora.

Neither of them could manage more than a few additional strides before the blast forced them to the ground. There was nothing to do but lie flat, faces down, and cover their heads as they waited for the rocks to stop raining on them.

When the worst of it was over, Ninan peered out from under his arms.

Qora looked at him with grim exasperation, then got to her feet and turned to gape back at the scene.

Rising slowly, ears ringing, Ninan coughed. "What the *hell* was that? What were you *thinking?*"

"I almost had him," Qora snapped.

"You almost had your head blown off by a firebomb!"

"I could have outrun it. We outran *that* one. At least I could've taken him out before he *launched* it at us." She gestured back at the pillars, some of whose tips were still visible through the tree branches, where the firebomb had since dissipated.

"I don't understand," he said. "I thought you liked that guy. Or at least tolerated him. Now you're risking everything to see him *dead*?"

And so much for that. Ruyan was injured, sure, but he was still alive somewhere back there.

Qora pursed her lips, then turned and stalked off.

When Ninan determined she wasn't going to respond, he followed her away from the blast site and into the woods that continued beyond the Rock Forest. "What happened?"

She continued as though he weren't there, clutching her pack straps and keeping a stalwart pace.

"I'm not saying you owe me an explanation," he added, "but considering you almost got me *killed*, it wouldn't hurt."

"I didn't ask you to stay there while I shot him." She stopped and spun around so fast, Ninan almost crashed into her. "You could've kept going."

"And you could have kept going when that pterodactyl carried me off, but here we are."

She clutched her pack straps more tightly. "What's that supposed to mean?"

It means that I don't know how to walk away from you now, Ninan thought.

It meant Qora wasn't just any random competitor anymore—although he wished to all gods and spirits that that wasn't the case, because this was seriously one of the last things he needed right now.

But regardless of what it meant, his attention fell to her elbow, as red liquid tracked down her arm.

"You're bleeding," he said. "A lot."

She looked down at herself, paling as she realized he was right. She let up on the strap, leaving a dark stain behind, and stared at the dripping gash on her palm.

"Here." Ninan took off his pack and removed his tattered poncho, from which he tore a long strip of material. He took Qora's hand and swathed the wound. The material soaked up the blood on contact, a red blotch that grew smaller with each layer he added. To his surprise, she didn't protest; she kept still until he finished, then turned her brown eyes on him.

"Thank you," she whispered flatly.

He nodded and gathered up his things. "Let's go."

〉〉〉

Far-off firebombs continued to explode, no doubt killing many additional competitors that had come after the first wave looking for the midpoint prize. Eventually Ninan and Qora progressed too far to hear them anymore, but Ninan wondered how many had died at the Rock Forest now, adding to the death toll from the previous night.

He also couldn't figure why Qora had been so reckless back there, why she'd turned vengeful. He knew she could be hotheaded sometimes, but she also seemed intent on getting through this competition *alive*, and he couldn't help feeling like there was something she wasn't telling him. Not that she *would* tell him. Why should she?

They traveled for hours in silence. Even during water breaks, Qora didn't speak—and Ninan didn't dare prompt her to.

As the sky grew pale, Qora slowed, dropping her pack. She seemed to be surveying her surroundings, which were practically a whole different world now. Abundant ferns, twisting ceiba trees with all their nooks, broadleaf palms whose trunks were sheathed in rows of their own dried fronds, dangling vines, fiery heliconia blossoms. She cast a weary, sideways glance at Ninan before she tipped her head, listening like she had the previous night.

All Ninan could hear was the same refrain of animal voices they'd been hearing for miles, not so different from the sounds of their homeland except for what seemed an increase in the number of small, chirpy flyers and distant monkeys. Few mammals could hold their own among the reptiles, but the denser vegetation of this ever-more-tropical side of the Terrain provided plenty of places to nestle and hide. Human travelers should have had the same advantage, only most weren't familiar enough with the plants and the topography to use them strategically.

"What is it?" Ninan asked.

Qora's jaw tensed. "Nothing. I just … I don't recognize some of these noises. There are new reptiles here."

"Plenty of travelers have survived out here with lesser skills than yours, I'm sure," Ninan said. "Anyway, it'll be dark soon, so …"

She nodded once. "Better find a safe place to lay your head, then."

Ninan hesitated, staring at her in disbelief. "You can't be serious. You really want me to go somewhere else?"

"*You* can't be serious," she argued. "We can't just … stay together. I appreciate that you haven't made an enemy of me, but we're not friends, either. That's not how the Venture works."

"What's the difference if I'm twenty feet away or two?"

"It's different." She opened her pack and tossed her rolled-up hammock on the ground.

"I have some food," he told her.

Qora unwrapped a mass of dried fruit, all stuck together. "So do I."

"Meat," he clarified, removing the package of cured organ meats from his supplies—the ones Mullu had looted for him before he'd reached the Rock Forest.

She met his offering with a shadowy glare.

"Come on. It's been a long day. You've walked eighteen miles. You need protein." He extended the package. "I know you're hungry …"

Qora tensed visibly, as though she were resisting him with every muscle, but he waited, fixed to the spot, refusing to back down. He could be stubborn too.

She glanced at the meat, with all its dried and gnarly pieces, likely fighting some war between her belly and her brain.

He raised an eyebrow.

Her nose twitched. "Fine. I'll eat." She sighed. "And then one of us has to go."

"Fine."

They arranged a few items to get more comfortable and then Ninan set the open package between them, taking a two-inch-thick piece.

"Looks like a heart," Qora said flatly. "Gods know what animal it came from, though …"

Ninan shrugged. "Avimimus, I'd guess."

When she gave him a blank look, he grinned, for once feeling like he had the upper hand on her, and feigned shock. "You mean you can't tell one reptile's innards from another's?"

She rolled her eyes. "It's not like listening to their calls.

How do *you* know, anyway?"

"Theropods—especially avimimus—have faster heart rates, and you can see it in the heart musculature." He sliced the organ in half with his pocketknife and showed Qora the inside. "See how the chambers are smooth? Less friction. Faster bloodflow. Faster heart rate. Simple."

Qora narrowed her eyes. "Why do you know all this?"

He flicked the knife closed and shoved it back into his pocket. "I may have come from money, but I'm not completely out of touch."

"Not *completely*," she agreed.

"Whatever life of luxury you imagine I've had, that's not the whole picture," he told her. "I spent a year working with quinoa farmers; I blistered my hands raw doing it. And last winter left most of the community struggling for food. Game was scarce— probably everywhere near Qhusi, so you might remember that too, as a hunter—and they butchered their few kills down to every organ. Nothing gone to waste." He stared at the halved heart in his palm.

Qora peered at its details, then looked back at Ninan. "What were you doing on a quinoa farm? I'm guessing you didn't *choose* to be there—not if you could afford not to be."

"Let's just say I found myself sort of … lost … from my family. The farmers took me in. I only started prizefighting a few months ago when taxes went up again. Figured my fists could earn some extra money."

"That's why you were there that day? At the Underground?" He nodded.

Qora didn't seem to know what to say. As far as Ninan had seen, she was always ready to spew plenty of tough words— until, of course, she didn't feel like talking, and then she was as impervious to conversation as raptor scales to rain.

After a moment, rather than admitting she'd misjudged him, she simply offered, "I heard once that avimimus hearts are supposed to be good luck … for a swift journey, I think. Or maybe it was courage, not luck. Although I'm not sure if that means eating one or just carrying it with you."

"That does sound familiar." Ninan presented her with one of the two halves. "In which case, godsspeed to us both."

She pinched it between her fingers, examined it, then slipped it into her mouth.

Ninan bit into the other half. It took at least a full minute to break through the cured, chewy texture, but the flavor was good and the meat was, appropriately, "hearty."

Once it hit his stomach, Ninan began to feel a warm sense of ease coming over him. It was incredible what a bit of nourishment could do after hours of walking.

When he looked at Qora, her eyes met his for an instant before the horns blared over them. He knew she was mentally counting them too.

Twelve … thirteen … fourteen …

Silence.

They sat with the information as darkness spread across the sky. Qora turned her attention toward the thick brambles beyond them, like she was seeking a divergent path. One that would lead her away.

Ninan got the sudden urge to speak up. In fact, he could scarcely control it. The words were already halfway past his teeth when he thought better of them. "You should stay." He cringed. "I would really like it if—I mean—I think it would be—"

No. Why had he even opened his mouth? He must have been more tired than he'd realized, and his weariness had weakened his self-restraint.

Qora shook her head. "Three times starts a habit—that's what my mamáy says—and if I stay with you again, that's more than halfway there."

"Not all habits are bad," he said.

"This one would be."

Whatever was swirling through his mind right now, he knew she was right. They could be allies for the moment, but the Venture only ever ended in conflict. There would be no co-champions.

Still, he couldn't keep himself from entertaining other ideas. Like the idea that maybe he didn't have to be alone tonight. He found it almost painful, trying to hold back all the words he wanted to say.

With effort, he managed to keep his response short: "Of course."

"It's not personal," said Qora. "Or … maybe it is. I don't know. You … confuse me, I guess. I'm not sure why you'd try to help me. I'm not sure why I didn't just leave you to the pterodactyls; that would have been the smart thing to do."

"It was 'on the way'," he reminded her.

"It was. But also … I didn't want anything bad to happen to you. Anything worse, I mean." She shook her head. "Gods, what am I saying?" She stood.

"Don't go," he said. "Please."

Gods, what am I saying?

Ninan stood and stepped in front of her. "When I saw you coming up the riverbank, taking down those pterodactyls, it was like watching the personification of those legends about the ancient Slayer Queen of Wilamaya killing monsters with her golden spear. I don't know how I had time to think about it when I was in the middle of getting shredded by flyer claws, but now I can't *stop* thinking about it."

Qora looked at him like he'd lost his mind. "The Slayer Queen ..."

"Sorry," Ninan said. "That was a strange thing for me to tell you."

"Except slayer queens always know the right thing to do, though, don't they? They're not scared of anything. They don't make stupid, desperate choices that get them trapped in impossible situations."

Ninan started to speak, ready to confess his own desperation, his own seemingly impossible situation, then stopped. "What do you mean?"

"I did something bad." She brushed a few loose hairs off her forehead.

"Bad?"

"Illegal," she said. "I'm no noble warrior. I'm just a dumb kid who thought I could make a lot of money fast—and now, no matter what I do, I'll be paying for it ten times over. With my life, either in servitude or in death. Unless I can get to the end of the Venture and win."

"The laws are a joke," Ninan said candidly. He'd seen many of them made on a whim to suit the qhapaq's personal needs or desires. "What could you have possibly done to get a consequence that severe?"

Her chest rose and fell. She shook her head again, like she was willing herself not to tell him. But finally, she said, "A raptoriva."

Ninan had to ponder this for a moment to understand her meaning. Qora was a hunter *and* a trader—he'd known that as soon as he'd upset her at the Underground. Meanwhile, there had been an influx of raptorivas and other exotic flyers migrating westward to escape harsh, volcanic conditions. And of course the qhapaq had people everywhere feeding him information, and he'd set forth laws regarding the capture and trade of wildlife, often for the sole purpose of seizing the best specimens for himself and—

Ninan felt himself pale.

The flyer in the gilded cage in the summit hall.

It couldn't have been the same—could it?

But it had to be. That cage was for the qhapaq's latest acquisitions. Qora would have had only weeks to pay her fine. The timeline coincided.

"I—that's—I'm—" The words all fought for position on his tongue.

Behind those words were others rising up in his throat. He wanted to tell her she'd been right from the beginning, that his reasons for competing were nothing compared to others'—to hers. The truth about his upbringing, his expulsion from that life, his plans to return to Kallpa House after winning the competition … He was ready to confess it all.

She shifted on her feet, then sat back down. "You think I'm terrible."

"What? No …" And since when did she care what he thought of her?

"I only did it because I had to." Her voice was almost desperate, pleading.

Ninan hadn't heard her plead before, couldn't have imagined it. He didn't know her well, but he sensed she was more likely to keep her desperation hidden, putting on the face of a snarling reptile for anyone who got too close.

Then she went on to explain that she'd done it for her

brother—a brilliant eight-year-old boy laden with theropox and hanging onto his life by a fiber. The sparkshade had been an impossible requirement, and then, just when it had been within her reach, the law had snatched away her means, along with any hope to recover from her mistake.

She also told of a medicine man who had prescribed pamparaptor liver, which had only made her brother hallucinate—a brief and confusing distraction from his symptoms—for a few hours before it had worn off.

Ninan glanced at the package of organ meats, considering the strange effects certain dinosaur parts were said to have. There were people in the north who swore by pachyrhinosaurus horns, ground into an ingestible powder that could provide superficial energy and wakefulness. Others soothed panic attacks with the calming effects of placodus oil. Many effects were scientifically proven, although some were traditional remedies with no basis in truth, and others were shameless gimmicks. There were so many it was hard to keep them all straight.

The "luck on a journey" that Qora had mentioned sounded familiar, and so did something about courage, but … it wasn't quite right. Avimimus was indeed a symbol of courage, which would have made sense. But courage could manifest in different ways—in braving danger, in self-sacrifice, in recklessness.

In speaking the awkward truth.

"Feet!" Ninan said suddenly.

Qora flinched. "Feet?" She blinked at him several times. "What does that have to do with—"

"People eat the *feet* for a swift journey. Feet—*walking*. Traveling. But the heart is for courage. Not just symbolically. It has an enzyme that affects the mind. It subdues fear, and … inhibitions."

Qora put her hand over her mouth.

"I swear I didn't know," Ninan said. "You know I'm telling the truth because neither of us have been able to *stop* telling the truth for the past half hour."

He couldn't deny he'd been tempted to let her keep talking—although he wasn't sure he could have hidden the truth about what he'd just realized even if he'd wanted to, with these enzymes working through him and breaking down his mental barriers. It was such a strange sensation, like everything he'd been thinking and feeling—things he'd buried—were all rising to the surface. And Qora's confession brought new things to consider, which he struggled not to say aloud. If he could win the competition—earn back his father's respect—he might have the ability to help; he might be able to get her charge dismissed, grant her family access to better medical care. He wasn't sure his father would allow him such power right away (the qhapaq would want to watch him closely, keep him on a short leash) but it was possible. He was also painfully aware that his own reasons for winning were completely trivial compared to Qora's, and maybe she ought to know—

"We're done talking now." Qora picked up her pack and began to gather her things into it.

"Wait—I won't say anything else," he told her. "I promise. Not a word. No questions, nothing. Just … stay a while longer." Spirits, he was practically begging her not to go. He knew he sounded much too eager, and it was even worse because now she knew he wasn't capable of being insincere—at least not until the effects of the heart wore off.

Qora shook her head. "You know I can't."

"Tell me you want to be alone. Say it and I'll know you're not lying—and I won't ask you again."

She stared at him, clenching her fists. She was holding back; she always was, but he knew it was more difficult for her now. Even though it was wrong, he was glad the heart had weakened her resistance. He found himself longing to know all the thoughts and feelings and stories she kept locked away, and hoping she might finally be inclined to allow him a better glimpse.

After a long moment, Qora finally set her things back down.

꙳꙳꙳

Ninan set out the oilskin tarp for them to sit on while they pawed through the rest of the dried foods they kept between them, wary of other strange effects they might experience. He handed her a piece of jerky made from the liver of another small theropod, and accepted a mass of Qora's sticky, dried mangoes that were tart and sweet.

Once he'd finished the mangoes and moved on to a string of twisted, dried intestine—this time having no guess as to what kind of reptile it had belonged to—he sighed through his chewing, wishing he at least had a bit of bread to go with it. If only bread wasn't so quick to go stale, or encourage mold …

As Qora watched him curiously, he tried to convey his thoughts by positioning his hands as though he were holding a small loaf. When she raised a brow, he then acted out the process of grinding amaranth, mixing it with other ingredients, putting it in an oven, removing it, cutting it, and eating it.

Her lips twitched with each of Ninan's additional movements, until she finally broke into laughter.

Ninan stopped, grinning.

It was nice to see Qora smile, although he had to admit there was something about her scowl that pleased him too.

Sometime not long after sunset, as they sat pensively in the glow of Qora's mystical mushroom jar, Qora began to drift off, and Ninan, although unfortunately inclined with the honesty to remind her she wanted to separate, was quick to follow her example before he could say it.

〉〉〉

When Ninan woke at first light, Qora lay still, her fingers gently resting on his knuckles. Something that had felt natural in Ninan's sleep-drugged state of mind began to take on new meaning. His pulse kicked up.

Will she feel that?

He kept still and took shallow breaths, afraid the slightest movement would bring them both to an uncomfortable, mutual awareness of a situation that neither of them would know how to address.

Decidedly, he slipped out from under her in calculated increments. He cringed with each subtle crinkle of the oilskin tarp as he crept across the surface. Once he was on his feet, he stepped back from where Qora lay, as though she were a firebomb that might detonate at the slightest disturbance.

More than anything, though, was his urge to urinate. When he'd camped alone, he'd had no grace about it, but with Qora here, he decided it would be best to go off a ways before relieving himself.

When he returned, he did so quietly, so as not to wake Qora, but he found her already up and alert, struggling to attach her quiver to her belt. He watched her for a moment, as her determined but impatient fingers worked the loop, a task made worse by her injury. Feeling as though he was interrupting her, he kept quiet while he approached, but finally felt inclined to ask, "Do you need help?"

In response, she spun around—and flung her fist at his face.

"The tighter the bowstring, the more pressure is built up behind it. When that happens, it only takes the slightest touch to trigger your bolt."

Ollan Kanchaya

TWENTY-FIVE

 but his face manifested in meaningless shapes and blurs.

Qora didn't think, she just threw punches. She lost herself in a flurry of arms. Panic swelled in her chest.

Her thoughts flourished like reeds on the lake bank—thoughts she'd stifled for days to keep her mind from dwelling on the fears they carried.

But the memories persisted.

The two men that had come for her at the ravine who would have punctured her skull with slingstones.

The painted man who had put a knife to her throat.

Ruyan's attack at the lake and his threats hissing in her ears long after she'd left him.

At once, Qora felt it all. The demonic spirit of every malicious arm and deadly weapon wrapped around her, wringing her out, cutting off her air.

She'd dreamed of those incidents the previous night. Not clearly, not in any order, but they had surfaced in her mind in fragments. At one point, she'd been standing in the woods, shooting bolt after bolt at some unseen enemy, and mid-air, each bolt had turned to a blade of grass that fluttered uselessly to the ground.

Now all her nightmares converged into a single figure. Her limbs seem to flail independently of her, automatic defenses with minds of their own.

"Hey," said a voice. "What's the matter? What's—"

The pattern of the voice was familiar, the depth and cadence. It was kind. Concerned.

Confused.

Everything jolted into focus: a quiver on the ground with scattered bolts, Ninan gripping her by the wrists.

Qora yanked against his hold but his arms were solid, keeping her in place. It was only because he let up for an instant that she had the chance to pull back and pitch another hit. He blocked. She struck again.

"Qora," he said through clenched teeth, parrying her fists, "It's me. *It's just me.*"

Another block. Another hit. Another block. Yesterday's wound leaked fresh blood, but she couldn't stop.

He doesn't want to hurt me.

And somehow it didn't matter. The only thing that mattered was the fact that she couldn't break free.

Ninan seized her wrists again, flipping her around and crossing her arms over her chest in one move. He wreathed her shoulders and dropped, pulling her with him until they were both sitting on the ground. When Qora writhed against his control, he only held her more tightly. She fought against him for at least a full minute.

And then she became aware of her pulse hammering in her head, a sting on the heels of each throb. Her strength seemed to evaporate with the sweat that formed on her skin. Her ragged breathing slowed. The sounds of the forest came back.

Swaying fronds, crinkling grasses, chirps and whistles.

Tears spilled down her face and she went limp in Ninan's arms.

"You're okay," he whispered, so close his lips grazed her ear. "You're okay. It's just me."

TWENTY-SIX

WHEN NINAN FINALLY LET HER GO, Qora wiped her eyes with the heel of her hand, then returned all her bolts to the quiver and stood slowly, turning away from him.

"I'm sorry," she whispered.

Ninan got to his feet and brushed debris from his clothes. "It's fine, I just don't understand—" He stared at the fresh floret of red that soaked Qora's bandage.

She tucked it against her body and bent to pick up her crossbow with her other hand, grunting as she slipped the strap over her head.

"What are you doing?" Ninan asked.

"What does it look like I'm doing?" She released a breath through narrowed lips and shook out her wounded hand.

"You're going hunting?" He reached for his own weapon. "Don't be ridiculous. Let me do it."

She flicked a sharp look at him.

"Not because you *can't*," he clarified. "Because you *shouldn't*."

"I can handle it." She started walking.

Ninan huffed as he trailed her. "*Can* you? I barely said four words before you flew into a rage. We're really not going to talk about that?"

"No."

What was going on? First she'd been an emotional wreck, flailing at him like he'd been trying to kill her, and now she was going to act like this was just a normal day?

"Hey …" He picked up his pace and fell into stride with her. He lifted his own weapon in demonstration. "We both know I could use the practice."

"You can practice as much as you want—just don't do it close to where I'm hunting."

He scoffed. "Are you always this scaly? At first I thought maybe I just caught you on a bad day—or a bad *week*, since the Venture isn't exactly a pleasant event—but now I'm starting to think it's just your personality."

She ignored him all the way to what was apparently a good climbing tree, as though she'd known all along right where it was. After a bit of hesitation that she tried to downplay as some critical examination of the tree, she pulled herself up with her good hand and got in.

For a few minutes Ninan said nothing. He waited below with his hands in his pockets, wondering why he didn't just leave her to it. Whatever this was, it was none of his business. Still, he couldn't make himself walk away, either.

As soon as Qora tried to pull the trigger, she sucked air through her teeth. The bolt shot out at a terrible angle that didn't even come close to its target. Small flyers scattered and Qora huffed her frustration. She did this twice more before looking back at Ninan, who raised a brow.

"Fine," she growled.

TWENTY-SEVEN

"BRACE THE CROSSBOW AGAINST YOUR CHEST," she said quietly. "No—closer to your shoulder."

Qora had allowed Ninan to climb into the tree with her, both of them now sitting between the branches that extended up around them like thick fingers coming out of the earth, a seat in the palm of a wooden hand. She reached over and adjusted Ninan's weapon. "There. Like that."

Ninan squinted one eye, panning the crossbow slowly from side to side. He paused, focused on the glimpse of a troodon—a bipedal omnivore, weighing around ten pounds—about thirty yards away, upwind of them.

"Higher," Qora whispered sharply. She nudged the crossbow so it pointed a hair upward. "The trajectory of the bolt drops over the distance. If you want to actually hit the target—"

"Okay—I've got it. Relax."

"I'm trying to make sure you do it right," she said. "Some mistakes will cost you more than a missed meal."

He glanced at her weapon, which she still held onto, despite having agreed not to try to use it for a while. "The 'mistakes' you're talking about—the ones that 'cost' more—did your military brother make a mistake like that?"

Qora avoided his gaze. "No."

"No?"

"No."

"Okay." Ninan stared at her meaningfully before turning back to his prey, a species whose hearing was limited in favor of improved attunement to ground vibrations. He adjusted his grip and squinted again, then took a shot.

The troodon jerked back and assumed a fighting stance as the bolt zoomed past. Qora and Ninan sat still as stone until the troodon relaxed and began to sniff the ground.

"So what's your deal, then?" Ninan asked, apparently unbothered by his failure to hit the dinosaur. He withdrew a new bolt while he waited for an explanation.

Qora glared at him, angry at the way his unkempt hair seemed to fall so nicely around his face. More angry that he didn't seem to care about how poor a shot he was. Angrier still that she wanted to tell him everything even without truth-inducing enzymes tempting her to do so. "It was me, alright? I'm the one who made the mistake. I keep making mistakes. Bad ones. And they follow me everywhere. I can't escape them. They creep into my dreams, even into my *waking* mind ..." Her stomach soured when she thought about how she'd reacted to Ninan that morning. Something had taken over, a primal survival instinct that hadn't had any root in logic. Or maybe there had been *some* logic to it; he was, after all, her competition—not quite an enemy, but not someone she should befriend.

"That's ... understandable," he said.

"I think I was ... testing you," Qora said. She frowned, trying to pick apart the exact reason for her outburst. "Testing myself *against* you, maybe. You startled me, and for a minute I was scared, but then I saw how ... how you didn't want to hurt me. But even though you weren't trying to hurt me, I was still helpless against you. And that made me angry. Like ... *really* angry."

"Because if you couldn't overcome someone who *wasn't* trying to hurt you ..."

She nodded. "Then what happens when the time comes for me to fight the next person who *does* want to hurt me?"

Ninan spanned his crossbow and loaded the bolt but didn't aim yet. "I guess that makes sense, but ... you seem to have handled yourself up to this point."

"I've been lucky," she said.

"You took down a swoop of pterodactyls—and destroyed your attacker in the process. And Ruyan clearly didn't get the better of you; I'm guessing whatever happened to his face was your doing."

Qora looked out at the trees. Her whole body felt numb when she remembered it. The way Ruyan had appeared so casually, so confident in what he'd been planning to do. "He didn't want to kill me," she said, letting anger replace her fear. "Not at first, anyway."

Ninan looked at her more closely now. "What do you mean?"

"He wanted to ..." Qora swallowed hard. "He wanted to ... *use* me. Use me and then just ... leave me there. Or kill me after, maybe. I ... don't really know."

It seemed to take a few seconds before Ninan understood her meaning. Then his brows pulled together. "Spirits," he muttered. "Why didn't you tell me after we left the Rock Forest?"

Qora tugged absentmindedly at her crossbow string. "I didn't want you to say you told me so. 'Word of advice' ... Remember?"

"What—You mean because of what I said at the entrance

trials? I overheard him say some crude things, but I thought he was all roar. I had no idea he'd actually … *try* something. You can't seriously think I'd feel smug being right about that."

"I don't know what I think." Qora shuddered and gazed off into the muddle of green, the tangle of branches and vines that seemed all too familiar in its winding, overpowering nature. The tangles inside her hummed with a similar energy, housing unseen monsters while overhead storms that came and went without warning. "Anyway, it's my fault. I let my guard down. It's completely my fault—"

"No," Ninan said. He set down his weapon and laid a hand on hers. She flinched slightly but didn't pull away. "Don't ever say anything like that again. You can try and blame yourself for a lot of things, but what *he* does—what anyone else does—is not one of them. Okay?"

Qora bit her lip.

"As far as just being lucky," he added, "well, I don't buy that either. You might feel like some of those other competitors can overpower you, but fighting's not all about strength or physical technique. You've proven that."

"Sure, but what happens when I'm out of resources? What happens if I'm cornered without any venom, or wild flyers to help me?"

At that moment, the troodon wandered closer, grumbling over what must have been some lost rodent meal in the ferns. Qora paused, analyzing it—green scales and violet markings and a row of scant feathers on its forearms. Meaty for its size.

She pointed her chin at the reptile and lowered her voice. "Focus. Pay attention to the details—the way it moves, the sound of its footfalls. You'll get a sense of whether it's about to move again."

The troodon stopped to dip its head into another fern, squawking at something between the fronds.

Ninan adjusted his position and drew a breath.

"Your breathing matters too," Qora added quietly. "Hold it before you trigger, otherwise the rise-and-fall of your chest will affect your aim. You're in control, but you have to control *yourself.*"

She was surprised at how well he was following her instructions this time, at how natural he was starting to look with the weapon in his hand. The lines and angles of his arms, the concentration on his face. The morning sun, still low and gradually rising, cast a gleam of copper light over him, and once again she saw that hint of regality she'd noticed at the Underground.

With a bolt at the ready, his breath held, everything braced, he squeezed the trigger.

Click.

His bolt pierced the troodon from the side, straight through both lungs. The troodon dropped.

Ninan gasped. "Whoa." He looked at the weapon in his hand with what Qora could only interpret as awe. Then he turned to her and grinned. "Thank you."

"For what?"

"For showing me I could do that. And now … it's my turn to show you what *you* can do."

TWENTY-EIGHT

"**REMEMBER WHEN YOU TOLD ME** to focus?" Ninan said.

Qora stood facing him, while the flames of a small fire lapped the edges of the troodon's skinned carcass, and nodded.

"I was aiming at the troodon and you said, 'Pay attention to the details. You'll get a sense of whether it's about to move again.' The same applies when you're up against a human opponent," he explained. "They have these … sort of … tells. A rhythm to the way they move. But you can't panic. Yes, you have to act quickly sometimes, but, again, like you said earlier, *you're* in control—you just have to control *yourself*. If you can ignore your sense of panic, the solution will become clear."

"Okay, but I don't even know what my options are."

"Start by looking for weak points. For example …" He gently took one of her wrists. "Your instinct will be to pull your arms back toward yourself. But that doesn't work against the weak point of my grip. See where my thumbs touch my fingertips? That's your opening. That's where you apply pressure."

Qora twisted her wrist against this "weak" point.

Ninan's thumb and fingers separated. "Perfect."

"But you're not holding very tight. Someone who wants to hurt or kill me will have a stronger grip."

"It's about maximizing your chances. Try again. I promise to use the full extent of my strength."

Qora tried again but Ninan was still locked on.

"Use the energy of your whole arm—your whole *body* if you can. And you need to do it with more speed."

Qora lifted her arm and performed the same motion as before, but with a quick, downward yank, breaking loose.

Ninan smiled. "There you go."

He showed her other techniques based on the same principle. A choke hold, for example, had a similar opening. Ninan explained how she could plant her foot and twist her body to slip backward and out, breaking the hold and pushing away. They went through different attack scenarios, everything from being shoved up against a tree to being tackled on the ground, practicing each one repeatedly.

Qora had been eager to get back to traveling the route, of course, but Ninan had reasoned that it was worth a brief investment of time, if it meant she could better defend herself later.

"Most importantly," Ninan said, "you have to determine where most of your power is. A lot of times it'll be in your hips." He stepped in closer and set her hips so they were square with his. They locked eyes and his face suddenly warmed. He cleared his throat. "That's your center of weight. Your center for full body movement. It's a good base and you can maneuver your legs under it for maximum effect. Twisting out of a hold. Pushing someone off. Working against those weak points and potential openings."

"It sounds so easy." Qora shook her head. "But trying to think clearly when there's a knife at my throat or when I can barely move ..."

"You can do it," he said. "I know you can. You know that moment when you're thinking to yourself, 'This is it, this is how

I'm going to die'?"

He could tell that she did. She must have known it too well by now.

"Yes."

"Don't think that."

"Oh, okay," she bit out. "I just … won't think that …"

"I'm serious. Just don't. Think instead, 'What's the way out of this? Where's the weak point? Where does my strength lie right now?' If you have enough time to think about death, you have enough time to plan your escape. Use that time wisely and try not to panic."

Qora took a deep breath. "I'll see what I can do."

"I hope you don't have to, but if the time comes again, I think you're ready. You have the power, it's just a matter of directing it to the right place."

)))

In the distance, the Volcano Kañay rose above the trees, a mountain with a tiny puff of smoke seeping from its vent. The sky was a hazy, dirty blue even from here, but Qora and Ninan wouldn't pass the volcano's base for another two days.

As they progressed, the broadleaf trees made way for spiny palms. The woods became more crowded, their clear patches narrowing with every mile. There was a palpable moisture in the atmosphere and waves of heat that set loose new scents—damp soil, decaying wood, and sweet florals.

In the afternoon, walking beside Ninan, Qora looked over at him. She took a deep breath and said, "Can I tell you what happened to my brother?"

Name: Spinaeosaur Uchuy (colloquially known as "sailbeast")

Average Weight: 1,500 pounds
Average Height: 5 feet
Average Length: 20 ft (due to extensive tail)
Features:
- black scales
- lateral thoracic feathers
- distinctive red spinal sail
- red striping
- conical teeth
- long fin-tail
- crocodilian snout

Notes: This specimen has manifested external features remarkably similar to that of a typical spinosaur (as intended) but with a ninety-percent reduction in size.

**From the scientific reports of the
Sumaqi Reptile Interbreeding Program**

TWENTY-NINE

FOUR YEARS AGO

"YOU'RE STILL TRIGGERING TOO QUICKLY," Ollan told Qora. He crossed his muscled arms, standing with the posture of a grown man although he was barely that. His once-perpetually tousled hair was cut short now, and he wore clean trousers and a shirt without wrinkles. Qora couldn't say he looked *different*, exactly; he still had the same honey-brown eyes and the same dimple on one cheek and the same habit of shifting his feet when he got impatient. But there was a rigidness to him now, something new trained into his features.

Qora sighed and loaded a new bolt. "What doesn't that even mean?" Her previous bolt protruded from the rump of the straw-stuffed likeness of a theropod leaning up against a tree in the distance. "It takes half a second to pull it."

"It's about sudden movement; you get too hasty with the trigger, your hand makes the weapon waver. You sway an inch here"—Ollan put one hand on the crossbow handle and another on the stirrup while Qora held it—"and you'll be off by a few *feet* over there." He jerked his head at the dummy.

He'd taught her dozens of rules already and she'd dutifully memorized and recited them back, at his request, but all she'd wanted to do was get her hands on the crossbow. She'd been itching for it. She might not have been so impatient, had it not been for the two weeks when he'd allowed her to follow him out shooting and watch—but *only* watch—without touching.

"We need to finish up and head home," Ollan told her. His authoritative tone was something about him that *hadn't* changed; in fact, it had intensified. Six years' difference in age had always given him the idea that he could tell her what to do, but his time as a young soldier had reassured him of it.

Not that that meant Qora was inclined to obey him.

"We've still got time," she argued.

"Mamáy's going to be annoyed as it is."

"Oh please. She lets you get away with *everything* now." Qora braced the crossbow against her shoulder, licked her lips, and slowly pulled the trigger. *Click.* The bolt sprang forward and landed a few inches to the side of her previous shot. "She's so glad to have you back, she wouldn't dare waste time being upset when you're around."

After Qora spanned again and loaded yet another bolt, Ollan lifted her elbow and nudged her spine into a straight line, adjusting her like she was a heap of clay on a turning wheel. "Yeah but she's also paranoid. I'm gone too long and she'll think I've been mauled by wild reptiles."

He was right. When they were younger, their mamáy had always let them play outside for hours if they'd finished all their work, partly to get them out of the house so she could get a minute to herself and partly so they could "use up some of that energy." But that was before Ollan had joined the Guard. He'd only been deployed in one attack, a joint-force effort with the Unuvians at the coastline when extracontinental troops had breached the naval blockade. Since then, many of the soldiers had been sent out for much less deadly work, like patrolling city streets or checking entrance documents and shipments at the borders. Still, any time Ollan was on leave now, their mamáy had barely let him out of her sight, if she could help it; she fed him double helpings at every meal and refused to let him lift a finger and knitted him extra clothing to keep warm before the weather had even turned particularly cold.

"Just a couple more shots," Qora begged.

Ollan crossed his arms again and nodded once. "Fine. A *couple* more."

As Ollan had instructed, Qora moved slowly on the trigger, pressing down in tiny increments so as not to throw off her steady position. The bolt cut the air in a crisp diagonal and lodged in the tree bark just above the dummy's head.

Ollan nodded again. "Better."

Qora growled and threw her head back. *Still not good enough.*

"You have a talent for this. I've seen grown soldiers take longer to train to this point," Ollan told her. "But you have to be patient."

"*More* patient?" she asked. "If you'd had your way, it would've been months before I laid a finger on this thing."

"Sorry for not being eager to put a military weapon in the hands of a thirteen-year-old."

"It's pretty small for a military weapon." She dragged her thumb down the length of the handle.

"The word you're looking for is 'compact,'" said Ollan. "Makes it easier to maneuver. Faster spanning. And better for patrols when I have to carry it around all day."

"Well, I want one of my own. It's the perfect size for me."

"Sure. Good luck getting Mamáy to agree to that."

Qora snatched up the last bolt in the quiver and stuck her tongue out sideways at him. She was about to say that their mamáy might agree if *he* was the one who asked permission, when a loud *crunch* stopped her mid-span. One look at Ollan and she was certain it was bad. He knew the woods better than her, and the fear in his eyes spoke volumes.

That's not normal.

Slowly, Qora and Ollan turned.

Staring at them through the trees was a large, black theropod, with a blood-red sail on its back.

It opened its long, crocodilian snout, and drew a gravelly breath, tilting its head.

Qora's whole body went numb.

The reptile was the size of a megaraptor, except for the sail—which added height—but had the visual features of a spinosaur. Qora knew well enough the image of a spinosaur; there were statues and heraldic devices and patriotic artwork everywhere depicting it. *This* creature's existence, however, didn't make any sense. There were no spinosaurs in Sumaq; the national symbol had come from the Old Empire, when all the lands (including those on which the giant theropods lived) had flourished under one ruler. If this was some smaller subspecies, it didn't belong here.

"Don't move," Ollan whispered.

As if she *could*.

Even were she not paralyzed with terror, Qora had no desire to inspire the reptile's natural urge to chase a running prey.

Still, when the reptile stepped one of its webbed feet toward them, she shuddered.

Then she remembered she was holding a loaded weapon.

The reptile locked its yellow eyes on them and roared.

Qora fired a bolt at its chest.

It roared again, but continued moving toward them, picking

up speed. It did not bleed, unhindered by the shot. In fact, the bolt seemed to have barely punctured the skin.

Qora screamed.

Ollan lunged in front of her.

With long, three-fingered claws, the reptile pinned Ollan in place. Ollan thrashed against the reptile's grip, blood already seeping from his side and soaking his shirt as Qora scrambled to retrieve one of the bolts she'd shot only minutes ago.

By the time she reached one, the reptile's teeth were closing over her brother's left shoulder.

"Ollan!" She took another shot, but it soared past the reptile. "Qora—run!"

She hesitated. She couldn't just leave him there. But his strangled voice carried that same authority he'd always used on her. *Do as I say.*

"Run!" he screamed again.

Pulse pounding in her ears, Qora snatched another bolt from the ground. She sprinted several yards, then stopped at a tree and pulled herself up into the branches, higher and higher until she felt dizzy. It was difficult with the weapon but she didn't dare go without it.

Another scream hit her ears. Muffled. Unintelligible.

When Qora reached a point of safety, well out of the way, she looked down to see the sailbeast dragging Ollan away, trailing streaks of blood. She covered her mouth and clung to the tree so tightly she started to lose feeling in her fingers. Her eyes welled so fast they stung.

Ollan wrestled to whatever extent he seemed able, but it was clear his injuries had already weakened him.

Qora felt a sense of detachment, like she was watching something unfold in a dream. It *had* to be a dream. Dreams were the only place in which things like this could happen, she told herself. Dreams were the only place in which mysterious creatures could emerge in lands they didn't belong and rip someone from safety so suddenly right before the eyes of a loved one.

Surely she would wake soon, clutching her chest in a panic, and find herself alone on a bedmat in the dark, startled but unscathed—and Ollan would be on his own bedmat at the other end of the house, sprawled out with his limbs loose from their blankets, snoring.

Amid his garbled screams, Qora could feel Ollan slipping away, a tangible shift in the air around her—a shift that shriveled her heart. She wanted to run after him. There had to be something she could do …

But within seconds, the sailbeast had disappeared with him into the thick of the woods.

When Ollan's screams went silent, Qora knew it was too late.

THIRTY

"**A SAILBEAST.**" Ninan's fists curled instinctively when he said it. His stomach churned.

He hadn't expected this to be Qora's story. He hadn't expected his own father to be responsible—or to feel somehow responsible himself. His chest tightened as he tried to take his next breath.

If Qora knew the truth about him, she very well might have never let him near her.

Qora nodded. "I ran home. My mamáy gathered the neighbors. We followed the trail, searched for hours, but never found his remains—just blood, and the military identification tag he'd still been wearing around his neck." She swallowed. "I didn't find out until later that the reptile had an actual name— that others had seen it, shared stories about it, decided to call it something. Some even said it was the result of a breeding experiment, under orders of the qhapaq."

Ninan felt lightheaded. He scrubbed a hand over his face.

"If I hadn't *begged* my brother to take me out there that day …" Qora said.

"It could have been any day," argued Ninan. "Any other day, and you wouldn't think you'd done anything wrong. You had no way of knowing."

"The point is," Qora said, "that I can't let anything like that happen again. My weapon always has to be loaded. And more importantly, *I* have to always be capable of shooting it."

"That might not be possible."

She heaved a slow and heavy sigh. "I know."

ↁↁↁ

The afternoon brought a mist of rain, which Ninan thought was inconvenient as they arrived within a region where the trees thinned out again and offered minimal shelter. This time, the gaps between trees widened into an enormous, verdant meadow.

As Ninan and Qora walked across the open space, it soon became clear why the tree growth was sparse here. Hundreds of wild stegosaurians covered the expanse, grazing.

"Gods in the High World ..." Qora said reverently.

There were several species milling about. Dacentrurus with spikes instead of plates. Kentrosaurus with plates on the front half and spikes on the back, and a large spike protruding from each shoulder. Hesperosaurus with yellow skin and rounded plates that reminded Ninan of mushrooms growing sideways in a scalloped pattern. Then there were the true stegosaurs, most of which stood at least ten feet high, and extended three times that in length—thanks to their tails—with a full back of dermal plates that angled up like tapered fans. Some had plates that were as vibrant and orange as flowing lava; others had plates that were sapphire-blue, or turquoise, or magenta.

The reptiles grazed lazily, some in clusters, others more scattered. All had color variations even within the same species, a chromatic display of scales, scutes, and plates that slowly shifted on the grass. So many shapes and patterns, like flower petals.

It would have been impossible not to walk among them, for how many there were and how far spread. Qora ducked to avoid a swinging, spiked tail. The reptiles hardly seemed to notice the humans in their midst.

Qora reached out to touch a hesperosaur, gazing up at its rounded backplates. She startled when the reptile reacted to her fingertips—a twist of its neck to glance back while chewing on a mass of leaves.

In Ninan's immediate line of sight, two stegosaurs separated to reveal a lively bunch of small reptiles behind them. The younglings (whose plates had not yet grown in) bounded back and forth, squealing, and swinging spikeless tails.

Qora crouched to pet one. It nuzzled her knee, then licked her hands. She shrieked in surprise. Ninan doubled over laughing.

Qora seemed like she was trying not to smile. "Oh, you think that's funny?" She lunged at him with her slimy hand.

He twisted away.

As he should have suspected, she was fast, and she caught him coming around the opposite side of a kentrosaur. He braced her shoulders to keep her at a distance but she managed to wipe her hand on his shirt regardless.

The stegosaurians grumbled lightly at the ruckus.

Ninan looked down at his front. "How *dare* you."

Now Qora laughed—for the second time, Ninan thought, and he enjoyed the sound of it.

It took him too long to realize he was still holding her, and they maintained this awkward pose until Ninan's attention fell to Qora's feet, where one of her boot laces had fallen loose. He released her as she bent to tie it.

With her injury, however, she quickly made a tangle,

struggling to manipulate the strings.

Ninan knelt in front of her and made the appropriate loops and knots while Qora bit the inside of her cheek resentfully.

Once he'd double-knotted the lace with a brusque tug, he lingered a moment. He slid his thumb over the leather at the toe. "Wait…"

He'd assumed the black boots were made of dromaeosaur, a common reptile for sturdy footwear, having large sections of black skin that their white markings did not touch. But up close he could see a hint of red in some places. And the texture was different from the dromaeosaur-leather products he'd seen before. Thicker, and with a much wider pattern—indicative of a larger reptile.

Qora drew her foot away and stepped back.

Ninan raised his eyebrows.

She clutched the straps of her pack.

They held each other's gaze for a moment, and then she nodded slowly in response to his silent question,

"The same sailbeast?" he asked.

"Yes."

He gaped up at her, still kneeling on the ground. "How?"

"I stalked it for months. Barely had a clue what I was doing, but … somehow … I managed to find it again. The tracks were hard to follow, but the rumors were easy. There had been other sightings. Then I found signs of it in the same area …"

"I think they have a homing instinct," Ninan told her. "Well, spinosaurs do, at least. Sailbeasts probably share that."

"Lucky for me." Qora dug the toe of one of the boots into the ground absentmindedly.

Ninan stood and brushed off his pants.

Qora started walking again, leaving the midst of the

stegosaurians as they chewed contentedly. Ninan followed, watching her to see whether she would continue her story.

"I learned a lot about hunting and tracking during that time," she said after a moment. "Even all those days when I didn't find the sailbeast, I took home smaller kills for meat, since I was already out there with a weapon. Then I realized I could trade some of them for their skin and teeth, sometimes even their bones.

"My brother had told me about the Underground once, a place where he and some of the other soldiers sometimes liked to go to watch fights or play low-stakes token games—a place where trades were made 'off the books.' That's where I met Sakay. He was still apprenticing then, in charge of petty trades, which is all I was able to bring in. Until ..." She glanced down at her boots again.

"You must have been ... so terrified," Ninan said.

Qora's chin trembled. "I finally found the sailbeast drinking from the stream. Except I wasn't ready. I'd gotten used to coming up empty, so I let myself breathe for a minute, let my steps get too heavy." She gripped the straps of her pack again. "It heard me the second I came through."

"What did you do?"

"When it attacked, I didn't have time to think. I just took a shot. My bolt sank into its roaring mouth—right where the flesh was soft at the top of the throat. Put an end to it once and for all."

"Spirits ..." said Ninan. He couldn't imagine what it must have been like for her to face such a monster, after what had happened to her brother. He also couldn't believe his father had let the sailbeast run rampant for so long without managing to recover it; then again, he supposed he shouldn't be surprised that it hadn't been a priority.

"When I realized the sailbeast might be valuable," Qora explained, "I had to drag Sakay and some other guys out to the kill site because the carcass was too big for me to bring in on my own. I told them I found it already dead, but Sakay wasn't falling for it. Eventually I had to tell him everything. The boots were his idea. He said he'd make sure I got a good offer, on one condition—that I keep some part of the reptile as a trophy.

"I never wanted anything to do with it, besides making sure it didn't live another day, but … I also knew I would never really outrun the sailbeast anyway. Physically I did, but what happened to Ollan will be with me forever, no matter how I might try to distance myself. It's always on my heels. So I figured, what difference would it make if I actually wore it there?"

Ninan looked at her seriously, in awe of her words. She already seemed to carry so much on her shoulders, and now she wore those boots like additional weights strapped to her feet. He wondered whether such a coping mechanism was more helpful, or harmful. Although he admired her resolve, his heart ached for her.

"The profit from the trade was enough that I could afford a dinoleatherworker, with more to spare. And I needed some good hunting boots, so …" She shrugged.

After a pensive beat, Ninan asked, "Do you regret it?"

She glanced at her feet one last time before turning her sharp gaze back on him. "No."

THIRTY-ONE

RAIN MISTED OVER THE ROUTE AGAIN, waking Qora and Ninan early the next morning. It hit Qora first, a smatter that filtered through the canopy. Ninan, sheltered below Qora's hammock, had startled at the building sound—a million whispering drums—and they both bolted up in a frenzy to gather the skyrock dust.

Without any discussion about it, they'd stayed together another night. Qora had been too tired to present the usual arguments, and if she had any hope of surviving now that her hand was injured, she figured she was better off with an ally. She would survive for Rimaq, if she could. She had, however, created a habit, one she prayed would not lead to her eventual downfall.

Once everything was safe and dry, they began their day a bit earlier than usual—already wide awake and packed—in hopes of gaining some extra ground. No hunting for today.

Moriche palms grew over much of the landscape, dropping dark red fruit. Qora and Ninan stuffed a few dozen into their packs and ate them on the move. It rained lightly and sporadically for the rest of the day.

They stopped in the evening to build a fire before dark, using Ninan's friction matches, of which he only had a few left. Unfortunately, though, the matchfire struggled to catch on the tinder they'd gathered, the driest of which still seemed to be damp.

When they finally managed to get a full fire going, the wood steamed and smoked like the volcano in the distance until its outer layers burned off. They fried a batch of sliced plantains on a flat river stone suspended over the flames, ate quickly, then pushed onward another mile before making camp, leaving the evidence of the fire behind them.

Then they rested by the light of the mushrooms. Qora sat next to a pile of violet feathers, the few short and coarse ones that had come from the forelimbs of the troodon Ninan had shot the previous day, while she cut notches into the tail end of a bolt for fletching. Ninan worked on something strange in his lap.

"What's that?" She nodded at the thing in his hands, some triangle made of three sticks and a few fabric scraps.

"A surprise," he said. "I'll let you know when it's ready."

Qora put up the hood of her jacket and lay back on the grass for a few minutes. The green glow of the mushrooms was strong tonight in contrast to the dark sky, thanks to the cloud cover that blotted out the half moon and threatened another day of rain. Without the mushrooms, she didn't think she would have been able to see her hand an inch from her face. She was beginning to feel like the miles ahead were the same, smothered in a near-tangible darkness and filled with a growing number of uncertainties. She'd never crossed the kind of terrain they had now ventured into; she knew how many competitors were left, but she didn't know which ones; and of course the conditions at the end of the Venture would be a mystery until the remaining competitors arrived. Meanwhile, Qora's family was waiting for her, and she had no way of knowing what things would look like for them when she got back—or whether she'd make it back at all.

What was more, she wasn't keeping up with her previous pace. Based on the pennant markers, she and Ninan had only covered twelve miles after the halfway point two days ago (for a total of eighteen miles that entire day), then fifteen miles yesterday, and ten today. Sakay had warned her that all Venture routes were designed to get more difficult as competitors progressed—selected and planned for worsening landscapes and weather—but knowing that didn't stop her from worrying about falling behind. She just hoped the other competitors were slowing down too. They had to be, didn't they? Everyone was wearing thin, running low on resources, facing new challenges.

"Tell me something good." Ninan suggested, as though he had sensed the tangle in her mind. Or perhaps he had a tangle of his own he wanted to avoid. "A good memory."

A good memory? Of course Qora had lots of them, but right now they were like the moonlight that was tucked behind those thick clouds. It was amazing how something as powerful as joy could be dampened so easily, the same way something as big and bold as the moon could completely disappear behind water vapor. Still, Qora tried to picture that moon at full brightness. Then the sun. The mountains. A warm day in Qhusi, when things had been simpler.

"In the summertime, when Ollan was still alive, my brothers and I always used to help pick mora berries for our mamáy," she told him. "She works with dye, so she needs all kinds of plants and things to use for pigment. But we always ended up eating more than we picked. And then we'd try to hide it but the stains—and the empty baskets—always gave us away."

"Gods, I'd kill for a bowl of mora berries right now," Ninan said. "With cream and cinnamon …"

Qora smiled vaguely. "Do you have brothers or sisters?"

"Two brothers," he said. "But we were never friends. Not even close."

"Oh. That's too bad."

Even though Qora wasn't looking at him, still lying back on the grass, she could hear the shrug in his voice.

"There was a boy my age in Thak. I'd only known him a year, but he was more a brother to me than the ones I was raised with." Ninan huffed. "He liked to tell stories around the fire— and he was so good at it. All the kids from the community would come sit and listen to him dramatize 'The Three Allosaurs' or 'The Littlest Raptor' or parts of 'Kuymi and the Tricorn.'"

"I love 'Kuymi and the Tricorn,'" Qora said. "That's my favorite story."

"Really? Mine too. Well, actually, it's a tie with 'Chaski's Charango.' I used to play my charango and pretend I was Chaski."

Qora sat up and shook her head. "No. You do *not* play the charango ..."

"*Used* to," he emphasized. "I haven't touched one in years. I barely remember which strings to pluck, and my calluses are long gone."

"I can't even imagine it," she said.

He smiled while he twisted strips of fabric into cords and stretched them across the triangle, securing them on both sides. Finally, he held up the finished product. "All done." From his upturned hand hung the triangular framework, with dozens of little cords suspended across, intersecting at the center.

"What is it?"

"It's a Qolqese cordshield," he said. "My mamáy is Qolqese; she gave me one like this when I was small—a protective charm against demons and nightmares." He handed it over, then sat back and draped his arms over his knees. "It's supposed to be better decorated, though. Colored strings that dangle down like a quipu, and you can tie knots for words of protection. Some have big tassels, too. That one's just plain ..."

"It's beautiful," Qora said quietly, touching the corners and turning it over.

She suddenly felt strange waves of elation moving through her, and before she realized she was staring at Ninan, his eyes caught hers. This mutual awareness seemed to last a beat too long and Qora had to look away.

"I kept mine by my bed to help me sleep," Ninan told her, breaking the tension. "Who knows what I was even afraid of, but my mamáy said her ancestors used to hang them over their beds for comfort. Of course childhood fears are simpler, and obviously what's happening to us now is so much *more*—"

"I love it," she told him before he could second-guess himself again. She hung the cordshield from a branch above her hammock, letting it twist and dangle close to where her head would be. "Thank you."

Ninan's mouth broke into a boyish smile. "Anyway, I know we'll eventually have to separate again, and I just wanted you to have *something*, you know? Not that you *need* it ..."

"Maybe I don't," she admitted. "But ... I want it."

At that moment, she suddenly developed a new fear—that she wasn't only talking about the cordshield.

ꗃ

As Qora slept, for once she didn't have any nightmares. Instead, she dreamt of smoke and ash and embers. When she opened her eyes, the particles that slipped through the holes in the canopy were pale and delicate; they floated like flakes of snow in the high peaks of the Willkapampa mountains north of Qhusi. Only these flakes were not made of ice—they were a product of fire.

A fiery heart sends smoke to the head.

Tisquvian proverb

THIRTY-TWO

NINAN RAKED HIS FINGERS through his hair to clear the ash that drifted overhead as he and Qora gathered their things. Qora's dark braids were specked, and black smudges marked the hammock and the tarp and their supplies well before they finished packing it all away.

They were still most of the day's journey from the volcano, and the fact that they could feel its effects at this range was ominous.

"Do you think we're in danger?" Qora asked.

Ninan shook his head. "I don't know. Kañay may be more fiery than usual. We'll need to be careful."

Ninan recalled the few times he'd traveled with his father over this area and seen the volcano smoldering. Once, from the safety of the pterobeast gondola, he'd seen it spilling fiery liquid that oozed down the mountain and into where the trees were thick, burning them as it went. Currently, the smoke appeared to be coming from the ground a few miles off.

"We should cover our faces," Ninan added, squinting at the diffused morning light. The sky was so hazy it looked overcast. "We shouldn't breathe this directly."

They tore strips from whatever spare fabric they had on hand, and wrapped their mouths and noses.

They tried to circumvent the location of the smoke based on where it rose, but a sultry breeze meandered through and carried it back and forth, making it difficult to pinpoint the source. Ninan imagined lava creeping through the woods, traveling far from the mountain's vent, searing the earth and overwhelming the plants, igniting everything it touched. A force gripped his lungs—some combination of the hazy air and the idea that they might not make it past Kañay alive.

They moved onward, with Ninan swinging his blade and hacking at the bushes and vines that grew closer and closer together with each mile.

"Spirits, I wish there were some other path." Qora panted. "It's only going to keep getting worse ..."

"There's an abandoned trade route somewhere near here, not far from the volcano," Ninan said. "One that predates the paved road. Something like that wouldn't take so much cutting, since the plants were cleared from it for so many years. But of course any of the connecting trails are probably grown over, so it would be pretty much impossible to find."

Not only had that route been visible on the secret map Ninan had lost to the pterodactyls, but he'd actually seen it once in person too, from the air, on a trip to Huandoy flying over this region. But that was seven years ago, and he doubted he'd ever be able to locate it, especially from the ground.

As they pressed on, they passed another grove of moriche palms. Ninan picked up two fruits that had fallen, inspected them for blemishes, and handed one to Qora.

They uncovered their faces to eat. One bite, though, and Qora twisted her face. Ninan did the same.

"Must be a bad bunch," Qora said through a mouthful before spitting it out.

Ninan was about to drop the fruit when something caught his eye. There was another castoff fruit—not Qora's or his own—lying in the grass, scaly red skin broken, exposing the orange flesh inside, distinct human teeth marks on the edge. And it was fresh; it hadn't browned or shriveled yet.

Ninan jerked his head around, looking for other signs, but as far as he could see, he and Qora were alone.

"Did you hear that?" Qora asked.

At first Ninan couldn't hear anything above the persistent hum of the forest. A gallop of wind. The howl of a monkey or the chatter of a rhamphorhynchus.

He waited, trying to pick apart the sounds the way Qora might. It took a second, but then he heard it. Far off, muffled.

A soft *boom*.

The sound faded and came again. Every so often there was another.

Qora squinted. "Firebomb?"

Ninan shook his head. "Don't think so."

They both looked toward Kañay, which smoked gently like an old man with a pipe. No glowing fire filled the chamber—at least, none that was visible. The explosions must have been coming from somewhere else.

Another sort of fire ignited in Ninan's chest, a fearful one that made his blood feel hot.

This can't be good.

"Let's stop for a drink," he said, in hopes of gathering himself.

No amount of water could fight the foreboding feeling that crept up his throat, but he'd take what little water was available to quench the thirst that made it worse.

They sat with their waterskins. He took a swig and wiped

sweat from his forehead. For some reason he had expected the water to be cool, to temper his insides, but of course the waterskins had warmed like everything else.

Qora glanced up. A few of the heralds flew over, progressing in a V formation. The white pteranodons screeched as if to announce themselves, as if their giant bodies casting dismal shadows was insufficient. Ninan looked at Qora, the scene reflected in her wide brown eyes. She caught him looking and smiled—a diffident expression rather than a joyful one.

"What?" she asked.

Ninan turned back to his water. "Nothing."

Certainly not her endearing, ash-smudged face. Not the way she held her shoulders like a shell against the horrors that awaited her, fighting to hide all her fears under the surface and denying them free reign. Not her poise with a crossbow or her ferocity against pterodactyls or the memory of her fingers against the back of his hand or—

He covered his mouth again, wishing he could filter out the thoughts that lurked near the edges of his mind as easily as he filtered out the smoke that lurked near his airway. The reality of what had happened to Qora affected him more than he was able to fully admit, worsening the longer he was with her, and now all he wanted to do was to find Ruyan and beat him till his insides came out.

"We'd better go," said Ninan.

The explosions grew louder. A crackling burst, then a crumble. An emptiness after the echo. Without any particular pattern, another sounded. This went on for at least a mile.

Suddenly, Qora stopped. She jumped back, gaping at the ground.

"What's wrong?" But then Ninan saw it too. A large crack

snaked through the dirt, and widened farther down, where smaller cracks branched off.

He followed the crack visually, watching it take up the length of the foreseeable route. He pulled Qora off to the side of it.

"We'll keep going," he said. "We'll try to avoid it."

Avoid the smoke. Avoid the crack. Avoid the other competitors and the reptiles and the poisonous plants. Avoid starvation, dehydration, getting lost.

Sure. No problem.

As they moved along, it was like the earth was breathing, a chest rising and falling, pockets of air filling with unseen gases that released in huffs of smoke and steam.

The explosions continued in the distance, while a muted burble intensified close by.

Up ahead, the crack took a sharp turn that cut off their path, something they didn't see until they approached through a screen of smoke. It opened wider now, at least three feet across, a rift revealing itself as the smoke thinned in the wind.

"What in the Five Terrains …" Qora whispered.

Fire gleamed from within, but didn't flicker—a vibrant orange against the broken, earthy crust, seething. Like some glimpse of the Grave World, its contents seeping up to kill.

Ninan swatted at new flakes of ash. "The lava flowing underneath must have split the ground."

Another explosion sounded, this time louder. And this time the source was clear.

Qora gasped.

Bubbles of lava were breaking through the rift and bursting up, spewing rocks and dirt.

"We have to get out of here," Ninan said.

But as the rift threatened them from one side, thick clouds

of smoke obscured the other.

"I think we need to get to the other side," Qora suggested. "Then we can look for a different route, opposite the smoke."

As they went to cross the rift, it spewed again. A single drop of lava flecked Ninan's sleeve and burned straight through.

"Agh!"

Qora tugged him back.

The fabric buffered the heat, but barely. A blister formed in a matter of seconds, searing and stinging.

Heat spread over Ninan's body in a suffocating blanket. He looked at Qora, whose cheeks were as flushed as his own felt. Smoke shifted all around them, altering their view.

There was another loud explosion. A man bellowed. Metal scraped metal. Pteranodons screeched, their wingflaps drawing smoke aside like a translucent curtain.

Qora raised her crossbow and Ninan drew his blade.

Several figures manifested. First, Ruyan. Then Takan. Then a Tisquvian competitor Ninan didn't recognize. Two heralds hovered.

Takan held his pickaxe against Ruyan's hunting knife, pressing him toward the rift. The Tisquvian lingered nearby, as though waiting to take advantage of whomever was left most vulnerable from this encounter. Bubbles of lava belched in their midst. Ruyan pounced on Takan, his arm cocked back with his knife in stabbing position when another burst caught him off guard. Rocks and dirt shot up and tumbled down, and Ruyan shrank with his arms over his head.

The Tisquvian made a move toward what Ninan assumed to be Ruyan's traveling pack, but as soon as the lava subsided, Takan snatched the pack first and made a run for it, leaving the Tisquvian empty-handed.

Ruyan's attention snapped to Ninan and Qora.

Qora and Ninan readied their weapons as Ruyan approached. Qora gripped her trigger and aimed straight ahead.

Ruyan sneered.

Then they witnessed the loudest, biggest explosion yet, and Ninan glanced up in time to see a chunk of rock hurtling toward Qora.

He tackled her out of the way, but he was too late to get them both in the clear. The rock bashed into the crown of his head. A searing, crippling pain ripped through him, collapsing him on the spot.

THIRTY-THREE

QORA GROANED. Ninan's body pressed down on her, his head resting on her collarbone. She wedged her thumbs under his chin to lift his face.

"Ninan." She panted.

He groaned, struggling to move.

Between his weight on her chest and the sound of Ruyan's approaching footsteps, Qora's breath went shallow.

Don't think about death.

How do I get out of this?

Using the same technique Ninan had taught her for getting out from under an attacker, she used her hips and a bent knee and a planted foot to move him, rolling him off of her and onto his back.

"Ninan," she said again. She knelt over him and gave him a few gentle slaps. "Come on. Get up!"

His eyes opened a crack and he clutched his head, grimacing. When Qora looked up, Ruyan lunged at her, his long knife angled to kill.

Meanwhile, the Tisquvian seemed to be assessing them from a distance, surely making note of Ninan's weakened stance and the plethora of supplies he and Qora possessed.

Reluctantly Qora sloughed off her pack for better mobility

and swung her crossbow in front of her as Ruyan's blade came down. The blade gashed the curved wood of the limbs and halved her loaded bolt.

Ruyan struck again. And once again, Qora blocked with her crossbow, but this time she skewed it, catching and trapping Ruyan's blade flat between the crossbow's curve and the bowstring. She twisted—and unintentionally flung both weapons into a mass of dense undergrowth.

Ruck.

Heat thickened the air, dampening Qora's focus.

Ninan was too close to the rift. He inhaled sharply and clenched his teeth as he struggled to get back onto his feet, with the Tisquvian slowly approaching.

Ruyan drew a second knife from his belt. Qora turned and sprinted, dodging another spew of rocks and lava, which separated her from him long enough to give her some headway.

Farther down the rift, the lava spurted high, a red fountain of molten rock. Some of the lower-hanging tree branches had caught fire, leaves burnt off and bark blackened. Qora hesitated, skittering to a stop. In no time, Ruyan's long strides closed the gap that was her safety.

A force buzzed in her arms and legs, an energy she didn't know how to direct.

Where's my way out?

Burning trees. Smoky clouds. Liquid fire.

There was no time to consider the risks. With all her might, and a running start, she leapt over the rift, heat waves scorching the soles of her boots, and landed in a crouch on the other side. On impact, she sucked in a sharp breath.

Ruyan stared after her, then down into the hot fluid. Something akin to respect flickered over his marred face.

The rift spewed again, puffing up the earth. It gurgled, splashing lava through the opening. Lava seeped up and flowed across the ground, oozing toward Ninan.

Ruyan's gaze followed the trail to where Ninan stumbled against the Tisquvian who, thankfully, didn't appear to be armed. Ninan fought back wearily, almost uselessly. Qora thought he must be seeing double, because he acted like he was fighting two men instead of one—which wouldn't have even been an issue for him normally, but in this state, he was basically doomed.

"Not only is he not going to save you," Ruyan said, "but you're going to have to watch him burn."

Qora held her breath as she watched Ninan, the fighter whose style and grace she had so reluctantly admired when she'd first seen him, now staggering drunkenly, taking hits to the face like he had no clue how to defend himself, making halfhearted swipes at his opponent. But there was nothing she could do from here—not with Ruyan intent on revenge.

She raced down the length of the rift.

Ruyan mirrored her, matching her stride for stride.

She juked the opposite way, but Ruyan wasn't fooled; he stuck with her like a shadow, permanently fixed to her every move.

In the lava's glow, Sakay's machete glinted from Ruyan's belt.

This wasn't working. There was only one option here.

I can't. It's crazy.

Her only way out was to go *in*.

She stopped. Ruyan stopped.

Qora's eyes flicked toward Ninan again, who managed to land a single punch, then jolted backward as lava spewed between him and the Tisquvian, splashing them both. Ninan remained unharmed—by the lava, at least, as it splattered his chest where the dinoleather vest beneath his shirt protected him—while the Tisquvian clutched his arm against what appeared to be searing pain. The Tisquvian growled through gritted teeth and smothered the flames that had erupted on his sleeve.

Qora turned back to Ruyan. Smoke slithered up, blocking Ruyan's view of her for a few seconds before moving away. She watched it happen several times, almost in intervals.

That was all she needed.

She turned and walked ten paces.

"Giving up so fast?" Ruyan called.

Qora clenched her fists, gathering her courage. She took a ragged breath. She counted to three.

One.

She turned on her heel.

Two.

The smoke moved between her and Ruyan again.

Three.

Her legs propelled her forward, faster, faster. Her bent arms cut through the air at her sides. Ruyan's eyebrows pulled together as the smoke cleared.

Qora launched herself over the rift and directly at him.

He cocked his shoulder and raised his knife—an instant too late. He collapsed under her. She took advantage of his surprise and wrenched his knife away. He snaked his legs around her thighs and grappled to regain control, flipping her. As she scrambled away from his grasp, she fumbled his knife and dropped it into the rift, where it sank and melted with a prolonged hiss.

Ruyan growled and slammed her down. Flat on her back, she had a clear view of the heralds, the underbelly of each pteranodon that circled over the brawl. Another explosion rained rocks on her and Ruyan. Qora squinted and turned her face to the side, but Ruyan glared down at her unfazed.

The flat of his hand came across her jaw, which sent a rippling shock from one side of her head to the other. Flashes of color swam around her and her eyes began to water.

Ruyan straddled her waist and pinned her wrists to the ground and dragged one of her arms to the edge of the rift. Waves of heat distorted the figures beyond, blurring and warping the charred plants and trees. Just being this close to the lava made Qora feel like her skin was going to boil right off her bones.

Don't think about death.

But she was not thinking about death; she was thinking about pain.

She screamed in a pitch she didn't know her voice could reach. Ruyan scrunched his reddened, crusted face in response. Despite her piercing cry, he pressed harder. Sweat dripped from his hair onto her neck.

And then something animal in Qora took over. Her pulse beat thickly through every part of her. Her muscles hardened. The searing pain in her arms pulled at her senses like a sparkcord on a firestick, striking an explosion from within.

She didn't even have to ask where her power lay.

She bent her knees and dug her heels into the dirt and drove her hips, pitching Ruyan so far forward he released her wrists to catch himself. While he fought to regain balance, Qora clamped her arms around the trunk of his body like a strangler vine and wrestled him down. She got a single look at Ninan—who had somehow managed to wrestle the weakened Tisquvian into a cloud of steam—before Ruyan dug his fingernails into her blistered arm. She screamed and wrenched herself away while he tried to get her under control again.

The Tisquvian, with skin inflamed and red as rocoto peppers, hissed out his pain, threw a horrified look at the rift, and seemed to decide on cutting his losses, darting off into trees. Ninan collapsed onto all fours, panting.

The pteranodons cried above, audible even through the continuous explosions. Rocks rained again, this time at the back of Qora's head. Ruyan grunted as dust fell into his eyes. Qora used his momentary blindness against him, feeling around for another weapon, anything he might still have on his belt. Her fingers found the hilt of Sakay's machete.

The next explosion brought a bubble of lava above ground that burst and oozed out near Qora and Ruyan. Failing to take back the machete, Qora rolled from Ruyan to avoid the flow, hoping to leave him to its fire, but he moved before it reached him. Then he lurched onto his feet and grabbed Qora by her shirt, dragging her back.

"You're going to burn," he told her.

He whirled her around to face the rift, a tight arm around her neck, the river of lava below them. She gripped his forearm, trying to breathe, trying to keep from panicking, knowing she only had a few seconds to get out of this before he shoved her down and the flesh melted from her face.

Don't think about death. Don't think about pain.

Where was his weakness?

Qora focused on the opening, the weak point where his clenched fist met his own shoulder to lock her in. Qora tucked her chin, stepped out, pivoted against him, and thrust an elbow at his ribs, slipping out from underneath and twisting back his arm. He winced and folded at the waist.

Holding him, she slipped Sakay's machete from his belt— and shoved him into the lava.

He made sounds like nothing she'd ever heard before. His body floated on the surface as his clothes erupted in flames.

Bubbles formed under his skin and danced like a rolling boil in water. His screams lasted only a second before the heat consumed him, revealing his bare bones, which were quickly buried as the lava churned over them.

THIRTY-FOUR

NINAN WATCHED BLEARILY as Qora threw her head back and fell to her knees, her arm flaring a bright red with the heat that had burned it. She'd killed Ruyan. That bastard had met the fate he'd deserved—and Ninan only wished the excruciating heat had been drawn out longer, to cause as much suffering as possible.

Head throbbing and nose bloody, he scrambled over to Qora as liquid fire nipped at her heels, and pulled her out of the lava's range just before it caught the hem of her clothes.

She panted as she came back to herself, then turned to him as tears spilled down her cheeks. He took her in his arms, barely able to stand but determined to give her something to hold onto, at least for the moment.

As smoke curled all around them and sweat streaked their necks and arms, he took a deep, sustaining breath and said, "Let's get the hell out of here."

THIRTY-FIVE

ALTHOUGH QORA AND NINAN HAD MOVED miles from
the rift now, the fight that had taken place there stayed with
Qora, the image of Ruyan's final moments seared into her mind,
a scar that would linger as much as the burns on her skin.

Both weary from their individual beatings, Qora and Ninan
had to stop and rest several times—much more often than
usual—while the heat, the smoke, and the terrain made for a
grueling afternoon. The only water for several long miles was an
isolated pond covered in giant lily pads. Wild compies leapt from
one pad to another, dipping their snouts into the water looking
for skimming insects and chewing on purple and pink lilies the
size of cabbages. Ninan only had the chance to admire this scene
for a moment before he vomited into a cluster of sword plants.

Eventually they found a brook with some wild yams growing
along its fringes. They stocked up on water and dug up several of
the yams to eat later, along with a few herbs.

Finally, the day faded, and Qora and Ninan began to look
for a place to stay the night. They'd managed ten miles in total,
at least matching their progress from the previous day.

The pteranodons flew over and the horns blared thirteen
times—only one new death: Ruyan.

As fresh air diluted the smoke behind them, they came across the cooled lava flows of Kañay, whose mountain was currently at rest. What had once been fiery streams of lava were now thick layers of black wrinkles, solid and tepid in some areas but still sticky and hot in others.

There was about half a mile of this blackness, with pockets here and there where the wrinkles still glowed orange like embers. Qora and Ninan took advantage of one of these and used it as a cooking fire.

While they sat and roasted the yams, Ninan sipped from his waterskin and Qora wrapped her burns and other wounds with bandages and salve.

The small yams cooked fast and the outsides were burnt, but Qora and Ninan were so hungry they didn't care. They ate them and drank the last of their water, and then sat listening to the soft crackle of tame veins of lava running through and dimly lighting the environment.

Ninan, only now seeming to be fully alert, reached toward Qora and touched the bruise on her cheek—the place where Ruyan had struck her. Qora flinched at first, but then let his thumb caress her. It was a strangely soothing feeling that made her pulse kick up.

"I'm so sorry …" he said.

Qora had the sudden urge to put her hand on top of his. "For what?"

He shook his head. "I should've—"

"What?" she asked softly. "Tried to defend me?"

"Yes."

"In *your* condition?"

"Yes," he said again, dropping his hand. He gazed out into the blackness around them.

"Everything's fine," Qora told him. "*I'm* fine. And Ruyan is dead now." Of course "fine" was relative, but Qora was too tired to pick apart the nuances of everything she felt. She'd finally killed a man, directly and intentionally, and she thought she ought to find the whole thing more disturbing, but more than anything she was relieved.

"Well, it could've been you," said Ninan. "I'd never be able to live with myself if that had happened."

He sighed and buried his face in his hands, then slid them up over his hair, releasing the smoky scent that had built up on him in the midst of all this fire and char.

"I didn't realize you cared that much," Qora said. "I mean, I know you're not heartless. I'm sure you *care*, but ..."

Ninan looked at her squarely. "Of course I care that much. Since the day I met you, you're just one curiosity after another. A mystery, pulling me in. Making me question things I thought I understood. You're bold and persistent. You shoot like it's easy as breathing. And maybe you're not always well matched against the monsters of this world, but you use every claw and tooth you've got, even when the odds frown on you. Honestly, I don't know whether to try to protect you or just get out of your way. More often than not, it seems to be the latter. It's confusing, and fascinating, and ..."

Qora pressed her lips together to keep from smiling. "And ... what?"

Not that it mattered what. What did she expect him to say? He was probably delirious, after everything they'd been through today. She shouldn't care. No—she *didn't* care. *Couldn't* care.

Still, his words and his gentle touch had stoked something inside her that was hard to ignore. Not even the heat of the environment or the heat of her burns could mask the new heat rising within her body.

"*And* … I … like … being near you," he said. "You're a bright spot … in the darkness, Qora."

Qora's cheeks warmed and she had to look away. "I don't know about that. I mean, I almost got you killed—a *few* times."

"It was worth it."

She narrowed her eyes. "I'm sure you don't mean that."

"I do."

Qora supposed he hadn't exactly proven otherwise. He'd tried to intervene at the river when the painted man attacked. Then he'd taken a flying rock to the skull at the lava rift so that she wouldn't.

She shook her head. "You know, sometimes I think you're not scared of anything."

"I'm scared of lots of things," he told her.

"Like what?"

"Like … never seeing my mamáy again. Or not being able to go back home. Or … finding out, at the end of all this, that I'm a completely worthless human being."

Qora wasn't sure what he meant by that, or what would have led him to need to prove himself by competing in the Venture, but for once she saw less of his confidence and more of his pain. What pain, exactly, she couldn't guess, but it was there. "I don't think you're worthless."

He chuckled bitterly. "No?"

"No," she confirmed. "I think you're clever, and kind, and you somehow manage to hold your ground in a fight even when you're about to collapse from a head injury …"

Ninan scoffed.

Qora curled her fingers where her wound from the Rock Forest still stung, and squeezed, letting herself feel it. "I'm … I'm really glad you're here … with me. I didn't want to admit it—

obviously—and I'm not sure why I'm admitting it now, especially without having ingested anything that would encourage me to. But, this competition has been … a nightmare … and it was so much worse on my own." Her eyes welled when she thought about Ruyan, and the men at the ravine, and the pterodactyls. Her voice broke. "It's just one monstrosity after another …"

Ninan immediately took both her hands in his, and this time, Qora didn't flinch at his touch.

"Hey," he said. "Don't fear the monsters—okay? The monsters … should fear *you*."

A spatter of rain hit her cheek, startling her. Another spatter sizzled when it struck the ground.

Ninan guided her chin with his hand until she met his eyes. "Okay?"

The whisper of a laugh tickled her throat as she blinked away her emerging tears. "I think you hit your head too hard …"

He smiled. "I hit it just hard enough."

Steam rose as the rain evaporated from the few pockets of trapped, hot lava.

Ninan leaned in, his face mere inches from Qora's. The throbbing from her burns and her beatings became a throbbing in her chest that was heavier and louder than all the others combined.

His eyes darted to her mouth. His fingers twitched against her jaw.

Her breath hitched.

For all the reasons she'd once resented him, she couldn't think of a single one right now. She even tried to conjure them, to remind herself why this was a bad idea, but she couldn't.

It was foolish. She knew it. And she wanted him anyway.

Closer.

Just a little closer.

Another inch and she could forget everything. She could fall into him and get contentedly lost.

But then … he stopped.

He hesitated, then seemed to deflate, and slowly withdrew himself. "We, um … we'd better get to shelter. Before the rain gets too heavy."

Qora's spine stiffened.

"It's been a long day," he told her. "We need to rest so we can try to get a head start tomorrow." He stood and started gathering things.

Qora was frozen where she sat, once a moving fire now solidified—like the lava under her. She watched Ninan securing the buckles on their packs as she sorted through dozens of words she couldn't form into sentences.

In silence, they located a cavernous opening, a tube of rock carved from lava that had long since flowed away and cooled—a perfect place to sleep. By mushroom light, Ninan laid out his tarp inside, while Qora spread her hammock flat as a ground cover since there was no place here to hang it. They didn't bother putting skyrock dust at the lava tube's opening because it would only rinse away. Qora hoped the weather and the smoky haze would deter the wildlife.

Qora and Ninan lay side by side, but there may as well have been a gorge between them. Every raindrop that pattered was like another tiny pang, the mark of another fragment of time that somehow held an eon, but before Qora knew it, the fragments pooled into a lucid dream that then became opaque, and she surrendered to the weight of the day and her wounds and her weariness, closing her eyes on Ninan, who had turned away from her now—in more ways than one.

When you find yourself unraveled, simply begin to weave, and Sky Mother will provide you new thread.

Sumaqi proverb

THIRTY-SIX

FOR A MINUTE THERE, Ninan hadn't been thinking clearly. Qora had been right when she said he'd hit his head too hard.

But pretending he wasn't thinking about her that way became increasingly difficult when she was lying next to him, when he could hear her breaths fill the gaps of sound between raindrops.

No matter how he'd tried to ignore those thoughts, they'd been building up there, right beneath the surface. Now they were breaking through like lava from the rift, fiery and out in the open of his mind, and he didn't know how he would contain them anymore.

It took everything not to drape his arm over her, to pull her against him and whisper that he was sorry. But he couldn't.

She didn't know that when he spoke about his family, he spoke of the qhapaq—the man who burdened the people with excessive taxes, the man whose dinosaur breeding experiments were responsible for the rogue and deadly sailbeast, the man who had vied for the "privilege" to hold this competition without a care for what desperate motivations might send participants to an untimely demise.

The spinosaur-and-shield emblem pricked at the back of his neck as badly as if it had just been needle-inked on him, only in a different way now. A permanent reminder that he carried the same blood in his veins as a man who could instantly destroy anyone that displeased or disappointed him.

Maybe Qora wouldn't blame Ninan. Maybe she'd understand that he was as much a victim to the qhapaq as anyone else, only he sometimes received mercy because of his bloodline and because the qhapaq hoped his son might be worth something someday.

Or maybe Qora would see Ninan for what he really was: a coward, who hid until he was forced to come into the light, complying with a tyrant to regain an inheritance he was beginning to think he was foolish to want.

Ninan fought with himself throughout the cycles of a restless sleep. Part of him wanted to wake Qora, to forget all the things that had held him back before. But another part resisted, telling him she'd never be able to see past his secret. Even if she could, what future was there for them?

Maybe if he'd just been Ninan from Thak, instead of Apo-Kimsa Kallpa, things could have been different.

>>>

Eventually, dawn faded in and the rain finally let up, leaving a heavy moisture suspended in the air that drew out hordes of mosquitoes. In between swatting the bloodsucking insects and packing up, Ninan and Qora's exchange of words was minimal and clipped.

"How's your head?" Qora asked.

The crown of Ninan's head was tender, with a lump formed over where the rock had hit. A dull ache hung behind his eyes, and a mental fog dampened his energy. Still, he only said, "Better."

"We should get moving," Qora said. "We need to make up some time."

"I'll gather fruit before we leave."

Ninan brought back four coconas and some açaí berries as Qora finished packing, and then they set off on the next leg of the journey, hoping to add a few miles beyond the fifteen or so they'd been able to manage as the land had changed.

The break in the rain was brief, though. As morning turned to midday, another downpour followed, this time with thick, dark clouds as the sky rattled.

The durable material of their packs kept everything mostly dry, but Ninan tucked the firestick into the oilskin just in case. As for Ninan and Qora themselves, it was only a matter of minutes before they were drenched like they'd taken a fully clothed swim in the river. It felt nice at first, the way it washed off all the sweat and grime from the past few days, but soon it was uncomfortable. The lesions on their skin became waterlogged, all salves having rinsed away long ago. And the rainforest floor was a swamp, a slog that slowed their steps.

They hacked at the foliage, blades flinging water, wet leaves and vines slapping down. Qora seemed to add a particular drive behind her machete, like every strike was an assault on some unseen enemy. She wore a tight bandage on her hand to keep the wound from splitting again, but Ninan was sure she was in pain.

As they moved onward, an unfamiliar class of palm trees grew prominently along their path, with long, straight roots visible above the surface of the ground, beginning partway up the trunk and angling downward like several wooden poles leaned together. Similar to a conical tent frame.

"Walking palms," Qora said blandly when Ninan continued to gape at them. "There's a legend about them. Supposedly the earth spirits can possess them and walk them to new locations—very, very slowly over time. I wasn't sure they were real."

Ninan shuddered at the thought of trees that could walk, especially with exposed roots that were nearly as tall as he was.

After a few more hours, they stopped to rest and eat. Qora draped the oilskin tarp around the roots of one of the larger walking palms, making use of the tent-like frame they created. Some had too many additional roots in the middle, but this tree had enough of a gap that they could both enter and take shelter, giving themselves a break from the full extent of the rain.

Even after another meal of fruit, Ninan's stomach groaned. They hadn't had meat in days. He suspected Qora felt the same. But there would be no making fires in this weather to cook.

"Still hungry?" he asked.

Qora sighed and nodded. "I think I saw mangoes when we passed the hill by the river, about five minutes behind us. I'll go back and gather a few."

"We can both go."

"Not unless we take everything with us," she reasoned. "It'll be better for one of us to stay here. The tarp's already set up."

"Then I'll go."

"You need to rest as much as you can. You won't get very many chances with how far behind we are."

Ninan's head still throbbed and he knew she was right, but he hesitated to let her go alone.

"I'll be quick," she said.

She took her crossbow and some bolts for protection, along with her machete in case she needed to go into the foliage, then pulled up her hood—as though both her hair and the jacket weren't already soaking wet—and headed off.

With Qora gone, Ninan felt himself relax. He hadn't realized how tense he'd been. After last night, the discomfort between him and Qora was tangible, and it had worn on him more than he cared to admit. As he waited for her, different kinds of emptiness rumbled against each other inside him—hunger and guilt and growing hopelessness—echoed in the thunder above the canopy.

He waited and waited. He couldn't tell how long it had been, but it felt like twenty minutes, at least. Half an hour, maybe.

Something's wrong.

But he remembered how slow they'd been moving in this new climate—how, even though Qora was stubborn about keeping speed, she was also wounded, even if she wanted to act like she wasn't.

Maybe it hadn't been as long as he thought it had. Surely hunger and boredom and never-ending rain could alter one's perception of time.

And somehow, he didn't think that was the case.

With each passing minute, his heart beat louder, faster, with more urgency. He walked several paces from the tarp, peering out over the path they'd cut, but no one was there. No hint of Qora, not even a distant figure. He squinted to be sure, knowing her green jacket would blend in, and visibility was poor right now.

Still nothing.

If she was lost and he left this spot, they may never find each other again—and he had all her things. But if she was hurt and stranded and in need of help, every minute Ninan waited here was a risk borrowed against her life. He had to find her.

Still, he had to account for other scenarios. What if Qora came back after he left? He gathered what scraps of fabric were left of the poncho he'd stopped wearing days ago, separated the copperskin lining from it, and shredded it to thin strips with his pocketknife, leaving the pieces attached together on one end. He twisted the strips into quipu cords and built a message into the knots and hung the cords from a low branch where they would be easy to see in case Qora came back while he was gone. Then he rolled up the tarp, grabbed Qora's pack and his own, and headed back the way they'd come.

There were traces of their journey, bootprints they'd left in the mud, the leaves they'd hacked away. It would have been difficult to get lost when there had been a clear path to follow.

What could have happened?

When he located the mangoes, there were no signs of Qora. What he found instead was a heavy waterflow that intersected the path—a flow that hadn't been there when they'd passed before—coming from the adjacent slope and carrying a significant amount of mud and debris. With a persistent humming in his chest and a hollowness in his stomach that now had nothing to do with hunger, he followed the flow. The mudslide gushed over a distance of three or four yards, and then washed down another incline. Right into the swollen, swiftly flowing river.

No, no, no, no, no.

Ninan jerked his head in every direction looking for any other clues, pleading with the gods he didn't believe in. He dropped the packs and clambered down to the platform above the bank, sprinting parallel to the river, screaming Qora's name. The rain was even heavier outside the canopy of trees. For several minutes he called, then waited, called, then waited. There was no reply but the echo of his own voice and the pelting rain and the fading thunder. Hopeless, he returned to the packs. His throat was raw, and his entire body shook when he thought of Qora swept under the rapids. He had let her believe he didn't feel the things he felt. And now she could be dead.

In the middle of his silent pleas to the water spirits, a sharp sting pierced his collarbone. Reflexively, he slapped himself.

Damn mosquitoes.

Except … there hadn't been mosquitoes since before the rain had picked up again.

His fingers twitched at the base of his neck, coming up against a fine, wooden dart.

He plucked it out, hissing at the pain, his eyelids suddenly heavy as he tried to examine it.

His vision blurred, as though he hadn't slept in days, a weight pulling at all of his senses. His muscles loosened without warning. He crumpled to the ground. Everything went black.

THIRTY-SEVEN

MUDDY WATER SPEWED from Qora's mouth. She coughed and gagged as she gripped the base of a grassplant. The rapids, swollen from rain and coursing at high speed, swiped at her legs. She'd been too preoccupied over the prospect of drowning to worry about water predators, most of which thankfully seemed to have sought deeper waters in this chaos—but she didn't want to take any chances.

Gasping, she flexed her arms, muscles taut as rawhide stretched over a drum, and flailed her lower half to propel herself up. When she clambered onto what was left of the bank—the thin ribbon of land that wasn't submerged—she dug her nails into the mud, clawing her way up until she was completely free of the river's pull, slipping and sliding, but grounded.

By the grace of the water spirits, her weapons still hung from her body, the machete on her belt, the crossbow strap across her chest. Except she'd lost all her bolts in the water; she'd watched them spill out of their quiver and float downstream like a school of slim, dead fish. And sometime, during one of her attempts to get a handhold on bankside wood or plants, the string on her crossbow had snapped.

Everything had happened so fast.

Stray branches and leaves had built up at the bottom of the

hill by the mangoes, packed tightly between two trees that had grown a few yards apart, with rainwater dammed up behind. The pressure had apparently been building. And then it had ruptured and sent a violent mudslide across Qora's path, whipping her feet out from under her.

Now she could be a mile from where she'd started, and that wasn't even considering the twisting of the river's flow, affecting where she was laterally in relation to Ninan.

Ninan.

How long had it been? How long before he would give up and go on without her?

The rain slowed to a mist, but Qora was so completely wet it hardly mattered either way. Catching her breath, she tried to reorient herself, to look for clues about her location. Unfortunately, everything was the same as before: vibrant green leaves, a deep gray sky, a wet sheen on every surface.

Maybe it was for the best, she thought, that she and Ninan had been separated. The tension between them was an unnecessary strain, something petty that Qora didn't need weighing her down. It didn't matter where Ninan was now; she ought to keep going, forget what she'd left behind.

If only Ninan didn't have all her supplies.

Could Qora make it to the ruins with just a machete and a crossbow—assuming she could fix the crossbow? She considered whether it would be worth the effort to get back to Ninan. One glance at the dense, seemingly endless jungle, however, made the decision for her.

Be precise or do it twice.

She had to think carefully and do this right, with every possible advantage. Especially because there was no "twice" in this situation. No second chances. Her death might bring her family *some* financial relief, but if there was any possibility she could succeed and finish the competition, she had to give it her all.

The logical thing would be to follow the river, to walk against it, opposite the way it had swept her. If she were to follow the same snaking route, eventually she'd end up back at the same place she'd fallen in. Hopefully.

Without allowing herself to think about everything that could go wrong—surprises in the landscape, a reptile attack while her weapon was broken, whether Ninan would have left their spot or gone looking for her or run into other competitors again—Qora started hacking a new path, with dread seeping in from all sides.

As she cut her way through, the rain stopped altogether and the air turned to steam. One minute, Qora was soaked in river water, and the next she was soaked in sweat, and the change was so gradual that she missed the shift—except that the sweat stung her wounds much worse than the water had.

Her jacket smelled like a wet dog, the lightweight wool trapping moisture against her. She squirmed under the fabric until she couldn't take it anymore, peeling it off and tying it around her waist. The long sleeves of her shirt were no better, stuck to her like a layer of dead, wet skin; she tore them off at the shoulder.

Immediately she regretted this.

The mosquitoes already buzzing around her by the hundreds descended on her bare arms, pricking her and sucking at her life force drop by drop. This urged her onward, as they landed on her in swarms whenever she stopped or slowed her pace, while motion and speed somewhat deterred them. Instinctively, her fingers tugged at her jacket, aching to untie it, to put it back on as a barrier, but the heat was its own jacket, and the thought of two made her feel like she couldn't breathe, couldn't think straight. If her body didn't suffocate first, her mind might.

It was difficult to be as alert as she knew she needed to be. She needed to pay attention to the sounds, the smells; she had to look for clues and signs of danger. Most of the tracks on the ground belonged to smaller reptiles, even if she couldn't identify them all, and a lot of the ruck piles were hours old. She tried to estimate the number of larger carnivores close by, to listen past the howler monkeys' low-pitched calls that overpowered many of the dinosaurs'. Flyers remained perched in the canopy, for the most part, while spider monkeys moved throughout, their tails like a fifth limb grasping at branches. While gazing up, distracted by the eerie sight, Qora nearly stepped on the remnants of a carcass—some small theropod, maybe having weighed fifteen pounds at its heaviest. Only a few shreds stuck tight to the bones, just enough to reveal the shape of the teeth that had fed on them: two sizes on the same jaw.

"Dimetrodon ..." Qora stepped back and glanced around. She crouched to look at the moist soil, where five-toed footprints faded somewhere into the leaves. Based on the size of the footprints, the dimetrodon would have only been six feet long, maybe, including the tail. The spinal sail probably wouldn't have come up higher than Qora's shoulders, not too big to be intimidating to a human—unless of course that human were to find herself without a weapon. Stocky-legged dimetrodons might *look* slow, as far as they appeared in illustrations, but they were said to be surprisingly fast and vicious. Qora thought of the woman at the city square in Qhusi, with her jar of "brain berry" dimetrodon eyeballs. *Breach the cracks of a broken mind! Heal an injured brain! Achieve mental clarity!* After experiencing the effects of eating that theropod heart with Ninan, Qora wondered whether the old woman might have actually been telling the truth.

Down at the river, a cluster of pterodactyl nests bobbed with the raised water level. Qora tensed at the sight of them, but there were no pterodactyls at the moment. She scanned the skies but found them empty of anything so large. Meanwhile, the nests floated, despite the heavy eggs they held, and despite their own heaviness in general. Qora marveled at how watertight they were, especially as one of the nests detached from the others and drifted off in the current like a little boat.

Rumberries grew all along the riverside, globules bunched up on bushes. Qora stained her fingers as she plucked them and stuffed her mouth, dribbling juices, not able to eat fast enough to calm her raging appetite. When she'd just about made herself sick, she collapsed in the grass, staring at her hands, suddenly reminded of her mamáy. Her mamáy's stained hands. Soft yarn dyed red.

A pang seized Qora's chest.

She was so far from where she needed to be. Not only from Ninan and the site where they'd stopped, but from the goal. The reason she was doing all this. Already at least a day behind and now she was going backwards—on purpose.

It took all her energy to stand back up again and keep moving, but she couldn't waste time. Not if she was going to find Ninan. Not if she was going to get home to Rimaq. She clenched her fists, holding on to the berry stains, holding on to memories of her mamáy, and gathered herself.

More hacking, more mosquitoes, more steam as the sun baked the soil. Rhamphos called to each other between branches and caimans waded along the slowing river current as the basin curved inward. Blue mononykus startled when Qora came hacking through the vines too fast. A protoceratops munched on lattice mushrooms and, instinctively, Qora moved her crossbow into position—forgetting momentarily that she couldn't hunt without bolts.

By the time she found a section of trampled grass and broken foliage, she hardly believed what she saw. She was sure it was some hallucinatory manifestation, a mirage she'd created out of desperation.

But she was positive this was where she'd left from this morning. The same clearing she and Ninan had cut around the walking palm, indentations where they had set their heavy packs, fruit peels scattered over the ground.

Except … Ninan wasn't there. In place of him was a makeshift quipu.

He'd left her a message:

MUST GO ON ALONE. SORRY. GOOD LUCK.

))))

Qora sat on a log, numb, staring up at the jungle's underbelly. Tears streamed from the corners of her eyes and collected along her jaw until they condensed and fell to her chest. The leaves wavered in a wind that offered no relief; it only added movement to the heat trapped between the trees.

The swollen bumps on Qora's arms begged her to scratch them, but instead she held the bundle of cords and ran her fingertips over the knots, pausing to pinch them like she could change their meaning.

Hunger and longing warred against her apathy.

She closed her eyes and pictured Ninan. His broad shoulders, his guarded smile. What had happened last night? Had she misread him? What she felt for him had shifted so subtly and so naturally, as subtly as her body had gone from river-soaked to sweat-soaked a few hours ago. Only this stung even more.

How could he have done this to her? *Why* would he have done this? He'd been the one to insist they stay together. She'd never asked a single thing of him, and now he was just ... gone?

It didn't seem like him—to leave her when they'd come so far, to take all her things with him. Had it all been just a long-game trick? Had this been Ninan's plan from the beginning? Use her to get through the worst of it, rob her of her tools, and leave her to die?

He's not like that.

But did she really know what he was like? Did she know *anything* about him? Maybe he was just like Ruyan, an actor with an agenda. Maybe he had set traps after all, with charms and false kindness rather than spikes at the bottom of a slope.

One thing she did know was that she didn't have time to think about this. She could argue with herself for days trying to make sense of it, wasting away mourning the loss of Ninan, but his motivations were irrelevant. All that mattered was getting back to her family—which seemed like an unattainable, golden dream now that she was stranded with practically nothing.

To make a new string for her crossbow, she would need an animal for its sinews. To kill an animal, she would need a working crossbow. And where would she sleep? How would she protect herself? She had no tools to make fire, nothing to sleep on, and no skyrock dust.

With less and less daylight left, she had to make a choice. She forced the last few tears from her eyes, wringing herself out, and stood.

While the heralds blew the horns before duskfall (eleven

times), Qora looked for things she could use—several small, sturdy branches; a wide, flat rock; bundles of grass; leaves almost as big as she was.

She twisted the grass into a long rope, made a stack of the giant leaves and rolled them up so they were easy to carry, and sharpened the branches to points. Sunset was pending, so she'd have to hurry. She gathered her new supplies and set off to look for the best place in the ground to suit her needs. Then, wiping a layer of sweat off her forehead, she took a deep breath and plunged the flat rock into the damp soil like a shovel blade, and started digging.

〉〉〉

A couple of hours later, Qora had hollowed out a cave for herself where the land sloped up into a mound, big and dense enough to support the space. With leaves, she'd lined the inside and strung together a curtain to hide herself. She'd broken ground once more to dig a small dinofelis trap, and now she waited, and hoped that a reptile would find its way to one of them.

In the complete darkness of her cave, Qora curled against the wall, feeling like it was all too appropriate that she was in the ground, because there were things she needed to bury. Bury the part of her that still hoped there was some elaborate misunderstanding and that Ninan was waiting for her somewhere. Bury the part of her that didn't think she could go back to doing this alone. Bury her pity, her sympathy, her compassion, and tomorrow emerge from this cave a vicious killer with a singular focus.

As fatigue tugged at her eyelids, she thought of Rimaq, his little face all splotched with pox, and her mamáy wearily catering to his every whimper, not knowing whether he'd make it another day, and Hakan working for the metalsmith with hands far too rough for a boy his age. And herself, with an accumulating list of challenges, and no reason to believe she would finish her task, alive or dead.

Then her mamáy's words came back to her, the phrase Hakan had repeated before Qora had left without saying goodbye. *Even grass has a blade.*

"There is always something that can be done," her mamáy had often said. If the bread had gone stale, she would cut it into small pieces and add chancaca and cinnamon to make rafañote. Once, when Qora had fallen and scraped her elbow, leaving a permanent blood stain on her white blouse, her mamáy had dyed the whole thing red to cover it. When Qora's weaving threads would tangle, her mamáy always knew clever tricks to salvage the design, to make something new as though that had been the idea all along.

In the face of mistakes, in lacking, Qora's mamáy had taught her to look for that fine edge that could cut through obstacles, that there were options even when all seemed lost.

No matter what else happened, Qora had to fight. She would turn scraps to fuel, and make war paint of her blood, and untangle this horrible mess.

Even though her promises may have felt as thin and flimsy as blades of grass, Qora said them aloud to give them to life.

"I'm going to win this competition—and I'm going to destroy anyone who gets in my way."

NINAN OPENED ITCHY, PUFFY EYES. He blinked slowly, watching his surroundings become more clear—although it wasn't much of a clue as to where he was. A blur of green … and more green. His neck ached, muscles tight and inflamed, but when he went to lift his hand to it, he found his arms immobile. Ropes cut into his wrists, and despite feeling like he didn't have the strength to keep his head up—let alone the rest of his body—he was vertical, his back held straight against something rigid and rough. *A tree?*

The daylight was milky, with the kind of chill—not exactly a chill, but something less than oppressive heat—that came only in the early hours, the sun's fire not yet fully blazing. But it couldn't be earlier than when he'd lost consciousness. Not unless he'd been unconscious through the night, and this day was a new one.

How long had he been here?

Some of the plants around him showed touches of humankind—vines cut, grass trampled. Then Ninan spotted two packs—Qora's and his own—open on the ground.

Beads of sweat eased down his face. There was smoke, a flickering flame.

A caiman carcass roasted on a spit of branches. Once Ninan

processed the smell, hunger gripped him like a predator.

"Good morning," someone said, as though this were the most casual situation.

Ninan turned his head too quickly and regretted it, his temples throbbing from the force. "Takan …?"

The other competitor rotated the caiman and tended to the fire. "How are you feeling?"

How am I feeling? Like there were blades cutting into the space behind his eyes. Stiff muscles and stinging cuts. He groaned and tried to focus, a new fog weakening his brain.

"What's going on?" Ninan's voice came as a dry croak. Deep in his chest he felt the urge to panic, to thrash, but an unseen heaviness held him still, kept him slow and mellow.

Takan moved to Qora's and Ninan's packs and sifted through the supplies. "Thought it'd be nice to spend some time together." He removed and examined each item from Qora's pack. Salve, mushrooms, hammock. Ninan's pack came next. Firestick, rolled-up tarp, pouch. Takan opened the pouch and gave it a sniff, then wrinkled his nose. "Is this really the best skyrock dust you could afford? As a prince of Sumaq?"

"I *was* a prince," Ninan reminded him. "You should know that. You implied the first time we spoke that you're aware of my history."

"Yes, and of the future you hope to attain. But it seems there's quite a bit of history you've forgotten."

"Enough with the games," Ninan said. "Who are you? How do you know me?"

Takan chuckled. "The games have only been my way of entertaining you, princeling. I didn't want to bore you. I thought it might be a challenge for you to retain information if it wasn't presented to you with a high standard of theatrics."

"My heritage hasn't given me the benefits you think it has."

"Really?" Takan stroked his chin. "Strange, then, that you'd risk your life to *restore* that heritage. That *is* what you're trying to do here, isn't it?"

Ninan had no response to that. It *was* strange. But his heritage was something he didn't think he'd ever be able to fully disentangle himself from, a life and a past that would never completely fade from his sense of being. While Ninan pondered this, Takan said, "How about I entertain you with a story, hmm?"

Again, Ninan was silent.

"Imagine a boy from Unu. Ten years old. Son of an uncommonly beautiful woman who was fortunate enough to find employment in the home of an esteemed Sumaqi ambassador. An ambassador so esteemed, in fact, that he has, on multiple occasions, had the grand privilege of hosting terrenal monarchs." Takan seemed to pause for dramatic effect, and then began to pace slowly. "Qhapaq Apo, as you might be aware, is very fond of Unu—the rugged hills and sprawling wetlands … The food … The women …"

"Yes, I'm painfully aware of his social activities and the tastes that drive him."

"So you *are* aware of what goes on in your household."

"Not aware enough to differentiate between the qhapaq's numerous conquests—although that should speak more to his character than to mine."

"'Numerous,'" Takan repeated. "Too many to remember, naturally. So many that they might as well be livestock. Nameless creatures to be used for their benefits and retired when they've worn out."

"That's not what I meant. I've never liked the way he carries on, the way he takes whatever he wants whenever he wants it.

I've been among common people, too, witnessed loving and loyal relationships, watched people capable of behaving with respect. My household has never functioned that way, but that doesn't mean I don't wish it did."

"See, I almost want to feel sympathy for you. And I would, except … How can I take you at your word when you've been doing everything in your power to get back into the good graces of that house?"

Ninan shook his head. "Nothing is that simple. If you'd just—"

Takan's knuckles sent a shockwave through Ninan's head. Only then did Ninan realize that, for the first time since he'd laid eyes on Takan, that the man wasn't wearing his gloves—and that the back of his hand bore the branding mark of the Three Crescents.

"I was *there*." Takan rubbed his knuckles, just above where his skin was raised and pink. "I was *at* Kallpa House. A decade ago. Brought there alongside my mother, who was given the room and board of a servant. Servant—because that's what she was. Not an equal, not a lover, not even a mistress, despite whatever title she may have had. I didn't understand at first; I thought her work would be similar to her employment in Unu: housekeeping, tending to guests. It nauseates me, how naive I was."

Ninan's stomach roiled. It was one thing for Kallpa House employees to willingly take on the mark, to give themselves in loyal service to the qhapaq and allow the hot iron to forever brand them as his; it was another for those who were brought in by command, without a choice in the matter. "Look, you *have* to believe me when I say—"

Takan struck him again. "I'm not finished."

Wearily, Ninan nodded that he understood, waiting for the spots in his vision to clear.

"I was allowed to accompany her to the castle," said Takan, "and live with her there, as an *incentive*. No more shining dinoleather shoes on the streets; I'd be well fed, clothed finely, educated by the tutors of Kallpa House." He laughed bitterly. "She told me it was an 'assignment' …. That it would be good for us both. But night after night, I watched her go to him, all made up like some offering to a sick and selfish god. And then I'd sit on the edge of my bed, waiting, shaking, clenching my fists, with only a vague understanding of what she was doing— what she was obligated to do—but knowing enough to give me nightmares." Takan stopped pacing, jaw firm, staring daggers. Finally, he relaxed and cleared his throat. "We were there for two months. Treated well, for the most part. Almost like guests. I've had a taste of your life, brief and limited though it may have been."

"You haven't had the slightest taste," Ninan argued.

Takan nodded. "Sure. And I suppose it was because you were *so* miserable with all your wealth and privilege that you couldn't help yourself. You had to vandalize the meager space in which I was allowed to exist."

"Vandalize? I—"

The word summoned the memory of paint—Sumaqi red, stolen from the stockhouse, typically used for placards and patriotic emblems—splashed across a splitting, wooden door. The words *whore* and *bastard* in his own eight-year-old scrawl. Words he'd barely known the meaning of, but he knew they would cause harm.

"Spirits …"

As if that hadn't been enough, he'd entered and torn the

rooms apart, too. Thrown clothes onto the floor, knocked over tables and chairs, mussed the bedding.

He tried to conjure what he must have been thinking at the time, what would have possessed him to do such a thing. All he remembered was that his father's attention had been fleeting. The qhapaq had barely acknowledged his own wives and sons, and yet he'd found time to collect additional women—and, in some cases, their children when he felt merciful enough not to separate them. Although now that Ninan thought about it, he realized it wasn't mercy, but convenience. After all, what good was a downhearted woman whose children were far away from her, and usually in poor conditions? Better for her to have a constant reminder of who else could benefit from the arrangement. Such a woman is much more compliant. Even female reptiles made better beasts of burden when kept near their young; otherwise, they were likely to resist, even despite the threat of skyrock.

Ninan remembered how he had felt the presence of these women and children in his home tenfold. Strangers coming and going. He hadn't yet come to understand his father's responsibility in the matter, hadn't yet learned to resent him; at the time, Ninan had still felt a fierce loyalty to the man, feared him but also admired him, believed that maybe others had been to blame for tempting or distracting him. Ninan had scarcely known the meaning of the words he'd used to shame Takan and his mother. All he'd known was that visitors were not welcome— at least not to him.

"I saw the whole thing," Takan said. "Watched you from across the passageway while you made your point."

"I'm sorry," Ninan told him. "I really am. I was a stupid child, and to me you were the reason my father hated me. One of many." He shook his head at the memory. "Are you really going to punish me like *this* for something I did when I didn't know any better? For … ignorant slurs?"

Takan scoffed. "Oh, is that all it was?"

"Do you think I didn't have demons of my own? Do you think it was easy for me to see my father bringing strange women into my home? Do you think being raised by a man like that, that I could have possibly known any better? I regret it. I do— *sincerely*. And not just because I'm bound. What could I possibly do to compensate you now?"

"You think that's the end of the story?" Takan replied. "No. There's more. There's the part where the boy and his mother were sent home. The part where the boy's father couldn't look at the boy's mother the same way anymore. She was different. Tainted. Maybe he hadn't wanted to see her that way, knew it wasn't her fault, and still, he only felt betrayal and disgust. In her absence, he'd taken to drinking pisco to keep himself numb; after she returned, he couldn't kick the habit, turned angry and lazy. The boy's mother spiraled into despair, grew to hate herself. Finally, the boy found her alone on the floor, breathless, with the stain of nightshade on her lips."

Ninan wasn't sure whether the mounting turbulence in his stomach was related to whatever he'd been drugged with or whether the ending of Takan's story was affecting him—or whether it was some combination of both. He *was* sure, however, that his face had paled considerably, because he was too dizzy to have any blood circulating particularly well above the neck. "There's nothing I can say to convey how sorry I am for what you've lost, Takan. I can't take back what I've done, and I can't fix what happened before or after. But you don't have to do this. Qhapaq Apo is your real enemy, and if you think hurting me will punish him, it won't; he doesn't care about me."

"He may not care about you, but he cares what you can do for him. He wouldn't allow you the opportunity to redeem yourself if it didn't benefit him in some way."

"That may be true, but killing me will only *inconvenience* him. It won't thwart his power."

"You're right," said Takan. "It won't. But when I win the Venture, when he names me champion at the homecoming ceremony, I'll be sure to put an end to his reign."

"How, exactly, do you plan on doing that?" Ninan twisted inside the ropes that bound him. His wrists were tied in front, while his body was bound with additional ropes, without slack.

"Pollenbane," Takan said. "Ever heard of it?"

Ninan shook his head.

"It's made from the pollen of k'acha-miyu. Once it comes into contact with human skin, it slowly poisons over the next several hours, eventually stopping the heart. Just one touch— during a congratulatory handshake, perhaps—from a gloved assassin. That's all it would take. No one would suspect a thing."

Ninan couldn't say he didn't want to see this happen. Then again, Apo-Huk would only take their father's place, and lead Sumaq in a similar manner. Regardless, he doubted Takan could really enact such a plan.

"Fine," said Ninan. "Do as you wish. Try your hand at killing the qhapaq. I won't stop you. But you have no need of me."

"Anyone with Kallpa blood deserves to suffer."

"I *have* suffered. My own father practically fed me to wild raptors. He encouraged my brothers to batter me on a regular basis as a test of my character and worthiness from the time I was small. This competition, in which I've been robbed, beaten, mauled by pterodactyls, nearly impaled—it's yet another test for me, not some opportunity for me to show off. I don't want to be a Kallpa—I'm not *fit* to be one—but I also don't know how to be anything else." Saying so much at once left Ninan winded and he had to take a deep breath.

Takan slow-clapped and stepped closer, examining Ninan like he was some strange specimen. "That all sounds very sad, but … there's also a special satisfaction that comes with seeing you this way, helpless and afraid. And the girl, well, she's been an excellent catalyst to your suffering."

The memory of the waterflow came back to Ninan with the sting of a thousand of Takan's darts.

Qora.

His mind was still sleepy, still processing where he was, what Takan had said. He hadn't remembered the circumstances that had led to this situation in the first place.

Where was Qora now? Had she survived? All this time Ninan had been trapped here, useless, while Qora might be desperate for help.

"You saw her," Ninan said. "Was she alright?"

Takan didn't reply. He only smiled and returned his attention to the packs he'd stolen. He also had his own pack at the ready, although it was different from what he'd been carrying before; it was dinoleather, sleek and impermeable—perfect for keeping out rainwater—and clearly stolen as well. Apparently without much assessment, he condensed all the stolen supplies into it, all food and tools and gear, even Qora's cordshield. "Good luck charm?" he asked, then shrugged and tucked it in along with everything else.

"Have you seen Qora or not?" Ninan demanded.

"I'd tell you, but that would deprive you of the lesson." Takan finished arranging his new things and approached Ninan again. "The person you care about? Not knowing exactly what's happening to her, whether she's alright? Whether you'll find her in the same condition you left her in? Who might have *touched* her ..."

"I will beat you until your skull cracks," Ninan growled. He twisted uselessly in his ropes again.

Takan adjusted his shirt collar. "Don't be silly. You won't be using your fists anytime soon. Meanwhile, poor Qora will be wondering where you've gone."

Ninan stopped fighting his bindings and snapped to attention. "So she's alive?"

"She looked like she'd gone for a *horrible* swim." Takan gathered some of the crossbow bolts that had slipped out of their quiver and set them and Ninan's crossbow together next to his newly arranged pack.

Blood pulsed hard through Ninan's limbs but dammed up where the ropes pressed against him. He spit on the ground because it was all he was capable of doing at the moment. "You've made your point, alright? Stop wasting time trying to sabotage me. You should be trying to get to Utula as fast as you can."

Takan nodded. "Yes, I should. But I was running low on supplies. You and the girl seem to have accumulated enough to last me till the ruins, along with some other things I've confiscated. Now I just need to increase my speed, and, as luck would have it, there's a megaraptor running loose—a failed capture by some other competitor, most likely—and I'm going to catch it. On a raptorback, I'll make excellent time."

"You'll never catch it," Ninan said.

"The lure I've set up won't be as effective as a dinofelis pit," Takan admitted, "but I don't have time to dig one large enough for a reptile that size."

Ninan narrowed his eyes, thinking of the spike that had

stabbed his leg, remembering how he and Qora had had to claw their way out of the earth. "It was *you* ..."

"You're familiar with my work?" Takan smiled sourly. "Glad to know my reputation precedes me."

"Your trap wasn't enough to kill me. Who's to say a simple lure will be enough for a raptor five times my size?"

"I've also got tranquilizers if the raptor is uncooperative." He removed a wooden blowgun from his belt, twirled it, and tucked it back in. The same tranquilizers he'd used on Ninan.

"Wow. You've thought of everything," Ninan deadpanned.

"Which is why I'm going to win."

"Then you should really quit wasting your time with me," said Ninan. "I don't care about winning anymore. Seriously. Just let me find Qora and make sure she's okay, and I'll quit the competition. I swear."

"Does she know the truth?" Takan moved back to the caiman at the fire, which was now charred and sizzling. He removed it, set it vertical, and sliced meat from the carcass. Its scent grew stronger, making Ninan's mouth water.

The truth? Those words burned like the friction of the rope against his wrists. Thinking of how Qora's family had suffered—was currently suffering. How she'd sacrificed everything, risked pain and personal violation and death. Thinking of how she'd managed to trust him in all this when everyone else had wounded her, betrayed her. How he'd hidden the extent of his past since the moment they met.

Takan laughed while he chewed, the juices of the meat dripping down his chin. He swallowed and wiped it with his sleeve. "That's what I thought."

"I'll tell her. Eventually. Whatever the consequences. But there's not much time. Let me go and I'll flag down the heralds as soon as I find her."

With the heralds in mind, Ninan turned his eyes toward the sky, but the canopy was so thick he'd be lucky to catch a single flash of the white pteranodons through the leaves. Mullu surely wouldn't be able to see him here like this, to know that he needed help.

Takan tilted his head and set another chunk of meat into his mouth. He approached, standing so close Ninan could smell his breath, which was both disgusting and intoxicating. "Interesting offer, but … no. Anyway, she's long gone. She had to spend a lot of time making preparations for herself without having access to her supplies, but she took off this morning. She'll be miles out by now."

"What makes you think she won't keep looking for me?" said Ninan.

"She has no *reason* to keep looking for you," Takan replied with confidence. He moved back to the fire and tossed dirt into it, extinguishing the flames.

Not far off, a megaraptor roared. Takan powdered his hands with Ninan's skyrock dust.

"No," Ninan said. "There's no reason she'd go on without me."

But of course he could think of plenty of reasons. Like her urgent need to get the golden spinosaur tooth and win. Or the way he'd confused her emotions at Kañay.

"She would if she thought you'd gone on without *her*," said Takan.

Ninan opened his mouth to argue, but the pieces started to come together before he could even finish forming a phrase in his mind.

Takan had shot and tranquilized Ninan not far from where he'd stopped to rest. He knew things about Qora and how she was faring. He had to have been watching them for hours. He would have seen them get separated, seen Ninan searching for her, seen the quipu …

"Why shouldn't she believe a message," Takan asked, "spelled out on something that belongs to the very boy she was looking for? Even if it's not the same message you wrote her."

Acid crept up Ninan's throat and he went limp inside the ropes.

If his eyes could be daggers.

The corners of Takan's mouth twitched up. "Now if you'll excuse me, I have a raptor to catch."

THIRTY-NINE

WITH SAKAY'S MACHETE, Qora added her own noise to the rhythmic ensemble of the jungle. Amid high-pitched trills, an underlying chatter, a punctuating *caw*, and small dinos growling over grubs, she flung her blade.

Swing—chop—swing—chop.

The sound of her footsteps shuffling through organic decay.

A grunt. Another shuffle.

Swing—chop—swing—chop.

This was supposed to make her feel like she was making steady progress, but in reality, she didn't feel like she was getting anywhere.

The jungle seemed to thicken as she moved. Trees grew closer together, the underbrush spread wider, and vines meandered and dangled like hundreds of territorial snakes that refused to let her pass.

In the time it had taken her to travel half a mile, she should have covered two or three, and she was already delayed from everything she'd had to do before she'd left that morning.

Her crossbow hung by its strap against her hip, once again loaded and functional, thanks to the fact that a compy had fallen into her trap during the night. She'd stripped the reptile's backstrap sinew, then dried, separated, and twisted it to make a new bowstring and repair her weapon. She'd even used the reptile's fat to grease the crossbow's metal flight groove, which had washed too clean in the river, and then she'd cobbled together a few crude bolts.

It had been worth the extra time, now that she was armed again, but what little hope she had of cutting through to victory was fading fast.

Without a map, she'd have to try to remember the route on her own, and hope to spot the red pennant markers to reassure her she was still going the right way. For the moment, she strayed from the bank as she followed a set of dimetrodon tracks that ran parallel to the route before diverging. Qora didn't want to veer too far off-course, but she couldn't stop thinking about that vendor with the dimetrodon eyeballs.

Breach the cracks of a broken mind! Heal an injured brain! Achieve mental clarity!

The memory made her shudder—all those dead, yellow irises staring out from behind the glass, swimming in some bloody solution.

But if the heart of a theropod could make her confess the truth, then maybe it wasn't so far a stretch to think a dimetrodon eyeball could affect her mind in other ways—give her the clarity and mental energy she lacked. She needed to think of a better way through this mess.

Swing—chop—swing—chop.

An ache spread from her chest to her limbs. In her mind, she zoomed out on herself, watching her body from the height of a pterobeast gondola. In this vision, the rainforest dwarfed her; she was a speck in the never-ending green, moving through an inch at a time, always approaching but never reaching Utula.

It was enough to make her stop for a moment and hang her

head back. With her hands on her hips, machete hilt pressed between her palm and her side, she squinted into the light that winked through the leaves.

But the light quickly dimmed under her stare, turning pale. Practically delirious, she almost thought she'd caused this, but a wind kicked up and she remembered the thunder, which grumbled again.

Behind a fern, three stocky lystrosaurs began to burrow underground, shifting dirt with downward-pointing tusks. Qora hadn't even noticed them before, with their dull scales and peaceful demeanor. She questioned their hasty retreat, but she lost her train of thought when the wind vented into the canopy, and then into the weave of the fabric of her clothes. Her sweat took on a chill, if only a slight one, and she released a pent-up sigh that shuddered on its way out. This had been the strongest, coolest wind she'd felt since Qhusi and her body came to life like a wilted plant after a bit of care. For longer than she should have, she stood still and let it soothe her, closing her eyes, clinging to the subtle drop in temperature that meant more to her now than an entire season's change in her home city ever had.

Birds and flyers took refuge in the trees. Compies and mononykus skittered into thickets for shelter.

The animals knew this place better than Qora did; she should follow their example and seek shelter too. But a new energy filled her and she drew on the wind's relief.

Swing—chop—swing—chop.

Everything leaned and swayed.

Even better.

Throw yourselves at my blade.

Less work for her.

The strength of the wind built until a rustle became a howl.

It cut through the mug, a godlike blade to aid the work of Qora's mortal weapon.

Together she and the wind could bust out of this monster's belly.

Then, in a mess of swaying leaves and fronds, among those rounded and plicate like fans, the yellow-mottled sail of a dimetrodon meandered through. Not just footprints, or crushed grasses, or ruck, but the creature itself.

Qora's pulse raced as she tried to keep it in her sights. She fed off the wind energy around her, cutting a path at twice her former speed. The wind warded off insects, lightened the air, pried apart the vegetation and revealed all that had been hiding within it. Breath of the gods, conveyor of wind spirits, an invisible urging hand.

But in a matter of minutes, it turned violent. Soon it was less a relief and more an opposing force, an invisible wall. Qora pushed against it. Then it started to push back.

Vines became whips. Debris took flight and swirled around. The sky shot rain in harsh diagonals, pricking her eyes. Everything darkened until it felt like dusk.

Before she knew it, she was struggling to stay upright. The jungle pummeled her from all sides and the sky unleashed a fury. She had no choice but to stop and take cover. She slipped in between the roots of another walking palm, hugging her legs and burying her face in her knees, once again having been lured into a false sense of security, and once again betrayed.

Kuymi stroked the tricorn's yellow frill.

The tricorn bleated and gently stamped her feet, nuzzling Kuymi but taking care not to strike him with the short horn above her beak. Despite the marks of the whip that striped her pebbled skin, she was docile, and craved affection.

"Someday we'll leave this place," Kuymi told her. He gazed up at the sky, where fine white lights streamed across the black of night, as they did each year at this time. It was an event that carried both sadness and joy—a reminder that another year had passed and Kuymi was still captive to the enemy. "Someday we'll run away and tell everything that happened to us here. Then, we'll go and live among the stars, so that no one can ever hold us or keep us again."

Excerpt from "Kuymi and the Tricorn"

FORTY

THE RAPTOR'S FOREST-GREEN SCALES SHIMMERED
when Takan brought her, reined and raging, back to camp. Amid
an intensifying wind, the megaraptor twisted her neck in protest
and made a sound halfway between a snarl and a squeal before
she swiped a three-pointed claw at her captor. Unfortunately she
didn't reach him.

She still wore a harness, with a heavy saddle on her back and
a bit between her jaws. The equipment was loose and tattered,
but otherwise could easily be put back into working condition.

"Good girl." Takan bobbed and weaved to dodge the raptor's
attacks. He jerked her dinoleather reins—a sick thing, now that
Ninan thought about it, binding reptiles with the skin of their
own kind—and she lurched forward. Takan ducked under her
gnashing teeth and she arched her body and swung her tail, an
inch away from clipping him. This dance went on until Takan
secured her reins around a tree.

Once Takan was finished with the raptor's restraints, he
checked on Ninan's, tugging on the ropes, testing the slack. He
slipped a finger into one of the ropes binding Ninan's legs, shook
his head, then tightened it. Ninan grunted involuntarily as it cut
into him.

Then Ninan's eyes met the raptor's. Marbles filled with

liquid gold, and onyx at the center. For a moment, she didn't thrash. She looked back at him, like they were sharing a thought.

A common enemy.

Takan was quick to brag about the ease with which he had snared her. "All it took was a troodon carcass and a trigger-activated noose—although it's a good thing I found her quick, because she was about to bite clear through the rope."

"Good thing," Ninan repeated without enthusiasm.

"They say raptors are intelligent," Takan added, ignoring his prisoner's contempt, "but I think I've made it clear to her who's in charge."

He reached to touch her muscled shoulder and she almost took off his hand—which she would have if she'd had full range of motion in her mouth and another inch of length on the reins.

Takan laughed and shook his head, patting the blowgun on his belt. "Bet you won't be so feisty with a little *medicine* in you." The raptor's nostrils flared. "If you're a good girl, maybe we don't have to use it. Up to you."

Before Ninan could stop himself, he scoffed. Takan strode over to him and thrust a fist into his ribs.

Ninan's flesh warmed with the swell of blooming bruises. He would have collapsed onto the ground if the ropes hadn't been holding him upright.

Takan pointed a warning finger as a drop of rainwater flecked his knuckle and rolled down the back of his hand.

Ninan took note of the change in the air, the accelerating wind, the way the animals all seemed to be diving back into their holes or touching down from flight. The raptor growled again and yanked against her ties.

Takan looked up at the clouds and the movement of the trees, and rushed for his dinoleather pack stuffed with loot, rummaging until he found Ninan's tarp and Qora's hammock.

He flicked open a pocketknife and slashed holes at the corners of both. He threaded ropes through the holes and strung up the materials in low branches, then gathered his supplies and enclosed himself in the shelter. The canvas and the oilskin billowed and flapped around him. The sound and the sight seemed to rile up the raptor even more. She roared at the skies as the rain picked up, water coursing down her scales.

The heralds flew over earlier than usual (probably to get ahead of the storm) and blew the horns ten times, then descended to safety—and not a moment too soon.

The air quickly turned violent. Ninan got a second beating from the broken, airborne twigs and branches, while water soaked his cuts. A few hours of this and he began to get a sense of what the Grave World must be like, lost souls tortured endlessly in the winds of disarray.

Ninan stared at the raptor again. He willed her to look back, holding on to the single shred of solidarity he had. Those golden eyes. That menacing stare. Their mutual misery. But for now, she just chomped uselessly at the bit, and Ninan couldn't think of a better metaphor for the situation.

FORTY-ONE

QORA'S BRAIDS WERE LIKE frayed, black ropes whipping over her shoulders.

She waited for what must have been hours, her clothes soaking wet, her face and arms chafing and raw in the wind and rain, an ache in her ears. The storm didn't end. It didn't calm down. The walking palm roots were no true shelter from the elements.

Wind whistled and whooshed around her. The clouds had blotted out all signs of the hour.

She continued to wait.

Soggy and beaten down, she curled her toes inside her boots and shifted against the ache in her muscles. She closed her eyes and endured.

)))

An eternity later, because Qora had become so attuned to the speed of the pouring rain, she startled when the rhythm slowed. But she didn't dare hope that this was over. It wasn't until the howl of the wind reduced to a murmur, and then to silence, that she raised her head to peek through the gaps between roots.

The sky didn't seem any brighter, which meant that this could be nothing but a lull as new storm clouds shifted in. Still, she waited for the chatter of the animals—those whose senses were keener than hers—before she unfolded her body, pushed up through the roots, and emerged to see the aftermath.

The scents of tree sap and wet wood embraced her in the breeze. The underbrush continued to sway gently, but everything was calm by comparison. Qora tried to find an opening in the canopy so she could get a good look at the sky, to gauge how much time she had lost.

Then a source of light drew her attention as the clouds thinned out like carded tufts of alpaca fiber.

It was a distinct fraction of a silver-white orb—the waxing gibbous of the moon.

Moon.

Qora's heart sank.

The entire day was gone.

And she had hardly moved an inch.

FORTY-TWO

WITH MORNING CAME A CLEAR SKY, the sight of which
Ninan had almost forgotten. But the air was still heavy with
moisture, so much that taking a breath of it felt like taking a
breath under water.

Of course the ropes across his chest might also have had
something to do with his breathlessness.

His limbs looked like they belonged to a corpse washed up
on the riverbank. A bluish tone overpowered the brown of his
skin, thanks to the watery bloat underneath. Blood was pooled
in all the wrong places, dammed up against the ropes that bound
him.

Before he was even fully awake, after a night of fragmented
awareness and the semi-lucid wanderings of his mind, Takan was
already up and struggling with the raptor.

But Takan was leaning too far back when he tried to mount
her, tugging her balance. She staggered and roared, bucking in
a wave motion that moved down her spine like the walk of a
centipede.

"Come on, you savage," Takan growled. He jerked the reins,
which he had readjusted along with the saddle, but the raptor
bucked circles around him and tangled his wrists in the lines.

The saddle was too tight, Ninan observed, and too low on

the raptor's ribs for her to support it comfortably. It should have sat above her seventh stripe—a good marker for the end of the rib zone. The discomfort alone would make her want to buck, and that wasn't even considering her growing contempt for the man trying to ride her.

Takan got his bearings again and made another attempt to mount, this time leaning in against the raptor before he swung his leg over. Meanwhile, the raptor curled her front claws and flared her nostrils like she was biding her time. She allowed Takan to get into the saddle now, but instantly flailed her tail and destabilized him, forcing him end over end into the nearest thicket.

Ninan shook his head. *You're supposed to snug the reins, scuteface.*

The raptor's eyes were wide and unblinking when Takan approached her again. She could keep this up all day.

Ninan tried not to smile.

"Stay!" Takan commanded when the raptor tried to move again. She snorted, darting her head in defiance. "Stay."

It also would have helped if he'd been using the right intonation to command her, Ninan thought, but he kept quiet.

After a while, Takan shot the raptor with a tranquilizing blowgun dart—just enough for a quick nap, Ninan guessed, based on her size—and disappeared. But not before checking Ninan's ropes again and giving him a good slap.

With Takan gone, Ninan raised his bound hands and bowed his head until the ropes touched his teeth, and then bit into the dry, twisted blades of grass and chewed like a hungry llama.

Never had he been subject to so many degrading things in such a short period of time. He was grateful the heralds weren't flying over right now.

He had to stop and take several breaks, over the course of nearly an hour, and finally broke through a narrower section of the rope, taking cuts to his already swollen lips, and spit out the grass that stuck to his tongue. The strain on his muscles to hold this position was almost unbearable, pressuring his bindings. It would take all day to get through at this rate.

Around the time he had decided to take another break, the raptor stirred. She cracked open her giant eyes and tried to lift her heavy head. Ninan clicked his tongue to draw her attention and she shifted her gaze toward him, blinking like she was trying to focus. With a vigilant glance at the break in the trees where Takan had disappeared, Ninan suddenly dared to hope.

At some point, Takan was going to unhitch the raptor again, and when he did, Ninan wanted to be ready—with an ally here at this camp.

"Hey pretty girl," he whispered. It was an idiotic thing to say, but she had to get used to his voice, no matter what sort of ruck came out of it. "You probably want to bite my head off, don't you?"

She snorted.

"Well, just so you know, I'm not like that other guy. I mean, I'm not a *great* person, but … I'm stuck here like you. See?" He made a show of trying to move his arms unsuccessfully.

The raptor was still waking up, not her usual feisty self yet. Ninan imagined if she were human, she'd be snippy and a bit sarcastic. She bore a familiar weariness—the weight of wandering through the jungle all these days—with a suppressed fire behind her eyes.

Ninan laughed weakly. "You know, you remind me of someone. I'm sure she wanted to bite my head off at some point too. Probably still does, come to think of it. Her name was Qora."

The raptor snorted again, her breath stirring up a mess of loose leaves. She pushed up off the ground until she was standing, unsteady and swaying as she moved.

"You probably have a name too, don't you? But of course there's no way for me to know what it is. Maybe I should give you a new one." He thought for a moment, then perked up. "Qoraptor. Yes! Qoraptor. What do you think?"

She took a few steps.

"You like it? That's it. Come to me, Qoraptor. Good girl." If he could get her close enough to get a better sense of his smell, combined with his very non-threatening stance, he could start to earn her loyalty.

She was weak-kneed and wary, but she was on her way, sniffing the air and inclining her head with curiosity. Gaining confidence now that she was up and about again, though, she took her next steps too quickly and reached the end of her lines.

"No!" Ninan shouted.

The leather cut into her neck.

She yowled.

Her yowls became roars and she clawed uselessly at the reins, gnashing her teeth again until she wore herself out and flopped back to the ground. The dart's poison, it seemed, was still affecting her. Ninan gave her a few minutes to rest, fully intent on trying to win her affection again, but the sound of footfalls on damp leaves told him Takan was on his way back.

Takan returned to camp, dragging a psittacosaur carcass. He tossed it at the raptor, who stumbled sleepily toward it.

She chewed the meat resentfully, snarling with each bite, munching improperly around the bit (which Takan should have removed first) but apparently too hungry to care. Ninan was sure she had never been treated this way by her previous riders. Lured to a trap, harassed, drugged, fed on the condition that she tolerate continued disrespect. As if she hadn't already been struggling enough to eat with that bit for however many days she'd been on her own after someone had probably killed her rider.

But the psittacosaur worked wonders. The raptor let Takan mount and stay mounted; she even let him walk her forward before she started bucking again.

Then Takan lost patience completely. He took a pinch of Ninan's skyrock dust and peppered the raptor's snout. She shrieked and squealed, and then all Takan had to do to control her was threaten another dusting. The raptor submitted.

Takan paraded her around the small camp, head held high, finding his rhythm. After a few laps, he brought her to a halt in front of Ninan.

"Now that I have this beauty," he said, beaming at the raptor and stroking her neck, "It's time you and I part ways."

"What a pity," Ninan muttered, keeping his wrist ropes tucked against his body to hide the notch he'd bitten into them.

Takan ignored the bitter tone. "Spirits willing, you'll die slowly and painfully. Starvation, parasites, losing one limb at a time to a carnivorous reptile …" He slid down from the raptor's back, now with the confidence of a seasoned professional, despite his graceless landing. "It's a shame I won't be around to see it. But knowing you're trapped here thinking about the girl, with nothing you can do to help her … That'll be good enough, I suppose."

Ninan breathed fast through his nose, knowing no threats he could make had any foundation, not when he was bound like this. But even though Qora was capable of taking care of herself, she was at her greatest disadvantage yet. The thickening jungle. None of her belongings. A horrible storm that must have set her back a whole day if she'd even managed to survive it.

"You're no better than the qhapaq, you know," Ninan said. "Selfish and brutal and merciless—"

Takan kicked him in the groin, forcing a hard pulse of nausea into his gut. Ninan folded—as much as a person could fold under restraints like his—and wheezed through the pain.

"Should I pass the girl on my way to the ruins," Takan said, "I'll be sure to let her know that the princeling sends his regards."

FORTY-THREE

QORA JERKED AWAKE when she hadn't even known she'd been asleep. She sat crimped into herself and weary. She peeked out of the walking palm again to see new daylight, which came in orange and pink on the eastern horizon, filtered through the canopy, trickling in among the green. A thin mist hung low, making her long for the cool and ominous mountain mists of Qhusi.

She climbed back out, with layers of half-dried mud on her skin, her scabs soggy but crusting again at the edges. She combed her fingers through her tangled hair and rebraided it while she took in the scope of the wreckage. The wreckage of her optimism, too. Broken pieces sprawled out mindlessly in an already mindless place.

Even though she was hungry enough to devour a giant sauropod whole, she picked up her weapons and headed off without eating.

She wasn't sure where she was going, whether she should even bother to take another step. When the earth could split open and bleed fire, when the wind itself could knock her off her feet, when friends could become enemies at a moment's notice … it hardly seemed worth the trouble.

It was only the memory of home that kept her moving. And the thought of Rimaq healed. The shard of possibility that she might see him and Hakan and her mamáy again.

She listened for the river's rush to determine which way was south, shuffling her feet as she followed the sound. Along the way, she found copoasu trees. There was plenty of fruit at the base, so she took one and busted open its brown shell with her machete, exposing the pale flesh inside. She scooped it with dirty fingers, stuffing her mouth, swallowing so much so quickly that she gagged, barely tasting the flavor that was like pineapple and banana and cacao all at once. She sucked on the remaining pulp, pulling out the juices, and gobbled up six whole fruits. Then a queasy ripple forced her to sit with her head between her legs for a few minutes before she could go on.

Once she was back in the thick of it, the jungle floor was a soupy mess as it gradually absorbed the stormwater. A lizard flared its patterned frills and snapped at swarms of mosquitoes that hung in the lingering moisture. When she realized the mosquitoes avoided the parts of her that were coated in mud, she quickly added another coating and filled in the gaps, a trick that let her hack a new path for a couple of hours in relative peace until the heat finally began to dry out the landscape, and many of the insects dispersed.

Even still, Qora would be lucky if she'd gone a full two miles in this. What was worse was that she was more than seventy miles short of where she needed to be to get to the ruins on time—which wasn't even considering what obstacles and dangers she would face trying to find and get the golden tooth—a thought she couldn't stomach any more than she could stomach the idea of eating dimetrodon eyeballs, which were a lost cause too, at this point. There was no hope for her that she could see, so she floated on the hope that she *couldn't* see, the grace of Sky Mother, the mercy of Light Father.

But that mercy was bestowed upon her sooner than expected. In the distance, several vaned spinal-sails shifted among round, toothed leaves. Heartened, she looked for a good spot in the trees, bit back her nausea, and readied her weapon.

❩❩❩

Because it was too awkwardly shaped to carry over her shoulders, Qora dragged the dimetrodon behind her until she could find a safe place to stop and cut out its eyes—far away from the other dimetrodons. Or maybe she was stalling while she searched for the *courage* to cut out its eyes. But she walked with the river in view, following its guiding curves until another set of tracks appeared.

Bootprints in the mud.

Leaves and vines cut, blunt ends dangling, scraps cast to the jungle floor and trampled underfoot.

She gripped the hilt of her machete.

Maybe it had only been Ninan. Or maybe it had been some other competitor who had come through a day or two ago. After all, the last time she'd seen any of the others was before she'd killed Ruyan. She and Ninan had lost a lot of time recovering from the lava rift, giving others plenty of opportunity to get ahead.

What would she say to Ninan if she found him? Would he fight her now? Did he have it in him to have acted so loyal when he'd never meant it, and then turn around and try to kill her like everyone else had? How did one confront a situation like that, if given the opportunity to do so?

A tread on wet grass made Qora think she was about to find out. She turned, expecting to see Ninan, but a swinging longblade and a flash of dinoleather armor confirmed her mistake.

Reflexively she raised her machete. Her blade scraped against the other—a grating sound that shot a chill between her shoulders. The man wriggled his weapon around hers, loosening her hold on the hilt, and flung the machete out of her hand. It landed in the grass with a *whoosh*. Qora ran, grasping at a hanging vine that she pulled tight across the man's chest. The man stumbled, unable to react in time to avoid it.

He had his own coating of mud, and his leathers were more of a mesh now, shredded and slit and burnt in so many places they couldn't possibly offer the protection they had before. Like Qora, he seemed to have lost everything, with the exception of a few items on his belt: a knife, an empty sheath where his longblade must have been, a waterskin, and a tubular object wrapped in a piece of oilskin.

While he was down, Qora slid her crossbow strap around so the crossbow was at her front, but the man was up again quickly. Qora spanned fast but didn't have the chance to load a bolt. She twisted her hips to avoid the blade, but he cut through the bottom edge of her jacket and sliced all three of her bolts in half.

Qora staggered backwards. The man swung his blade again and Qora arched her body away, but not before taking a deep cut to her chin.

Wincing, she put all her power under her legs and ran again, diving into brambles and bushes. She shoved her way through, getting scraped and scratched with every move.

The man hacked at the leaves, but Qora burrowed in deep where he couldn't reach her. She kept stone still as blood dripped down her neck, holding her breath and hoping she'd make herself too much trouble for him. If only there hadn't been a spider the size of her fist scuttling across the toes of her boots. She released an involuntary shriek. The man moved toward her as she tried to push through to the other side, kicking like a cat that had stepped in a puddle.

"Let's make this easier on both of us," the man shouted. "I don't want to have to kill you, but I need that weapon. Give it up and we can part ways peacefully."

Qora knew he wanted her to think he was the one with the power right now, but he wasn't. Without a projectile weapon, he couldn't hunt efficiently, and he wouldn't make it to Utula if he died of starvation first. And who knew what he'd have to fight at the end. She was sure a blade was barely going to cut it—literally.

Ignoring his negotiations, Qora saw a break in the leaves where some dinosaur had trampled foliage and made a subtle path to the river. She snapped branches by hand, clearing a rough way for herself to get to it as the man cut closer and closer. With his blade at her back, she made it out into the opening, at which point she sprinted straight to the riverbank. One more cut and the man was on her heels again.

Qora's crossbow was still spanned. She felt for what were now half-bolts on her belt, all tips flat except for one that seemed to have splintered. That would have to do.

While she ran, she pulled out the splintered bolt, awkward and short, and set it into the spanned crossbow. She spun around and aimed low at a large hole in the dinoleather. Pulling the trigger was painful—the first time she'd taken a shot since her injury—but she did it. The bolt sank into the man's leg and toppled him. He dropped his longblade but forced himself up, shouting obscenities while she spanned and loaded the two completely blunt bolts and shot them one after the other.

One bounced off his shoulder, where Qora had tried to exploit an oozing wound, and the other bounced off his groin. Even without piercing him, this pained and disoriented him long enough for Qora to gain some distance and hide herself in a row of bushes that grew parallel to the water.

"This is a waste of energy!" the man yelled into the open air.

Qora made herself small and forced herself to inhale slowly until she caught her breath.

"You're completely unarmed now!" His voice was louder, closer. "There's nowhere you can go that I can't catch you!"

His feet made suctioned noises in the bank's mud as he approached. He knew she was in one of these thickets—he just didn't know which one.

Yet.

Rumberries dangled into Qora's view and she watched them closely, a gauge for her own stillness; they would only sway if she did.

The man stopped a few feet away. She caught glimpses of him—a swatch of hair, a blur of his torn shirt under his perforated armor—peering between the leaves. He paused. Then his blade came down hard, chopping through the brush and rustling violently.

"You move once and I'll see it," he warned. "You sit still, and I'll get around to you eventually."

He slammed his blade down again, so close Qora almost screamed. She held her breath again, her mind racing.

His logic was sound. There was no way out of this unless she gave up herself and her weapon. One more strike and she was dead.

The man stood directly in front of her now. Her only advantage was his height. He was looking somewhere above her head, otherwise he would have been able to see her. She stared at his belt.

And his belt was exactly what she needed.

She should have realized it sooner. Under that piece of oilskin was her salvation. *A firestick.*

She tried not to think about how much she needed that firestick intact; how this might be her only chance at another one after she'd lost her own before the pterodactyl attack; how, even though it was the closest thing she had to a weapon right now, it seemed like such a waste. On the other hand, she would have a hard time winning anything if she was dead. Being able to signal the Watchtower should be the least of her worries.

She had to believe she could find an alternative signal. She'd managed to create resources before when there had been none. She'd continued to survive despite the odds. She hadn't come this far to quit here.

So, as the man's blade came down for the third time, she launched herself forward and tackled him, tearing the firestick from his belt and peeling off the oilskin. As he recovered, she pulled the sparkcord. Damp on the outside, the firestick sputtered at first, then it hissed and lit. Qora jabbed the flame in his eye.

His blade hit the ground with a tinny clunk and he screamed, thrusting the heel of his hand into his eye socket. With his other hand, he grabbed Qora's wrist and redirected her aim. She twisted against his thumb and forefinger and pulled down fast to get free, then pointed the firestick at him again as it shot out, red sparks sizzling. She got to her feet and picked up the man's longblade, wielding it over him. The firestick was about to burst again and she raised it, letting the blast go high. It squealed and exploded in the air.

If this had worked once by accident, it could work again on purpose, she thought. A clarion call to airborne reptiles to come and take this competitor away.

Visually, she planned her escape back into the trees as she listened for pterodactyls. The seconds were long and agonizing. Her heart pounded in the silence.

And finally, a piercing cry filled the air.

"To run, you must press your feet upon the earth so that it may propel you forward. To soar, you must harness the wind so that it may carry you. The forces of nature remain at your service, and the creatures who live among them will guide you in their use."

Shaman Sisa Achirana

FORTY-FOUR

TWO MINUTES EARLIER

TAKAN LOADED UP THE RAPTOR, packing supplies and weapons behind the worn saddle.

Ninan hadn't been able to bite a good chunk out of his rope since Takan had returned from hunting. Not that it mattered much. Even if he got free, he'd be empty-handed.

The raptor's saddle straps dug into her loin and she shifted inside them, but Takan threatened more skyrock dust when she didn't stand still, so she kept quiet.

For an instant, the raptor looked at Ninan again, and Ninan thought surely she must recognize his empathy, the way they both writhed under their individual restraints, their mutual hatred for the man who had restrained them.

Ninan knew there wasn't much time, that he ought to just take a chance, try a command while Takan was distracted untying the raptor from the tree. It was a risk to the raptor, though. If she'd really wanted, she could have dragged that bastard halfway back to Qhusi, but she was tense, eyeing the skyrock dust warily. Even though the dust was weak as a generalized repellant, it would sting like death if Takan got enough of it in her eyes or nose. And Ninan certainly didn't have the freedom or the strength to defend her from him.

Takan slipped his foot into one of the stirrups, hopping on the other foot to give himself a jump up to the saddle. Between hops, he swayed off balance, suspended between ground and mount.

This is my chance.

Ninan stared the raptor down, waiting, willing. Finally, she looked back, and he saw a flicker in her expression.

Takan swung his leg to mount.

Ninan whistled.

The raptor snapped alert, jolted forward, and knocked Takan flat.

Takan rolled and dove for the skyrock dust.

The raptor flinched.

"Leave her alone," Ninan demanded.

Takan stood and took the raptor by the reins. He approached Ninan, raptor in tow.

The raptor thrashed lightly but allowed him to lead her.

"Trying to play the hero …" Takan said.

Ninan spit into his face. "Who's playing?"

Takan cranked back his arm with his hand fisted tight. Ninan cringed as he cried out: "Assail!"

Instantly, the raptor swung her tail like a whip, lashing Takan across the chest with so much force he crumpled. She pinned him with her front claws. He swatted, screaming and grunting. She gnashed her teeth and tore open his shirt. Red marks materialized on his skin like swift paint strokes on a sheet of canvas.

The raptor's growl rippled through Ninan's bones.

Soon there was so much blood Ninan had to look away. But it didn't help; even without a visual, Takan's cries scraped at the corners of Ninan's mind.

Ninan knew he could make it stop, command the raptor to back down. He was half tempted, considering.

Takan pleaded for Ninan to end the pain. Between his pleas and the raptor's vengeful growls, Ninan almost didn't hear the burst in the distance. It was only when Takan began to fade out that a flare of light shot above the trees to the east, stealing Ninan's attention.

Qora.

It was desperate and ridiculous, but Ninan wanted it to be her. He wanted to believe Qora was close enough for him to reach, that she was calling out to him in fire. It didn't matter that he was tied up and that Qora didn't even have a firestick. After all, the *last* time a firestick had been deployed prematurely, Qora had been the cause. Ninan's chest swelled at the idea and a rush filled his body that made him think he could tear through his ropes with willpower alone.

Luckily, he didn't have to.

He watched the sparks, committing their location to memory. East, about two miles off.

"Cease!" he shouted.

The raptor stopped, leaving a blood-soaked Takan and raising her head. Ninan called her to him and commanded her to bow and open her mouth, and then he raised his bound wrists to her teeth, cutting the ropes with several quick passes over the serrations. With his hands free, he untied the additional ropes, rubbing the sore spots on his skin as he quickly evaluated the camp.

Everything worthwhile between Qora's pack and his own was now in a single dinoleather pack, along with weapons— including the blowgun Takan had used to knock him out—and it was already secured onto the megaraptor. The only thing missing was the pouch of skyrock dust, which he snatched up, pursed closed, and shoved into the pack. Some of the dust had spilled, but what was left would have to do.

The rest of the plan was simple.

With sore but nimble fingers, he adjusted the raptor's straps, climbed into the saddle, and steered her toward the sparks. As the red lights faded, a swarm of blue figures moved toward the same location.

Ruck.

Ninan squinted to be sure, but his heart felt like lead. If Qora was there, he'd have to hurry.

FORTY-FIVE

QORA WAS ALREADY HALFWAY to the protection of the trees as her attacker scrambled helplessly away from descending pterodactyls. Two of them dipped down to squabble over him, but one clasped his ankle, sweeping him into the air and dangling him upside down. He grunted and flailed, and Qora could only think of the last time she'd witnessed such an incident. His shifting weight jerked the pterodactyl's flight off course, but only just. The second pterodactyl returned to lay claim, and both pterodactyls pulled in opposite directions, forking the man's legs like a tree branch, and he released an ear-splitting scream that faded to an echo as he was carried off and out of Qora's sightline.

Distracted by the horror, Qora stumbled and fell flat.

As she got to her feet, she spotted the heralds soaring in the distance—close enough to see the action but far enough away that their presence wouldn't interfere—just before a swoop of five more pterodactyls descended. Qora gripped her fallen opponent's longblade and swung high. She hacked at the reptiles. They hissed as she nicked their skin, recoiling briefly, though none let up enough to give her the chance to run again.

What have I done?

Gradually, she inched backward, hacking in front of her. Pterodactyl blood spattered her face and clothes, a red so dark it was almost black. The smallest of the pterodactyls was particularly agile, avoiding her strike and clamping onto her arm; it pulled her two feet off the ground as her dangling crossbow clapped her navel. She plunged the longblade into the pterodactyl's underside, piercing the soft tissues where leg and belly merged, forcing the blade deeper until the reptile's wings began to droop and it released her before it collapsed. Before she even hit the grass another pterodactyl darted forward. It snapped its enormous beak, clicking its fine-point teeth. She slashed its neck and spilled a stream of blood.

Two down.

The remaining three pterodactyls hovered eagerly. The first swooped in and tangled its claws into Qora's hair, grasping at the top of her head. The second lunged at her weapon and clutched the bare blade. Qora gripped the hilt with both hands and put all her weight onto it, grunting as sweat, blood, and humidity weakened her hold and the weapon slipped away. She cowered as all three pterodactyls surrounded her. There was no way out, and she had no way to fight them. She didn't think they even planned to carry her off; she was certain they intended on tearing her apart right here.

Claws slashed and scraped at her. She barricaded her face behind her arms. Yellow eyes and blue skin flickered through the gaps of her defense as the pterodactyls tore holes in her clothes and her flesh. In the chaos, she caught a glimpse of an open mouth, wide enough to sever her head from her body, ready to snap shut. She condensed herself, trapped, nowhere to retreat.

Worse, there were heralds watching, who would help her easily if they wanted. But instead they were simply going to watch her die, and then report it to the masses as a riveting story.

The pterodactyls squawked and squealed, digging in. For a

moment, Qora wished she had died at the lava rift—because at least that would have been quick. But suddenly the reptiles' cries turned sharp, defensive. Something pulled them back.

A raptor's roar. A swift and heavy tread.

Why in the Grave World's pits would a megaraptor attack a swoop of pterodactyls?

Taking advantage of the distraction, Qora scrambled to her feet and ran. She didn't have to glance over her shoulder to know the pterodactyls were close behind; their wings fanned a rush of air at her back, and their shadows fell over her like fine, black veils that billowed in the wind.

The entire pursuit between the reptiles and herself played out in silhouettes cast on the ground stretched out in front of her. Her feet raced over the shapes but she couldn't seem to outrun them.

The pterodactyls swooped and rose and swooped and rose, clawing at the raptor, who roared and gnashed. Someone was riding the raptor, but she couldn't make out who. A competitor she didn't remember? Someone who had been lost in the jungle all this time, only to emerge and help these monsters take her out during the last leg of the competition?

A cacophony grated her ears until the click of a mechanical weapon punctured the noise.

One of the pterodactyls took a nosedive, soaring over her head and plunging face-first into the silt of the riverbank with a bolt in its head.

The raptor's snout eased into Qora's periphery. It darted its head forward, angling low for speed. Qora's lungs seized and her legs went leaden, but she pushed herself faster. The final two pterodactyls swooped down and she cringed, waiting to feel claws on her shoulders and teeth cutting into her neck, but instead the raptor veered laterally and sped alongside her, roaring and snapping at the flyers.

When she looked over, she almost choked.

Ninan sat on the raptor's back, pushing and guiding it like a riding warrior in battle. He wrapped one of his forearms in the rein lines, securing himself as he slid sideways on the saddle and hung low enough to reach out to Qora. They gripped each other, wrist to wrist, and he pulled her up.

At first, Qora wasn't sure what he was trying to do, the way he maneuvered her so that she ended up straddling the raptor backwards, facing him as they rode. Then he handed her a quiver of bolts.

Understanding his meaning, Qora accepted the ammunition, hooked her legs over his, and braced her crossbow over his shoulder so she could load it.

Aiming, however, was a whole other game.

Not only was the target moving, but so was she. Everything shuddered and shook in her view. She held her arms rigid and clenched her jaw.

At least the pterodactyls were big and close.

She sank a bolt into a belly—not immediately fatal, but the best she could do with her hand sore and throbbing. Then she punctured a wing. Two more bolts to the chest close together, which jolted the reptile backwards and sent it hurtling away. The last one took her three shots: another wing puncture, one to the neck, and finally, a bolt straight to the eye. It shrieked and fell at a downward curve as the megaraptor swept Qora and Ninan into the foliage away from the bank and out of the heralds' view. The pterodactyl crash-landed into the trees in a tumult of rustling and snapping branches that spewed small birds like sparks from a forge.

Qora released a breath and melted against Ninan, her head collapsing on his shoulder. With his arms on either side of her, his muscles tightened as he pulled the reins to slow the raptor.

"Halt."

The raptor slowed to a trot, then a saunter, trampling and breaking the underbrush with its large body.

Once it had come to a complete stop, Ninan and Qora sat together for a few seconds, chests colliding with heavy breaths. There was blood and sweat and filth all over them, thick like a paste. Qora peeled herself back and looked at him.

There were so many things to say, to ask, she didn't even know where to start. But it didn't matter, because as soon as she opened her mouth to speak, Ninan pulled her to him and kissed her.

Everything seemed to pause around them. The sound of the river and the animals and the wind were nothing but a mutter against the sound of Qora's heartbeat.

"I'm sorry," Ninan whispered breathlessly against her mouth. "Was that okay?"

Qora closed her eyes and nodded, trying to calm the thumping in her chest. "But I thought—"

His lips were on hers again, then her chin, her cheeks, her forehead. He paused to trace her jawline with his thumb. "Whatever you thought, it was wrong. Whatever you saw, it wasn't true. I'd never leave you." He kissed her again and again and again. "Never."

Through the lens of affection, copper gleams like gold
and tears shimmer with the luster of pearls.

Sumaqi proverb

FORTY-SIX

NINAN EMBRACED QORA, soaking her in. "I'm sorry," he whispered into her hair.

"I really thought you left," she said.

"I hoped to all spirits you wouldn't believe it when you saw the quipu."

"I didn't *want* to. But then I remembered the night before, at the volcano. I thought you—I mean, it seemed like—"

He released her. "I know. I was stupid. It was just … being that close to you, looking at you and the way you were looking at me, I felt …" He hesitated. What could he say? That he'd been scared out of his wits? A complete coward? "There are things about me that might change your mind. Everything you thought about me before, my family's money … That's only the beginning." He let a tuft of hair fall into his face. A thickness built in his throat and his hand trembled against hers. "The truth is, I'm … I'm …"

When he failed to hide his pained expression, struggling with his words, she only smiled, and consoled him with another kiss. "I don't care," she said. "You don't owe me anything—and that includes explanations."

"Well *that* seems too good to be true," he said through a weary laugh.

"There's so little good in all this. I think we should accept whatever good we find, and not question it."

She kissed him again and his whole internal argument fell away, even if only for a minute. Her lips on his lips, her arms around his neck, his hands on her waist. For the moment, he could pretend he was someone else who wasn't bound by his own mistakes; it was an illusion he didn't want to shatter with the truth.

They returned to the river to let Qoraptor drink while Qora and Ninan washed. They each took turns while the other kept an eye out for predators, but having a megaraptor nearby made them automatically feel safer. Qoraptor snarled when anything came close, even little compies, or the colorful macaws that flew back and forth to the adjacent clay lick.

Ninan explained all that had happened during their separation, how Takan had captured him and manipulated everything. Qora didn't ask why Takan had targeted Ninan specifically, and Ninan realized she didn't have any reason to; every competitor had reasons to sabotage the others.

"That must have been awful for you."

His stomach began to sour as he thought about the story Takan had told him, the forgotten history between them. "I deserved it."

She frowned. "Why do you say that?"

"Because I've made mistakes. Bad ones. I've treated people poorly. I haven't always had noble reasons for doing what I've done."

Qora listened quietly as she rinsed the mud from her arms and face, revealing new wounds Ninan hadn't seen before, cuts and bruises hidden underneath. The distinct scratches of pterodactyl claws, a blade gash on her chin, whip-marks from windblown thicket switches.

"That doesn't mean you deserve to be tied up and beaten." She caught him staring at her wounds and shrank back, turning her face away. "I'm sure it looks worse than it is."

Ninan inched closer and pulled her into him, firm but not too tightly since he suspected she had injuries everywhere. She was stiff at first but slowly relaxed when he slipped his fingers between hers.

She looked up at him. "This is going to complicate things. You know we can't both win."

"Perfect—I don't want to win."

"What?" Qora narrowed her eyes.

"For me, this was never about winning the spinosaur tooth; it was about winning back an inheritance. Winning back favor with my family—and with a lot of other people who don't really matter. It might not make a lot of sense, but what happened with Takan made me realize … I don't want their favor. I don't want anything from them. Not anymore."

"So … you're going to surrender?"

He shook his head. "I'm staying in the competition—but I'm staying for *you*. I'm going to do everything I can to make sure you get to the end."

"Ninan, that's ridiculous. You can't do that. Stepping down is one thing, but continuing to *risk your life* …"

"What's my life worth if I don't use it for something? I certainly wasn't doing anything useful before."

"Ninan …" she said again.

"Qora."

She sighed and glanced at the megaraptor, who lapped up water gracelessly.

"Her name's *Qoraptor*," Ninan informed her.

Qora put a hand on her hip. "It is not."

"It is. I told her so and she likes it." He grinned. "She's scaly, but she's loyal, and she knows how to put a guy in his place."

Qora gave him a playful shove.

"Like I said—scaly."

"You haven't seen scaly yet. Just wait."

Ninan pulled a stray leaf out of Qora's hair and leaned in close. "She's also quite a ... lovely creature."

"You're only saying that so 'she' won't bite you."

"Maybe. But that doesn't make it any less true." He kissed Qora softly.

She kissed him back, over and over until she was nearly breathless, and then, after a moment, turned her eyes vaguely toward the sky, which was empty for the moment. "We'd, um ... better be careful. There'll be eyes on us again soon. We don't want to cause a scandal back home."

Nodding, Ninan brushed her cheek and thought about the stories that would spread if the heralds were to catch a glimpse of them like this. Or worse, what the coordinators might do to try and turn them against each other, tear them apart, or make a spectacle of their feelings. "You're right. Best to get back to business." He cleared his throat. "What can I do to help?"

Qora sighed. "Well, I lost that damn machete again. Along with a dimetrodon."

He arched a brow.

ↄↄↄ

Once they reoriented themselves, it wasn't too difficult to backtrack to where Qora's last scuffle had begun—and Ninan listened as she explained it all in great detail along the way.

346

At first, Ninan assumed there would be a bit of a hunt for the items, but a gang of unwitting, orange velociraptors gnawing at the belly of some animal corpse was like a flare in the shady jungle depths.

Ninan reached around Qora and patted Qoraptor's neck. "Okay, girl … I'm going to need you to scare off those little demons, alright?" The megaraptor snorted in response. "Ready … Assail!"

Qoraptor rushed the gang. All the velociraptors raised their heads at once, bloody jaws still open. At first, they gathered like little warriors on the front lines of a battlefield, hissing and clicking to defend their scavenged meal. But as Qoraptor released a violent roar, the velociraptors scattered. They paused every few yards to look back and hiss again, but eventually they filtered so deep into the trees that Qora and Ninan couldn't see them anymore.

Spotting the machete, Qora slid off the megaraptor's back and landed in a crouch. "This is the second time I've had to go back for it." She slipped the blade back into her belt. "Such a headache—just like its owner. Somehow Sakay still manages to be a pain in the hindquarters even when he's not around."

Ninan chuckled. "Well, you were already planning to come back for … *this*." He grimaced at the half-eaten dimetrodon, most of its middle torn to bloody shreds with several organs missing. "You sure this is necessary?"

Qora nodded. "Now that you're here, too, it's even more necessary than before. It's supposed to heal the mind *and* the brain. I just wanted some mental clarity to help me figure out what to do next, but you still have a head injury from the lava rift—and I'm sure multiple beatings from Takan didn't help."

Ninan had gotten so used to the splitting headache and

constant throbbing, he hadn't even thought about it. Most of his body had been hurting since a few days into the Venture, so it hardly seemed worth worrying about. Not when his very life was hanging in the balance daily.

Qora crouched over the dimetrodon's head, which was still intact, and clenched her teeth as she put a small knife to the reptile's eyeball, turning slightly away even though she'd need to give it her direct attention to do this. Ninan braced himself.

When it was done, she stood before him, her face gray with horror, and presented two, slimy globs in her cupped hand.

Ninan winced as he took one for himself, and nearly dropped it when he felt the slimy texture between his fingers. It was an inch in diameter, with a gold iris looking back at him. Qora's still had a bit of connective tissue stuck to it. Ninan suppressed his gag reflex as Qora pulled the collar of her shirt over her nose and mouth.

"So, do we bite it?" Ninan asked. "Or … swallow it whole?"

Qora's voice came out muffled. "Bite it, I think."

Ninan took a deep breath. "Okay. Let's get it over with."

On the count of three, they popped the eyeballs in and choked them down. It was like a dense grape, with a springy texture that burst under the pressure of Ninan's teeth. Except the liquid that came out was salty and his tongue nearly ejected the whole mucusy mess. He pursed his lips and forced himself to swallow, gasping violently afterward and spitting out the taste. Meanwhile, Qora was still doubled over with her hands on her knees, chewing fast with her eyes squeezed shut. The second her throat flexed, she raced to the traveling pack for a waterskin and chugged.

Sometime in the midst of dry heaving and lying curled up on the ground, something else set in.

"Gods in the High World ..." A tingly, numbing sensation flooded Ninan's brain. Gradually, the pain in his head began to subside. Warmth and tranquility and relief replaced it.

Qora sat like a statue, and then a smile crept onto her lips.

〉〉〉

"It's this way, I know it." Ninan steered Qoraptor into the thick of the jungle while Qora held on from behind. The mental images were coming to him so fast, he couldn't barely process them. He saw the aerial view of the whole region, the same as when he'd been seated in that pterobeast gondola seven years ago looking down. He also saw the secret map he'd lost, clear as though he were holding it in front of him, with every topographical and mathematical detail. The abandoned trade route—now at least a decade out of use—was just on the other side of this impassable jungle, waiting for them.

It had taken them three hours to get six miles, even with Qoraptor, thanks to the thickening underbrush, but it was still faster than they would have gone on foot. Qoraptor grumbled but obeyed, braving vines and brambles while Qora and Ninan cut what they could with their blades. They pressed on until, finally, in the afternoon, they broke through to an open space.

Open, at least, by comparison.

The packed-dirt road, which had never been paved by modern methods, was overgrown in places, although patches of it were visible between grasses and small ferns. Plenty of plants sprawled over its surface, and many had wended their way upward, but none were so large as those on either side of the path. The years of heavy usage had stunted the plant growth. It was still too cluttered for a person to move quickly on foot, but it was nothing for a large raptor.

Ninan and Qora gazed ahead at the long clearing, and Qora's arms around Ninan's waist seemed to tighten instinctively. Ninan clicked his tongue and the megaraptor took off running.

Now without having to cut dozens of branches to clear just a few feet, they raced for the ruins at speed, only taking short breaks for Qoraptor to drink and rest her legs.

Qora's heightened senses allowed her to recall and match the sounds of the more exotic dinosaurs to those she'd tried to commit to memory during the past few days, with no effort at all, and from a greater distance. Hunting came even more easily to her than usual, now that she seemed to have the ability to predict animal movements by something as subtle as a change in the pattern of their breath—which she could hear yards away.

Under the influence of the "brain berries," Qora and Ninan were unstoppable. Pin-sharp focus, total recall of long-forgotten information, strong senses, and improved insight. The rest of the day was a blur of progress.

Ninan was also grateful to find his head injury much improved—no more persistent throbbing, no more dizziness or nausea from the pain.

Once the sky began to darken, they stopped for the night, having added ten miles following the trade route for a total of eighteen (including the progress Qora had made in the morning and Ninan having used her pre-cut trail and the riverbank to catch up to her on Qoraptor).

If they could keep going the next day at fifteen miles per hour—a comfortable pace for Qoraptor—that would put them within thirty-five miles of the ruins before the old trade route veered southward. Then cutting through at two to three miles per hour after that, they could expect to arrive a few hours after dawn on the last day of the Venture. It was a tight schedule, but at least there was hope. As long as someone else didn't find and seize the golden tooth first.

The heralds' horns blared seven times.

Qora and Ninan made camp and, with some firepowder from Takan's supplies, built a brilliant fire. They cooked Qora's kills and ate until they were so full they couldn't move.

Qoraptor tucked her legs under her body and curled up resting her head on her front limbs. She looked so docile like that, Ninan thought. Not like the vicious killer she could be when circumstances called for it.

Ninan and Qora used the remaining skyrock dust to encircle themselves. There was less now that Takan had wasted so much, barely enough and the ring had to be much thinner. They lay together in Qora's hammock. Outside the ring, the fire died down, and Ninan watched sleepily as the glow meandered through the embers. Qora's head rested on the crook of his arm, and her eyelashes fluttered as sleep overcame her. It was too hot to be so close, but after losing her for two days Ninan didn't dare put too much space between them, especially not for the sake of his own comfort, which he'd been without often enough lately that he hardly remembered it.

As he slept, he had two minds. The brain berry still affected him, somehow allowing him to be simultaneously alert and at rest. His body seemed capable of perceiving the details of his surroundings and piecing them together visually in his mind's eye, although the sights blended with his sleepy, nonsensical thoughts. As the effects continued to fade, he wondered what it would be like if the effects were at full force, if he would have been able to see everything as though he were wide awake, while still experiencing rest.

At dawn, when the sun peered up and cast pale light from below the horizon, Ninan dreamt of the previous night's fire. The flames moving together. Merging into a sly yellow serpent, hissing and elongating and turning dark. The sound was so real his pulse thundered in his ears. The serpent grew as thick as an arm and as long as eight men laid end to end—not simply a snake anymore but a serpentosaurid. Faster than Ninan could react, it slithered over him and Qora, wrapping itself around them, around the hammock, encasing them in a canvas cocoon. Ninan couldn't breathe. He fumbled for his blade, but the serpentosaurid was so tight on him he couldn't move his arms above the elbow.

Then it became clear that this was not a dream. Daylight reached full bloom and in it Qora's face drained of its natural color, turning purple. Ninan cried out in a stunted voice while Qora choked beside him. The serpentosaurid constricted, crushing Ninan's ribs, binding his lungs. It swiveled its head until they were eye to eye and flicked a forked, black tongue. Its body made a wave crest as it poised to strike. Ninan watched helplessly.

A deadly hiss. Muscles clenched as it drew back to build momentum. Jaw wide and fangs bared, dripping with venom. A mad dart forward.

Ninan braced himself for the piercing cut of those fangs when a vicious roar rattled his ears. Qoraptor leapt into view and chomped down on the serpentosaurid.

But the snake wasn't deterred. In fact, the bite spurred it. Its scales rubbed together, creating a dry, rasping noise.

With enough body length above Qoraptor's biting jaw, the serpentosaurid twisted and struck Qoraptor twice. Qoraptor yowled, and chomped down again. The serpentosaurid hissed in short bursts and struck back. The two reptiles battled with fangs and teeth and claws, and all the while, Qora and Ninan were bound together losing consciousness.

It was only when Qoraptor sank her teeth close to the serpentosaurid's head that Ninan sensed any difference in tension. Enough to stretch the length of his arm that was free.

Ninan grazed the hilt of his blade, effortfully walking his fingers down until he got a firm grasp. He bent his arm and brought the blade up against the snake, pressing with all his withering strength.

He dragged the blade back and forth with what little range of motion he had, sawing into flesh and spine, losing a fraction of consciousness with each push and pull. The serpentosaurid still clenched around him and Qora, emitting a long, strained hiss that crept into Ninan's ears and made him cringe.

Qoraptor snarled and gnawed the snake with her teeth, but she was losing strength too. A low whine erupted in her throat. The venom must have been agony in her veins.

Weakly, Ninan continued to saw. The pressure on his body was so intense he half expected his skull to split a rift right down the middle.

If he could just keep the blade in place. Cut deeper. Deeper.

Even though it was morning, stars flashed around him and his vision blackened and the grip of death began to pull him under.

But in an unexpected rush, his surroundings flooded back— too many colors at once, too bright, too stark—like nails driving into his bones.

The tension let up. Qora and Ninan both gasped.

Qoraptor groaned and slumped down.

The serpentosaurid still lived, bloody and shredded, wavering drunkenly but coming for them again. Finally, Ninan yanked his arm free and swung at the serpentosaurid's throat, the narrowest place right below the jaw. The severed head hurtled away as the body slapped to the ground.

Panting and nauseated, Ninan wriggled out of the snake's scaly mass and all but fell out of the hammock, nerves raw and buzzing. He stumbled to help Qora, unwrapping full yards of thick, serpentine flesh to free her. She coughed and gagged, burrowing into his shoulder.

For several minutes they held each other, catching their breaths, trying to make sense of everything. Ninan didn't know how long they clung together, both too stunned and repulsed to speak.

The serpentosaurid was dead but remained partially coiled around one of the trees to which the hammock was tied—three feet off the ground. There was a trail in the jungle floor that showed a record of the serpentosaurid's every move, the way it had dragged leaves and dirt under its heavy body. Visually, Ninan followed the shape and landed on a dark green heap.

"Qora," he whispered.

She didn't move until he said her name a second time. She looked up, then covered her mouth as tears brimmed her eyes.

Without a word, they hurried to Qoraptor. Her toothy jaw was slack. Bloody gashes marked her neck, shoulders, and snout. Ninan felt her chest for movement, desperate, trying to catch a rising or falling motion in between the throbbing of his own pulse. Qora listened at her snout.

Nothing.

"She's gone," Ninan said finally, trailing his fingers over her scales. His heart pinched.

Qora shook her head, cheeks glistening with tears.

The serpentosaurid carcass twisted all around their camp like a narrow river, its shimmer not so different from light on a body of water. Even though it was dead, Ninan shuddered at the sight of it, at the power in its length and thickness, at the way it remained clenched in different places.

"The skyrock ring isn't even broken except for where you and I stepped on the tarp," Qora said. "It's like the serpentosaurid … climbed right over it."

"It wasn't a strong ring to begin with. Especially not when we're running so low on dust."

The bigger the breed …

Ninan ached as he looked over Qoraptor's dead body, her golden eyes wide open.

Qora and Ninan sat and stared at her. Even though there was no time to waste, it seemed wrong to just walk away, to act like this didn't mean anything. This animal had been loyal to Ninan, saved his life, helped him save Qora's. They'd had a bond, however brief, in their time captive to Takan. Qora must have been thinking all her hope of reaching the ruins and getting back to Qhusi in time to help her brother was gone now, without Qoraptor's speed and protection. They were still behind schedule with more than fifty miles remaining, and even though only a few competitors remained to hinder them, they didn't know what else awaited them in the jungle. After the serpentosaurid, who knew what might be next?

Qora grasped her own head at the crown, weaving her fingers into her hair.

"We're not finished yet," Ninan assured her. "We'll keep following the river." He tried to sound encouraging, but he knew they'd never make it on foot.

"The river …" she repeated.

"I mean, that's the easiest—"

Qora perked up. "The current's fast. It swept me full miles in no time at all. If we could harness that speed, that would be even faster than Qoraptor ..."

Ninan nodded halfheartedly. "This last leg would be ideal for going by water; the river curves out of the way in some areas, but even with the extra miles, at *that* pace ..." The current moved at two to three miles per hour, and if they paddled consistently they might be able to add another two for a total of five. "Except, I don't think either one of us knows how to build a raft."

Which was too bad, since the river led straight to Wiqi Falls, where the ruins of Utula stood.

Qora got a far-off look in her eye. "What if there's something already built?" She stood, looking toward the water even though it wasn't visible from here.

Ninan got up and stood beside her, trying to see what she was seeing. "I don't follow."

"We'll need something to paddle with, obviously," she said, mostly to herself, "and probably some big leaves to coat it with, to cover the smell. Of course we'd have to get it *empty* ..."

"*Qora.*" Ninan braced her shoulders. "What are you saying?"

Her eyes drifted until they met his and it was like he'd woken her from a trance. "We *are* going to get to Utula on the river. In a pterodactyl nest."

FORTY-SEVEN

"WE'VE NARROWLY SURVIVED two pterodactyl attacks already," said Ninan. "You really want to push our luck?"

Qora heard his voice as if from behind a cloud, muffled, while her mind worked.

The pterodactyl nests could certainly support the weight of two humans; after all, they could support multiple pterodactyls. The nests were also watertight, because Qora had seen one float away when the river was swollen. And the nests were spacious, with raised sides that would keep passengers secure on rough rapids.

The only real problem would be keeping the pterodactyls away while Qora and Ninan stole one.

"I'd rather take time to build a shoddy raft," Ninan said as they walked parallel to the riverbank. From there they were protected by the trees, but near enough to the edge of the canopy that they could see through to the water and catch sight of any nests that might be clustered alongside it, scouting while they followed the route so they didn't lose more time.

"It won't be that hard to get a nest." Qora stripped twigs to make more bolts. "We'll use Takan's blowgun. We can tranquilize any pterodactyls we see, shoot any we can't tranquilize, and we'll stay under the trees until we clear them out so we have a safe place to run if they attack. This won't be like the other times;

we'll catch the pterodactyls off guard while they're resting, not draw them to us fast with a firestick. And the darts will be subtle; we won't upset the whole colony by causing abrupt pain with a bolt."

Ninan looked at her sidelong and ripped a couple of large leaves from a plant without losing the rhythm of his gait. "Shouldn't you save the darts for Utula? No matter what you're up against, it'd be better to have tranquilizers on hand."

"There's at least a hundred darts in the canister; I looked. We can spare a few. Besides, we won't even have the chance to use them at the end if we don't get there on time, right?"

He sighed and nodded. "You're crazy, though. You know that, right?"

Qora skimmed her knife over the bolt and smiled.

The riverbank was mostly clear except for birds and small flyers, and a group of protoceratops drinking at the water's edge, but otherwise Qora and Ninan were alone. No one came to airdrop supplies anymore, probably because there was almost no one left to fight over them.

Within a couple hours, Qora pointed to the bank. "There."

Ninan peered down.

It was much smaller than the colony they'd encountered the previous week. Here there were five nests, about thirty-five eggs divided between them, and fourteen adult pterodactyls perched throughout the cluster, with no young hatched yet. One pterodactyl flew off and another soon landed and took its place. Some of them snacked on piranhas, dipping their beaks into the river and coming back up with a mouthful of gnashing fish.

"So which nest do we go for?" Ninan asked.

Qora shrugged. "The one closest to the far-side edge? That way, we can break it off and push it right into the current."

"Good idea. I don't want any trouble, and we'll want to get out of here as fast as we can."

Ninan set to work on making paddles from young trees with sturdy, narrow trunks. He used the machete like an axe, hacking a growing dent until he was deep enough to snap the whole thing with a push. Qora collected the remainder of the leaves and made calculations to determine how many darts it would require to knock out each pterodactyl.

A single dart could knock out a human for around twelve hours—depending on weight—or a thousand-pound reptile like Qoraptor for around one hour (according to Ninan). The pterodactyls were probably closer to five hundred pounds, and it wouldn't be necessary to tranquilize them for a long period of time. Thus, a single dart for each pterodactyl should suffice.

While Ninan prepared their pack and all other supplies they might need, Qora situated herself in a hiding spot with a strong vantage point—a climbable tree so she could angle down at the pterodactyls, but not so high up that she wouldn't be able to jump down and make a run for it if she needed to.

When they were all set up, Ninan came to Qora's spot. He handed her the blowgun with its canister full of darts. "You're a much better shot than me with any weapon."

Qora accepted the blowgun and admired the fine work of the darts, the tiny plant-fiber fletching, the tips dyed red with paralyzing poison, the fact that there were so many of them. This had been a hobby of Takan's as much as a resource, she could tell that much. Traps, snares, toxic weapons. He must have been feeding himself well.

"Alright," Qora said. "Ready?"

"Ready."

With the loaded blowgun in hand, she aimed for the first

pterodactyl, inhaled deeply, and blew.

With a sharp *ffffpt*, the dart zipped out, piercing the pterodactyl's neck.

Less than a minute later, the pterodactyl swayed, its body going soft, its head flopping like it was too heavy to hold up, and thunked down.

The other pterodactyls squawked and yipped, a couple of them nudging their fallen companion.

Ninan gave Qora an encouraging nod, so she repeated this with all the pterodactyls until the last one lay unconscious. They exchanged a glance, picked up their things, and headed for the cluster.

They had to tread carefully along the soggy bank, which was littered with arapaima bones. Ninan boosted Qora into the first nest, then handed her the pack, paddles, and leaf coverings rolled up together like a large green scroll, and climbed in after her. They clambered over the nests, some of which were still on land connected to others that touched the water, until they reached the one they'd set their sights on, holding their noses.

The pterodactyls appeared as though they were dead, all limp and splayed out.

Qora held her crossbow to her chest.

Once they reached the nest, Qora handed Ninan the eggs one by one and he set them into another nest. They threw in their supplies, climbed in, and began the detachment process.

The nests were bound together with some unsavory reptilian secretion. It was flexible and strong, a mess of gluey white globs that ran deep into the framework. Ninan and Qora pushed off at the same time, straining and grunting. But the nests barely creaked.

The nest that Qora had seen floating off the other day must

have been a rare malfunction in pterodactyl tactics, she thought.

"Let me try the machete." She handed her crossbow to Ninan, then wedged the blade between the two nests, guiding it back and forth to make a deep cut, but finding the substance incredibly sticky, so much that she almost couldn't pull the machete out once she was in the thick of it. Finally, she wrenched out the weapon and flung it onto the pack with a huff, hands on her hips as she thought about what to do next.

Ninan, without warning, raised the crossbow and shot. Something heavy dropped behind Qora and the nest bobbed vigorously under it.

When she turned to see what had fallen, a half-dead pterodactyl flapped in the nest, probably the one that had flown off earlier, now returning. Its angry wings whipped like a boat sail in a windstorm and shoved Qora into the water. Amid the sound of her own splashing—and her screams, as no fewer than six piranhas nipped at her thighs—the crossbow clicked twice more, and then Ninan's hand shot into the water to grab her. The nest snapped and cracked at the joint. Qora and Ninan crouched low, balancing on the rim, both of them reeling, Qora's heart hammering as she tore off the three piranhas that still clung to her knees. Her weight and Ninan's weight and the weight of the dead pterodactyl and of all the belongings tore the nest from its cluster. Instantly, Qora and Ninan were caught in the river's current, gliding onward at high speed.

They scrambled to get the paddles set up. The nest spun slowly and provided a dramatic, panoramic view of the water road. Qora couldn't help but laugh.

Being out in the open—*really* out in the open, not a fear-for-her-life sprint away from the rainforest—felt like breathing for the first time in weeks. The sky seemed wider and bluer, the air fresher, the possibilities immeasurable.

"Sky Mother provides for us," she whispered.

ᗺᗺᗺ

Once they had settled themselves with the river's flow, it was time to address the problem of removing the pterodactyl. It was so heavy that despite their combined strength and the leverage of both paddles, they barely managed to rotate it halfway. Even if they could manage to lift it up onto the edge, Qora figured it would probably capsize the nest.

"I think I know what we have to do," Ninan said.

There were only so many options, and Qora could already see where he was going with this.

She grimaced. "Don't say it."

"It's the only way. It's too heavy."

"Can't we just—"

Ninan handed her the machete. "Heads? Or tails?"

The reptile was big, but its limbs were narrow under all that wing membrane, its bones light. That, at least, was to their advantage. They started with those, each taking a side. Then Ninan worked on the head while Qora handled the body; after all, she'd helped butcher enough reptiles for meat to have a good idea where to start. Every cut spilled more of that blackish blood, and by the time they'd finished, they both looked like they'd been involved in a massacre. The nest floor looked like they'd given it an intentional coat of paint.

"Bet you're thinking stegosaur slime isn't so bad now." Ninan wiped blood from his neck but somehow added more.

Qora wrinkled her nose in response.

Ninan grinned and gave her shoulder a pat, leaving a bloody

handprint on her sleeve.

She gasped and returned his handprint with her own on his chest. Then he reached for her hip and simultaneously pulled her up against him. They swayed together for balance as the nest bobbed in the water and he steadied her in his arms. He brushed his thumb over her chin.

"Why don't we … finish and get cleaned up first," she suggested. His lips were tempting but she didn't want this blood on her longer than necessary.

Ninan dropped his arms. "That's probably a good idea."

Neither of them could stomach the thought of eating the pterodactyl, but they kept a portion anyway—a loin cut—because it would be a waste not to, and tossed the rest overboard for the dakosaurs and the piranhas. The water predators converged on the raw meat from all sides, audibly chewing and tearing it from the bones and sending out ripples behind them.

Qora and Ninan drifted away on the water, glassy with the reflection of all the verdure and the sapphire sky, and let the nest carry them safely.

The smell of the nest wasn't so bad now that they had moved on from the cluster, where guano and sludge had surely been gathering underneath for months, maybe years. The fresh water made a world of difference. Qora unrolled the leaves and lined the nest's interior until everything was smooth and green, hiding all evidence of the slaughter they had committed.

Whatever scent lingered seemed to deter most other reptiles, some territorial mark of the pterodactyls. Thank the gods it was good for something, Qora thought.

The heralds flew over once, pausing to assess this strange new development, and then disappeared when it was clear there would be no further action for a while.

Once they'd gone, Ninan's fingers found the hem of his shirt and pulled it up over his head. He shook out his hair, which was stringy and matted as it skimmed the back of his neck. His shoulder muscles flexed when he leaned over to drag the shirt through the water, blood flowing off like an excess of red dye. His copper-toned skin gleamed in the sun, with a watercolor map of old and new bruises splotched over it.

Ninan watched the river on the opposite side of the nest and waited for Qora to drag her own clothes through the water. It took her a while to convince herself it was safe, to bare any part of herself. She repeatedly glanced over to see if he was peeking, but he kept his gaze forward, his elbows on the rim and his palms forming visors on either side of his face.

"Can I turn around now?" he asked after a few minutes.

"I don't know …" Qora said. "I think maybe I'll let everything dry completely before I put it back on. Think you can wait a while longer?"

She said this already fully clothed again, having wrung out her shirt and pants and put them back on. Thanks to the blazing heat, they were already half dried.

Ninan groaned but she could hear a weary smile on him when he said, "You're killing me, Qora."

She exaggerated a sigh. "Okay, fine. You can turn around."

He lowered one hand and turned with leery measure. Before he even got a full glimpse, he tackled her to the bottom of the nest. He positioned himself over her, his forearms pressed to the floor at her sides. "You have no idea what you're doing to me."

She gazed up into his bruised face where so much mystery lay. "I guess I don't."

It was hard to believe he could find her appealing when she looked like some dinosaur had already chewed her up and spit her out. Her appearance was a far cry from the days when her mamáy would dress her up in a beaded blouse and embroidered skirts, and arrange her hair into an intricate plait, and remind her that a good marriage could strengthen two families, before dragging her off to social festivities held among the locals of her district. But here and now, she was completely unembellished—except for the claw marks and the bloodstains and the bruises, of course.

Ninan must have been a sight before, though, she thought, with all the money his family must have had. What would he look like if she could see him in his usual element, combed and cleaned and dressed to make an impression? Would he be the same boy? Would he be allowed to consider her the way he did now?

Qora had already decided a while ago that she would rather not know where he really came from, whatever it was that made him feel so guilty. Who knew if their ways of life could ever overlap? She'd rather go on like this, in ignorance. Feeling his heartbeat while she held a fistful of his shirt, his breath a breeze on her cheek, his lips pressing into hers gently like he was afraid to hurt her, like he was suppressing an eagerness she suddenly wanted to unleash.

If they died, there was no reason to worry about the things in Qhusi that might so easily keep them apart. She slipped her hand around the back of his head and kissed him with full force, and the way he looked at her afterward said everything she ever needed to know about him.

))D

The heralds blared their horns six times, and daytime burned to night like a fire turning wood to char, a flaming sunset that dissolved to black, with stars like sparkling white embers.

364

The heavily starred Sky River flowed like a stream of spilt milk, reflected in the water—the kind of sight that never would have shown through the jungle canopy.

The figures in the star groups were the brightest Qora had ever seen, drawing out the dark silhouettes between them. The Serpent, The Seven Llamas, and The Sauropod, all coming to drink from the Sky River's celestial waters. Beyond them she located Kantuta Flower, Raptoriva in Flight, Astrodon, and the legendary Kuymi and the Tricorn.

Ninan brought the nest to a stop. Qora threaded a rope between a breach in the nest branches to make a handle to pull it ashore, and together they heaved it up under the trees a safe distance from the water.

Ninan made a paste of the skyrock dust and spread it around the nest's rim; it dried quickly into a permanent ring of protection around the cradle where they would sleep.

The pterodactyl loin was bitter meat, chewy and tough, but Qora was reluctantly grateful for the chance to eat fresh meat without having to hunt.

Afterward, they took stock of their supplies. Ninan had managed to bring all the things Takan had stolen—whatever Ninan and Qora had had in their packs, plus additional items from other competitors, and most importantly, another firestick. Qora silently thanked all the gods and spirits for that, vowing not to get herself into another situation where she'd have to use it as a weapon.

Then Ninan unrolled the map on the ground and sat before it with his arm draped over one knee, hair falling into his face. He traced the river line with his first two fingers. "We left just before the river snakes away from the route"—he pointed to the spot—"and stopped just as it snakes back, leaving us just fourteen miles short of the ruins now. We've probably had to travel close to fifty miles because of the curves adding length, but that's still thirty-seven miles of progress toward the ruins—in *one day*."

Qora scooted closer, looking over his shoulder, scanning the map herself. "That means we've doubled our pace. Not our early pace, of course, but our fastest since the halfway point at least. That's ... amazing."

They would arrive at Utula a few hours after taking off in the morning. Then they could finally search for the golden spinosaur tooth, and hope to survive whatever was guarding it.

Ninan shook his head in disbelief and turned to Qora and cupped her cheek. "Qora, the nest was *brilliant*."

"Well, it was the only logical solution."

"Logical? To rob a swoop of flyers?" Ninan spit a laugh.

Qora shrugged. "They know this environment better than anyone. They're already armored against it. And now, we are too."

FORTY-EIGHT

NINAN AND QORA CONTINUED TO MOVE fast on the river. Ninan gazed at the endless greenery, relieved at the thought that without the nest they would still be miles behind and hopelessly hacking through the jungle one branch or vine at a time.

They found early on that they would need to construct a cover, however, now that they didn't have a constant roof of fronds over them. They fashioned a few poles similar to what they'd used for the paddles, with the tarp strung over the top—a meager but sufficient shelter from the brutal sun and what was sure to be coming rainfall.

Qora used a single paddle to rotate the nest and whirled them all around to look at everything.

Long sections of the river didn't have walkable banks; trees and bushes grew right up to the edge, leaves dangling into the water and brushing it with a lazy caress. Other sections had tall, eroded sides from the sometimes high-sweeping current, baring ruddy dirt and stray roots.

Before noon, Qora and Ninan hit a calm stretch that didn't need much navigation. The water split the rainforest like a jagged, polished blade, and the sky was filled with downy clouds that diffused the sun and softened its heat.

Within the hour, they should reach Wiqi Falls, a cascade

said to spill down in feathery white streams, spraying mists that carried divine knowledge.

Qora slid her fingers between Ninan's as they lay on their backs. The humidity built between their hands and Ninan couldn't help but think that there were so many ways she could slip out of his grasp in the coming days, so many ways he could lose her.

But of course he'd lose her no matter what. He'd been acting like there was no "after this" because, for so many days, it had felt like there wouldn't be. In the beginning, it had felt like he would be wandering forever. Alone. Always looking over his shoulder. Hunger scraping his belly. An endless loop of torment. But now, with the end in sight, he had to seriously consider how things would be when they returned to Qhusi—since they very well might return.

"What if we don't make it?" Qora asked. Sunlight kissed her closed eyelids and her chin trembled as she spoke. "What if ... what if we've come all this way, and made it through all these things, just to die here at the very end?"

There was a dull ache in Ninan's limbs that had nothing to do with his wounds. He squeezed Qora's hand, feeling her individual knuckles with the individual pads of his fingertips. That golden tooth would be mounted somewhere, giving the illusion that it was just within reach, and then some horde of scaly demons would emerge to prove otherwise. A small part of him hoped he and Qora *would* die, because it was the only way they'd ever really be free of all that was working against them. He didn't know for sure what he believed about the hereafter, about the High World and spiritual rest, but he sensed that whatever came next was going to test them in ways they couldn't yet imagine.

"Then we die together."

She rolled over to face him. When he mirrored her, she put her forehead against his and sighed. She stroked his jaw, sending chills through his body.

They stayed this way for a long time, neither of them wanting to get up to see the last stretch of landscape before they traded their temporary peace. He pressed their lips together and drew her close, but Qora pulled away and sat up so abruptly he almost thought he'd offended her. Then she tilted her head, aiming her ear at something.

Ninan rose and peered over the rim of the nest to scan for predators.

No pterodactyls in sight. No caimans or dakosaurs. Nothing but the water's glimmer and the same repeating mass of trees on either side of the aquatic road. No sounds but the usual buzz of jungle fauna. Except—

"You hear it too, don't you?" Qora moved to their paddles and plunged one into the river, concentric circles rippling around it. She began to paddle intensely, pushing the nest toward the bank as fast as she could.

There was a burble that was too loud for these smooth waters, a rush that implied a heavy current. But they were sliding along like a fleck on a puddle of oil. There were no rapids. No breaking waves. No whitewater to account for the static hush that swelled in the distance.

The scent of the misty spray hit Ninan before it peeked above the vanishing point ahead, catching a flare of light that split into a multicolored beam.

Ninan lunged for the other paddle and dug into the water. "I thought we had more time!"

As they paddled, the nest barely drifted from its original

course. They would need at least four people to move it across at a reasonable speed.

Ninan's arms went rigid, his grip fierce on the paddle. Qora held her spine straight as a spear shaft as she plunged over and over. Ninan tried to sync with her rhythm, to give them a greater combined power.

The current picked up as they neared the waterfall's drop-off. Its mist condensed and beaded on them like sweat.

Qora shouted, "Come on! We can't let it go over!" But her shout was like a whisper in the volume of the flow.

They moved inches at a time, every lateral progression canceled by the force that swept them downstream. Ninan's face was wet not only with mist but with the splash of his urgent strokes.

They pushed closer and closer to the bank. For a moment, it seemed like they might make it—until the nest struck an eddy that sent them spinning, a force that slammed them both against the nest's inner wall. They drew both paddles into the nest to keep from losing them, and collapsed together, out of breath and soaking wet, as the nest began to keel.

"Quick!" Ninan shouted. "Grab the rope!"

The tow rope was tied in a bundle opposite where they sat, at the back end that rose fast against the drop. Qora threw herself as a counterweight, then held tight to the rim to brace herself. Ninan followed.

"The firestick!" Qora's eyes darted to the pack as it slid to the other end of the nest.

Ruck.

The treated dinoleather material of Takan's stolen pack was impermeable, but if completely submerged, everything inside would get wet through the opening.

Ninan crouched and held onto the rim with one hand and stretched out his full arm span, reaching for the pack. He grasped it by a single strap and only managed to curl two fingers around it, his joints burning under its weight.

And then they were airborne.

Ninan's heart and lungs clenched.

Not yet.

What he'd previously thought about contentment in death—he suddenly regretted it with every cell of his body. His limbs and his veins and his bones all screamed that it wasn't time, that he hadn't meant it. That he was not ready to let go.

His mouth was open like he was screaming, and he was sure he must have been—with his diaphragm strained so tightly it felt like he might eject his soul through his throat—but he couldn't hear it. All he could hear was the violent wall of water and the blood drumming in his ears. Qora clung to the ropes and closed her eyes and scrunched her face. Ninan imagined she was crying out like he was.

Their bodies couldn't balance against the angle of the nest. Every second, they were a breath away from breaking loose. He got a third finger around the pack strap and curled his hand shut. He firmed up his grip on the nest rim.

For an instant, it was like they were hovering, suspended, and that the watery surface below was zooming up to meet them rather than the other way around. The droplets in the mist were like thousands of pinpricks. The mist itself was all consuming and surrounded them in a blanket of white.

A shroud.

Ninan remembered a particular gondola flight, so high that he and the attendants had passed through a cloud pillar that had looked white like this from the inside. Being younger, he'd thought the High World could be so simple—the lightweight feeling of soaring above the earth, the perceived comfort of spirits he couldn't see. Now he didn't know what to think, but he believed there were forces much stronger than humankind. Forces that could bury him like he had never existed.

The far end of the nest pierced the water first. The nest rocked violently when the near end followed, catapulting Ninan from his place. He let go of the pack as the impact launched him into the shearing forces where the waterfall churned into the bottom pool. At last, he did hear a scream, but it wasn't his own. It was Qora's, garbled and fading fast. The recirculating current sucked him under.

He kicked his legs and paddled his arms, but the water only pulled him back again. With every kick and stroke, he diminished the quality of the air in his lungs. His muscles craved energy. His lungs begged him to release the breath he was holding, but he shook his head like he could will away this desperation. His ears ached with pressure. His skull throbbed like it was going to implode. Soon he could barely move. He struggled for as long as he could, an eternity trapped in a minute.

He couldn't fight it anymore. His mouth exploded and a flurry of bubbles skittered over his tongue and past his teeth and he watched them float up and away. He forced himself not to inhale yet, defying nature. Defying logic. But there was no logic here, not when he was stuck between worlds. He wasn't underground, wasn't above it. He was … elsewhere. Between the living and the dead. If he didn't inhale, he would die. If he *did* inhale, he would die.

His body sank. The urge to inhale grew more powerful with each second that passed, but he managed to hold onto his will a moment longer, and then another. Then his foot struck something hard—a boulder.

With one last hope and one last scrap of willpower, he kicked off.

He broke free from the circulation, but was doubtful he could make it to the surface in time, before a spasmodic lurch in his throat would drag water inside of him. His body went limp. He thought he heard his name, the smallest of muffled sounds.

Two hands cuffed his wrists and he felt himself floating. He broke through the surface of the water and gasped for air, a painful relief burning his throat. Weakly, and with Qora's assistance, he clambered over the edge of the nest and flopped down inside, coughing and sputtering. Everything around him spun except Qora, who knelt beside him, shaking.

Ninan propped himself up on his elbows, waiting for everything to come into focus. Suddenly, he remembered where they were. Or where they were supposed to be. Then he pushed up to a sitting position, against Qora's protests, but he toppled onto his hands and knees when his weakness got the better of him.

"Where—" he rasped, looking past the edge of the nest.

He saw it in reflection first, all wavy and distorted by the fine ripples of the current. Then he looked up.

It was small for a fortress, but still impressively wide and high. Four cylindrical towers rose up at each corner, with walls spanning the distance between them. A shorter, defensive wall lined the perimeter but was now mostly broken. Battlements topped every wall—the defensive squared openings typical of the castles in the lands where the Kastillans had come from. Much of the castle was crumbling, and moss filled the cracks, but the structure remained otherwise flawless and beautiful.

Qora's eyes fixated below, however, on the castle grounds.

The entire frontal tract was a mud-bed of human skeletons and mauled corpses at varying degrees of decay—some of which looked vaguely familiar from the sendoff—with weapons and broken supplies and copper firebomb shells scattered between them. And there was no growth, just earth trampled bare, the imprints of death in the soil. Even the surrounding jungle had been worn down, trees broken or bent unnaturally apart as though they were averse to whatever lay between them.

Thunder rumbled remotely, something Ninan didn't think much of until it occurred to him that there were no clouds at the moment, no obvious foreshadows of a storm.

Qora and Ninan exchanged glances.

Then, from behind the fortress appeared a massive black creature with a red spinal sail. If Ninan hadn't felt his pulse thumping so heavily, he would have thought his heart had stopped.

In an instant, the spinosaur approached the bank and opened its mouth to release a deafening roar. From here, its individual teeth were distinguishable—and one of them was gold.

SPINOSAURUS (*spi-noh-SOH-russ*)

Clade: Theropoda **Length:** 50-60 ft **Weight:** 7-9 tons

Large spinosaurid theropod dinosaur. This longest-known terrestrial carnivore bears a massive crocodilian skull, conical teeth, robust forelimbs, and incredibly powerful hindlimbs, balanced by a long and heavy tail. Distinguishable by a brightly colored sail that runs the length of its spine.

The Runaqan Compendium of Reptiles

FORTY-NINE

QORA COULDN'T MOVE.

The Venture had taken its premise to a new level. The object Qora and Ninan sought was not only *guarded* by a monster—as so many of the game's prizes had been before—but this time, it was *part* of the monster.

Ninan nudged her as he reached for a paddle, although he, like her, couldn't seem to form any spoken words, or take his eyes off the spinosaur.

The spinosaur stepped into the water, its giant head coming toward them, golden tooth gleaming, and suddenly it was as though Qora's nightmare had burgeoned all at once, a hundredfold increase in size and savagery. In the spinosaur's raging jaws, she saw the resemblance of the sailbeast, teeth digging into Ollan's neck and shoulders, blood seeping and spurting. Her stomach went sour, body trembling. The dinoleather boots that were stuck to her feet were no longer the symbol she'd wished them to be, a meager vengeance in the face of a towering demon.

Ninan paddled the opposite direction and pushed toward the bank across from the ruins, but Qora knew—she was certain—they wouldn't be able to outpaddle the spinosaur. The spinosaur looked like some binary of evolution, equipped with the powerful legs of a walking land predator but the webbed feet and wide, rudder-tail of a sea monster.

Another step into the water—an easy motion for the spinosaur that quickly closed the gap Ninan had paddled so furiously to create.

This was how it always ended for Venturers, Qora thought. Weeks of trying to survive, cheating death, wearing themselves thin as mosquito wings, only to die before the real battle had even begun. Maybe this was how it ended for humankind in general: barely eking out an existence, haunted by the horrors of the past while the future held nothing but impossible barriers.

The spinosaur roared again. Then, as its gnashing teeth came down, it jerked back. It turned its fury toward another prey—a competitor who had somehow managed to wrap a rusty chain around one of the spinosaur's hind limbs. And then, as if from nowhere, the heralds appeared.

Thanks to the distraction, however, Ninan gained some distance. Qora steadied herself enough to take and use the paddle on her side of the nest before the whole thing spun.

The other competitor launched a fistful of skyrock dust, coating the spinosaur's dark scales and sending up a cloud around its head. The spinosaur thrashed and roared.

The second the nest struck the opposite bank, Qora and Ninan climbed out, their feet slipping on the silt as they dragged the nest ashore. From what they now hoped was a safe distance, they watched. The competitor jabbed a longblade into the spinosaur's ribs, but the blade only made a shallow cut. With a single snap of its jaws, the spinosaur tore the man in half.

Struck by a scene that reminded her so closely of the worst day of her life, Qora covered her mouth and sank to her knees.

⟫⟫⟫

Qora's grip on Ninan's hand must have been making his fingers go numb by now, but he hadn't said anything. With approximately four hundred feet of distance—and a small body of water—between them and the spinosaur, Qora forced herself to sit on the bank and face the reality of the situation.

The spinosaur dragged the rusty chain for a long time before finally flinging it loose. The chain must have been a remnant of the fortress, something left behind by the Kastillans before they'd been driven out. Qora wondered what other potential supplies might be inside, but she doubted it would be anything powerful enough to kill a reptile that large. Maybe if there happened to be a cannon.

"It's male," Ninan said. "Female spinosaur sails are less vivid, almost pink, and smaller—at least in the compendium illustrations."

Qora wasn't sure this mattered, although at least they wouldn't have to worry about the potential for a nest of spinosaur hatchlings nearby, or some juvenile brood they might have to fight off. One spinosaur was more than enough to deal with.

She had to focus, to block out her memories. She had to make an objective hunter's assessment. She had to observe the way the spinosaur moved, the way his muscles shifted, to determine where his organs were likely to be. His shimmering black scales seemed to slide back and forth over his joints, stark and stunning and menacing. The red sail stood out on his back, the color of fresh blood, the color of the dye bath outside Qora's house, the color of death. How could he be so horrifying and so beautiful at the same time? Additional marks of red striped his back and limbs, blended like a painter's careful brushstrokes. To see this in person felt like both a privilege and a punishment.

Qora had limited knowledge about spinosaurs; they were

foreign creatures who rarely ended up north of the Pirqa mountain range. But it was said they used their sails for intimidation and herding prey both in water and on land, with the lower portion of the sail containing fat stores that allowed them more time between meals.

She connected similarities between the spinosaur and the sailbeast. Firstly, an animal that didn't hunt often was difficult to follow; fat storage meant fewer meals, which meant less ruck to identify; maintaining that fat storage meant less movement, which meant fewer tracks.

"The fact that he kills so often isn't natural," Qora told Ninan. "Most reptiles kill to eat."

"Well, based on the way so many of the bodies have been left to rot, the spinosaur's clearly not eating them. So, I'd have to agree."

How many of those bodies had been competitors? Qora wondered. And how many had been local hunters who had stumbled upon the spinosaur by accident, drawn in by the prized tooth? How many had been innocent, with no harmful intentions, and had simply been in the wrong place at the wrong time?

All throughout the Venture, Qora had imagined that the golden tooth would be hidden someplace hard to get, but she'd never imagined it would be *in the mouth it came from*. Spirits knew how the coordinators had managed to get it gilded. There were legends of other lands in which select humans had the ability to turn things to gold with their touch, and although these were nothing more than children's stories, she couldn't help but think that magic would have been the only way to accomplish such a thing. More likely, the coordinators had sedated it somehow, although even the most potent skyrock products would barely control a beast that size—weighing tens of thousands of pounds. Ninan seemed particularly frustrated by the idea, with whatever the coordinators might have up their sleeves that defied common knowledge.

Understanding and exploiting a reptile's limitations was half the battle, though—more important than size or speed, as Ollan had said. Except Qora didn't have the faintest idea how she would extract the tooth. She would have to kill the spinosaur, set off the firestick signal, and hope the still-rooted tooth would be sufficient to win.

As Qora and Ninan continued to observe, they were soon drawn to the sound of shouting amid the broken trees across the pond. Two competitors emerged, one in pursuit of the other, each bloody and bruised.

At this point, heralds had been taking shifts in pairs, one pair in the sky at all times constantly patrolling the area. With most other competitors dead and only a few remaining, all of whom seemed to have already set up camp or were nearing the area, there was sure to be action every few hours or less.

Meanwhile, the spinosaur had been busy drinking at the bank, so much so fast that Qora half expected the water level to drop noticeably before her eyes. The spinosaur, too, turned his attention to the commotion.

As one of the competitors drew a blade, the spinosaur swept toward them, clamping his jaws over the first as the second fled back to the jungle's depths.

Qora wanted to cover her eyes, but she didn't. This was no time to shy away from what she would soon be facing. She couldn't cower this time.

Of course that was easier said than done, when she hadn't yet gotten close enough to be in any immediate danger.

The spinosaur chomped twice and then left the first man's

body mangled on the ground as he stomped off in pursuit of the second. A game, he seemed to think. Qora and Ninan witnessed the second death only by sound—branches snapping and an uproar of shifting leaves, then a loud scream abruptly cut short.

An hour or so later as Qora hugged her knees to her chest, heart still racing and unable to let herself relax, she spotted someone else at the top of the fortress, hiding between the battlements.

"Who's that?" Ninan asked.

Qora squinted. It was a lithe, tattooed woman with her hair tied in a low knot, carrying a spear. "It's the Allpan," she told him. "With the spear. We saw her at the Rock Forest. I can't believe she survived that firebomb." And clearly she'd survived a lot *more*, since she'd managed to make it here to the ruins.

The spinosaur moved across the grounds, pausing to listen when any of the jungle noises turned especially loud. As he neared the fortress where the woman waited, Qora held her breath.

The woman unwound a length of rope, which ended in a grappling hook. She hurled it at the spinosaur's back, and the hook caught in his spine. He grunted as the woman leapt from the battlements, clutching the rope, and yanking it tight when her feet landed. The spinosaur twisted his neck, snapping his jaws at her. She walked her hands up the rope and pulled herself toward the spinosaur's rearing head. When she reached the base, she plunged her spear into the scales. The spear appeared to be tipped with a smilodon tooth—one of the few things that could break through tougher scales like this.

The spinosaur bellowed, baring a dark, cavernous throat and a gleaming tongue, his pink buccal flaps stretched to full capacity at the corners of his mouth.

Suddenly Qora felt herself transported. She was thirteen

years old again—slinking through the woods, crossbow in hand.

After three long months of stalking the sailbeast, there it was: black throat gaping at her, tongue long and pointed with a tip that rose and curved like a snake ready to strike. A string of saliva dangled from its jagged teeth. With one panicked click of Ollan's crossbow, Qora shot a bolt into its mouth—a clean puncture to the soft palate. The reptile collapsed on the spot. Qora trembled, panting. Warily, she approached the beast and looked into its dead eyes before she shot it twice more for good measure.

Coming back to herself in the present moment, Qora studied the spinosaur's mouth, the way it opened.

The woman had been trying to exploit a similar vulnerability, Qora thought. The base of the head, to get to the brain. But it wasn't going to work. Not if the spinosaur was as genetically similar to the sailbeast as it appeared to be. There was a reason people made armor from dinosaur skin—and this skin was first rate.

"No ..." Qora whispered aloud.

"What is it?" Ninan asked.

The woman held onto the spear as the spinosaur thrashed, but the movement was too strong. The spinosaur flung her to the ground, where she fell between his massive legs. She scrambled to get back up but a webbed foot came down on her, pinning her in place while she wailed. Then the spinosaur inclined his head toward her, grasped her with his claws, and sank his teeth in.

Holding back the bile that threatened to rise in her throat, Qora turned to Ninan and said, "I only know of one way we can be almost sure to kill it."

Ninan squeezed her hand and nodded. "Let's get to work."

FIFTY

THE PLAN WAS TO GET UP HIGH. Unlike the fallen competitor, however, they wouldn't risk getting too close. Ninan helped Qora devise a plan to draw the spinosaur to them from a safe vantage point, and from there—if possible—Qora would make the fatal shot. Failing that, Ninan would scatter Takan's pollenbane in hopes that they might be able to poison the spinosaur slowly over the several hours that followed (provided such a large reptile was susceptible to it), and they would also bring Takan's blowgun and exhaust the entire supply of sedative darts and hope that it would be enough to slow the spinosaur long enough to get away.

Ninan gathered wood and cut it to size while Qora stripped it down for bolts. He then built her a fire so that she could perfect the bolts, bending them over the heat to make them straight.

It was midday by the time they'd amassed a good supply of ammo, and they hadn't eaten yet. Eventually, Ninan pried Qora away from the bolt tip she was whittling and insisted they take a break for some sustenance.

"We can't fight that thing on an empty stomach," he told her.

"Fine," she said, "But no hunting. I don't want to waste a single one of these"—she touched to the pile of bolts—"on any animal that isn't the spinosaur."

"Fair enough. I'll go see if I can find any wild root vegetables. We can roast them on the coals now that the fire is dying."

He went off a ways into the trees, but stopped when he came upon a clearing. The ground was covered with fallen leaves and other plant debris, but for some reason, nothing grew for several yards in each direction. Curious, he took a few steps into it—and both legs immediately began to sink into the soil.

Their hands will rise to meet any who may dare to stumble over the gates of the Grave, and by your fear they will know you, as clearly as the cadence of your voice or the contours of your face—and by your fear, they will hold you.

From "The Pits of Tapuy" by Hatun Walla

FIFTY-ONE

IT MUST HAVE BEEN ANOTHER HALF HOUR that Qora continued to work, until she paused to massage the cramping in her hand and realized Ninan had been gone much longer than necessary. She scoured the immediate area, through the opening where she'd seen him leave, looking for signs of him.

There was a trail where he had hacked deeper into the blanket of green, and marks in the dirt where he'd pushed aside leaves, probably to look for any cassava that might be hiding among them.

A muted sound caught Qora's attention. She strained her ears through the layers of noise. Howling monkeys, birds calling back and forth, the distant rush of the waterfall.

A human boy's grunt.

The grunts grew louder as Qora moved toward them, until she reached a clearing with a wide area of bare rainforest floor. And Ninan was in the middle of it, buried up to his armpits.

"Stop!" he shouted when he saw her, raising a muddy hand. "Don't take another step."

When she glanced at her feet, the earth appeared to be solid, flat, and unthreatening—and yet, Ninan was sprouting out of it like a thistle, his legs somewhere underneath like the roots he was supposed to have been digging for.

"This whole thing is a pit." He panted, sweat glued his hair to his temples. When he moved his hips in demonstration, the earth around him moved too—but only slightly—a viscous fluid with a deceptively ordinary surface.

"Where does it start?" Qora scoured the underbrush until she found a long, sturdy branch. She held it out to him.

He shook his head and reached out, wrapping his fingers around the end. "Basically wherever nothing's growing."

"It's like the 'Pits of Tapuy,'" said Qora. "Spirits of the dead reaching up from the Grave World to test the bravery of those who fall. They know when you're afraid. The harder you fight, the tighter their grip on you."

Ninan grunted again as he struggled against the mud that seemed to suck . "That's a nice metaphor, but not very helpful."

"It's literal, too. You're not supposed to fight it. If you panic, it sucks you down."

"I've figured out that much. Except, staying still isn't exactly doing anything for me either."

"Okay, so move, but … slowly."

He huffed and looked down at himself. "Okay."

With the gentlest motions, he made progress. The silty mud began to budge. Ninan got a leg up, and from there angled his body laterally until he was basically floating—although the mud was so thick he was more like a corpse emerging from a grave. Then, finally, he freed both legs and crawled to where Qora could offer an arm for support, and together they freed him from the foul pit.

"Come on," Qora said. "Let's rinse you off."

Ninan cleaned off most of the mud at the waterfront as Qora finished up the bolts. With the bolt supply complete, they worked on a rope that would span the fortress from top to bottom in case they needed to drop quickly. Qora separated grass into bundles while Ninan twisted them together, folding the length of the growing rope onto itself until it formed an additional, fortified twist, and gradually wove more grass into it. Qora's wounded hand had healed enough now to form a good scab, but she wrapped it tightly for extra protection.

They finished everything in the early afternoon and loaded up the nest. Then they waited as the spinosaur stood at the water's edge, dipping his head under. When he reemerged, he held an arapaima between his teeth and chomped to break up the meal. A bulge rolled down his throat and disappeared. When he was finished, he wandered off into the half-trampled jungle of his territory.

Now that the spinosaur had taken its leave, they were ready—and so were the heralds, who kept close.

In the nest, Qora and Ninan pushed off, and quickly paddled across the pool, banking a few yards from the fortress grounds. They jumped out and sprinted for the ruins, both armed with crossbows and quivers. Ninan carried the rope, looped over itself and attached to his belt, along with his final smoker and a couple of matches—in case of emergency. Qora kept the pollenbane and the darts.

As soon as they got close, Qora covered her mouth. Ninan gagged.

The mud was embedded with skeletons—half-buried rib cages, and skulls with mouths wide open like they were crying out. Leg and arm bones protruded from all directions. Strewn among them were skeletons with a bit more "meat" on them, bodies close to complete decay but still clinging to a final, tawny sheen of humanity, and others who were filled out and basically untouched except for the puncture wounds of spinosaur teeth and the maggots and worms that fed on their bloated flesh. Qora was reminded of the compies back home, who would sometimes play too much with the rodents they wanted to eat, eventually losing interest in them and leaving the food to rot. She shuddered and swallowed hard and tried not to inhale.

Ninan, covering his nose, gestured for Qora to follow him around the fortress walls to the far side. There, they found the entrance: a gaping, rectangular hole where doors must have once been, now broken wider. After a brief check of their surroundings to make sure they were still in the clear, they entered.

Inside what would have been the main hall, dividing walls were broken down to piles of rubble scattered across the first level. The second floor, too, had crumbled, with only the nubs of its supports showing.

It was easy to see how the spinosaur could fit inside comfortably. He would have been able to stand up straight if he wanted to. He may have even been the one to bust open such a spacious lair for himself; no doubt his head was thick and dense enough to do it.

The broken walls allowed Qora and Ninan to see through to an open space and even into the corner towers, where a stairway spiraled all the way up.

Ninan followed Qora up the stairs. Air rushed over her skin when they reached the top. All the dead bodies were spread out below, filthy and pale, with gelatinous blood built up in their cavities.

Ninan put a hand on her shoulder. "You alright?"

She nodded, not because she was, but because she had to be. "You?"

He echoed her thought. "No other option, is there?"

When she shook her head, he embraced her from behind

and took a deep, trembling breath. He trembled so much, Qora could feel it under her feet.

Wait—that can't be right.

Ninan and Qora both looked to the green, where the trees swayed in response to a force that told of more than moving air. The vibrations traveled up the walls.

The flying heralds eased inward, a warning in and of itself. There would soon be something to see.

Qora tensed. The spinosaur came into view, swaying with the movement of his enormous haunches, head bent forward. The pressure from Qora's pulse made her think her veins were going to burst. Her arms and legs shook violently. For a moment, she was not a hunter anymore; she was a little girl, panicking in the wake of a monster.

Qora and Ninan adjusted their position and prepared their weapons: blowgun and darts, crossbows spanned and loaded, quivers upright and within easy reach, rope coiled with an adjustable loop knot.

The spinosaur neared the fortress, snorting forceful gusts, his scales gleaming individually as they shifted over taut muscles. He pressed new footprints over old ones, overlapping shapes in the mud.

Qora pressed her fingers against her crossbow tiller to keep from shaking; it wouldn't do any good for her aim to be anything but perfectly still.

The spinosaur stomped back and forth and picked at the corpses, nudging one with his snout, clawing at another with his webbed foot. Then he lifted his snout and sniffed. The inhalation howled like a windstorm.

Spirits, Qora thought. His lungs must have been the size of the bulk sacks of grain the ankylosaurs transported in Qhusi.

The beast paused and jerked his head, his gaze falling where Qora and Ninan waited.

"*Ruck*," Ninan whispered.

Instinctively, Qora withdrew—as though she had anywhere to go—but Ninan put his palm on her back. "Now!"

The spinosaur bounded toward them, shaking the walls again. Qora steadied her hands and braced the crossbow and squeezed the trigger. Her bolt pierced the roof of the spinosaur's mouth, at the back of the hard ridge. The spinosaur growled and snapped his jaw shut, splintering the wispy bolt with no effort.

The golden tooth was prominent, long and coated in blood that highlighted several dings and dents in the soft metal. When the spinosaur roared, it came with a breath like a gale force wind that stank of organic decay.

Ninan stood ready to shoot but waited for Qora to try again. She spanned and aimed, but the spinosaur reared his head so violently, the bolt barely reached the far side of the hard palate before it was crushed.

"The snout's too long." Qora shakily loaded another bolt. "I need a wider opening to get at the back." Maybe this wasn't going to work. While the sailbeast had had similar features, it had also been less than a tenth of the size; the length of a single bolt had sunk deeper in its smaller body.

The spinosaur snapped his jaws, gnashed his mismatched teeth, roared and twisted himself trying to reach the Venturers.

Qora struggled to hold her weapon steady and waited for the right moment, for a good view of the soft flesh where the throat began.

The spinosaur stepped back, then lunged forward, thrusting his head at the tower wall like a battering ram. The whole thing quaked and swayed. Cracks spidered out from the point of contact. Stones broke off and crumbled into the mud, dusting the spinosaur on the way down. The outer half of the tower began to collapse—and Qora and Ninan retreated from the edge just in time to avoid falling right into the reptile's waiting jaws.

"Darts!" Ninan said.

Qora handed them over.

In an instant, Ninan had the blowgun to his lips, spewing darts that landed like pins on the spinosaur's snout and head. The spinosaur widened his jaw to emit another rageful growl—not wide enough for the shot Qora needed—but was otherwise unfazed. He pounded the wall with his head, again and again.

In the meantime, Ninan (wearing Takan's gloves to protect his skin) took the pouch of pollenbane and turned it upside down, letting it fall over the spinosaur's head in a yellow dust cloud. The spinosaur growled before emitting a forceful sneeze, but continued to batter the wall.

Steeling herself, Qora waited for the sedative to take effect, but it didn't seem to be making any difference. Agonizing minutes passed, and yet the spinosaur remained at full force. "The darts must not have punctured deeply enough."

Ninan nodded. "Time to go, then." He loosened the rope attached to his belt and handed it to her, then readied the smoker. "You get started. I'll distract him."

Qora's feet were like boulders attached to her legs, a weight that rooted her to the spot. How could she go down there?

Another strike shook the entire structure. Qora kept low and braced herself for more tremors. She tried not to think about the fact that, once she and Ninan rappelled to the ground, they'd be in an open range with nothing to protect them. They couldn't outrun the spinosaur; he may have been too big to be fast, but a single one of his strides was worth ten of theirs.

Qora hurried to the worn battlements on the opposite side. She threw the loop around one of them and pulled it snug, tugging the rope a few times to test it.

Ninan delayed the spinosaur's next attack, landing an impressive but ultimately ineffective bolt between the eyes—huge amber orbs with almond-shaped pupils. They were probably the only vulnerable spot Qora and Ninan would ever be able to reach.

If we could blind him ...

Qora's stomach clenched. Killing an animal should be quick and painless; blinding him would be cruel—especially if they weren't able to kill him soon afterward.

"Come on!" she shouted.

Ninan lit the smoker and dropped it. It landed on the bridge of the spinosaur's snout, puffing and clouding his view. It disoriented him long enough for Ninan to get to the rope, rocks tumbling behind as the tower continued to sway.

"I'll go down first," Ninan insisted. "That way if he catches anyone, it'll be me."

"You don't have to do that," she told him, but he was already lowering himself. Qora grabbed the rope after him, clenching it with her legs and feet for extra support. Ninan's boots squelched in the mud as the spinosaur emerged from around the corner, rattling Qora's head with a roar.

Ninan sprinted for the bank, luring the spinosaur away. Qora loosened her grip on the rope and slid down, coarse fibers scraping her palms raw before the landing pains shot up her shins.

The spinosaur had already caught up to Ninan and stretched forward with an open mouth.

Qora screamed at top volume. "No!"

For an instant, the spinosaur turned his gaze on her. Ninan ran *toward* the spinosaur, then veered to the side and sprinted past in the opposite direction. The spinosaur growled and turned to catch him, but his girth made him slow to rotate. Halfway into the turn, the spinosaur stopped, eyes set on where Qora stood. His enormous tail went swinging like a thick whip as he stalked toward her.

She glanced down the bank, trying to gauge how long it would take her and Ninan to get back there. With the spinosaur charging, and knowing she had nowhere to go that he wouldn't be able to catch her, she aimed her crossbow. She clenched her muscles to steady herself. She took a deep breath.

Don't shake.

Don't flinch.

Don't trigger too quickly..

She sank a bolt into his eye.

The spinosaur skidded to a stop, a single bound away and screeching, while Ninan came up from behind, spanned and ready.

Roaring and flailing, the spinosaur fixed his remaining eye on Qora, right before she shot again, fully blinding him.

"Run!" Ninan said.

They raced to the nest, the spinosaur close behind with darts coming out of his body like porcupine quills as he stumbled after them. The heralds soared above, following the action.

Qora and Ninan weaved unpredictably, but the spinosaur stayed on their heels, his other senses apparently sharp to their scent and the sound of their tread.

When they reached the nest, they leapt in so forcefully they didn't even have to push off; they drifted right into the current. The spinosaur stopped where the nest had been banked. Ninan grabbed Qora's wrist and pulled both the paddles into the boat, putting a finger to his lips. The spinosaur paused at the edge of the water and smelled the air, aiming his head in all directions like he was sorting through different scents. He huffed dismissively.

Qora and Ninan drifted out to the middle of the pool, and it was only then that Ninan tried to paddle again, as the current had begun to carry them downstream.

The spinosaur growled and strode back to the fortress.

〉〉〉

Qora and Ninan approached the opposite bank, pulling the nest onto land. They climbed out and collapsed on the damp silt and Ninan allowed himself to go flat, lying on his back and spreading out his arms. Qora folded her legs against her chest, resting her forehead on her knees, panting. Her heart pounded for several minutes, gradually slowing to a normal pace— although "normal" these days was surely elevated, from being on constant alert.

The heralds slowed their motion, swept over the scene once more, then flew back to some indistinguishable jungle location where they must have been camped, and dropped below the canopy.

"I'm sure the spinosaur could swim across the pool if he wanted to," Ninan said wearily. "Maybe even wade. His legs are probably long enough to touch the bottom."

Qora nodded with her eyes closed. "Good thing he can't see." It sickened her, the thought of what she'd done, wounding an animal and leaving him alive to suffer. No matter how monstrous he was, it wasn't right. A hunter was supposed to make a clean kill, not cause suffering.

"But he can still smell," Ninan said. "Although he didn't try to follow us over like I thought he would."

Qora thought back to the way the spinosaur had seemed to analyze their scent, almost like he'd been confused. "He must have smelled the pterodactyls. What was left of them, on the nest."

"If we'd built our *own* raft," Ninan said, "we'd probably be on the other bank with all those corpses. Looks like your wild idea saved us in more ways than one."

Qora was grateful for that, of course, but she wasn't sure it mattered. They could only deter such a large and predatory creature for so long before they ended up like the other competitors.

For several hours they kept an eye on the castle, waiting for glimpses of the spinosaur, hoping that by some miracle the pollenbane had had some effect on him, but they saw no such evidence. At one point, the spinosaur blindly came to the water again, this time only to drink, and submerged his entire snout, rinsing away the fine yellow dusting completely, and continued stalking around as though it had never touched him.

"So what's the plan now?" Ninan raked his fingers through his hair.

Qora shook her head. "I don't think there *is* another plan. We don't have time for it. That's what I really need—*time*. Time for as many tries as it takes to make that shot deep enough to kill. Maybe even from a lower angle. But the spinosaur's enormous; it's not safe for us to be on the ground with him. One wrong move could cripple or kill us both. If I could just *restrain* him somehow …"

That first competitor had had the right idea with the chain. A massive leash. But clearly that had been a faulty method.

"There's no other sensitive areas you can target?" said Ninan.

"I already hit both eyes and that didn't kill him. Nostrils might work if the snout was shorter, but it's not. I have to get at something vital. The mouth is his only real vulnerability close to an area like that. I mean, you saw what happened to the others when they tried to break through the scales."

"So heart and lungs are out of the question."

"Pretty much all organs below the neck."

"What about some other form of poison?" Ninan offered.

"I haven't seen a sinorn since we came out of the mountains, so I don't know where I'd get venom. I'm not familiar enough with any other poisons. There are curare plants, I'm sure, similar to what Takan might have used in those darts, but that's mainly a paralytic; who knows how much it would take to be fatal? Not to mention I wouldn't know those plants by sight, or how to extract anything from them, or a better way to get it into the spinosaur's system."

"Me neither."

They sat on the bank a while longer to think it over. Qora whittled an experimental bolt tip, something broader and sharper, while Ninan fiddled with the wet silt, digging his nails into it, making a fist and squeezing it through his fingers.

Above them, a single pteranodon circled the falls.

"That time of day again," Qora muttered, gazing up at the underside of its wings. The flyer dipped into a turn, its rider's form backlit by oncoming dusk. She squinted, stretching her neck toward the trees where the flyer descended as though such a small motion would give her a better view.

"Something wrong?" Ninan asked.

Qora blinked. "Do the heralds ever ride two to a flyer? I could've sworn—"

Ninan stood and looked to where she was facing, but only

the flyer's white wings were visible before the entire silhouette disappeared.

"Maybe if one of the flyers is injured and the heralds had to double up." Ninan shrugged.

A few minutes later, all ten heralds appeared, single riders on individual pteranodons as usual, for the final round. Qora and Ninan waited for the horns to blare, but there was no sound to be heard.

Qora frowned.

"No more horns when there's five or fewer competitors," Ninan reminded her.

"Oh, right." She bit her lip. "There were six horns last night, and then we saw four die today. So that means …"

Ninan squeezed another fistful of silt. "Just you and me."

Qora could hardly believe it. She wished that being one of the last two competitors was reassuring—because at least there was no one else vying for the prize, no one who would ambush her and demand that she hand over her weapons and supplies, no one who would shoot at her with slingstones or get her up against a tree with a knife to her throat, no one who would dig holes in the ground with spikes at the bottom to impale her.

Maybe she ought to try and think like Takan. All it would take would be a spinosaur-sized dinofelis pit, but she couldn't imagine how long something like that would take to dig, or how deep it would need to be to trap a reptile with such long, thunderous legs.

She watched Ninan for a moment, with his hands in the wet silt, then suddenly stopped whittling and stared at him. A crease formed between her eyebrows.

"Oh no …" Ninan said. "I know that look."

Qora noted the residual mud on his clothes. Without having

figured out how to get out of it, Ninan might have been stuck in that pit for days and even died there.

"What is it now?" he asked.

"Sky Mother provides for us again ..."

"What do you mean?"

"I was thinking we could set a trap," she told him. "But nature may have already set one that we can use."

FIFTY-TWO

EVEN THOUGH THE SPINOSAUR was blind now, he didn't slow down. He tromped around as menacingly as before, although he was more vocal, and every time he groaned, Ninan saw Qora go stiff.

Inhumane, she had said.

"He would have killed us both," Ninan reminded her. "It was necessary."

With a crude broom of bundled, wiry twigs, Ninan now cleared a path on the jungle floor, shifting aside leaves and debris so that he and Qora could walk as noiselessly as possible when the spinosaur came—and it would come. It had to. Qora had already cut the way through that would lead from the bank directly to the sinking pit. After that, it was a matter of luring the spinosaur across the pool.

"We'll have to use ourselves as bait," Ninan said.

Qora nodded gravely. "The spinosaur clearly isn't hungry, but he does seem to hate humans. Why else would the fortress grounds be cluttered with those bodies? It's almost like … a warning."

"He must have been captive. Abused or something," Ninan suggested. "It would make sense. The Venture coordinators had to get him here somehow, manipulate his homing instinct to *keep* him here, gild his tooth … That couldn't have been easy—or humane."

"But we can use that hatred to our advantage. He'll want to follow us over, if we give him the chance."

To make their human scent stand out, Ninan caked the nest with thick clay-soils to dampen any remnants of the pterodactyls and skyrock dust. "So it won't distract or deter the spinosaur," he said.

They gathered a reserve of clay to cover themselves afterward. Once they had the spinosaur on their own bank, they'd want to mask the very scent they'd used to lure him.

Qora then set up a small offering to Sky Mother—a tiny fire surrounded by rocks, in which she burned a handful of wild herbs and flowers she'd dried by the bank earlier, along with some holy wood cut from one of the local species of bursera trees. She spoke prayerful words as the heat diffused the fragrance of the offerings, and then she wafted the smoke over herself and Ninan, who didn't protest despite his usual reservations—because, if the gods did exist, he wanted them on his and Qora's side.

"We've invoked Her," said Qora. "Now it's time for us to do our part."

Ninan sensed her faith to be fragile, but she clung to it in these moments, and he didn't blame her.

Their last day to kill the spinosaur and win the competition came closer and closer to its end. A fearful high made Ninan's head throb. After all these preparations, the evening was already upon them.

Qora stood next to the nest as she looped up the slack on the rope. She'd been quiet most of the day, and Ninan guessed he had been too, both of them working and focused, sometimes on separate tasks. But once they set this plan in motion, there would be no turning back, and there were so many things Ninan wanted to say to Qora, things he didn't know if he'd have the chance to say later.

He caught her by the wrist and drew her in close.

"I want you to know," he said, "that no matter what happens—"

She shook her head. "No promises. That way, if we don't survive, then nothing gets broken."

"And if we *do* survive?"

The question was for himself as much as it was for her. He definitely didn't have the answer. And the thought of not seeing her again after this …

It was like he was under water again, lungs desperate for air.

But there didn't seem to be any way to keep her. He'd racked his brain trying to think of something, but his father would watch him like a condor when he returned. It was best that the qhapaq didn't find out about anything or anyone that was precious to him.

Qora's eyes were watery, but they didn't spill over. She took a step into him and rested her head on his chest and whispered, "Let's worry about that when we come to it."

When.

So full of possibility. And yet, it felt so out of reach.

With a gentle hand, he held her, and then he tilted her face up to meet his, and he kissed her like he could drink her in, like nothing else mattered, like it was the last time—because, no matter what happened, it would have to be. He memorized the way she felt, clinging tight to her essence, shutting out everything else. It was the saddest, most beautiful lie that he told himself, that it wouldn't completely destroy him to let her go.

Finally, he did let her go, and the inches between them

suddenly felt like miles. They certainly would be once she found out who he really was. He would have to tell her. But she was right; better to worry about that when they came to it. No more distractions from their task.

And so, they began.

))))

With no one left but Ninan and Qora to watch, the heralds had been at the ready. They flew over the falls and the ruins, spreading out, assuming their usual formation.

The spinosaur was somewhere inside the fortress. Ninan and Qora pushed off in the nest, paddled toward the ruins, and paused at the water's edge. From there, Qora shot several bolts at the fortress wall, which splintered and ricocheted when they hit. Ninan hadn't been so sure this would work to rouse the spinosaur, but a few seconds later, the clatter of broken stones echoed from inside, shifting with the spinosaur's movements.

Ninan's stomach turned as the spinosaur came out into the light, eyes oozing with a yellow fluid congealed and mingled with blood, bolts still intact inside the eye sockets. He glanced at Qora, who seemed to be holding her breath.

The spinosaur sniffed the air, then the ground, following the invisible trail to where Qora and Ninan sat waiting and ready to paddle for their lives.

The spinosaur tromped beyond the castle ground, then down the bank. He jerked his head, nostrils flared. He gave a long, low growl.

Then, something in that eyeless gaze told Ninan the spinosaur had caught their scent—and locked onto it. Qora nodded at him and they eased backward, careful not to splash.

With their movement, the spinosaur crept forward into the pond after them. One foot plunging in, then the other. A few drops of water spattered Ninan's cheek.

Ninan and Qora paddled with slow but meaningful strokes to put more distance between themselves and the large reptile, a delicate balance to keep him close enough to smell them but not close enough to sink his teeth in. Carefully, they led him on.

The spinosaur's body displaced so much water that a crosscurrent swelled under the nest, a lift and letdown that forced Qora and Ninan to hug the rim for stability. Qora pinched her lips tight and winced.

As the spinosaur swam, wake lines formed behind him, spreading out from his shoulders. His thick, enormous legs shifted the undercurrent and stirred the sediment, turning the water a cloudy brown.

The spinosaur was fast. Faster than Ninan and Qora had anticipated. Sure, he was tentative in such an open space without his sight, but his strokes were as big as his land-strides had been. Qora and Ninan weren't even halfway across and he had already come within a few inches of catching them.

Imagine if he could still see, Ninan thought. A shudder traveled down his spine as he pulled on the paddle again.

Three quarters of the way across.

Almost there. Maybe a hundred feet to go, Ninan guessed, before glancing warily at the spinosaur. This had to work. The sun was already so low; there wouldn't be time to try another way.

Qora's shoulders tensed visibly as she paddled. She released a ragged breath and pulled the paddle in long, forceful drags.

One final drag and the nest bumped the bank. Qora and Ninan climbed out and slid into the water, rinsing their scent.

As they ran for the clay, the spinosaur sank his teeth into the nest with a gargled snarl, tearing the rim from the base and clawing at the remnants looking for his prize.

Ninan and Qora coated themselves in clay, then took their weapons and clambered up the muddy incline just as the spinosaur abandoned the nest, whose broken bits bobbed and floated as the current tugged them downstream.

Ninan cast a longing glance over his shoulder as he and Qora raced to their places on either side of the cleared path. They crept behind designated trees, each with a loaded crossbow, a quiver of bolts, and a sharpened blade.

They waited for the spinosaur to step on land. The reptile put his nose to the ground, marking the dirt as his nostrils widened.

Qora caught Ninan's eye. They said nothing. Neither of them moved, but they spoke to one another in a gaze. They were ready.

And then the spinosaur began a lethargic turn back into the water.

Qora didn't hesitate. She turned her crossbow on him—loaded with a new, finely sharpened, broad-tipped bolt—and took a shot.

Click.

It was enough to get the spinosaur's attention. He roared and angled his head toward them, twitching his hindquarter where the bolt had struck and bounced off. He crept back and put his nose to the ground again.

Across the path, Qora's hairline glistened with sweat that bled into the clay on her skin.

She tilted the quiver so she could reach inside and reload, but a handful of bolts slid out and clacked as they fell.

The spinosaur's next roar shook Ninan's skull.

Qora stopped dead for an instant, then took off in a sprint as the spinosaur lunged.

Branches bent and snapped under the spinosaur's weight. Despite the path Qora had cut for this purpose, the reptile was so large that his shoulders scraped the trees and his feet crushed the blunted underbrush.

Ninan shot at the base of the spinosaur's tail, giving Qora time to get ahead. But now the spinosaur came for Ninan.

A click echoed from further down the path and another bolt struck the spinosaur's thigh. He turned back on Qora. Gradually, Ninan and Qora herded the spinosaur to the pit, enticing him between them. Qora baited him onward, Ninan drew him back, she advanced, the spinosaur chased. As they all neared the pit, the spinosaur grew impatient; his chest rumbled, and he clawed at the earth with his enormous feet, raking like a gigantic bull about to charge.

Come on. Just a little deeper.

The spinosaur pursued Qora again, but he was getting too close. She was using double the bolts to urge him on faster. When he rotated, he exposed his loin. Ninan aimed for it, sinking a painful shot that actually stuck between the scales.

That should have been enough to turn him back to Ninan, but the spinosaur kept going.

Ninan shot again and still the spinosaur paid him no attention, thundering after Qora.

No, no, no.

Qora sprinted like she had the day of the sendoff, as though there were dozens of armed hunters ready to take her out. There was only one hunter now, but he was worth a battalion.

Ninan followed at full speed, stumbling to keep up.

The pit was within his sights.

The blinded spinosaur was none the wiser. He dipped his head and bared his teeth and he was about to come down on Qora's fleeing form when she took a running leap and launched herself into the clearing. Ninan's breath stalled.

The spinosaur's first foot sank in.

Then the second.

He tried to step out, but the suction anchored him. He bellowed at the open, lavender sky with its pink clouds. His legs only sank deeper and locked tight.

They'd done it. The spinosaur was trapped.

But … Where was Qora?

She should have landed somewhere safe, come to a stop and settled in between the trees so she could prepare to make her first calculated shot—an injury to the tongue, which would be fleshy enough to cause pain and force the whole mouth open wider.

It seemed cruel, yes, but in a twisted way it was the only humane thing to do. Competition aside, the reptile had to be put out of his misery, and they'd have to expose that fatal spot to do it.

Then Ninan saw her.

She gazed up, wide-eyed, at the spinosaur railing over her—with her own right leg sunk up to the knee. The rest of her body was positioned awkwardly outside the boundary of the pit as she tried to pull herself free, but she found, as Ninan had, that it was not that simple. She couldn't run. And if the spinosaur were to realize she was within reach …

Ninan understood now how it must have been for her to find him here the previous day. It was disturbing, the way she seemed to come right out of solid ground, as if ghastly creatures were vying for her soul below the surface—only now there was a ghastly creature *above* the surface too.

She was at a bad angle and in no position to do what she needed to—forcibly bent in a pit and hunched off center. Scenarios played out on her face: Free the leg first? Try taking a pointless external shot that might give away her position while she was trapped?

No, Ninan thought, she couldn't even do *that*. She'd used the last of her bolts; the spill had left her short. And here she was, caught without ammo in a vital moment, the very thing she was always trying to avoid.

The spinosaur continued to rear his head. Qora didn't take her eyes off him as she slowly drew out her leg, shifting side to side to encourage the saturated soil to move and release her. Ninan kept his crossbow at the ready, skirting the edge of the clearing to get a better aim; if nothing else, he could disorient the spinosaur.

His pulse consumed him as he waited, as the spinosaur's angry cries stung his ears, as Qora wrestled the earth just a few feet away from the biggest monster either of them had ever come across.

An eternity later, Qora strained against the pit one last time and pulled the final length of her leg free—with an audible squelch.

The spinosaur lengthened toward the sound, jaw wide and snapping blindly. Ninan took two shots while Qora stumbled to safety. She panted as she looked to Ninan for a solution—for ammo. He quickly removed his quiver, ready to toss it over.

Then a rope looped around his neck, constricted, and swept him into the air.

"Ninan!" Qora screamed.

Ninan couldn't breathe. His body weight worked against him. He clawed at his throat to get his fingers under what seemed to be a type of noose.

A figure dropped from the trees, landing in a crouch, winding the other end of the rope around his own wrist. "I told you to watch your head, princeling."

FIFTY-THREE

THE SUN HAD NOW BEGUN TO SET behind the falls, a reddish glow bleeding over the three competitors and the beast. Qora rushed from the spinosaur, stopping halfway between the pit and the tree where Ninan hung.

Takan—practically a walking corpse—stood several feet from Ninan. Deep gashes striped his arms and face, crimson and congealed, crusted on the edges, crossed with stitches. He wore a patch over his left eye. But despite his wounds, something seemed to have fortified him.

And he'd set yet another trap, with Ninan tied like a wild reptile. Ninan's face contorted as he supported all his weight by his neck and the fingers he used to space the rope from choking him completely.

"What are you doing?!" Qora screamed.

Takan grinned and lowered Ninan until he was only a few inches off the ground, and suspended him there.

Heat spread through Qora's limbs like lava. Everything came back to her at once. Her family's hardships, her desperate attempt to fix it all with the raptoriva, this horrible competition that had been her only hope. Losing Ninan and finding him again, only to potentially lose him again. Competitors who *just wouldn't die.*

"How do you know I even care whether he lives?" Qora bluffed.

The heralds had drawn closer now, circling low above the trees, wingflaps forcing wind into the leaves and jostling the branches.

Takan sneered. "I had him bound long enough the other day to learn plenty about the both of you. And I've watched you together since I landed here. You're completely enamored by him. You've let him slither his way into your heart—and now he'll be your downfall. So accept the consequences; drop your weapon and let me finish this competition as Unu's champion."

Qora's stomach roiled as she imagined Takan lurking in the trees throughout the past day, watching them map out their plan. He would have known exactly where she and Ninan would be standing, exactly where to position himself so that he could ensnare Ninan. He might have been able to devise a similar trap for the spinosaur on his own, Qora thought, had he not arrived weak and injured; instead, he'd trapped Qora and Ninan into trapping the spinosaur *for* him, setting himself up for the win.

Ninan's kicking legs slowed. His strength dwindled. The spinosaur bucked and roared, flailing his head and struggling to pull his feet from the sinking pit.

"The heralds will see that you're cheating," Qora told Takan with a pointed, upward glance. "Everyone will know."

"That narrative can be easily spun. 'A last-minute interception by a determined competitor who survived against the odds and faced his would-be murderer, taking back the victory that was rightfully his.'" He scoffed. "Give it up, Qora. Let me win, or let Ninan die; make your choice."

Let this man take her last chance to succeed, or sacrifice the boy who had come to mean something to her, who had helped her find her way here.

Don't fall victim to a false dilemma, Qora thought. *There must be a way to have both.*

As Qora grasped the hilt of the machete on her belt, she remembered Sakay, the day he had given it to her—*lent* it to her.

"Or I just kill *you* right now." She withdrew the blade and pulled it back long enough for Takan to flinch, then hurled it at him. The blade plunged into the flesh between his chest and shoulder. He released the rope with a screeching groan and Ninan collapsed into the dirt, coughing and wheezing and gulping air.

Takan dropped, his face twisted in agony. He screamed at the machete lodged in his muscle.

If only she had hit him a little to the left, she thought. She would've finished the job.

Be precise or do it twice.

"You should have just let me kill him," Takan growled, clutching himself. "You think he's worth saving? He's not. If you knew who he *really* was—"

Qora went to him and wrenched out the machete, forcing an agonized grunt from his mouth as blood trickled out of the wound. "I don't care."

"No?" Takan panted, wincing. "Are you sure? Because whatever it is that's kept you in this competition—and I imagine it's something you desperately need the reward for—he could have given it to you from the beginning. He's had access to all kinds of resources, even had one of the heralds providing him support early on whenever there was a chance for it."

The spinosaur thrashed and roared in the background.

Qora shook her head. "That doesn't make any sense."

"He's lied to you. He's let you suffer for weeks." He hissed through his teeth.

"We've suffered together. He's saved my life."

Takan sucked in a pained breath and dragged himself backward. "And in all those instances, he didn't bother to mention ... that he's an *heir to the wealth of Sumaq*?"

Ninan continued to cough and gasp. He reached out to them, as if to interject, but he couldn't seem to form any words.

Qora looked to Ninan, thoughts swirling to make sense of this. Too much was happening right now—a raging monster that needed to die, a threat to Ninan's life she'd barely thwarted, and now ... an accusation like this?

"What do you mean 'heir'?" she demanded.

"I should think that would've come up at some point," said Takan. "I mean, considering that this is Apo-Kimsa Kallpa. The Third Prince."

Despite the chaos, everything around Qora seemed to stand still. Her head throbbed like someone was drumming on it with a mallet. Noises blended together, turning white. *Apo-Kimsa Kallpa? Prince?*

It had to be a lie. Ninan had been brawling like a savage the day Qora had met him. He'd spent a year on a quinoa farm. He *couldn't* be ...

But she remembered the way he'd spoken about his family, a family she had assumed must be wealthy and important. She remembered how they'd apparently extended him some chance at redemption among their ranks if he should win.

And then she remembered a day sometime during the previous year when she'd passed through the city square after trading a pair of aquilops to Sakay for their quills; people outside had been making some racket over the Kallpas, one of the lesser princes. Stripped of title and inheritance at only seventeen.

Ninan had started to tell her something the other night—

"If you don't believe me," Takan added, "check the back of

his neck. He's marked. You really haven't caught a glimpse of it yet? I would've thought you'd seen *plenty* of him by now …"

Qora drew back the machete, ready to end the other competitor this instant, but the look in his eyes stopped her cold. He was staring past her. His fearful gaze rose to something behind her, *above* her.

The spinosaur's footsteps shook the ground.

Footsteps.

She spun to see the spinosaur with his hind limbs partway coated in sludge, globs clinging to the scales as he towered over her. She backed away.

Takan grimaced and clutched his wound as he forced himself up and followed Qora's lead. He stumbled, and with clumsy footing he snapped a brittle branch under his heel.

The spinosaur lunged.

Qora didn't even have the chance to react before something heavy knocked her sideways. From a new, low angle, her cheek pressed to the ground, Qora caught a glimpse of the spinosaur's jaws closing over Takan—blood gushing down his body in rivulets. Takan let out a scream that quickly drowned in a gurgle.

Ninan—no, Prince Apo-Kimsa—lay beside Qora, half *on* her, straining. How he had mustered the strength to tackle her out of the way (again) had been a miracle.

Qora hurried to stand, reaching for Ninan to help him, but he barely made it to his knees before clutching his throat as he erupted with involuntary coughing.

Crushing Takan between merciless, grinding teeth, the spinosaur gnawed on Takan's limbs and then spat them out. They plopped down like wet logs.

Ninan continued to cough, drawing the spinosaur's attention.

Following Ninan's example from the previous day, Qora ran the opposite direction, shouting, making all the noise she could to lure the spinosaur away. But Ninan's coughs, stifled weakly behind the hand that he'd clamped over his nose and mouth, kept the monster focused. The spinosaur widened his nostrils, inhaled deeply, snarled.

"Here!" Qora shouted.

The spinosaur didn't acknowledge her. He seemed to sense that Ninan was an easier prey, injured and weak.

Ninan crawled to his weapons, which he had dropped when Takan had strung him up so abruptly.

It was Ollan and the sailbeast all over again: Qora, boltless, watching like a fool while a monster charged at a boy who meant so much to her, time somehow slowing *and* accelerating within the same moment.

Not again.

A fire blazed inside her, a building pressure that should have propelled her, and yet, she was also frozen. Stuck between fighting and failing.

That's when she noticed the tendons of the spinosaur's legs as he walked. Taut and glistening above the line of the pit's filth that still caked his scales. A ring where the scales had worn thin, as though he'd been shackled.

Held captive. Abused.

Somehow vengeance and mercy were allies in this.

No more hesitation, Qora decided. She brandished her machete and raced toward him.

The spinosaur swung his enormous tail and Qora ducked into a roll, tucking her weapon against herself. His nostrils flared again, audible with his heavy breath. She got to her feet and lengthened her stride, then slammed the blade down on the tendon, ripping through the weakened skin and slicing all the layers beneath.

This time the spinosaur didn't roar, he shrieked—a bloodcurdling noise that could shatter glass. His leg-joints buckled and he twisted his neck until he was looking right at her. She wrenched the blade out and turned to run again, but it was too late. The spinosaur's mouth was wide open. Finally the gaping width she needed, but now his jaws were coming down over her. A rumble filled his throat and engulfed Qora in hot, fetid moisture. Her pulse pounded in every part of her body. Her heart hammered so hard it hurt.

She was not supposed to think it, but she did. *This is it. This is how I die.*

What was her way out?

Maybe there was none. Not this time.

Ninan got to his crossbow and unleashed a bolt on the spinosaur's twisted spine, the last thing Qora saw before the spinosaur closed her off from the outside world. Her instinct was to cover her head, accept her fate, brace herself against the pain until death released her. She had so little strength left. This monster was so much bigger than her. He could move her with his breath alone. Who was she to try and take his life? He could trample her like grass, and she would fold and sink into the earth—the only thing grass could do under pressure.

In these final moments, she saw her brothers, their bright smiles and young faces, the multicolored wool caps they wore to keep their ears warm in the cold, the way they cared for the compies with so much tenderness, the men they had the potential to become. And she saw her mamáy, the fine lines around her mouth, the way her fingers moved when she arranged newly dyed yarn to dry, all her wisdom and the phrases she spoke to pass it on. *Even grass has a blade.*

Qora's fist tightened around the machete hilt in her palm. Maybe she still had something left to give.

She still had a cutting edge.

No panic. No haste. Pure calculation, fully dedicated to whatever consequences might follow.

Before the spinosaur's teeth could cut her, she stepped onto the singular, gilded fang and pushed off, propelling herself deeper inside. She raised the weapon, putting all her force behind it, and shoved it into the roof of the spinosaur's mouth. He howled over her, his breath suffocating hers. She twisted the blade deeper. She yanked it out and stabbed again, and again, and again. She screamed as she did it, louder and louder with each attack. Another stab, another scream.

The spinosaur's jaw slackened, separated, displaying that golden fang. A rattle moved up his throat like demons cast out of the Grave World. But Qora didn't stop until every muscle went limp, one by one.

His body slumped. Qora held onto the machete still lodged in the soft palate, waiting for everything to settle down, trembling as she forced herself not to let go. Her fingers ached against her grip. Her boots slipped on the spinosaur's enormous tongue. Her breaths were sharp, separated, rhythmic.

Finally, the monster stilled. Qora slid down, eyes brimming, as she yanked the machete free and peered through the opening between the spinosaur's teeth, through which she could see the darkening orange tones of the sun making its final descent.

>>>

Panting, Qora tried to climb out. The jaw was heavy, but Ninan was on the outside ready to lift.

417

Spirits—he's alright.

Together they made enough space for Qora to fit.

A dozen failed bolts littered the ground. Ninan's quiver lay empty.

Ninan went to Qora with open arms and they collapsed against each other. At least for this moment, Qora didn't want to think about what she knew, or what it meant. She absorbed Ninan's warmth, different from the heat that radiated from her own body and the feverish climate—the warmth of his life, which Takan and the spinosaur had failed to destroy.

The sun had almost completely disappeared below the horizon, with nothing but a sliver remaining before twilight. Ninan removed the firestick from his belt and handed it to Qora.

She stared at him, unable to fathom that she was actually doing this—signaling the watchtower because the spinosaur was dead by her hand. But it was more complicated than that now.

She hesitated.

Ninan, like he knew what she was thinking, bowed and lifted his hair, baring the back of his neck.

The Shield of Sumaq was bold on his skin. Inside the shield was the image of a spinosaur, so much like the one she'd just killed, only this one was foreboding for an entirely different reason. Her jaw trembled as she tried to form words she didn't know how to say. Instead, she said nothing.

Ninan nodded at the firestick. Qora pulled the cord and raised it high and it sparked and glowed against the falling night as the sun disappeared, informing the Watchguards that she had vanquished the beast to obtain the tooth.

The victory was bittersweet—but she had succeeded.

FIFTY-FOUR

IT ONLY TOOK A FEW MINUTES for the Watchtower guards to arrive, with lanterns like stars on the move. The Head Watchguard herself—as evidenced by her uniform—glided down in the pterobeast gondola while four pterobeasts followed, carrying additional watchguards. They landed and disembarked.

Ninan and Qora stood and bowed to greet them.

"Good evening," said the Head Watchguard. Her red jacket and copper helmet were bold against the dark green of the jungle. "I must say, I didn't expect to find *two* competitors here—at least not without conflict. Whom do I have the honor to congratulate? Which of you delivered the fatal blow?"

"She did," Ninan said. His raspy whisper stung like he was swallowing knives—although it didn't sting half as much as the look on Qora's face once she'd seen the emblem on his skin.

The Head Watchguard regarded him skeptically, then reached out to one of the other watchguards and received a handkerchief, which she used to shake Qora's bloody hand. "Well done."

"Thank you," Qora replied flatly.

Ninan suspected she wasn't proud of what she'd done and was even less inclined to hear praise for it.

"This year's Venture is now complete," said the Head Watchguard. "Please allow us to escort the new Venture champion back to the capital."

"What about Ninan?" Qora glanced at him with a conflicted but hopeful expression.

"We were instructed to carry only the champion back to Sumaq," said another watchguard. "I'm afraid you'll have to find your own way back, young man."

Qora shook her head. "You can't just leave him here. Not after everything …"

"I'm sorry," the watchguard replied.

"He's not just any competitor," Qora argued. "Ninan, tell them who you are."

"Well, technically I'm not anyone." *Especially not now*, he thought, letting his gaze wander over the slain spinosaur—the spinosaur he was supposed to have found and conquered on his own. The gilded tooth protruded from its slacking jaw, close enough to reach out and touch.

"Give them your birth name," Qora said.

Ninan locked eyes with her briefly, almost apologetically, knowing that to say it out loud would be like salt in an already painful wound. He sighed, and spoke it like a recitation: "My name is Apo-Kimsa Kallpa, of the House of Kallpa."

All the watchguards stared at him, faces like cold granite.

The Head Watchguard looked him over, took a step in his direction, eyes roving. Without prompting, Ninan bent forward and pushed his hair off the back of his neck to reveal the emblem.

"Well," she breathed, "It's an honor. Champion or not, you've earned the respect of the Five Terrains."

ꑭꑭꑭ

Before they departed, the Head Watchguard instructed

420

her comrades to remove the spinosaur's head from the carcass. Qhapaq Apo had apparently told them that since the golden tooth was such an impressive feature *within* its original setting, the plan—provided a Sumaqi competitor won—had been for the watchguards to return the entire severed head to Kallpa House for preservation.

It was impossible for Ninan to look away. The guards sawed through bone and flesh, spilling an unbelievable quantity of blood. It took all the guards to get the head into a rope net suspended between three spare pterobeasts, and they came away looking like they'd just come from the slaughterhouse.

"You'll be sure not to let a shred of him go to waste," Qora said to the Head Watchguard. "Won't you?"

She said "him" like the beast had been an old friend, and she said it with a sadness in her eyes that baffled Ninan, but also endeared her to him even more. It must have been eating her alive, the things they had done to him.

"Kallpa House and its associates will feast on your victory," the Head Watchguard assured her. "And I guarantee the qhapaq will have his leatherworkers fashion you a souvenir."

Qora gave a terse nod but didn't look directly at the officers. She didn't want to remember this; it wasn't like her boots; she'd had no vendetta against this creature.

Once that was settled, the other pterobeasts departed and then Ninan and Qora boarded the remaining pterobeast, seating themselves on a bench that lined the interior of the circular gondola, taking opposite sides with two watchguards in between.

There wouldn't be any horns while passing back over the route, the watchguards told them, since there were no other competitors to alert. Instead, Qora would be announced only as they reached Qhusi.

The Head Watchguard stood outside the gondola to see them off. "I look forward to seeing you both at the welcoming ceremony in Qhusi in a few days," she said. "Safe travels."

"Rise," commanded the piloting watchguard. The pterobeast spread its wings and lifted them away.

The spinosaur's headless carcass shrank beneath them, and all Ninan could think was what a miracle it was that they were sitting here, flying home.

Then he remembered what awaited him there, and despite the heat, he shivered.

Rare is the one who weighs the faults
of others without pressing on the scale.

Sumaqi proverb

FIFTY-FIVE

THE ATTENDANTS PROVIDED Qora and Ninan with water and food. Qora drank until she was sick, but when it came time to eat, she still couldn't rid herself of the mental image of the spinosaur's severed head. As it was, her stomach had already been churning with worry over Rimaq, over what would happen next, over all that had already happened and what it meant for her future.

Once she'd managed to quell those thoughts, she took a moment to look at Ninan and the heritage that loomed over him. Suddenly every memory she had of him was tinted in a new hue.

The cocky, dirty prizefighter at the Underground? He had been a prince of Sumaq.

The competitor with the smoke bombs, luring unsuspecting aggressors to his camp? He had been a prince of Sumaq.

The boy who had kissed her on the back of a megaraptor after she'd nearly been ripped to shreds by pterodactyls? He had been a prince of Sumaq.

All his cuts had leaked royal blood.

And worse, that blood was the same blood that ran through the veins of Qhapaq Apo, the man whose rogue sailbeasts had killed innocent people—killed Ollan—and whose merciless

424

governing caused suffering all throughout Sumaq.

Qora wasn't sure whether the brunt of her pain stemmed from Ninan's connection to Kallpa House, or simply from her not having known the truth sooner. Regardless, she didn't think she would ever be able to look at him the same way. Even though he couldn't be blamed for the crimes of his father, she feared what he might be capable of.

The ride would be a few hours long, which should have been plenty of time to discuss it all, to ask questions and have them answered. But with the watchguards in the gondola, it would be impossible to have a private conversation.

There were so many things to consider, but Qora's thoughts, of course, turned back to Rimaq, whether she still had time to help him or whether his condition had worsened to the point where he might be impossible to save. She also thought of Hakan and her mamáy, how they must have been so worried by her absence, and wondered if they'd ever be able to forgive her for leaving the way she had.

She only planned to rest her eyes for a minute, but when she opened them, she found herself sideways, her upper body lying across the length of her part of the bench. The air was chilly, a coolness she hadn't felt in a long time. It was as though a fever within her had broken.

The watchguards handed out blankets, an almost foreign idea to Qora, who had been desperate to let her skin breathe for so many days she'd almost forgotten what it felt like to ache for cover and warmth. The scent of the misty mountains beckoned her now.

"Welcome home," said the pilot.

Qora sat upright and gazed out over the landscape, the tiny buildings in silhouette under the full moon as cloud wisps glided over them. Ninan sat quietly across from her, one knee bent with his foot on the bench, his chin resting on his hand.

Whatever lies he'd told, her heart still twinged at the sight of him. The truth of who he was had consequences, but the idea that Takan had thought he could persuade her to trade Ninan's life because of them had been idiocy.

Two of the watchguards blasted a fanfare so that all the local citizens knew the champion had returned, and even though it was the dead of night, people still came out to see, gawking up and cheering, and rousing others to do the same.

They passed over Qhusi's streets and across the dip between mountains until they landed at the front terrace of Kallpa House. Its chiseled walls were gray and foreboding behind the mists, which diffused the firelight from the beacons that marked it in the night.

The pterobeast dipped and soared into a smooth landing on one of several stone-paved pads that covered the clifftop where such traffic arrived and departed. There were other gondolas, without pterobeasts attached, apparently ready to carry nobles and staff to various locations at daybreak.

Qora gaped at the castle's magnitude, never having imagined it could seem *so* much bigger up close. The tiers of land that had been cut and scaped on either side were vast enough to host hundreds of large dinosaurs or provide training grounds for an entire army. The castle itself had multiple towers of stone surrounding a central courtyard that featured a granite spinosaur within a dry fountain. Qora stopped in front of it and looked into its blank eyes.

"It must appear a bit paltry to you," one of the guards said. "now that you've seen the real thing."

Qora regarded him silently before he ushered her and Ninan

past the fountain where a familiar herald greeted them coolly.

"Mullu." Ninan gave a nod. He turned to Qora and told her, "This is the qhapaq's chief attendant."

Qora nodded once too.

"This way," Mullu told them. After they ascended a grand staircase, Mullu led them through a long corridor and finally through a set of enormous doors to a grand foyer, with polished obsidian floors. Sconces flickered, turning the surface into a dark, lapping lake. Qhapaq Apo, with several additional attendants, descended a set of shallow steps.

The qhapaq halted at the sight of Qora and Ninan together, and looked to Mullu as if for explanation.

"I'm not the champion," Ninan said flatly. "She is. And she knows who I am."

After a moment of speechlessness, the qhapaq stepped forward and acknowledged Qora. "Congratulations."

"Thank you so much," Qora said, "for accepting us at this very late hour." She forced a respectful tone as she bowed to him. Internally, though, she could only think how much pleasure he'd had at their expense, the publicity they'd brought him with the conflicts that had nearly cost them everything.

There was tension in his voice. Reluctance. "It is a privilege to accept the winner of this challenge, day or night."

Even though Qora wanted to pin him to the wall with a bolt, there was a more pressing matter that superseded everything else.

"It's an incredible honor to meet you, and I couldn't be more grateful for the opportunity to be your champion," she continued. "But I only entered this competition for one reason, and that was to help my brother. Would it be possible for me to go to him right away?"

He furrowed his brow.

"She needs sparkshade," Ninan told his father.

A flicker of understanding passed over the qhapaq's face, but without emotion. "Because you've brought me the spinosaur tooth," he told Qora, "and because I have important matters to discuss with … *Ninan*"—he glanced at his son—"I will approve your request, and provide you with the appropriate resources to aid what ails your brother. But you must return tomorrow at midday and we will discuss preparations for the homecoming ceremony to be held three days from now."

"Thank you." Qora had to bite the inside of her cheek to keep from releasing a feeble sound. This man was her benefactor now, a fact that choked her like a haze of smoke—and yet, the relief that she would have what she needed almost cleared it away entirely.

Almost.

Qora looked over at Ninan, not sure what to say after all their time together—and having an audience here—but he wasn't looking anyway. Instead, he followed his father solemnly down a dark corridor as the guards followed, leaving the foyer in darkness.

FIFTY-SIX

NINAN FOLLOWED HIS FATHER to the menagerie, where a stone path snaked between cages that housed an array of exotic dinosaurs. No matter how many times a day the cages had been cleaned, though, the smell of ruck and straw and raw meat never seemed to diminish. It was a carnal smell, Ninan had often thought; the darker side of the life cycle.

Each cage contained its own habitat, complete with equally exotic plants, and slabs of rock to mimic boulders or mountainsides. Torches lit the pathway.

The qhapaq, wearing a new ring with a faint purple stone in it, approached one of the cages where a multicolored theropod fed from a trough close to the bars. It stood approximately three feet high and flaunted a thick coat of feathers, primarily red, with small sections of blue and green like a macaw.

The qhapaq reached inside and stroked the dinosaur's golden snout. The dinosaur made a low trilling noise, almost a purr. Ninan arched a brow and peered into the cage to get a better look.

"You're wondering why he is so attentive to me," the qhapaq said to Ninan.

The dinosaur leaned into the strokes like a loyal pet, like it had no memory of the skyrock used to control it on a daily basis.

"I call this breed 'iridosaur.' A hybrid of the North Coast dromaeosaur and the scarlet avimimus. Both parent breeds are quite obstinate, so it required some effort to get him to come around," the qhapaq admitted. "He wasn't the hatchling I'd hoped for. He was scrawny, pugnacious. Took off two of my handlers' fingers, despite his small size at the time."

Ninan couldn't imagine this particular dinosaur to be difficult—not with the way it was behaving now. It wasn't just obedient. It was … *loving*. Affectionate. Completely docile.

"I grew impatient with him at first," said the qhapaq, "as you might imagine. Threw him to the wild to die, thinking perhaps a new genetic combination might prove more successful, but … somehow, he survived. The handlers found him less than a mile from the castle grounds, sleeping in a burrowed hole, and feeding on wild compsognathus." The dinosaur pointed his snout at Ninan and sniffed in his direction. "He'd made a meager life for himself, but he was growing weak. Mercifully, I chose to bring him back and give him another chance."

Ninan didn't like where this was going. His father never spoke in such a narrative voice—not unless it was to make a condescending point.

"To my surprise," the qhapaq continued, "I discovered that with the proper methods, he became compliant. He seemed to realize that it was better to follow my command, and receive the benefits of my care, than to rely on his own devices for survival in a world in which he was never designed to live."

"That's a touching story," Ninan said flatly, "but I'm extremely tired. Am I allowed to sleep at Kallpa House, or are you planning to send me somewhere else in light of my failure?"

The qhapaq chuckled. "Failure? Perhaps. Although I wouldn't go so far as to call it such." He stroked his chin. "I can always control the angle: You were a *selfless* hero, let's say, who chose to step down rather than take the glory for yourself, hmm? Or some crusader for the welfare of endangered reptiles? There are multiple directions we can take. Then again, I'm not sure any of them will be necessary. You haven't yet heard the public's reaction to the stories about you. You've become quite popular, in fact. So many tales of bravery, of your clever means to survive. I don't suspect they'll be terribly disappointed that it wasn't you who retrieved the golden tooth."

"The golden tooth that was *still attached* to the monster that was guarding it? How did your handlers manage to capture a spinosaur from beyond the Pirqas and subdue it long enough to *gild one of its fangs*?"

"We're developing some very promising methods for dinosaur control. They may have once ruled the earth, but now … it's our turn."

Bleary-eyed, Ninan shook his head. "You're sick, you know that? Sick that you would put an animal through this, not to mention complete strangers and *your own son*."

"But now you know you can overcome all odds—and everyone else knows it too." The qhapaq moved on to another cage, where a special breed of miniature, pink triceratops greeted him. "I'd almost given up on you, you know." He let the triceratops nuzzle his knuckles. "Although I did have multiple contingencies."

"Of course."

"For instance, there's a boy around your age in the Kichka District who resembles you quite well—and reasonably so, as the two of you are closely related."

Ninan scoffed. "Only one? Surely there must be dozens."

"This one had the Kallpa nose," the qhapaq clarified,

without any regard for Ninan's insult. "I might have passed him off as you, with enough grooming and training. Although, I much prefer your rise to fame through the Venture. Lookalikes are risky."

"Sure, but all you'd have to do is tattoo the terrenal emblem on his neck," Ninan said facetiously, "and no one would think to question his legitimacy."

So much for a permanent symbol, Ninan thought. His father had often acted like he could wipe it off with a damp rag whenever Ninan didn't cooperate.

"In any case," the qhapaq said, "while I lament that you did not bring home the victory, I believe you are worthy to resume your duties to your Terrain."

Resume his duties. Live under the qhapaq's careful watch. Never step out of line. Put his own ambitions and feelings aside. What had he been thinking when he'd agreed to this?

The qhapaq looked at Ninan meaningfully. "My own son—a Venture survivor. A prince who proved he could endure without the kingdom's resources. You'll be a bridge between the lowborns and the highborns, an everyman with royal blood. More importantly, a man whom the other terrenal leaders respect."

Never mind that Ninan had had *plenty* of the kingdom's resources, and had still managed to fall behind.

"'Other terrenal leaders'?" Ninan asked. "What does that matter?"

"Well, I can't very well promise you in a matrimonial arrangement if you're disinherited."

Ninan felt himself pale.

Matrimonial arrangement?

Of course he'd assumed his father had had some ulterior motive for allowing him the opportunity to return to Kallpa

House, but it could have easily been pride—growing political tensions that might be relieved by having one fewer stain on the family name, one fewer disgrace of a son, an additional honor bestowed upon the household through an interterrenal competition that everyone would rally around. Instead, the qhapaq had set up Ninan to be a prize *himself*.

"Matrimonial …"

"I couldn't really offer up my disinherited youngest son who had no accomplishments to speak of. And Paqari of Tisqu holds too high a position to be suitable as a second or third wife to one of your brothers; thus, I had to devise a plan to elevate your status—or, more accurately, to get you to do it yourself."

Ninan's lungs tightened and he swallowed hard as a wave of sickness crested inside him. "You can't do this," he rasped.

The qhapaq clicked his tongue. "Ah, yes. You must also be wondering how I could do such a thing to you *right now*—now that you've developed feelings for the Kanchaya girl." He cocked his head in mock sympathy. "Even from a distance, the heralds know how to read competitors—how they affect one another, what they … mean to each other. Of course I had to spend a great deal of money to keep them quiet, otherwise those kinds of rumors could jeopardize the arrangement. I wouldn't want your future wife to think you were pining after some lowborn."

Ninan just stared at him, feeling his breath stall. What had he done? He should have run from Mullu in Thak when he'd had the chance.

Maybe he still *could* run. Not right now, but sometime in the night. Sometime in the next few days or weeks when he could prepare himself, make a plan, gather supplies and arrange transportation.

"Even after all you've had to endure," the qhapaq said, "to

your fragile, youthful mind, this is the worst thing I could ever do to you—isn't it?"

Ninan narrowed his eyes. "No."

The qhapaq raised an eyebrow. "It's not?"

"I mean, 'No, I won't do it.' I won't be a part of whatever scheme you've got going on. You're trying to build an alliance with Tisqu, you're hoarding money and skyrock, and for some reason you're playing some sort of god with these reptiles. I'm sure that only a fragment of what you're planning—and whatever it amounts to can't be anything good. I'll have nothing to do with it." Ninan turned on his heel.

"Do you really think it was a *question* when I brought you back to compete in the Venture?" the qhapaq said at his back. "Did you honestly believe you had a choice in *any* of this? By the grace of the gods, you cooperated without me having to get forceful, but you still have much work to do, Apo-Kimsa."

Ninan halted.

The qhapaq came up behind him. "I'd hoped you'd have some pride in your heritage, but it seems some things never change …" He looked to one of the guards at the entryway and made a flicking hand motion that Ninan only saw in shadow. The guard nodded and disappeared. "Thankfully, I've had Mullu help me procure a bit of insurance."

Now Ninan spun back around.

Boots marched through the corridor, punctuated by the sound of jangling chains. When the guards appeared in the menagerie, a young man struggled against them, grunting through a gag.

Ninan stepped toward Pidru instinctively.

"Does this young man look familiar to you?" the qhapaq asked.

Catching himself, Ninan stood back and said, "I barely know that farm boy. He has nothing to do with this. Let him go."

"Alright," the qhapaq said. "If that's the case, then I suppose it wouldn't upset you if my guards were to fetch a *second* prisoner from Thak, whom you might claim you also 'barely know.' The little girl—what was her name again? Tamya ..."

Pidru shouted through his gag and struggled again, until one of the guards bludgeoned him with a skyrock staff.

"Stop!" Ninan cried.

The qhapaq motioned for the guards to ease up. "I'll let him go," he assured Ninan. "Once you agree to my terms."

"I agree to the marriage and you leave him and his family alone?"

"Regardless of what you agree to tonight, there will be a patrol of my guards stationed outside this boy's community in Thak, watching his family's every move, ready to slit throats at my command, until the marriage is legally bound and consummated. Should you step out of line at any point leading up to that moment, I will kill every citizen of Thak, one by one, whether you know them personally or not, beginning with this one."

Ninan looked into Pidru's pleading, rage-filled eyes, and deflated. The only real brother he'd ever had, in chains despite his innocence, with his entire community—the community that had become Ninan's, too—stuck like commodity reptiles waiting for slaughter. He returned his gaze to the qhapaq, who loomed over him, a monster whose demons would chase Ninan to the ends of the earth if he ever tried to run.

"So," said the qhapaq. "What will it be ... *Apo-Kimsa*?"

FIFTY-SEVEN

LANTERN LIGHT FILLED THE HOUSE as Qora's mamáy rose, visible through the window, like she'd been waiting. She would have known the competition had ended at dusk, and she certainly couldn't have missed the horns on Qora's way back.

Qora all but stumbled out of the gondola before the watchguards had even fully landed it.

Her mamáy came out and stood before her without a word, eyes welling. Qora froze, waiting, not sure what to say. After how she'd left things, she wasn't sure what her mamáy might think of her now, whether she'd even want her back.

But then her mamáy drew her against her chest, holding her so tightly that all of Qora's wounds began to throb—and Qora didn't care. The pain was nothing to her now. And whatever hurt she'd caused by leaving for the Venture could be discussed later.

Hakan soon emerged and came to add his arms and his tears.

Through tears of her own, Qora asked, "Rimi?"

She followed them to Rimaq's bedmat and everyone knelt around him. His skin was sallow and crusted, his breathing labored. There was a hollowness in his countenance that hadn't been there before, a deepening against his cheeks.

"We can't get him to eat." Hakan pushed the boy's oily hair from his forehead. "The physician said it could be any day now"

"Then let's get this medicine in him." Qora unstopped the vial and put it to Rimaq's lips, using her thumb to press her brother's chin and open his mouth.

Rimaq groaned when Qora touched him.

"Rimi, it's me. Please, you have to drink this," Qora said.

His jaw was slack, and some of the silvery sparkshade dribbled out. She closed his mouth and waited until he swallowed.

Rimaq grimaced and the muscles on his neck stiffened, but he took it.

There was no sign of any change in his condition for a long time. Qora's mamáy offered her some corn cakes and milk, which Qora declined in favor of watching Rimaq in the lantern light. She lay beside him and analyzed his every twitch, the rhythm of his breath, waiting for a flicker of hope that he was responding to the sparkshade.

Please.

She prayed to Sky Mother and Light Father, to the sun and moon spirits, to the stars, to any celestial being who might listen, as if sheer pleading could will Rimaq back to health. Qora believed she had done her part to get what her brother needed, through these weeks of fighting to get to the Venture's prize so she could bring home a cure. Now, the only thing left to do was wait.

Her mamáy stayed close by, performing her usual care rituals—cooling cloths on Rimaq's forehead, pillow and blankets adjustments, ointment on scabs. When she'd finished, she took another blanket, one she'd knitted herself years ago from baby alpaca fiber, and drew it up over Qora's shoulders, where she then placed shaky but firm hands. Her maternal energy seemed to soak into Qora's bones, a comfort that Qora had missed but never forgotten. Her eyes filled with tears almost instantly, and her mamáy brushed them away just as she had when Qora had been small, when Qora had wounded her knee or woken from a nightmare.

Her lungs spasmed as she fought to breathe between the sobs that lodged in her throat.

Her mamáy cradled her head. Qora wanted to sink into her, but she wasn't sure how, after all that had been said and done. But, seeming to sense Qora's hesitation, her mamáy drew her closer, held her in tighter, and suddenly Qora felt it—the firmness she'd been longing for.

You are still mine. I still love you.

"I'm so sorry, Mamáy," Qora choked out. "I'm sorry. I know it was my fault. I know you can't ever forgive me. But ... I'm sorry."

"*Forgive* you?" she whispered.

"For—for Ollan."

"Oh, spirits, Qora. I ... I never meant to let you think ..." She shivered. "I've suffered, yes. So much. Every day. But I never meant for my pain to be yours, for you to think that I haven't forgiven you—that there was ever anything to forgive. No." She shook her head, pressed her eyes closed. "It's you who must forgive *me* for keeping you at a distance, for ever allowing you to believe I didn't love you as much as I do."

Qora sat up. "But you must be angry with me. For begging him to take me out there. For not ... bringing him back."

Her mamáy lifted a strand of Qora's hair from her eyes and stroked her glossy, wet face. "You couldn't have known. No one could have."

"And for the trade? For the Venture?"

"I was angry that you left," her mamáy admitted. "Because it's the worst thing, as a mother, to not be with your child. I kept imagining you hungry … lonely … hurting. And I couldn't get to you, couldn't help or comfort you. It ripped me in half, aching for you, longing to go to you, while Rimaq needed me here."

"I'm so sorry," Qora said again.

Her mamáy shrugged one shoulder. "Maybe that's what motherhood is—a heart torn to pieces, feeling everything at once. It was the same … that day. I was devastated. And yet, so incredibly relieved and grateful that you were still alive." She took a deep, steadying breath. "I've traded my anger for pleading. Pleading with the gods and spirits. I don't know whether it was those forces that brought you back to me, but I'm certain the actions you took played a part—that because you fought your way through, you survived."

"It was your voice—your words—that gave me strength in the end," Qora told her. "You've fought your own kinds of battles, and you've been so much braver than me."

She took Qora's hands and smiled through tears. "We grow brave because we simply don't have the option not to."

)))(((

Qora vowed not to sleep until she knew for sure whether Rimaq was alright, but her own body overpowered her. A heaviness pressed against her resolve. Sleep washed up over her muscles and bones in waves, pulling her deeper with each recession. Her vision blurred. She blinked against it. She blinked again. She wasn't sure when she stopped.

As daylight crept into the house, Rimaq opened his eyes, just barely. With a hint of color in his cheeks, he squinted at Qora and whispered, "Is it the High World?"

Tearfully, Qora sat up. "No, Rimi." Her voice quivered.

439

"You're here with us—and you will be for a *very* long time."

⟫⟫⟫

Later, while her mamáy and Hakan had taken Rimaq out to the meadow for some fresh air (allowing Qora a few more hours of sleep), Qora woke to a rap on the door. Still filthy and dressed in the same clothes she'd been wearing for weeks, Qora shuffled to answer it.

She rubbed her eyes. "Sakay?"

He cradled a sack of quinoa and stared at her with his mouth open. "Sweet serrated teeth …"

For a second, she forgot that she must have looked like death. But one glance down at herself, at the blood and the dirt, and she remembered all too well. She wrapped her arms around herself like it might shield Sakay from the horror.

He dropped the quinoa and crushed her in his arms. It was strange, coming from him, but she didn't question it; she absorbed his warm, woody scent. Then he took her by the shoulders and evaluated the damage. Bruises, a dried-up cut on her chin, nicks all over, a swollen bottom lip.

"The stories they've been telling about you …" he said. "You were … incredible."

"You mean the brutal deaths I caused? The harm I inflicted on a reptile I should have killed humanely? Being a key figure in a bloodbath publicized for entertainment?"

He blanched. "I guess it's easy for the rest of us to forget it's more than a story."

"I'm just … glad it's over."

He gave her a flat smile and squeezed her hand.

"Anyway," she said once he let go, "I'm glad you came. You

saved me a trip. I have something for you."

She retrieved his machete, which she'd propped against the wall by the door. Sakay held out both hands and she set the blade across them.

"I used it to kill the spinosaur. I'm sure you'll hear all about it soon enough, when the fictionists start getting the word out."

He looked it over, flipped it. The blade was stained and crusted, but still sharp. He sighed and handed it back to her. "*Kantuta*, this one is definitely on me. You've earned this."

"I had no idea it would be so incredibly expensive."

He shrugged. "I drive a hard bargain."

She couldn't help laughing.

"Hey," he added, "How'd the prizefighter make out? I heard he got to the end even though he didn't win."

"We … haven't really spoken. The qhapaq has a lot of plans for us. We've both had personal things to attend to. You can imagine how it is."

She was sure the stories had at least given him an *idea* what Ninan meant to her. If nothing else, he seemed to catch the subtle drop in her tone that she had failed to disguise. But he didn't push her to say more; he just nodded. "Yes. I can imagine."

ꙮꙮꙮ

Even though Qora had bathed and tended to her wounds at home, the instant she arrived at Kallpa House—after having someone retrieve her in a gondola to fly back to the otherwise-inaccessible castle—the qhapaq had a team of assistants set to work on her.

The qhapaq's own physician examined her. She coated Qora's skin with a thick, red substance that had a wet, spongy texture and smelled like meat, spreading it over her deepest cuts and gashes. Qora had to sit still for almost an hour to give it time to work. During that time, the wounds tingled and itched, and Qora struggled to keep from fidgeting and scratching. But sooner than expected, she began to feel relief, all pain subsiding. When the physician removed the substance, Qora stared at her skin speechlessly.

Every wound was gone, like it had never existed. Not a scratch remained.

"What—How—?" Qora stuttered.

"Spinosaur marrow," the physician said.

Qora felt a pinch in her chest. The mystical bones of the spinosaur, the creature she had brutally killed, had been the source of her healing. Wounds erased. Cuts without consequence. If only the wounds in her mind could disappear so easily.

Next, she was bathed in a copper tub, with fine soaps and scented oils. Two ladies' assistants, Jaylli and Michiq, combed her hair and trimmed her fingernails.

The ladies took her to a room where they had laid out several dresses for her, made of qompi cloth with detailed floral embroidery around the collars, hems, and cuffs. There were turquoise and brass earrings, woven sashes, sandals with dinoleather straps, and necklaces inlaid with rosinqa, opal, and citrine. The thought of these items on her common body made her dizzy, but her fingers burned with desire as she touched the rosinqa.

Jaylli and Michiq tried everything on her in combinations, arguing over what looked best. They lined her eyes, added golden powder to her cheeks, and arranged her hair so that it hung free and smooth. In a green dress and opal beads, they paraded her over to the qhapaq, who waited in the summit hall.

On the way, gilded dome-top cages displayed magnificent colored flyers: a teal and blue eudimorphodon with white spots on its back, a fuchsia epidexipteryx with yellow tail feathers, an orange nyctosaur with a cranial crest. They squawked at the passing group.

As the three girls entered the summit hall, there was yet another flyer. When Qora saw it, her whole body went numb.

Adjacent to the throne itself, in some sort of cage of honor—gold, like the others, but with more flourishes on the bars, and a tiny lintel over the door—was a reptile Qora never thought she'd see again.

"Well, well," said the qhapaq, standing and circling her before she even had the chance to process what she'd just seen. "You ladies could have told me this was a different girl and I would have believed you."

Jaylli and Michiq beamed, while Qora stood like a boulder, heavy with shock and fixed to the spot.

"Which is why," he continued, moving with his hands behind his back, "this is a gross failure on your part."

Qora's heart thrummed. Only half listening to the conversation, she tried not to stare into the cage, but the only thing she cared about right now was the flyer inside—four-winged, small, with scales as green as Qora's dress. A raptoriva.

"I beg your pardon, Your Majesty?" said Michiq.

The flyer turned, stretching its neck. On the underside of its lower jaw was the same mark. That splotch of red.

Something inside Qora sank.

But the qhapaq didn't notice her hardened exterior. "This girl is the champion of Sumaq. She has slain a full-grown spinosaur. Everyone remembers what she wore during the Venture," he said. "It's all been depicted in the artwork, described in the stories. This—what you've put her in—is the costume of a gentlewoman, not a huntress. She's a warrior, not a beauty."

A tempest raged under Qora's skin. Here she was, in the same room with the very creature that had led her to this situation. The victim of her crime. The qhapaq had caged her like a prize, with no idea that it was Qora who had funneled her to him.

"What would you have us do, Your Divinity?" Jaylli asked. "We can't put her in the clothes she came in. They're ruined and filthy."

"Then recreate them in a higher quality. Have the seamstresses use them for a pattern … the clothes, the boots, everything. While we're at it, have the armory make her a special crossbow, solid metal with matching bolts. And a dinoleather quiver."

The order was enough to make Qora snap alert.

"Don't look so surprised." The qhapaq chuckled. "I want only the best for my champion."

She nodded, swallowing her feelings like she would swallow a large pebble. "Of course. Thank you."

He sent her back to her dressing room, alone, to wait until her new clothes were ready. She glanced at the flyers on the way back, wondering where they had come from, and from how many other traders the qhapaq had confiscated them. How many of those traders had been like her? How many had been swindled, jailed, fined, and forced into servitude? She thought she'd managed to escape that fate by winning this competition, but it turned out that, in a way, she was exactly where she'd started.

"My champion."

Distracted by this idea, she returned to the room and opened the door so abruptly she startled herself—particularly as she discovered that the room was not empty.

Her heart stammered.

Standing by the window, showered in brilliant white daylight, was Ninan.

He turned as Qora entered, and everything about his appearance was different. Qora almost wouldn't have recognized him if it hadn't been for the way he carried himself, that same regal posture she'd noticed that day at the Underground—and now, it made sense.

Her cheeks flushed under the haze of gold powder. But even though she wore a mask of cosmetics, she felt more vulnerable dressed like this, all feminine parts decorated. Her blood pulsed like drumbeats.

Ninan's eyes widened and traveled the length of her. "You're …"

"Don't get used to it," she said. "Your father hates it. I'm a warrior—not a beauty."

"You're both," he whispered, locking his gaze on her. "You always have been. To me, at least."

His wounds, like her, were gone, no doubt from the same treatment, his dark skin smooth and unblemished. Even though it was a good thing they were both healed, it somehow felt like an erasure of all they had experienced together.

He was dressed differently now too, in a black tunic with red shapes woven on the edges, a wide belt, and gold cuffs on his wrists. His true form.

"You tried to tell me the truth," Qora said. "That first night after you found me again. I just never thought you were hiding the fact that you were … a *Kallpa*."

"You were right not to let me tell you. If I had, we might have fooled ourselves into thinking there was something that could be done about it. Here in Sumaq I can't hide under a dirty poncho. You can see me as I am—a privileged heir—and not be convinced I'm anything better."

"So … you wanted to win the Venture, to get back"—she gestured around the room, a fragment of the vast property—"all of *this*?"

"Basically. Yes."

Qora had paid little attention to the news surrounding the qhapaq's third son last year. Politics—the personal affairs of leadership, at least—had never interested her, and so it had never occurred to her during the Venture that a Kallpa could be among the competitors. "Looks like you didn't have to win after all."

"My father was satisfied enough with my performance," he said without emotion.

Performance. The word gutted her.

"And what about—" she hesitated. "I mean. You and I—was that just—"

"I know you can't have a high opinion of me right now, and I don't expect that will change. But I was told you'd be here today and I wanted to see you, to let you know that I'm sorry. For whatever that's worth."

His refusal to acknowledge what she was sure he knew she was trying to say was yet another cut, another burn. It tore at her, and her breath quickened.

"I think you and I might see worth differently," Qora said. "Something that means nothing to you may be incredibly valuable to someone like me. You may never understand the fears that follow poverty, and how little it takes to give a common person hope for a single day, only to have it crushed again before the sun sets. And the people you meet and hold close for a moment may be disposable to you, but to me they're everything. So, I do accept your apology, for what it's *worth* to me: words as faint and thin as the mists on these mountains."

She pursed her lips to keep the tears from spilling.

Ninan shrank back slowly, as though she'd slapped him.

Qora willed him to speak again, to offer her some grand explanation that would make everything alright, but he didn't. Maybe because there was nothing to say, because even if his feelings during the competition had been genuine, it didn't matter. He was a prince. And she was just some girl.

A sudden knock at the door made her flinch.

Jaylli and Michiq gasped when they saw Ninan, and fell into bowing, but he waved off the formality. "Apologies for the intrusion," he told them. "I'll leave you to it."

Once he'd gone, Michiq said, "The qhapaq has decided it would be best to make use of your time here while you wait. We're to show you to the courtyard to practice what the qhapaq would like you to say at the homecoming ceremony."

"Of course," Qora replied.

She followed them down the hall and thought of the raptoriva in that ornate cage, as the qhapaq's words whispered through her mind again.

"My champion."

The spiritual and the scientific need not be mutually exclusive. While the abundant and unusually large meteorites—colloquially known as 'skyrock'—that have fallen upon our soil are composed of tangible minerals and metals, and are likely the result of the explosion of some celestial body, they undoubtedly hold a special power from beyond this world. How else could it be that what is, apparently, misguided debris, should allow humankind to flourish among these great reptilian beasts, were it not an intentional gift from the divine? The human race was indeed meant to control the dinosaurs, if we can but harness the power so abundantly given.

**From *Celestial Spheres* by Quyllur Chaska,
Sumaqi astronomer and mathematician**

FIFTY-EIGHT

THE MISTS HUNG BOLDLY over the grounds of Kallpa House, like they didn't care that there was a castle carved into *their* mountain. They hid Ninan and his shame as he stood on one of the tiered plots cut into the mountainside—made grassy by the qhapaq's groundskeepers—and aimed a crossbow at one of several wooden figures resembling human men ("dupes" as the combat trainers called them).

Click.

He spanned, loaded, shot—spanned, loaded, shot—spanned, loaded, shot—each sound escalating his fury. The figure directly ahead of him was pockmarked with the holes of other bolts, which unfortunately had hit nothing that would have been definitively fatal on a sentient living counterpart. Its etched face stared back at him unimpressed.

Typical Apo-Kimsa, Ninan thought, having struggled all morning to focus. Everything Qora had taught him seemed to be fading, because all he could think about was how devastated she had looked in her beautiful new clothes, how much the truth about him had cut her—how blindsided she was going to be when his father announced the *engagement* in front of everyone at the homecoming ceremony tomorrow.

Then, of course there was Pidru, and everyone in Thak, who

449

would now be living under the scrutinizing watch of the qhapaq's guards for the next few months. Ninan hadn't even been allowed to apologize to his friend before Mullu had dragged him out. Gods knew what Pidru must have thought of him, what he'd *been* thinking ever since Mullu had collected Ninan from the quinoa fields—and now this.

Ninan forcefully shot another bolt—a miss. He growled and tried again, but this time he pretended the dupe was Takan.

Watch your head, princeling.

Anyone with Kallpa blood deserves to suffer.

The bolt shot out and struck the dupe's groin. Ninan chuckled faintly.

Then he heard his father's voice in his head. *A point for my son ... in whatever game he thinks we're playing.*

Now Ninan stared at the dupe and imagined a gilded, dinosaur-skull headpiece on top; a flowing Sumaqi-red robe; a face with that tipped-up-nose way the qhapaq always had of looking over everyone.

Acting as a common Venturer. How convenient that you already embody the part.

"How convenient that I'm the one holding a weapon," Ninan muttered.

Whoosh—the bolt lodged between the dupe's eyes.

The sound of applause pulled Ninan from his fantasy, and he spun to see a regal man approaching him, grinning at the unwitting performance.

"Impressive." The man strolled across the manicured grass. Over black hair, he wore a bronzed headpiece similar to what Ninan's father wore, but this one was cast in the shape of a triceratops skull. His Unuvian-blue robe matched the sapphire rings on his fingers—at least eight rings spread out among them all.

"Qhapaq Izhi. Your Majesty." Ninan panted, bowing his head. He'd forgotten that some of the visiting foreign leaders would be touring the grounds, to view the recent additions. He had barely recognized the qhapaq of Unu, having met him only once during a diplomatic counsel, while abroad with his father, several years ago. Thankfully the man's clothing was elaborately patriotic, which helped Ninan to place him quickly. "Something I can help you with?"

"You've grown quite a bit since the last time I saw you." Qhapaq Izhi looked around. "Impressive shooting range."

"Bigger than the previous one." Ninan sighed and raked his fingers through his hair.

"Fit for a champion."

Ninan could only think of Qora, how she could have pierced every target, dead center, on the first try. "If only there were a champion here to take advantage of it."

Qhapaq Izhi cocked his head. "You know, I still can't quite figure why someone like you would choose to compete in the Venture in the first place. Risking your life in a fool's competition."

Ninan narrowed his eyes. "I'm sure you know very well why."

Izhi pursed his lips, dampening a smile. Ninan had no doubt the man had spies in all rival Terrains, trained to sniff out political intrigue like a herald's pteranodon was trained to sniff out a corpse.

"Let's say that I do."

"I don't have to tell you I'm a gamepiece—that I serve whatever function my father needs me to. It's nothing new that men like you and my father like to skew things to your advantage. "

"Skewing does come with the territory. Although I have to admit it can be quite expensive—and tricky—especially during events like the Venture. Reviving Takan, for example, was no easy task."

Ninan narrowed his eyes. "I beg your pardon?"

"You left him at the threshold of the Grave World," said Izhi. "He required much marrow for his wounds, and sparkshade for a rapidly spreading infection."

Ninan's pulse began to race.

Do the heralds ever ride two to a flyer?

Takan had been delivered to the ruins—and Qora had seen it. Ninan had brushed it off as some irregularity in the heralds' patrol.

He thought, then, how easy it must have been to procure such expensive cures for Takan as part of a game, while Qora had had to trek more than a hundred miles and face enormous beasts to be able to afford what her brother needed.

"I hope you don't take offense at this information," Izhi said. "It would be absurd to do so; all the Terrains cheated in some manner or another."

Ninan's breath grew heavier.

Izhi added, "You don't really think a serpentosaurid came out of nowhere, do you? They rarely migrate west of the volcanic region. Too 'cold' for them, believe it or not—even in the jungle. But the Qolqese can be very sore losers. They didn't even have a competitor left in the Venture by then, but they would have rather seen anyone but Sumaq put forth a champion."

Nauseated, Ninan turned away, fingers practically crimping dents into his crossbow handle.

"Even *you* cheated, remember?" Izhi said over Ninan's shoulder. "Accepting gifts from what should have been an impartial herald …"

"I didn't want to do any of this," Ninan replied bitterly.

That wasn't the full truth. He *had* wanted it, in theory, at the start of it all. But …

"You didn't?" Izhi flashed a falsely sympathetic smile. "I heard that you're to be restored to your former glory. A prince of Sumaq once more. Does that not please you?"

Ninan ground his toe into the grass and looked off toward the city, the view of which was hazy through the cloud mists. "What if I said it doesn't?"

Izhi leaned in close. He lowered his voice. "Then … perhaps we can have a real conversation now."

Steadying himself, Ninan glanced at the edge of the plot to see whether anyone else might have been watching. But of course his father didn't need to have him watched now, not when he was holding knives against Pidru and Tamya. "What about?"

He echoed Ninan's previous response. "'I'm sure you know very well' what about."

Ninan loaded another bolt and took an offhanded shot at the dupes. "I'm sure I don't." The bolt struck one of the legs at an angle.

"I can certainly understand why you might be hesitant," Izhi replied, "after all you've been through. After your father threatened the only people who have been allowed to treat you well."

Ninan prepared another bolt but didn't load it, only curled his fingers around the metal, and looked sideways at the Unuvian qhapaq.

Izhi continued. "I can understand why you might refuse to entertain the possibility of having a discussion with someone you believe has acted unscrupulously—albeit in a competition that is inherently unscrupulous—even though I was no more desperate than your father was to see a champion of my own Terrain take the stage. But more importantly, you ought to know—if you don't already—that your father's determination to win is robust, and that there is a much larger gameboard on which your father is moving pieces."

"He's always been a 'big picture' type of man." Ninan placed the bolt back in its quiver. "So what?"

"Excessive and increasing taxes. Spending cuts. Skyrock prices driven up while buyers are denied. Skyrock shipments to Tisqu—and unusual activity with the Tisquvians in general. Suspicious use of an old military stronghold. None of that catches your attention?"

"I'm aware of those allegations."

"Then I'm sure you're also aware that your father lives in restless shame over the Old Empire's 'lost lands.' You might have even heard him prophesy that the Terrains will 'come together again.'"

"Sure."

"But he's not referring to a peaceful reunion."

"I've had my suspicions," Ninan said. "It wouldn't surprise me if he were planning a war. But what does it matter? His predecessors have tried to regain the lost lands before and it's never worked. I obviously don't want more people to die, but … What exactly do you expect *me* to do about it? I'm not anyone anymore, even with my title restored. I'm as subject to him as anyone else."

"Subject, maybe, but your place in his household grants you access to knowledge few others have."

Ninan scoffed and picked at a bit of rough cuticle around his fingernail. "You overestimate my usefulness. My father's trust and respect for me hangs by a fiber."

Qhapaq Izhi put a hand on Ninan's shoulder, making Ninan flinch. "Then reinforce it," he told him. "Do whatever it takes to make him believe you're the son he wants you to be. Use that famous smoke of yours to blind him to your true motives."

"And what will that accomplish?"

"With the information I've gained, and your restored access to Kallpa House, we might accomplish a great deal."

"What information could you possibly have that could change things?"

"Your father's pending alliance with Tisqu has nothing to do with protecting the islands—which is what he's going to claim at the homecoming ceremony—and everything to do with the army he's breeding there."

"Army?" Ninan scoffed. "Why would he need additional soldiers on Tisqu? He already has plenty of—" He furrowed his brow. "Wait …"

Ninan thought about his engagement to the princess of Tisqu, which would secure ties. The way his father seemed to be stockpiling additional funds even though Sumaq had seen little improvement from them. The paranoia over every ounce of processed skyrock *and* its raw materials.

"We're developing some very promising methods for dinosaur control."

His father would have needed huge amounts of skyrock, and funding to develop these new "methods"—funding he could have obtained easily through higher taxes and fees and fines.

And then that word about the army. *Breeding.*

Like the iridosaur. Like the sailbeasts.

The logic must have played out on Ninan's face, because Izhi confidently said, "You've begun to understand."

Ninan's reply came out in a voice that hardly sounded like his own. "My father's going to take back the lost lands in a war. A very *unconventional* war."

Izhi nodded gravely. "You must understand that even once I share this information with the other terrenal leaders, no matter how we combine forces, we won't be able to defeat an army like that. Not considering the resources I believe Qhapaq Apo has developed."

"What resources?"

"I believe he has managed to refine and purify a particular skyrock formula that is stronger, one that works in reverse. While skyrock tends to repulse reptiles, this formula somehow *appeals* to them. They can't resist it. It's enticing in a way that overpowers their will and, in some cases, their logical instincts. Other forces seem to have no influence on them in its presence. So not only will he have an army that is expendable, easily replenished, and easily controlled—unlike humans who cannot simply be bred in massive numbers for war, must be trained extensively, and may waver in their dedication—but no opposing force will be capable of interfering with it. Do you understand the severity of what I'm telling you?"

Ninan's instinct was to drop to his knees. Every ounce of resolve seemed to have left his body and nothing remained to keep him standing. "What about the Tisquvians? If they knew the truth, they'd break the alliance, wouldn't they? And leave my father without an island on which to perform these ... experiments?"

"I'm afraid not," said Izhi. "Your father has promised Qhapaq Achik that he will retain sovereignty over the Isle of Tisqu—with some stipulations, of course—and all of its surrounding islands, for his compliance. He's a willing accomplice."

"But we both know my father won't make good on those promises."

Izhi nodded. "So you know that if you do nothing, your

marriage and the alliance with Tisqu will proceed as planned, and countless cities and people will be destroyed within the coming year, while all of Runaqa will be subject to your father and his unstoppable, unprecedented power."

Ninan shook his head. "How do you plan to stop him?"

"We need information, interception of messages and shipments, knowing when and where any preliminary attacks might occur. But essentially, my plan is to locate the dinosaur army, and destroy it before it's ever deployed."

"And if that's impossible?"

"Then we'll need to build our own armies," Izhi said. "Except we can't do that unless we gain access to your father's new methods and technologies. I have spies, but what they can do is limited. Your father has already sniffed out a handful, and they've paid for it with their blood."

"What makes you think I won't pay for it with *my* blood?"

"You might. Although it does seem you have a talent for acting. In Thak ... In the Venture. So, act accordingly now. Play the role."

It was an appealing idea, Ninan thought—fighting for something, taking down his own father, stealing from the qhapaq that had stolen so much from everyone else. Less appealing, though, when considering the risks involved, the man he would have to cooperate with in order to accomplish it.

But it was more than just his own safety at stake. It was the safety of people like Qora, like Pidru and Tamya, of the soldiers on opposing sides who would try to stop this madness.

Ninan didn't answer, but he let Izhi see the flame of decision in his eyes.

Izhi tipped his chin in acknowledgement. "I'll reach out to you when it's time to take the first course of action."

FIFTY-NINE

BEFORE QORA EVEN STEPPED OUT of the gondola, the loudest, most staggering cheers and applause overwhelmed her ears, voices whose vibrations rattled her bones. The ceremony had drawn so many more people than Qora had expected, a crowd that spilled out of the city square boundaries and onto connecting streets.

Over the cacophony of chatter and cheers, many were chanting something in unison. It took Qora a moment to mentally arrange the syllables and make sense of them.

Rap-to-ri-va! Rap-to-ri-va! Rap-to-ri-va! Rap-to-ri-va!

At the same time, some members of the crowd were waving green triangle pennants, while others raised canvas banners with green raptorivas embroidered on them.

Qora stiffened. *They know*, she thought. *How could they know?* Not even the qhapaq seemed to have known. She'd paid her fine quietly the previous afternoon.

But while the mists were good at hiding secrets, she had to acknowledge that she wasn't a simple girl among them anymore. She'd been watched by the Five Terrains, her name and attributes publicized. It shouldn't have surprised her that people would go looking for information about her, and that eventually they'd find it. Now, it seemed her crime with the raptoriva would follow her forever.

She didn't realize that she'd stopped in her tracks until Jaylli nudged her. "They're asking for you. Don't keep them waiting."

"Why are they calling me that?" Qora stared numbly at the mass of people, afraid to move forward.

"Because of your final battle with the spinosaur. You know, like 'The Spinosaur and the Raptoriva'—from *Asiri's Apologues?*"

Qora paused, remembering.

The raptoriva, angry that the spinosaur had disrespected her ... blinded him with the tiny claws of her feet. The spinosaur shrieked in pain, and the raptoriva flew down his throat and shredded his insides ... then crawled up from his belly and out of his mouth.

It was only a symbol. A poetic device.

She tried to hide her deep breath of relief. She drew it and released it slowly, nodding. "Right. Of course. Sorry ..."

Thank the gods. These people had no idea about the raptoriva the qhapaq now kept for his pet.

It felt strange, receiving this kind of attention, having so many people acknowledging her, offering their support.

Jaylli and Michiq both urged her to ascend the platform.

The spinosaur's head was on display here, staged with its mouth open, propped by wooden dowels hidden inside the flesh, its golden tooth polished and gleaming. The qhapaq's workers had removed the bolts from its eyes—which were grisly enough in their damaged state without such details—and washed off most of the blood. Qora had gladly accepted additional prize money in lieu of keeping the tooth as a trophy, although the money had already been more than enough to live on even after paying her fine.

As Qora climbed the steps, she caught sight of Ninan among the highborns who stood at the back, dressed in a highbornman's formal black and red robes. Again he was clean, his hair coiffed to reflect his class, and he stood with his hands clasped behind his back. He looked so beautiful it killed her.

Monarchs from all Five Terrains were seated to one side. The qhapaq and his three quyas were at the center, while the princes Apo-Huk and Apo-Iskay sat on either side of them with their corresponding wives. Along adjoining sides were the leaders of Qolqe, Allpa, Unu, and Tisqu, here to support the end of this year's Venture before they each vied for the privilege to hold the next one. The monarchs from Qolqe and Unu came in traditional sets (qhapaq and three quyas), while Quya Urpi of Allpa sat alone, and Qhapaq Achik of Tisqu sat with his primary quya and a much younger female—their daughter, perhaps—who couldn't have been much older than Qora.

Jaylli and Michiq instructed Qora to take her place beside the spinosaur head, facing out to the crowd. Qora wore clothes that looked like her own, but the new dinoleather boots were rigid and her jacket was the wrong shade of green. She held her metal crossbow and dinoleather quiver for show, but they felt cold and unfamiliar in her hands.

Horns blared the national fanfare, inciting more cheers and chanting. The qhapaq rose to take the front of the stage. He acknowledged Qora, and she bowed in return. The audience also bowed, a sea of heads that bent and rose again in waves before the qhapaq began his address. As Qora looked out, she saw girls throughout the audience wearing green hooded jackets similar to hers. A few of them clutched little raptorivas carved out of wood.

Thanks to the acoustical design of the city's gathering square that faced the viewing platform, the qhapaq's voice rang out loudly enough for everyone to hear. "The Terrain of Sumaq is pleased to announce the winner of the fifteenth quinquennial Runaqan Venture: Qora Kanchaya!"

The crowd raised their banners along with their voices, chanting again, and this time with more unity and vigor.

Rap-to-ri-va! Rap-to-ri-va! Rap-to-ri-va! Rap-to-ri-va!

"Like the fable of old," the qhapaq continued, raising his own voice and gesturing for them to quiet down, "*this* raptoriva, too, stood small, and she, too, blinded the spinosaur and destroyed him from the inside out. He swallowed her before she thrust her blade in a deadly blow. None of us, nor the spinosaur himself, could have anticipated such a feat. Yet here the Raptoriva stands before us today—and we couldn't be more proud."

Rap-to-ri-va! Rap-to-ri-va! Rap-to-ri-va! Rap-to-ri-va!

After a bit more noise, he introduced the monarchs from each Terrain. An attendant held Qora's weapons for her so that she could receive gifts. The Tisquvians provided bouquets of prized tropical flowers. The Unuvians gifted a silk pouch of the highest quality Unuvian cacao. From Qolqe, Qora received a string of jade beads.

Lastly, Quya Urpi of Allpa bestowed a rose-gold medallion etched with her Terrain's smilodon. She laid the medallion around Qora's neck, lingering when she'd finished. She touched her fingertips to the metal, then pressed her cheek to Qora's. The Allpans were more affectionate, Qora remembered, and sometimes greeted one another this way, although the proximity made her blush. With lips now close to Qora's ear, the quya whispered, "My name is refuge." The quya stepped back and locked eyes with her, some silent message Qora didn't understand. She was about to ask when one of Qhapaq Apo's attendants escorted the quya away so that he could place another accessory onto her: a necklace with large trapezoidal brass plates strung together on brass chains—the adornment of champions, the qhapaq said. She was heavy with adornments, and heavier with the weight of everything she'd done to earn them.

Then it was time for Qora to say a few words, the lines she'd been asked to memorize for this purpose. This pre-written speech was a lot of the same nationalistic raptor-ruck the qhapaq often used when he gave his own speeches, paired with a recounting of the events that had led Qora to this victory, including Rimaq's illness, her family's financial struggle, her debt and desperation. She felt as though she were naked in front of everyone, meant to inspire them with her vulnerability, a sort of calming element in the midst of a political storm, and yet she saw in her mind once more the image of the caged raptoriva in the summit hall.

She concluded with: "There is hope for us all to overcome whatever trials befall us. If a young girl like me can compete against those who are stronger, who are better armored, who are intent on killing, and then go on to thwart a terrorizing giant, there isn't a single one of us who can't work hard and see the results we so greatly desire, to fulfill our sincerest needs. Of this, I am living proof. Sumaq is a Terrain of champions; I am merely one of them."

Qora tried not to audibly suck in her next breath, after having exhausted the previous one to keep her voice steady and her lines sharp. The applause that followed, however, was more than enough volume to cover her presentation flaws. She nodded her thanks and forced a smile, even though her insides felt as hollow and small as a charango guitar.

Once that particular cacophony had calmed, the qhapaq addressed the audience again, pausing meaningfully on the platform before he spoke. He strained his face like he was damming up a flow of emotion before he finally said, "Now that we have celebrated our champion, it is time for a very important revelation."

The crowd marinated in confusion. Qora glanced at Ninan, who stood like a block of granite in his fancy clothes; his jaw flexed, but otherwise he remained still.

"While this year's great Venture includes all Terrains of the Runaqa, its events have brought about an incredible change in the land of Sumaq, individually. And now that so many are gathered here today, I would like you all to witness it."

The qhapaq made a motion to Ninan, who stepped forward and removed his robe. Underneath, he wore the simple clothes of a Venturer—not unlike what he'd worn when Qora had known him on the route, but which, similar to her own clothing, Kallpa House tailors had recreated with materials suitable to a higher status. He had to be presentable, of course, but the qhapaq would have wanted him to look his part, the part people had been hearing about these past weeks, the character Venture artists had depicted from the heralds' descriptions.

Members of the crowd murmured at the display, some whispering their recognition.

"Ninan."

"Is that supposed to be Ninan?"

"That's Ninan, isn't it?"

Ninan came to the front and stood beside Qora, close enough that his knuckles grazed the back of her hand, sending a spike of energy up her arm. In that instant, all her anger melted, and her breath turned ragged at his touch, and she wanted nothing more than to slide her fingers between his and squeeze. She hated that she still felt this way, after everything she knew now—despite the fact that Ninan was the Third Prince, the son of a tyrant whose careless operations and merciless laws had led her to this competition. In that instant, none of it mattered.

Qhapaq Apo continued. "This is not just any competitor. You

know him as Ninan—a few of you may even know him as a boy from Thak, or perhaps as a lowly prizefighter. But you may have not realized that his reputation precedes him." He paused again for dramatic effect. "This is a young man who once failed to live up to his heritage. One who, like many of you, was easily led astray from his duties. One who allowed his youth and his pride to hinder him. But also one who has struggled and suffered to restore his honor. One who performed with astounding skill and bravery at the entrance trials. One who nobly entered the Venture; fought to defend himself and, at times, others; survived; and endured to the end. He has humbled himself—repented with full sincerity— and finally returned to the House where he belongs. This is *Apo-Kimsa Kallpa*, my son, the third prince of Sumaq!"

Gasps spread like they were contagious, some interlaced with excitement, others with confusion or anger.

"This prince is the beneficiary of *my* forgiveness," the qhapaq continued, "and he will receive yours as well. You will take this as law. Prince Apo-Kimsa has participated in our grand Venture as a common man and proven that he can, with none of the advantages of his birth, succeed on his own merits. He deserves your respect, your praise, and your awe. He certainly has mine."

Mullu came around with a wooden box that contained a headpiece—a ring of bronzed dinosaur teeth—and presented it to the qhapaq. Qhapaq Apo set it on Ninan's head, to the sound of more applause and whispers of shock as everyone fell into bowing.

"Your prince is a young man who has faced and overcome the same challenges that many of you have—and beyond. He has experienced hunger. He has experienced debilitating pain. He has experienced lack of shelter and safety. He has known what it is to risk his own life to protect someone in danger. He has fought monsters and won. Look at the man who stands above you and know that he is one of you.

"The spirit of unity is strong in the Terrain of Sumaq. Let us never forget who we are, what we stand for, and that every day we grow in strength as we strive for prosperity for all."

Ninan took Qora's hand and raised them both. He didn't look at her. He held on a second longer than Qora would have expected, pulsing once before letting go. Qora didn't know what to make of it, whether he had meant to convey lingering feelings for her, or if it was a sad attempt at goodbye.

The qhapaq took over again. "Now, I have one final announcement. Today is indeed proof that Sky Mother has smiled upon us—and proof that blessings come in threes." The Tisquvian qhapaq stood, provoking more confusion from the audience. "I am pleased to announce an upcoming marriage that will fortify both Sumaq and the island nation of Tisqu."

Qora's stomach dropped. *An upcoming marriage …*

She wanted to turn to Ninan, to see some reassurance in his eyes, but she didn't dare shift her gaze. She steeled herself, keeping watch on the crowd that stared back at her.

Ninan's brothers could still take more wives, she thought; neither had more than one at the moment. Or maybe it was an arrangement for a lesser Kallpa relative.

But Qora thought about how rigid Ninan had been the last time she'd seen him, and then about the way his hand had lingered a moment ago, and something told her this announcement wouldn't be inconsequential.

Qhapaq Apo smiled. "At the onset of the equinox, approximately four and one half moon cycles from today, your beloved Prince Apo-Kimsa will be wed to Princess Paqari of Tisqu, of the House of Huapaya."

Qora's heart felt like a rock in her chest. For a moment it

didn't even seem to pump. The news cut through her again and again, sharp as her machete in the spinosaur's palate.

The Tisquvian qhapaq rose in acknowledgement, along with the princess, both of them nodding to the audience.

Qora stared at Princess Paqari, a fierce beauty with dark skin—darker even than the majority of those on the mainland—and long spiraling curls. The princess was graceful, composed. Meanwhile, Qora felt the chill of her own sweat breaking out against her brow, and feared her knees might buckle underneath her.

"For the few weeks prior to the wedding," Qhapaq Apo added, "the couple will embark on a goodwill tour of Tisqu's outer islands on the grand ship *Velosaura*, to convey Sumaq's loyalty in person.

"We are all looking forward to this consolidation, especially as outside forces seek to prey upon Runaqan lands. We must unite." His solemnity turned again to spectacle and he raised both his hands and his voice. "To the union of Apo-Kimsa and Paqari! To the union of Sumaq and Tisqu! And to the Raptoriva, who has brought us glory!"

Even though Qora had managed to survive the Venture, she felt like a small part of her had just died.

〉〉〉

After a torturous afternoon of greeting strangers, shaking hands, and recounting tales she never wanted to speak of again, Qora was finally allowed to leave. Jaylli and Michiq arranged for a decoy gondola to be sent to her house so she could slip away without drawing another crowd of fans, and provided her with an unremarkable, brown, hooded cloak, since she certainly wouldn't have made it far in her more iconic clothing. She then met with an attendant on raptorback to transport her at a delayed interval

When she arrived home, however, hundreds of people continued to wait for her, hoping to catch a glimpse, to say they'd spoken to her or had had the privilege of standing in her presence.

Hakan, with authority beyond his years, stood at the door and explained that Qora was not home, that she would be consulting with the qhapaq for days and there was no point standing around for her. He scanned the crowd and almost passed her over, but then his gaze fell to hers. With an almost imperceptible jerk of his head, he motioned for her to go.

Qora sighed heavily and told the attendant to leave. She didn't want to return to the city, though. All she wanted was her mamáy and her brothers and a warm bowl of quinoa and compy eggs while she sat on the rug by the fire.

Unfortunately, she would have to settle for the next best thing. As the attendant brought her to the Underground, she laughed bitterly, internally, at the irony that this seemed to be the only other place that felt a little bit like home. It occurred to her, however—if only for an instant—that this may have had more to do with the young man running the place than she would have liked to admit.

The attendant waited for her on the street while she entered.

Inside, Sakay mopped up spilled pisco and gestured before the traders. "And so the man said to his friend, 'I don't have to run faster than the puma; I just have to run faster than *you.*'"

The men erupted in laughter as Qora slipped into a chair at an empty table near the back. Without the faintest reaction, Sakay excused himself and came over to where she sat, taking the seat across from her. Casual as ever, he said, "Didn't expect to see you in here quite so soon."

"Yeah, well ... I couldn't really go back to my house, so ..."

Sakay glanced at the gamblers, who were engaged in their tokens and cards. "I'm flattered. There were plenty of other places you could've gone."

Qora looked down at her hands, which should have still been covered in scars—but weren't, thanks to the marrow she'd so brutally obtained—and twisted her fingers together. "Not really. Not anymore."

"I caught the end of the homecoming ceremony."

Her eyes burned. She blinked to keep them dry.

"The whole time ..." He shook his head. "The Third Prince?"

"I don't really want to talk about it."

"I don't really blame you. But it's a really good thing you came, because I'm supposed to give you something."

Give her something? What could he possibly have to give her?

"What do you mean?"

He dug into his pocket. "You're in luck; I have it on me right now. Then again, I only got it an hour ago. Didn't have the chance to put it away."

When he withdrew his hand, he was holding a mysterious object wrapped in fine, red fabric.

"What is it?" Qora held it still wrapped, shaky at the thought of opening it.

Sakay shrugged. "No idea. I figured it was private. Coming from Ninan, it didn't seem right for me to—"

"This is from *Ninan*?"

Suddenly she felt lightheaded.

"He came in dressed a lot like you are now—all inconspicuous and brooding. Shifty and paranoid he was being watched. Apparently fame isn't his thing either."

Once Qora got a sense of the shape of the object, she could

already tell what it was. Even under the fabric, there was no denying it was triangular. Ninan was returning her cordshield. A farewell gift and a feeble condolence. Closure. But Qora didn't want it. Why would she want another reminder of what she could never have?

"Are you going to open it?" Sakay urged her with his eyebrows. "Come on. I'm dying to know."

"You are not."

"Fine. But I'm curious. I wouldn't *mind* knowing."

She stared at it for at least a full minute before mustering the courage to lift one of the corners. One fold at a time, she revealed the cordshield.

Only it wasn't the token she'd been expecting. The framework was the same, but the cords were different. They were dyed now in an array of colors, and there were knots tied into them. A message.

Her pulse raced as she put her fingers to it, deciphering each word, knot by knot.

Sakay raised an eyebrow. "What's it say?"

Qora's voice turned urgent. "He brought you this himself? You're sure?"

"Yeah, I'm sure. I think I know what he looks like." He lowered his voice. "Why? Is something wrong?"

"No, nothing's wrong. Nothing at all."

She stared at the cordshield in disbelief. Her fingers explored the knots, rereading them to convince herself the message was real. Its full meaning was cloudy, but what she saw was like warm sun on her skin.

I HAVE A PLAN. WAIT FOR ME?

ACKNOWLEDGMENTS

First I'd like to thank Rocco and Bellamy, the ones whose YouTube dino videos inspired this book. That said, I guess I should also thank Pinfong! "If Dinosaurs Were Still Alive" stuck in my brain and got me thinking of a world where humans and dinosaurs might coexist. This isn't actually possible, since larger mammals only ever came to exist because of the *absence* of dinosaurs, but that's why this story is fantasy :)

Nano, as always, thank you for your love, encouragement, and support, and for being the sounding board I need (even if my scene descriptions sometimes make you sleepy). Also, thank you for helping me make my map layout a little more realistic with your water knowledge.

Jennifer, my first beta reader, and the first person to read this whole thing besides me (although it was very different back in 2020), thanks for pushing through it and giving me great notes!

Zach, thank you for being the *next* person to read the whole thing for me, and especially for saying, "When can I read the next one?" when you finished it.

Walker, thanks for always being ready to give me feedback on a full manuscript (often with short notice), especially this one, with all its weird little details.

Also, thank you to other Keystrokes writing group members who helped workshop some of the early chapters!

To Alexandra Levick at Writers House, thank you for reading my whole book not once but *twice*—in the midst of all your responsibilities as an agent—and for your encouraging words and thorough analyses. Even though you weren't able to take it on, just knowing that someone like you had *any* interest in my book helped me believe is was worth the effort to keep going with it.

Emily Thiede, Sandra Proudman, and Shannon A. Thompson, thank you for all your work during Pitch Wars in 2020 and for your generous notes and advice even though I wasn't a mentee. It was Emily's idea to give more magical/mystical properties to dinosaur organs, which was key in several scenes, and one of my favorite new concepts.

Kristin J. Dawson, again, thanks for being a great writer friend and for reading a bit of this book as well. No matter how busy you are, you've always taken time to give me advice.

Zoe, thank you for being willing to help a weird random girl on the internet by answering some of my questions about Peru and the Quechua language (both of which have a large influence on this story's world).

Derek, my fellow dino story writer, thank you for catching additional errors and hyping this series for me on TikTok! (Readers: If you liked this book, be sure to check out Derek Borne's *Dino Rift* series too).

Special thanks to TrifBookDesign for the cover, and to Dan Brown for the interior drawings. You were both so great dealing with my "art direction" and using your extraordinary talents to make the elements of my story come alive in graphics.

Lastly, a big thank you to all my readers. It sounds cheesy, but I'm seriously so grateful for you—especially those of you who have given rave reviews and been eager to read more of the series. It means more to me than you could ever know.

AVAILABLE NOW!

ABOUT THE AUTHOR

VICTORIA RIVERA is a graphic designer and mom of two kiddos. She has a bachelor's degree in English and has worked as a copy editor, proofreader, and designer at newspapers and magazines.

She was born and raised in Oregon but currently lives in northern Utah and misses the rain.

When she's not writing, she enjoys doing DIY projects, playing Beat Saber, rage-cleaning to good music, and reading (obviously).

For updates on books, **subscribe to her email list at www.toririv.com**. Follow her on **TikTok (@tori.riv)** for a glimpse into her day-to-day activities and other bookish things.

If you enjoyed this book, please leave a review on Amazon and/or Goodreads. Your feedback is greatly appreciated!